COMPLETE PRIDEAUX GHOST STORIES

FEATURING THE
PRIDIAS/PRIDEAUX
FAMILY FROM THE
11TH TO THE 20TH
CENTURY

A CIP catalogue record for this title is
available from the British Library.
ISBN 978-0-9954609-6-6

www.paganuspublishing.co.uk
First Published in 2017

Paganus Publishing
Ruthin
Denbighshire

Paganus Publishing

FOREWORD

The Complete Prideaux Ghost Stories are weird and unusual tales about 28 generations of the de Pridias, now known as Prideaux, family. My family and my ancestors. Each generation is my blood link from 1011 AD and reaches through my grandfather Clifford who died in 1963, to me. The last story in this collection is about Clifford Prideaux. I haven't yet written about Dorothy, Ann Agnes or Richard Fulke Paganus Prideaux. The stars of my tales lived in the places I write about, walked the lands, which more often than not they owned and played with the people I describe. They took part in great historical events and knew, Kings, Earls, Priors and poets, including Geoffrey Chaucer. They fought in famous wars and sided with well-known individuals and were enemies of others.

I have taken liberties with the stories that are told, but surprisingly much of it is - almost true. The prayer exists, the staff belonging to Henry VIII, the books and the documents. John Prideaux was the Bishop of Worcester and I have written about him in far greater detail in **The Bishop and The Witch**. I do have the cherry pits too, although I am better at growing them than making pies. I see dead people and I have seen the hooded man.

The stories can be found in shorter volumes in **Cornish Prideaux Ghost Stories, Devon Prideaux Ghost Stories, A Ghost Story, Prideaux Ghost Stories, More Prideaux Ghost Stories, Collected Prideaux Ghost Stories** and **A Christmas Story.**

CAST LIST

1. RICHARD DE PRIDIAS LORD OF PRIDEAUX
   1011 - 1051

2. PAGANUS PRIDEAUX de PRIDIAS LORD OF PRIDEAUX
   1040 - 1100

3. RICHARD de PRIDIAS LORD OF PRIDEAUX
   1070 - 1122

4. BALDWIN de PRIDIAS LORD OF PRIDEAUX
   1109 - 1165

5. NICHOLAS de PRIDIAS LORD OF PRIDEAUX
   1135 - 1200

6. RICHARD de PRIDIAS LORD OF PRIDEAUX
   1160 - 1225

7. RICHARD de PRIDIAS LORD OF PRIDEAUX
   1180 - 1250

8. SIR GEOFFREY de PRIDIAS
   1200 - 1270

9. ROGER de PRIDIAS
   1224 - 1291

10. PETER de PRIDIAS
    1260 - 1316

11. SIR ROGER PRIDYAS
    1294 - 1347

12. SIR JOHN PRIDEAUX
    1320 - 1357

13. GILES PRIDEAUX
    1345 - 1410

14. SIR JOHN PRIDEAUX
    1380 - 1443

15. WILLIAM PRIDEAUX
    1422 - 1472

16. JOHN PRIDEAUX
    1461 - 1523

17. JOHN PRIDEAUX
    1505 - 1568

18. JOHN PRIDEAUX
    1540 - 1620

19. THOMAS PRIDEAUX
    1571 - 1641

20. THOMAS PRIDEAUX
    1610 – 1680

21. PETER PRIDEAUX
    1651 - 1725

22. PETER PRIDEAUX
    1695 - 1749

23. PETER PRIDEAUX
    1733 - 1810

24. THOMAS PETER PRIDEAUX
    1768 - 1842

25. JOHN PRIDEAUX
    1796 - 1871

26. MATTHEW PRIDEAUX
    1838 - 1888

27. GEORGE PRIDEAUX
    1871 - 1926

28. CLIFFORD PRIDEAUX
    1902 - 1963

29. DOROTHY PRIDEAUX
    1936 - 2010

30. ANN AGNES PRIDEAUX

31. RICHARD FULKE PAGANUS PRIDEAUX

CONTENTS

BLOOD OF THE LYON MEN

Featuring Paganus de Pridias, Lord of Pridias (1040 – 1100)

Every time Pagan rode back to his clifftop home, his mood would rise and fall in equal measure. He loved his land - every rock, meadow, tree and stream on it, but recently he returned to it more slowly.

His mother had told him that he should marry and continue their blood line and she had decided that Ethel of Fowey, daughter of Gaston Polred, was the ideal match. Ethel was a pretty girl and had a decent figure but she did not ride nor use a bow and she hated Nos, his constant companion.

Pagan shouted to Nos and he ran back to his master and continued to lope alongside the horse.

"Don't get too far ahead of us Nos, there are hunters who will take you to your next life earlier than you plan. And I cannot do without you."

Nos looked up at his companion, tongue lolling and tail relaxed and moved in a comfortable step as they crossed the moor. Pagan had just spent the past few days at Zennor negotiating a deal for some of the crystals which were plentiful on Pridias land. Most had to be dug for but recently some of the crystals were becoming visible at the cliff front. Pagan sent women to collect any they found on the beach when the tide receded and children were sent to collect any crystals they found higher up the cliff.

"I hear that gold has been found on your land too," said Alain de Prous during the negotiations. "And I want in."

Pagan had laughed at that and drunk more mead, knowing that Alain had a band of men who would be more than willing to fetch the gold themselves, defended or not by the Pridias clan.

"There has been gossip about that on other land too. The Saxon bastards were always interested and never found anything on their many raids through my lands."

"We have new masters now," said Alain.

"They are not my masters," snapped Pagan.

"And we'll give them the same welcome we gave Cola and his mates," chuckled Alain.

Pagan finished his drink and asked,

"That will be easy enough and I can count on you?"

"Always. After what those bastards did to your father, you can always count on us. Your mother has done a good job of raising you."

"She is your sister, the blood is right, isn't it?"

"Yes, and that is another subject I want to discuss."

Pagan looked up, curious.

"What?"

"I have a niece, your mother's niece too, who has been living over the water since she was a girl."

"Ireland?"

"No France, Normandy to be exact. She has been living in a convent there. She is now come of age and in need of a husband."

"And you want me to suggest someone?" Pagan was feeling that this discussion was going to end with him having to agree to something he would later regret.

"No lad, you know what I mean. You are to marry the girl and then we shall be joined officially and we both will have a reason to work together."

"No! Mother wants me to marry the Fowey girl because that family has helped us since Richard's death and if I come back with any other arrangement, we shall be at war with them and they live nearer to my land than you do."

"You told me yourself you don't want to marry her! You have nothing in common except for being neighbours."

"And your girl is better? What's her name?"

"Tristen, your mother knows of her although she has never met her. She was born in Cornwall and moved to Normandy when she was one. Her father had been killed in a similar way to Richard and so her mother took her to safety."

"Whereas my mother stayed on our land and taught me how to defend it and keep it. There was no way that she was letting those idiots take control. We Pridias have had control since before that Christ fellow they keep forcing upon us, was born."

"It's the same for all of us. We own the land and every invader wants to steal it or sell it when they leave. It's not theirs, it's ours."

"And their beliefs are not ours," agreed Pagan.

"No. This Jesus may have been a good man but I don't see why we have to leave our old ways behind."

"It's only control. Once Rome could no longer afford an army here, they decided to have the Church hold our eternity in their hands and it's all bollocks."

"You don't believe that God holds your destiny in his hands then?"

"No! I believe I hold my own destiny. What happens to me is my own decision and no one else's."

"You would get on very well with Tristen. She was put into that convent when she was young and she wants to leave before they do the whole head shaving and committing to marriage to Jesus and all that crap."

"So, you want me to save her?"

"Yes, and I want you to save her blood. Her line comes directly from Melusine like Jehanne and me, but Tristen's blood is purer as it comes through both her parents."

"There seems to be only a few Melusine descendants in the world. Not all of them want to breed I heard."

"Tristen wants a life and children."

"Not a husband?"

"I don't think a husband is high on her agenda, but she must have one if she wants any sort of life."

"Marry her to one of your sons then!"

"No. I have valuable contracts from them already. I want you to marry her and then we can trade and I will fight with you. I shall write to your mother and she will agree. She owes me."

Jehanne probably did owe Alain a lot. After the death of her husband, she and the ten-year-old Pagan would have lost all the estates without assistance. The favours she accepted had long arms and marrying Pagan to Ethel was repaying one of those favours.

Alain and Pagan embraced and he set off home, accompanied by Nos and Ddu, the black horse he had bought from a merchant when he docked at Fowey a year ago. The promised boat load of more Spanish horses had failed to arrive but Pagan remained hopeful. Pagan rode across the moor southwards and tracked through the wood until he reached the northern edge of his lands.

The family had been Lords here since part of the clan moved from flooded Lyonesse to the cousin ruled lands near Fowey. The Pridias Lords had originally taken their name from the southern edges of their lands – the clay cliffs. The meadows and woodland on the estate was intermittently broken by crags and streams and marsh and ended with the old hillfort caped with trees and rocks. The old wooden stockade compound had been replaced with a huge stone wall surrounding an inner village and Pridias Hall. This afforded them a view to the sea and the bay which culminated at Ponts Mill, their own harbour.

As he rode across the crags, Pagan began to remember the time he wanted to forget. The day that the men had come on their horses with their torches and their swords.

"Run to your mother Pagan," his father had shouted. And run he did, to the hidden beach where he knew his mother would be swimming and he could shut out the noises of the fighting and shouting and the terrible screaming. When he told his mother what was happening, she hid him in a cave safe from the high tide and said she would be back as soon as she could. Then she ran up the rocks to the cliff top and was out of sight. Pagan could hear noises of frightened people and clashing swords but saw no one until the following morning when his mother returned to him and she seemed to have aged 10 years.

Richard de Pridias had been stabbed, beheaded and left against the stone stockade sides along with several of his men and some of the women and children. The raiding party had come to steal horses and the gold they believed the Pridias family had. They only got as far as they did because the invaders usually soldiered for the local Saxon trouble causers and they were not ordinarily challenged or crossed. By the time Richard realised that their aims were murderous, it was too late. The Pridias fought well but were swiftly overcome, a penalty of not being battle ready.

When Jehanne Melusine de Pridias came running into the battle, her family were all but overpowered. She picked up her dead husband's sword and swung it above her head before almost cutting the man she believed to be his executioner, in half. The man screamed and begged her for the death stroke but she only laughed and walked away before killing two more attackers. Jehanne screamed instructions at her people and soon the remaining bandits, including their leader, were cantering away, taking less with them than they had brought.

Jehanne called some of her own men as she mounted Richard's horse and they followed the raiders. Others from their village took care of the injured and two were instructed to row across the bay and fetch help. They were then to ferry back with help, for it was too far to ride inland to the bridge and ride back downriver. Jehanne had her bow and skilfully used it alongside her men, killing four escapees before they reached the Pridias boundary. Jehanne ordered that their bodies be dragged to the edge of the wood where she said the wolves would get rid of them. The only person to escape was the hooded leader whom Jehanne later learned was the real executioner and apparently, no one knew his identity, or was saying.

Following this terrible event with the support of her family and neighbours, she brought up her son as the Lord of the Pridias lands and taught him everything she knew, which was considerable. She brought in tutors only when necessary. Pagan loved her, respected her and feared her. Jehanne's familial line was as formidable as his, if not more so and everyone knew her skills. This was the woman that Pagan was now to tell about Alain's proposal. Jehanne knew they needed support, but she would not want to alienate her neighbours.

When he walked inside the great hall, he saw his mother standing on the balcony looking out across the bay to Tywardreath. He walked and stood by her side. Nos pushed his head under her hand, forcing her to stroke him.

"How did it go?" she asked.

"He will help us and trade with us but on one condition."

"There is always a condition with Alain. What is it this time?"

Pagan looked at his mother. Her blonde-red hair was silhouetted against the setting sun. It hung long and straight to her waist allowing it freedom, while most other women covered theirs with a wimple. She wore her overdress of black and gold long over the underskirt, in a style contrary to her contemporaries. Although in a vow of perpetual mourning for her husband, she nevertheless wore jewellery about her person and her hair, the jangling of which would announce her arrival.

"The other women will soon follow my fashion," she said to her maid, Gertrude.

Whether they would or not, Jehanne was more beautiful at 50 than many women half her age. Men admired her and women envied her. She was a goddess the like of whom Pagan wanted as a wife and they both knew that the Fowey girl was not up to scratch.

"He wants me to marry some cousin of mine who doesn't like living in a Normandy convent."

He was surprised when Jehanne grabbed his arm and asked, "Who?"

"Some girl called Tristen."

Jehanne put her hand to the pendant dangling among her many neck decorations.

"I thought she was dead."

"Not very dead Mother. I told him I could not marry because you have promised me to the delightful Ethel."

"I can soon get you out of that," she said.

This was an unexpected reaction, Pagan had expected anger and refusal.

"You go and bathe my son, you stink after your journey and I shall ride to Polred and meet with Gaston. If Tristen is still alive, then you shall marry her and keep our line pure."

Nos went to follow her and Pagan called him back. Jehanne had wolves of her own, all of which were related to Nos. The de Pridias family believed in purity of blood, whether within their own clan or with their animals.

She held her hand up as she walked away, signalling no more talk and hitched up her skirts as she ran down the wooden stairs to the ground. Pagan watched her pull herself on to her horse and ride away, accompanied by two guards. He crossed from the balcony to the edge of the wall and saw them gallop away from the cliffs and beach towards the bridge, two miles upstream which they would have to cross in order to ride back towards Tywardreath and beyond.

Gaston Polred had the lands down to the wood-covered headland. The property was divided by a small river that culminated in a pool stained red by the minerals and ore it ran through. Gaston had helped her a great deal following Richard's death and had asked her to marry him several times. His own wife died two months after Richard, after a fall from the cliffs at the headland. Some said that Gaston had been involved in the raid and wanted Jehanne and her lands. While Pagan was too young to take control, there was plenty of gossip about what could happen in the years between an heir being ten years old and his coming of age.

As it turned out, Jehanne was more than capable of running the show and kept Pagan close and her people loyal and so needed no husband. The same gossips believed that getting Pagan to marry Ethel was the next best thing for Gaston Polred.

Jehanne was an excellent rider and they arrived quickly at Polred Hall.

"My dear Jehanne, I am so pleased to see you!"

Gaston embraced her warmly and beckoned the priest who was with him to leave them alone. The man bowed and walked to the side of the hall.

"In need of spiritual guidance Gaston?"

"No, my conscience is clear. I was discussing the wedding plans, is that why you are here?"

"Yes. I have come to tell you that the marriage cannot go ahead as my son is promised to another."

"Since when? You cannot go back on this contract!" Gaston was instantly angry, a state his men were used to seeing but one he had never yet shown to Jehanne. He could see his hopes of marriage and control over the lands across the bay slipping away.

"I would not go back on a contract Gaston, but I have only recently discovered that the girl Pagan was promised to when he was a child, is still alive."

"Has she been resurrected from the dead?"

"Something like that. We were told she was dead when she was eight, not long before my husband was murdered. She caught the plague in Normandy at her convent and apparently died. But I have heard only today that she survived and I cannot in all conscience proceed with the marriage between Pagan and Ethel. It would go against God."

Jehanne looked over to the priest for confirmation and he nodded his agreement. She thought Gaston was going to explode. He smashed the table with his fists and threw a bowl at her head,

"Gaston! Control yourself! This is no way for a civilised man to behave!"

Gaston lurched across the room and grabbed Jehanne by the throat. She put her own hands up to his in an attempt to remove them.

As they struggled, her many stranded necklaces broke and her gold symbols, one containing some of Richard's possessions, fell to the ground. Gaston did not stop his attack but Jehanne was now empowered and she ripped his arms from her neck. Then she struck him hard in the chest and he fell back against the tall candle sticks. The noise finally brought assistance in the shape of the priest and two of Gaston's servants who ran to lift their master while the priest came to the side of Jehanne.

"My Lady, are you hurt?"

"Only slightly Father but he has broken my necklaces which are very precious to me. Please help me collect them."

He picked up the chains and pendants and it was then that Ethel walked in to the room.

"So, I am not to be your daughter, Jehanne?"

"No, my dear. You will have to wed your Lystwithiel fellow now, Ethel. Not such a good breeding line but at least you won't be alone."

"Like you?" replied Ethel.

Jehanne walked over to the girl, slapped her hard and said,

"Don't cross me Ethel."

Jehanne left and rode back home, smiling.

*

Tristen Melusanne arrived at the Pridias home in a procession constituting twenty men and four women. Jehanne and Pagan watched her arrival from the walls. The double line of horses and their riders rode in front and behind the horse which held his bride-to-be. She was dressed in white and wore a veil and cloak which completely covered her face and form. It seemed that Pagan must wait before he could view the woman he had agreed to look after for the rest of her life.

As they neared the house, a drum beaten by one of her outriders echoed. A single beat in time with their horse-steps brought Pridias villagers out of their homes until, without instruction, they lined her route.

Pagan looked at his mother and saw that she was looking at the procession more intently than she had ever looked at anything. He hoped all this was going to work out. He had agreed to the marriage contract but had no intention to be constantly at the side of his new wife.

Pagan had been surprised at the change in his mother following her return from visiting Gaston. She seemed more determined and focused. Writing back to Alain she not only agreed to the marriage but demanded that Tristen was brought home from Normandy and immediately despatched to their estates. Jehanne would only say that it was imperative for the family to keep Tristen safe.

As the procession arrived at the gates they were opened by guards and the procession moved through in time to the drum. Just before Tristen rode under the archway she looked up and Pagan swore that she left her horse and brought her face into his. But he must have been mistaken for she soon vanished from sight under the gateway and now they must descend the stairs and welcome the group. Tristen did not speak, her maids instead asking about her quarters and giving a list of demands to which Jehanne readily agreed. Tristen floated behind her maids into the rooms allocated to her until the wedding could take place at the church dedicated to Saint Blaise at Landreath which lay southwards along the cliffs.

There was a tall stone cross near the site which the Saxon invaders had helped erect and carve. It had been there for almost one hundred and fifty years and lay just inside the wall encircling the Pridias village. It was considered magical by the villagers and was often decked with flowers and charms.

"When do I get to meet her?" asked Pagan.

"At the wedding tomorrow."

"She might look like a boar!"

"She won't. She's a Melusine like me. She will be clever and beautiful and skilled." Jehanne put her hand to the jewelled pendant box hanging at her breast and whispered, "Now we shall know. Finally."

Pagan knew that the only thing his mother wanted to know was who had killed his father and he wondered how Tristen would be able to help.

He forgot all about the problem by the time he stood at the cross waiting for his bride to arrive. Tristen arrived attired similarly to her arrival yesterday. Her dress and tunic were threaded with gold and jewels and her cape was made from a pale fur and bordered with gold. Tristen brought no money to the contract although Jehanne said she brought more than wealth. She said that his new wife assured their protection against the upcoming and apparently unavoidable land grab by the Norman invaders.

Pagan dictated the details of the days following the wedding to a young monk who often visited the area. It seemed that the Church was looking at establishing a monastery across the bay if the money could be raised. The monk was disturbed about some of the elements of Pagan's story but knowing that miracles happened often, dutifully transcribed the words in his excellent hand.

This is what was written.

Shortly after our wedding it was obvious that my mother Jehanne and my wife Tristen were more than aunt and niece. I have always been aware that Jehanne had abilities unusual to all but the most accomplished of sorcerers. Now I learnt that my wife had the same skills and together they decided to achieve two initial goals. Firstly, to discover the identity of the man who murdered my father and secondly, to save and secure the Pridias ancestral lands. Our lands have, from the beginning of man's memory been in our possession and they run the length of the cliffs to the south, down to the sea and beyond the river to the east to Golant, to the north we own parts of Lanlivery and Luxulyan and beyond to the feet of the moor and to the west we own Stenalees and beyond. We own lands at St Breock and St Issey and beyond to the north coast. Our Hall is perched at the cliff edge at the bay and has a perfect view of the sea. This William man who has incorrectly termed himself King, has no rights over our Celtic and Kernewek lands.

My father Richard de Pridias had been killed and beheaded when a raiding party came to our home. My mother Jehanne and some of our fighting men saw off and killed most of the men, but were told that the man who stabbed and removed the head of the popular leader of their lands had escaped. No one had recognised him because he wore a leather hood but it had been reported that before he took the final deadly blow he removed it.

Jehanne had supervised the burial of Richard and only told me years later that she had removed my father's eyes. I was shocked to hear this news. I believed to that point that the box pendant Jehanne wore all the time contained only Richard's hair. Jehanne had always told me that she carried my father with her wherever she went but had failed to mention that it was his eyes.

I refrained from asking how she removed his eyes as I did not wish to know. Even though we live in such violent times, I have killed no one whereas I know of twelve men killed by Jehanne. She was not so weak as me in this regard.

We are told that the final sight of a person before they die is reflected in their eyes and the last thing Richard saw was his murderer. Jehanne said that she would wait until she was able to view the reflection. The eyes were kept in separate airtight compartments in the gold box, so that one could be removed without tainting the other.

At Pridias we have a building further along the coast which is used for meditation and worship. There is a central table with candles, bowls and a gold crucifix. On the circular walls are hundreds of candles on three layers of shelves, some of which are always lit. All the candles are lit when it is very cold or when there are special ceremonies. We celebrate our own beliefs in addition to the enforced Roman Christianity, ignorance of which would mean great trouble for us if commented upon by our neighbours to the self-righteous Bishops.

It was here that Jehanne tried her first experiment with my help. At almost midnight on the night of the Winter Solstice, all the candles were lit. The door was locked and instructions had been given that we to be disturbed under no account. Jehanne placed a silver mirror on the altar and Richard's left eye was placed on a raised gold plate in front of it. Behind that and in direct line with the mirror and eye was another plate containing some minerals which Jehanne said she had bought from a sea merchant at great expense quite recently. She spoke out aloud to my father's spirit and asked that he help us in our task.

The mineral was lit and it shot a hot bright light through the eye and it was there! A milky white image on the glass of a man and even the sword shape was visible. We held our breath as the image began to clear and then as a strange wind circulated the room, the mineral spluttered and stopped and the image faded.

It was over and we were none the wiser. Richard's eye was decaying before us and we both knew that our chance had passed. I had not known that Jehanne had asked Tristen to bring more mineral with her from France where merchants could obtain it more easily from the Arabian countries. The Melusine women would be able to work better together she told me.

Meantime, I supervised our farming and hunting and ensured the building work was done and soldiers trained and the fishermen had their nets ready. I spoke to visiting monks and saints and allowed hermits to travel through our lands and stay and rest in return for prayers and medicinal skills. I organised the mining and sale of the crystals and through only a few trusted men – gold.

Jehanne and Tristen would talk often and meet in our own chapel and discuss – I didn't know what. Then one day I was told that they were ready for the second and final experiment. I was also informed that I was to be present at this momentous occasion which was destined to succeed. This time it took place on the Summer solstice and with a full moon, it almost was not dark enough at midnight. By the time we shut the chapel door and lit all the candles the atmosphere was set fair and we were sure we would get a result. I never stopped to think what we would do when we saw the image. Jehanne said, "I will avenge your father Pagan, it is not of your concern."

We followed the same process as before and even I was aware that Tristen added energy to the proceedings. This time when the minerals were lit there was enough light to last almost a minute and there, reflected on the mirror was a face we recognised immediately.

It was Gaston Polred.

It took the three of us one hour to reach the stone and wooden home of our supposedly good neighbour Gaston. The Saxon, Cola had once been in overall governance of Polred lands but now that the Normans were taking control in England it was only a matter of time before he would have a new master. That night none of us were interested in outcomes as we were set only for revenge. Tristen was as determined as anyone who had known him personally. Jehanne was correct, there could never have been anyone other than Tristen for me.

A servant peered through the small hatch in the main door of the Polred Hall revealing only his dirty hood and grizzled face. He told us that his master was not at home. I told him I did not believe him and would kill him if he did not open the door. He said if I threatened him again he would send out fighting men and I informed him that I would kill them one by one and we argued in this childish manner until Jehanne stopped us. She asked where Polred was and the servant said he had ridden along the cliff tops and then down through the woods towards the headland at the edge of the bay.

We mounted again and rode down the coast track, feeling the sea spray from the high tide as the increasing wind threw it in our direction. We did not speak when the sun began to rise at our backs and brought into view a scruffy looking man on his horse. As we approached, he turned around and then dismounted.

By the time we were in front of him, Gaston shook and whimpered and said. "I am sorry Richard. I wanted your lands and your family and your life and tried to get it. I was wrong and will be punished for it. You have come to collect me and I am ready."

We looked to our right flank and out of the rays of the rising sun, rode my father in the same black and gold tunic which has always represented the Pridias family. Jehanne moved her horse towards his horse and Richard raised his hand to stop her and she understood. He patted his sword, the same sword I now carried and smiled. To Tristen he bowed and then he rode towards Gaston. Richard suddenly kicked his horse to a gallop and Gaston turned to run away and in so doing he ran straight over the cliffs. Richard continued to ride over the cliff and did not fall. As the sun came completely over the hills and bay to our rear, Richard and his horse vanished.

Gaston's servant and three armed men rode up behind us and then towards the cliff edge. "I saw Richard de Pridias chase him over the cliff," said one.

"His spirit did," said another.

This is exactly what happened and I want it to be on record for future generations to take note. The next time my father was seen was at my mother's deathbed many years afterwards. This is a true account

Paganus de Pridias

Lord of Pridias.

THE PATTERN OF ONE

Featuring Richard de Pridias (1170-1122)

Richard de Pridias was sitting on the beach at the base of the cliffs watching his wife Morwenna and his son Baldwin play in the water. They were trying to teach him to swim but Baldwin had no aptitude, instead preferring to play with the wolves. Richard a non-swimmer himself, had empathy with the boy.

It was a perfect sunny day and the sea was calm. He could see boats ferrying men across to Tywardreath and coming in from the bay with fish and crabs. The larger merchant and fishing boats crossed the end of the bay on their way to Fowey and back. Some ships travelled eastwards to other Cornish ports and across the Channel to the Normandy coast. The seabirds swooped against the cloudless sky and down to the water, hopeful that some of the food the family ate might go their way. Sadly for them, crumbs went into the mouths of the wolves and any attempt to steal was met with dangerous snaps and growls.

Richard stood up and brushed the sand from his leather tunic, the action encouraging Nosbach to run to his master and push his hand onto his own muzzle.

"Come on boy, we have to work."

"Can't you stay longer?" asked his wife.

"No. Tristen wants me to look at some documents about the Priory. They are intent on finishing it apparently."

Subconsciously they looked across their bay to the church perched a little back from the Tywardreath pier. To the seaward side was a tall wooden scaffolding tower covering the consecrated stones supposed to be used when the initial building blocks were laid in 1088. The building had been inconsistent, sometimes money ran out or was suddenly withdrawn and the local workmen starved or feasted or went back to sea, per the current state of play. Deaths of authority figures, both pastoral and legal and arguments over land and rights had delayed the project and 34 years on they were only partway through the build and still arguing. Now Richard was to attend a meeting with the delegated and ruthless Canon Ordagar and sign a treaty promising fighting men and money and land. If he didn't, they would be under yet another threat to have their own land taken from them. His late father Pagan had fought tooth and claw to keep the Pridias lands and Tristen his widow, had cast her spells. These incantations were performed in the early days with her mother-in-law Jehanne and following her death, alone. So far, the incantations had been very effective.

Richard kissed his wife and son, patted his leg summoning Nosbach and ran up the cliff. Richard hadn't ridden down, preferring to walk through the meadows to the beach. Even as he moved away from the beach towards Pridias Hall he could not help looking back at the sea. He could never tire of living here.

The grass, sandwort, orache and purslane and sedge quickly gave way to yarrow, lady's bedstraw and mint. He knew that a little further upriver he would find flag iris in yellow, blue and white, marsh marigolds and mallows. As he neared the edge of the tree line, the wood sorrel, woodruff, garlic and sweet nettles let out their heady scents. The trees, oak, beech, ash and alder hid the birds, squirrels and further inland at the dark centre of the wood the wolf families, boars and deer roamed.

He could never risk losing these ancestral Pridias lands to the Norman carpetbaggers who now enforced their self-serving laws. He must do what his family had always done, playact subservience and proact rebellion.

His mother waved at him from the wall and he fondly remembered his Nain Jehanne doing the same thing before her death seven years prior. Jehanne had been put to rest alongside Pagan and Taid Richard so carefully by Tristen and two of their local hermits. Jehanne rested in her specially designed coffin in a blue and silver threaded gown. Her pale red hair had been braided elegantly with gold and crystals and laid over her arms which were crossed over her breast. Unlike so many women, neither Jehanne nor Tristen needed to braid the hair of donor women into their own in order to make it look thicker and longer. Some women even added long silver cups and tassels at the hair ends to achieve the same effect. There had been discussion from others that Jehanne's dead arms should be held in prayer over her breast, but that idea was swiftly vetoed. Jehanne believed in her own power and would not bow to an outside idol, perhaps interpreting the Bible teachings rather better than the Bishops had.

Tristen met him as he walked through the gate and they made their way over to the chapel. Richard swung the heavy door open and they both entered before closing it firmly and bringing across the oak bar.

"I cannot wait long Tristen, I have to meet at Tywardreath and go through the convention for the future of our lands."

"I know my son. You must not panic, we shall retain them and secure our future."

"Spells and potions?"

"I trust that you are not joking Richard. Keep your focus on how you want your life to play out."

Richard said nothing, he was aware of how it worked and knew that he must never imagine anything he did not want to happen. He wanted to tell his mother about the feelings of impending doom he had hanging over him. She would tell him to change his thoughts and lately he was finding that advice irritating.

"I am, Mother. Now, what do you want me here for?"

"Seven years."

"I don't understand."

"It is seven years since Jehanne passed. It is time to collect her bones and relics."

"I'm not doing any of that," Richard said with a harshness in his voice that he had not intended to convey.

"You won't have to. I will do it and Geraint and Myfor will help me. There will be nothing gooey left on her bones, you know that's why we wait seven years."

"I know Tristen, it just seems a bit...like witchcraft."

Tristen caught his arm with a strength that defied her 74 years. She looked like a 30-year-old and he thought of Jehanne and the day she died at 95 years old. She had spent the day at the beach, walked back and gone into the chapel. She was a very fit and young looking – supposedly, old lady. Tristen had found her when Jehanne failed to return for her evening meal and she soon went about her Melusine business on Jehanne's body. The funeral had been a splendid affair.

Geraint and Myfor were two of her assistant monks whom she was teaching herbal medicine in return for their regular prayers for the more religious Pridias villagers. The rattle on the chapel door soon revealed their arrival for the task.

"I am going, Tristen."

"Where is the meeting?"

"Polred Hall. I am to meet Ordagar the Canon and the Polreds are supplying a place to meet."

Tristen looked up and said, "Beware that slimy weasel Ordagar and the Polreds. They are still holding a grudge. Here..."

Tristen took a pendant from her neck. "Wear this around your neck. It will keep you safe."

He took it and walked outside, putting the pendant into a tunic pocket. He had no intention of arriving with a feminine necklace to such an important meeting.

His escape was stopped by his mother shouting from the chapel door.

"Wait Richard, I want you to take a letter to the Canon."

*

He handed the letter to Ordagar as soon as he was shown into Polred Hall.

"Thank you, I always like to hear from the Lady Tristen. She is a special person."

"Yes sir. I think so."

"She has managed very well since your father passed to his higher reward."

"Yes, she has accepted that your God saw fit to send that storm while he was out on a previously calm sea."

"My God?"

"I suspect he is more yours than mine sir."

"Perhaps, perhaps."

Ordagar poured Richard a drink and then pulled a chair away from the table and untied the parchment.

He read it carefully and read it again and rolled it back up and retied it.

"Do you know what it says?" he asked.

"No sir, I have no idea."

"Then I shall not tell you but please tell her yes, I shall be honoured to accept. Now, let us discuss your rights to the lands across the bay."

"I like to think that we are entitled to the lands. The Pridias family have lived here since before Lyonesse fell, and hundreds of years before that."

"You are related to King Mark?"

"And by definition Tristan and Iseult? I heard you have been searching for their meeting place."

"An interest of mine I'm afraid."

"They met at Golant, by the church there. And King Mark was based at the hill fort over there," Richard pointed to the north east. "At Castle Dor."

"I have heard that. Perhaps you can give me a tour one day?"

"Certainly. There are some very interesting places on Pridias land too," said Richard, spotting an advantage.

"Hmmm. And you think it would be a shame to let the land fall into the hands of a Norman?"

"I do."

Ordagar handed him a roll of parchment,

"I don't read this fancy Latin script," said Richard, handing it back.

"By all means, I can tell you what it says."

Ordagar walked over to the window and began,

"One Knights fee in the manor of Pidias, to hold to Richard de Pidias and his heirs, except an acre of land in Carnubelbanathel for which the monks of Tywardreath rendered annually to the said Richard 20d for all customs, &cc, as written in this charter of convention between Ordagar the Canon and Richard de Pidias."

"It's Pridias."

"I will have it altered. Do you agree to the terms?"

"Do I have any choice?"

"My Lord FitzTorold will take all the lands if you argue. This way you get to keep everything and from what I see here there is a substantial acreage and perhaps it is worth bowing to another to keep it."

"And Carnubelbanathel?"

"If you let the monks continue to use it, that helps your case. I certainly have put forward the argument."

"Thank you. I don't expect that Polred is happy about this?"

"He doesn't know yet. He also doesn't know that he will be losing control over most of his own land to the Crown. He won't be happy."

"May I ask why you have been so helpful to our family?"

Ordagar laughed.

"The Melusine blood has influence in more places than you could possibly know."

Richard nodded,

"With a Melusine Nain and Mother I have seen plenty, don't you worry."

"I would like to hear about it. As you know…"

"It is an interest of yours."

"Yes, and a good job for you that it is."

"I am sorry sir. I did not mean to sound rude. What did my mother tell you?"

"Now that is where I must plead privacy. Ask your mother."

When Richard left Polred Hall and the young servant girl had smiled at him as she let him out of the door, he decided to ride over to the Priory site. There were a few workmen around but they were only half-heartedly dressing stones and erecting stockade fencing. The wooden scaffold surrounding the area where the tower was to be looked as though it would have to be rebuilt before any more serious work was to be done. The Priory was not half-finished and there didn't seem an intention that it would begin soon. Richard expected that his demanded financial contribution in return for his land would help.

Richard looked out to sea where ships sailed against the clear blue sky. He had to put his hand to his eyes against the bright sun which was gradually slipping down to the horizon. He looked back to the bay where he could see his Hall atop the old fort and the woods which caped the seaward side and the meadows which stopped at the clay cliff and the beach below. The tide was going out and that meant only the ferry and the smaller boats were using the water. Further up river and miles out of sight, was the bridge everyone used to circumnavigate the bay but near Ponts Mill, there was a lower causeway which could be crossed at the lowest tide. Here the traveller must be very quick and have a certain knowledge of the tide times.

His horse was becoming restless and as he bent to stroke him Richard heard howling. He saw Nosbach at the clifftop on the other side of the bay and the wolf had seen him. The wolf jumped down onto the beach and began splashing in the water. He started to wade in and Richard shouted out to him to stop but Nosbach couldn't hear him. The wolf began to swim and Richard didn't know what to do for the best. Shouting would only encourage him and if he rode back to the bridge, Nosbach may panic. He should have brought him to the meeting. They usually went everywhere together.

Then he saw Tristen running down the meadow to the cliff edge and Nosbach turned his head, hesitated and then began swimming back to the beach. Tristen waved to Richard and all was well again.

"Your mother is a clever lady," said a voice behind which revealed itself to belong to Ordagar.

"I thought he was going to drown."

"You love your wolf?"

"I do sir. We have a few at home."

"I always wanted a wolf."

"They take a lot of looking after and like to roam free."

"Yes, and I am always wandering around the country. I have to go to the north coast later this week."

"It is better that a wolf stays in his own hunting ground even when he has a master. They cannot be chained anywhere."

"I am sure. Tell your mother I will be back in seven days and we can do the thing she suggested then."

Richard smiled and kicked his horse on. The workmen nodded to him and Richard cantered through the village towards the bridge. The people looked at him with envy or scorn depending upon their own view of Lords and their lands.

Richard eased his horse as he arrived at the causeway. It was quicker to go home this way and he was worried about Nosbach. The water was now low enough and as it was a receding tide it could only get drier. It would save him almost an hour on his trip and he was sorely tempted to try it. He saw Nosbach and Tristen standing on the bank opposite and she waved. Nosbach was edging forward.

"Come on boy, lets risk it."

His horse twirled and spun and refused to move ahead. Richard kicked him and squeezed his legs, forcing him forward. The horse put one hoof on to the sand but as soon as he felt it sink a little, he reared and pulled back. Richard was not a cruel man and decided not to frighten the animal unnecessarily and so dismounted. A boy he knew came to him and Richard hailed him.

"Can you ride, boy?"

"Sir - yes my Lord."

"Do you know who I am?"

"You are the Lord of the Pridias sir."

"I am and you are the son of Philip the smith at Tywardreath."

"I am, sir."

"Take my horse back to the bridge and bring him to my Hall. You will be paid and I shall send you back on the ferry. No need to guide him, just hold on. He will know the way, so no ideas about gadding off on a longer ride."

"Right sir. You can rely on me sir. My Lord, are you sure about crossing here?"

"Of course, don't you worry."

"Only it seems a bit..."

"Get going boy."

The boy jumped easily on to the horse who accepted him without trouble.

"My Lord, I would like to come and work for you and take care of the horses or something like that. There is no work for me here and I do like wolves too."

Richard looked up at the raggedly-dressed boy sitting on his beautifully turned out stallion and said,

"See how you get on with him. We will talk when you bring him to me safely."

"I promise, my Lord."

Richard patted his horse and the boy turned him upstream. He heard a noise from the opposite bank and saw Nosbach standing on the far end of the causeway. The wolf had no fear of the receding water. Tristen waved again and stood behind the wolf. Richard walked forward and felt his boots sink into the sand and he withdrew them immediately. He had imagined it would be drier but when Nosbach began to bark Richard couldn't resist the urge to cross. He walked purposefully towards his mother and wolf and tried to ignore his wet legs and tunic. He also chose to ignore the shouts from the Tywardreath bank because he couldn't see what that was about.

It was several seconds before he realised that he was struggling to keep afloat and the weight of water on his tunic and sword was pulling him under. He was choking and spluttering and in his confusion felt his mind racing between panic and disbelief. There had been no water and it was a receding tide. It was not possible that the water was now above his head.

"Tristen!" he shouted. "Nosbach, help me!"

Richard was trying to keep the panic out of his voice as he splashed and struggled and his mouth went under again. Nosbach was at his side and Richard grabbed for him but couldn't reach. He saw Tristen on the bank and shouted, "Mother! I need help!"

He heard more shouting and some screaming and a little voice shouting, "Father! Shall I fetch the boat?" It was Baldwin and Richard couldn't bear that his son would see him drown.

"Baldwin! Go back to the Hall!" But his words could not be heard as his head was under the water. He felt a slight urge to cough and then it was over.

He was on the Pridias bank with Nosbach licking his face and Tristen standing over him.

"Is Baldwin alright?" he asked.

"Baldwin will be fine. He is a good boy and will make a good man."

"Hello my son. We weren't expecting you just yet."

It was Pagan and the woman was not Tristen, but Jehanne.

"I am dead?"

"Drowned, Richard, like me."

"You only swopped one time for another. Nothing to fear here. See? We have the lands and the sea and not one thieving Norman or Saxon or Polred can take it from us."

Richard sat up and looked around. Pridias looked the same and there was the sea and his parents and a man who looked remarkably like Pagan.

"Why? Why have I drowned? I have just secured the lands!"

"Ordagar is a liar and a poisoner and wants Pridias," said Jehanne.

"He will fail however. Baldwin will keep the lands. Tristen will see to that."

"I saw Tristen and Nosbach on the bank," said Richard.

"You saw me and Nosbach drowned when he tried to swim over to you. He is here too, playing with Nos."

Richard fell back on to the bank, unable to take it in.

*

Morwenna hugged Baldwin to her breast and they both sobbed.

"Is Father dead? Like Nosbach?"

Morwenna continued to cry and Tristen put her arm around the both of them before returning to her son's body. She closed the eyes on his wet face and beckoned over her monks.

"Take him to the chapel," she instructed. "Ordagar did this."

"How do you know?" asked Gwyn, Richard's chief guard.

"Trust me Gwyn. I know and we shall have our revenge. Ordagar poisoned my son so that he hallucinated and he will die for it."

Richard was taken to the chapel and washed and dressed ready for his internment. Jehanne's dry bones were already washed and had been split into three gold urns.

"One for the Priory, one for our chapel and one... well I won't tell you where that has been kept until you are older, Baldwin. But be assured Jehanne will protect our lands and the family and their interests."

"I am the Lord Pridias now Nain Tristen, but I am not yet prepared."

"I will stay alive until you are ready, Baldwin. You will be as good a Lord as your father and all your fathers before. Richard shall be kept here alongside Pagan and Taid Richard."

"Where are my other Lord Pridias buried?"

"On the moor. They will rise when they are needed. But always know this Baldwin, a Pridias lives forever."

She hugged him tight and nodded across to Gwyn.

He would deal with Ordagar, however long it took. The letter would ensure that he found him.

THE BRIDGE OF INCIDENTS

Featuring Baldwin de Pridias (1109 – 1165)

"Are they still arguing about that?"

"Yes, and I have again informed them of our position. The lands are ours and not Cardinham lands."

"I don't know how many times I need to tell them. More than I have already done it seems."

Baldwin was tired. He had been Lord Pridias for 34 years following the sad demise of his father Richard. During that time, he had agreed to help where he could with the now completed Priory at Tywardreath in return for the security of his own lands. Once the contract had been signed, he backed off from the deal, watering the commitment down in his own favour. He learned swiftly that once the local labourers and craftsmen had taken their wages for building the Priory, they had no desire to fund the monks in their judgements and lectures. They had their own hermits and experts in plants for medicine or poison and had no need of these self-righteous interlopers who came to save the Cornish lost souls. Baldwin and his family would always side with their own people. Tywardreath Priory and their Benedictine 'black monks' would have to rely for the most part on handouts from their sister monastery in France.

He had also had a bridge built upriver from the sea moorings at Ponts Mill and the sea causeway where his father had drowned. Baldwin remembered the day he saw his father walk into the sea because he believed that the causeway was dry. He had watched him drown and then seen his lifeless body dragged to shore. Tristen, he thought of Nain so fondly even now, said that Ordagar had poisoned Richard and she had made him pay. Ordagar was soon dead too, a victim of unidentified armed villains on his way to the north coast. Osbert was the Prior currently and had initially taken up the role in 1130 while he supervised the last years of completion until 1135 when the Priory officially opened for business. Osbert had hoped for a constant influx of paying locals worshiping and asking for forgiveness, instead he had a queue of men demanding favourable treatment in whatever deal they had in mind.

Shortly afterwards King Stephen had established his murderous control of England and money and food soon became scarce. There were hundreds of starving and ruthless strangers roaming the lands and willing to kill for food. Any person rebelling against the King was tortured and executed horrendously in the castles Stephen began to build around the country, several of which were in Cornwall.

That was when Restormel Castle began its life at Lystwithiel and where many lost their lives. Baldwin had struggled to keep his people fed and his lands his own. He had ensured that his animals were kept safe and guarded from the starving vagabonds who roamed the countryside ready to kill whatever came into their path. These unwelcomes would steal, kill and eat horses, wolves and cats when cattle, sheep or poultry could not be found. These villains were either executed and buried in secret or thrown outside Pridias boundaries as a warning to others. Hungry Pridias inhabitants would be sent to the hermitage or the Hall for sustenance.

The hermitage was on the western side of the bridge that Baldwin had built. A portion of the alms from the hermitage and the use of the lands surrounding it, went directly to the Priory in return for assistance when necessary.

The bridge was stone and timber built and substantial enough for carts to cross. It was on the River Par, north of the sea harbour at Ponts Mill, to where small ships would sail and dock. It had been Pridias men and Pridias money that had built it, but the Cardinhams and the Turstins were trying to lay claim to it. King Stephen was now dead and he sought to gain support of the new masters. Baldwin Fitz Turstin was trying to use as proof that it was he who had built it on his own lands, because the bridge had come to be known as Baldwin's Bridge. He had used King Stephen – a personal friend, he insisted – as a threat and Baldwin de Pridias had told him what to do with his threats. Now, Fitz Turstin did not feel so secure.

It was Baldwin's nineteen-year-old son Nicholas who was currently informing him of the new claim to the bridge. Nicholas was born the same day the Priory had been declared complete and open for business and he was considered locally as a 'special child'. Why that should be so when his mother had died during his birth condemning Baldwin to a celibate life, had confused them both.

Jehanne, Tristen, Morwenna and Gwen were all dead and there were no Pridias daughters. Soon it would be time to find Nicholas a wife and perhaps he would produce more children than the family had managed to date.

"Is Turstin still backing him?" asked Baldwin.

"Yes. They are making a push before the new King has a clean sweep and the past twenty years are put behind us. I expect they want to make a final claim to the bridge and hermitage and I am not allowing it to happen."

"Neither am I, son."

The bridge was a useful trade route as prior to its construction, travellers had to go much further inland or use the causeway or ferry across the bay. Now travellers paid a toll to an armed guard or two and part of this toll was given in alms to the hermitage. Other travellers wanted to call at the hermitage to visit with the resident sage who had more than likely come from Ireland to Padstow and then across the moor. There had always been a friendly welcome at Pridias from before remembered time. Now this little chapel gave them a place to stay and meditate and heal. The hermit collected their monies and the Priory had their portion. The Priory would sometimes send a monk of their own in order to make sure that nothing happened there which was against God or the King Stephen.

"Alright Nicholas. It will be fine. Now, there is something I think you should know."

"Not another family secret, Baldwin!"

Nicolas pulled a chair from the table and sat down. He accepted the offered wine from his father and smiled. Throughout his formative years, he had learned of the skills of his Mother and Nain. He knew of the wolves and their almost psychic abilities. He knew about the mysterious death of Gaston Polred and many healing miracles. Nicholas knew that he must not talk about any story which resembled witchcraft or event which could not be ascribed to God. Spies were everywhere and the perpetrator was soon reported, dragged off to a secure place by armed men and tortured until he came up with some random names and then he was still executed in a terrible way.

"Another secret Nicholas, you need to know all of the Pridias secrets to pass on to your son when you marry."

"I hope you are not yet contracting a wife for me?"

"No. But as you are the only Pridias blood after me, you must waste no time."

"Not very prolific, are we?"

"Not in this world, no."

"So, tell me."

"The bridge, you remember why I built it?"

"Because of Richard drowning and I know he was poisoned by the lying, thieving Canon. He too is dead and I am glad about that," answered Nicholas.

"Yes, because of my father and because of trade, the income from which has helped us and the Priory."

"And subsequently kept our property safe from all idiots."

"Indeed. But there is much more to it than that. Tristen summoned something to protect us and the bridge before she went. She helped as much as she could, even after your mother died. Sadly, she could not stay with us forever and so she left us a permanent guardian who cannot be paid, swayed, killed or removed. The guardian is ours forever and has protected us and our lands so far. These Cardinhams and Turstins cannot take any of our properties or people while the guardian exists."

"I have seen no guardian. Is he one of our men? Or a Melusine witch I don't yet know?"

"We both have Melusine blood, do not mock. The guardian lives at the hermitage by the bridge," chided Baldwin.

"One of those saints?"

"The guardian is no saint. In the wrong hands, he is the exact opposite of a saint."

"I am intrigued Father. May I meet him?"

"Tonight there is a lunar eclipse. We can only see him during an eclipse. So tonight, I will show you."

"It will be the third lunar eclipse this year, so they aren't that rare."

"I didn't say they were rare, just that is the only time we can see him."

Nicholas smiled, he loved his father but still felt the need to remind him of how clever his son was.

"In fact, there was a lunar eclipse on the first day of this year!" added Nicholas.

"One more word about lunar eclipses and I will eclipse you round the head," said Baldwin.

They both laughed, their close bond since Gwen died had matured and remained as Nicholas grew up.

"Tell me Baldwin and I promise I shall listen quietly."

"Disperkel..."

"What does that mean?"

"That's listening to me, is it?" asked Baldwin.

"Sorry Father," said Nicholas.

"Disperkel is the name of the guardian, because that is what he does. He gets rid of people by making anyone with any evil in their thoughts ill and unable to continue across the bridge. They think they are dying or going to fall over the edge of the bridge or become so ill that they must return to their beds. Many have been so driven by fear that they have gone straight to the hermitage and confessed all their sins. This has been quite profitable although we cannot hide the income from the Prior as many of these saints and holy men are too holy for our own good. You know quite well about the torture houses and the snake occupied cells at the castles and how many of our friends and neighbours ended their lives in such places. And how so many of their servants starved. Those Benedictine monks were and are liars, thieves and have been complicit in all of the murders, tortures and unsustainable taxes. They have been well rewarded for their sordid acts and are now feared, reviled and avoided by all who should be looking to them for help and advice. I am not a Christian as you well know Nicholas but I do know that we are all part of a higher intelligence. That is the reason I also know that these monks will suffer a worse fate than those they have made to suffer in return for material gain. Disperkel has kept us safe and will continue so to do as long as we meet his needs. Don't worry, there is no sacrifice, human or animal and nothing unnatural must be done for him or to him. I saw your expression change, but do you think that Tristen would conjure a spirit that required any such thing? A Pridias and Melusine Lady would do nothing so dreadful. I have told you before that when we pass, we literally pass to our own lands with our own ancestors and Disperkel lives in both worlds and he is only visible properly when there is no night or day. Tonight, is such a night."

They renewed their drinks and Baldwin continued.

"When we built the bridge, it was in a particular style and only part of it is visible to the uninitiated. The only initiated are of our blood and currently there are only two of us on this side. You and me. It seems it is far more difficult to persuade a Pridias to leave the Promised Land to come here than to return there." Baldwin stabbed his finger on the table to illustrate his point.

Baldwin got up and threw his fur cloak about his shoulders then tossed Nicholas his. They both looked tall and superior in their black and gold tunics and carrying heavy, gleaming crystal-hilted swords. Their high-ranking soldiers wore a black and gold chevron over-vest to identify them from the Cardinhams or the Turstins or any of the other Cornish families of old. Baldwin had ensured that all his men, women and horses kept themselves tidy and polished even during the darkest of the Stephonian times.

The two men went outside into the snow and Nicholas began to head over to the stables but Baldwin put a hand on his arm and held him back.

"We shall walk Nicholas, it's too cold to leave the horses by the bridge and the walk will do us both good."

Nicholas was conscious of his limp and thought that his father might have been a little more considerate instead of forcing him to walk. The damage to his leg had occurred during his traumatic birth and Nicholas was constantly aware of it, particularly when he talked to any women.

But, he was respectful of his father and so strode eastwards with him across the cliff top fields towards Ponts Mill. They descended through the woods to the path at the cliff top where the hermitage sat. It was built into the rocks, the cliff face forming the back and sides and roof of the chapel. The front was stone built with a heavy oak door. In the porchway hung a lamp which held a large candle. The small stained glass windows reflected the candles which burnt inside. The hermitage had been built in the style of their own chapel at Pridias Hall, only smaller.

The hermitage was protected by a castellated wall, one side of which extended to the bridge. The bridge was stone built with oak gates at either end and patrolled by a guard who used the stone gate house as a base. The bridge walls were castellated and tall and the tiny cottages along either side of the bridge floor were occupied by loyal Pridias tenants. Because it was the highest crossing place of the River Par before it fell into the sea, it was considered a prize and had been coveted by others for the 15 years since it had been built. No one had won it from the

Pridias although it had not been for want of trying. The older bridge and earlier crossing place was near Luxulyan and was quite a round trip for anyone wanting to get to Tywardreath or Fowey who couldn't use the ferry and daren't use the causeway.

Tonight, the bridge looked at its best. The lamps at either end of the bridge and the lights in the cottage windows shone through the snowflakes and cast yellow light on the river. Just below them on the high tide, several fishing boats and two merchant ships swayed and clanked at their moorings. There were only a few people about and they wore cloaks over their heads as they trudged through the snow homewards. Baldwin and Nicholas were recognised and acknowledged as Lords of the manor by all. The ships' crew were aboard their vessels ready for the night.

Baldwin clapped his son on the back as they arrived at the bridge gate.

"My Lords!" said the guard.

"All well tonight? "asked Baldwin.

"Yes, my Lord, it is a quiet night."

"I am glad to hear it. Family well?"

"Yes, my Lord. The children are celebrating the solstice at home with the wife but some of the neighbours have gone to the moor." The guard felt safe talking to his Lord in this way. Others would have reported him to the Priory and he would have been dragged from his home and his family killed.

"I hope they have a pleasant night and I want you to know that we appreciate your working on such a night." He handed him a coin and the guard put it in his pocket quickly.

"Thank you my Lord and you also Lord Nicholas. Are you crossing the bridge tonight?"

"We would like a walk to the far end and back if that is alright with you? I like to see the cottages in the snow."

"Of course, my Lords," and he opened the gate for them.

The men entered the bridge and strolled through. Faces came to the windows or the porches and then the occupants smiled and waved when they recognised their Lordships. The tiny cottages looked so warm and cosy with smoke coming from the chimneys and lamps at the window.

"Seren and Ddu would have loved this walk," said Nicholas of their wolves.

"Not when we meet the Disperkel," said Baldwin.

They walked to the far end and just before the gate, turned to the wall to look upriver. Baldwin pointed to the sky and Nicholas saw that the eclipse had begun.

"Quick," he said to his son and opened a door in the far bridge tower which had not been visible before. He dragged Nicholas through and soon they were underneath the bridge on a previously unnoticed stone ledge. Nicholas shivered and was about to speak out, but Baldwin put his fingers to his lips.

The ledge was lit by lamps, though tended by whom, was not obvious. Suddenly a low growling noise echoed down the walls. Nicholas began to experience the freezing shivers he usually did when he thought that there was a spirit about. He envisioned that some kind of demon with his eye hanging out would soon crawl towards them, one arm outstretched and finger pointing. He must have made some sort of involuntary squealing noise because Baldwin whispered harshly,

"What is the matter with you?"

Nicholas didn't answer.

They shuffled along the ledge, holding tightly to the wall and Nicholas was conscious of his lameness and hoped they would not need a speedy getaway. They had walked so far that he imagined that they must have reached the other side of the bridge. His guess was correct as Baldwin climbed a few steps and opened a door and soon they were standing at the home gate. The guard grinned and let them out onto the path and he bid them goodnight.

"What was that for?" asked Nicholas. "We just shuffled along a narrow ledge on the outside of the bridge and we could have walked across the top?"

His father was laughing so much that he bent over.

"It's good to know about every angle of your properties!" he said.

"I thought I was to meet some horrible monster that was going to come up from the river!"

"No, he doesn't live in the river. He lives in there." And Baldwin pointed to the chapel.

Baldwin walked over to the door and knocked. It was opened immediately and they were welcomed in by a man wearing a monk's robe of grey wool brought together around his slim middle with knotted cord. He also wore a hooded grey cloak which had snow all over it.

"Been out Patrick?"

"Yes, I have, just got back in. I knew you would be here soon. Come on in quickly, the moon has almost gone."

He pulled them inside and drew the wooden bar across. Baldwin had designed the chapel this way, for with the rock face making three sides and a small securely barred door, it would be very difficult to impregnate with force. The roof overhang and the tiny glass windows completed the secure cell.

"No time to offer you a drink both. He will be here soon."

The candles went out with a strange breeze and they were in darkness. Nicholas went to the window and could no longer see the moon. In fact, he couldn't see the bridge and the houses upon it. That did not make sense as there was no reason not to see the cottage lamps. Before he could successfully work through the problem he was aware of a change in the atmosphere of the room. His skin was crawling and he was so cold.

"Nicholas, will you turn around?" asked Baldwin.

As he did, Nicholas saw his father standing next to the hooded monk. Baldwin was laughing and pointing at the monk's face. Nicholas moved closer and closer until he was directly in front of the man.

"Go on! Move his hood back!"

"No, I daren't!"

Baldwin put his hand to the cloak hood and gently lifted it backwards. There was nothing there, no one. Nicholas froze. A little light came in through the window as the moon began to escape its own cloak. As it did so, a skull began to appear in the hood space where there had been nothing before. The moon gradually became brighter and as it did, flesh appeared upon the skull bit by bit. By the time the moon was again free of its shadow, the monk was returned to life.

"What have I just witnessed?" Nicholas asked breathlessly.

"I am the Disperkel," said the monk. "I protect you lot!"

Baldwin was still laughing, he enjoyed the trick.

"My son, I know I told you of a terrible demon, but although our friend is a strange man I agree, he is quite safe to us."

The monk removed his cloak and folded it neatly onto the table. He held out his hands to Baldwin who took them gladly and shook them.

"This monk will live here forever, so long as there are people of our blood in this land. If they leave he will wait until a Pridias returns to the land again. He has prevented the followers of the Devil King from reaching us."

"Forever. You will protect us forever?" asked Nicholas.

"I will and I will be here even after the sea retreats expanding the land to the edge of the bay."

"He always says that," confided Baldwin.

"The sea will move away from here and the land will rise. Your Pridias Hall will one day sit a long way back from the cliffs, leaving fields and roads and many houses and people. It will retreat far back from the Priory and there will be no harbours or ships up here. I might not like it here quite so much then but Tristen has said that I must stay."

"Oh. Right," said Nicholas.

"Come on home boy. You have met our Disperkel now and can visit anytime you like."

"And ask you questions about God?"

"Not God boy. Not as the Priory monks tell you. The chapel monks' faces will change over the years, but the Disperkel will always be behind his mask. God doesn't come into it."

The men walked back out into the snow and the jolly hermit monk closed the door again.

"So, he is an actual spirit guard?"

"He is. Isn't he great?"

"I suppose so. He wasn't really who I imagined I was going to meet."

"That is because your soul is pretty good. If it wasn't, your experience would be of hell itself."

Baldwin and Nicholas walked home by the coast path. The tide was moving out and the beach and rock pools just becoming visible in the bright moonlight. The snow still fell, but their fur cloaks kept them warm. Ships at sea were visible as a shadow silhouette and cottage lamps burned brightly against the dark walls. Looking across the bay they could see twinkling cottage lights there too. The brightest lights came from the Priory and the pier front at Tywardreath.

"The Priory is wasting our money on lamps and candles again," muttered Nicholas.

"It seems odd when the Disperkel tells us about all of this being land," said Baldwin, waving his arm in the general direction of the sea.

"He must be a witch of some sort to know that," mused Nicholas

"He's a good man. A good Disperkel."

They laughed and turned uphill to walk back to the Hall. It wasn't until they were enjoying a meal later that night when Nicholas realised that he was no longer lame.

THE HANGED MAN

Featuring Nicholas de Pridias (1135 – 1200)

Nicholas was regretting yet again having been persuaded by Alana to do it, but every time he mentioned it to her, she would flounce out of the hall and say that she could never understand him. How the moaning woman could say that was beyond him. She was more than aware of the things he had done to keep her and their lands safe.

He married Alana Cardinham in 1158 as the final solution to the skirmishes between their families in hope that peace could break out. Osbert, the Prior at Tywardreath had intervened and with a substantial financial payment from Cardinham's father and from Baldwin de Pridias worked out a contract that even the new King could not fault.

Sadly, the couple did not get on and once Alana had produced the twin boys Richard and Herden, their roles had been fulfilled and they lived separate lives. Alana spent a great deal of time at Restormel and it was at Nicholas's insistence that the boys remained at Pridias with their wet nurses.

The King Henry, who was a small improvement on the last, nevertheless had troubles of his own and had several times called upon his Lords to assist him in France while he fought to restore lands there.

Nicholas has been forced at 47 years of age, to travel with twenty Pridias fighters to fight for their King. Nicholas had received the princely sum of half a mark for his expenses which were many times more than that. The journey across the sea with the horses on the boats was troubling enough but luckily, they all arrived safely and no man nor horse were lost in the battle.

Nicholas was glad to return to Pridias where he regaled his family and friends with stories, not too embellished, about their travels and was ignorant of the fire he had lit in the minds of his sons. This was around the time that Alana went from Ladylike indifference to open hostility towards her husband. She had enjoyed free reign while he was in France.

The boys had been competing locally in tournaments and now wanted to train in order that they could compete around the country. Nicholas then told them of the young King Henry who was to be trained by the renowned William Marshal and they were mesmerised.

If truth be told, Nicholas had also become more than interested in the fun and had assigned a tutor to his young sons from among his own ranks of men. They would practice for hours along the cliff top meadows, from Pridias to Biscovey.

By 1189, the boys, now men, were both married. They often travelled to France and remained there for months at a time, following the tournaments wherever they led. Richard was the father of a nine-year-old boy, but the weaker Herden had no children. Neither minded leaving their families or their lands, the first Pridias generation to do so for a considerable time.

Henry Fitz Count the Earl, had demanded that at the young Richard must remain in Cornwall and be ready to fight or work for the King and take his duties as a Lord seriously. Richard was the first-born twin and so Herden was deemed freer to leave.

"There are already four Pridias Lords available for him!" complained Richard. "You, me, Herden and my boy Richard. If Herden ever gets his own wife with child, then there will be more! I want to be in France where I am making a fortune collecting ransoms. More than we make on this rotten bit of land. Make Herden stay!"

Nicholas had put his foot down and Richard responded by leaving his son with Nicholas and taking his wife Guinevere, his horses and his men to France. Nicholas then had the bright idea of passing off Herden as Richard to avoid fines and this worked for a long time. They were finally discovered when news began to arrive at Cornwall that Richard de Pridias was doing so well in France and Spain.

Twice Nicholas had been fined for making false claims about his sons, but the Earl was sympathetic, having boys of his own. Following the second fine of 1192, Nicholas sent a stiff message to Richard, who did not receive it as he was already on his way home, having badly injured his leg at the Tournament. When he returned and was lying at Pridias Hall with his wilful wife looking after him and their connection renewed with their now twelve-year-old son, Nicholas told him that if he did not stay at Pridias he would be disinherited.

Herden, who had been manfully and willingly looking after their estates while his ridiculous brother had been away on his jollies, took himself into the woods and hung himself from an oak tree. Alana blamed Nicholas and blamed Richard and blamed Guinevere, the slut of a wife she considered her to be.

Today, Alana had come into Nicholas's study to inform him that she had seen Herden in the woods and he had spoken to her. Nicholas did not believe her, which he realised was a little mean as he knew full well that such things could and did happen. Now that she had left him alone, he felt guilty and wished he had his father to confide in. He would have known what to do, although times had changed everything so much that he felt that once he died, memories and links to the old days would be gone. His own children had been such disappointments.

It wasn't as though he didn't have enough to worry about. Even the lands were now referred to the Manor of Pridias of Priory of Tywardreath and his son Richard did not seem to care or understand. The new King Richard spent a lot of time abroad or planning to go abroad and needed a goodly amount of income. William de Wrotham had been given the task of raising money from tin mining in Devon and Cornwall by Hubert Walter, the Archbishop of Canterbury. He was appointed the First Lord Warden of the Stannaries on 20th November 1197.

These new laws meant that anyone connected with tin mining could only deal with the stannary courts and were exempt from Parliament in London. In some ways, it was helpful and in others meant that Nicholas's mining interests were being badly affected by local political influence.

Nicholas was looking through some of his current holdings and was wondering how he could add to them,

Great and Little Pridias,
Lestoon,
Levrean,
Rosemullen,
Trevanney,
Trenince,
Ponts Mill in Luxulyan.
Stenalees in St Austell,
Grediow in Lanlivery,
Biscovay in Landreath,
Carroget,
Kilhalland,
Rosegarth,
Penpillick in Tywardreath.
Gubbavean in St Issey,
Nanscowe in St Breaock,
moieties in Golant,
Bakers.

It was becoming more difficult so to do, with the Prior and the monks controlling so much of what went on in the area and the secret political alignments that were tricky to foretell.

He got up from his desk and walked over to the window. He could see his Lordly line altogether in the walled garden, an addition he had decided to create after seeing so many wonderful gardens in the south of France when he had been there. It was ironic that his son Richard now found such pleasure in furthering its creation rather than gallivanting abroad.

There, playing some kind of ball game were his 40-year-old son and his wife Guinevere, their son Richard, now 20 with his wife Morgana who held their new born son Geoffrey. Richard and Morgana had married at 16 and were already the parents of two boys, Baldwin and Reginald who were playing around the garden too. They were laughing and relaxed and enjoying themselves. That was until he saw Alana stride into the garden, still nimble in spite of her 60 years and apparently announce to them that Herden was haunting the woods.

He would have to go out and join them.

Nicholas was not as nimble as his wife, his worries and the fighting in France had affected his stamina. His healer told him that his heart was sad and wanted to go home. Nicholas could not argue with that and as there were four generations of Pridias Lords alive, he knew that he could leave the estates in... That was his problem, he did not consider Richard to be a pair of safe hands.

Baldwin would have known what to do and the only way he knew to ask him was to die and then it would be too late.

By the time Nicholas reached the garden, the party had split.

"The Richards have gone for horses so that they can check the woods for Herden," said Alana, arms folded and triumph in her voice.

"I shall join them," said Nicholas and turned to go.

"I shouldn't bother my beloved husband, you cared nothing for him when he was alive and rewarded his devotion and hard work with rejection."

"Herden was weak and he sulked rather too much for a Pridias. If he hadn't been a twin of Richard, I might have doubted his origins."

Alana walked towards her husband as though she would strike him and then thought better of it. Nicholas may well strike her back.

"He was your son Nicholas. As much of a son as Richard is."

"Herden was the one who kept reporting us to the Priory, you know that don't you? He would have had me imprisoned if he had not been stopped."

"I don't believe you."

"It's true. He killed himself because he knew I had found out, nothing else."

Alana walked to Morgana who was clutching Geoffrey, frightened of the scene she was witnessing. She handed the child to his grandmother when she held out her hands.

"Sweet, sweet baby boy," said Alana and Morgana stood, nervously awaiting the safe return of her son.

Nicholas rode into the woods following the trackway he guessed his boys had taken. He was accompanied by Alain and William, two of his men who he hoped would help him with this unusual search. He had not needed to explain, for gossip had shot through the Hall and its surrounds when Alana came home crying and screaming.

A few minutes into the woods, they came across the two Richards, the youngest of whom put a finger to his lips as they arrived. He pointed in front of them and they could see what he could see, a man hanging by the neck from the same oak tree that Herden had killed himself. This man was decomposing and stinking and swinging.

Nicholas put his hand to his mouth to suppress a shout. His son and grandson were frozen on their horses that stood stock still. His men dismounted and walked bravely and deliberately to the swinging corpse. They could not recognise the body because the head was weathered and the tongue black and extended. The man was naked and could not be identified by his clothes.

"Shall we cut him down sir?" asked William.

"Yes, yes indeed. Who is it?" said Nicholas.

"It is Herden," said his son. "He was speaking when we arrived."

"What nonsense!" exclaimed Nicholas.

"I am telling you Father. That swinging corpse spoke to us and said that he was Herden."

"He knew our names," added Richard junior.

"Everyone around here knows our names," pointed out Nicholas, eager to remain the sensible leader.

"But he's a corpse. I think that makes a difference," said his son.

The servants laid out the said corpse and manfully refrained from gagging at the stench.

"You two must have been overexcited after Alana said she had seen Herden. I do not recognise this corpse so ask around and find out if anyone knows him. Then take his body to Tywardreath and have the monks deal with it. I will not be accused of covering up any deaths."

Alain remained with the body and William returned with the others so that he could collect a cart. Nicholas searched for his wife on their return to the Hall to tell her that she was mistaken. He could not find her and was informed that no one knew of her current whereabouts. While he searched for her in the tower which faced the sea, a favourite haunt of hers, he noticed how rough the sea was becoming. Even though their bay was relatively sheltered, the little ships were still struggling to stay on course. He saw on the west bank at Biscovey that a bonfire was lit and he wondered vaguely why. It was away from the houses there, but very large. The wind and rain which looked like it was on its way would soon put it out, he thought.

There was a hammering on the door and Nicholas opened it.

"Sorry my Lord, the Lords Richard have asked that you come down to the courtyard. Something funny has happened they said."

Nicholas followed the servant down the steps and outside where he found his son, grandson and Alain and William. The cart containing the body was in the middle of the yard and not on its way across Baldwin's Bridge and down to Tywardreath.

"What's going on?" he asked.

"It spoke again, my Lord. It said it was Herden and had come to say he was sorry."

"Really it did, my Lord," added William.

It seemed they had put the body on the cart, covered it with sacking and set off for the bridge. They followed the river down from the woods on the rutted track and were horrified when the sacking began moving and a voice came from it. They jumped off the cart and drew their swords and used one of them to raise the brown sacking. The voice continued repeating, 'Sorry, I am so very sorry.' They were sure it came from the corpse but when they looked at his leathery face there was no sign of life or speech.

"Just like we heard, what do you think it means?"

Nicholas stopped for a moment and then asked, "Why do you think it was Herden?"

"The voice was his, my Lord!" Nods all round meant they all believed that to be so.

"I am sorry!" was the wail from under the sacking and to a man they jumped backwards.

"Pull that cover off!" instructed Nicholas.

His son gingerly pulled it off and revealed the decaying corpse with a voice emitting from the blackened mouth. It was saying over and over again.

"I am sorry, I shouldn't have told them and I shouldn't have killed myself. I didn't mean to hurt Mother."

Alana was listening now and crying,

"Herden! My boy!"

Richard said, "This isn't right!"

"I am not dead, I cannot leave without forgiveness!"

"Nothing to forgive, little Hickadon!" said Alana, resorting to her baby name for the boy.

He stopped talking and Nicholas beckoned that the sack be put over him again.

"We must perform another service at the chapel!" said Alana. "Fetch the monks, they will have to be involved."

"We have already buried him once, they won't do it again! They can't!"

"Should we check that he is in the chapel before we make fools of ourselves?" asked Richard junior, quite reasonably.

"Good thinking," said his father and led the way to the chapel that had witnessed weddings, christenings, burials and spells. The normally closed door was open, the chapel waiting for them and they entered.

"The candles have gone out," noted Nicholas. "Light them, William."

As soon as light was thrown around the dimly lit room, the storm began outside. The rain was sideways and torrential and the temperature had dropped sharply. Cloaks were being pulled tighter around shoulders and held there with folded arms. No one was feeling secure.

Nicholas took his Lordly role again and went down to the crypt. The family had the chapel extended underground and lined with stone in order to keep the Pridias bodies intact. Jehanne and Tristen had taken care of bodies in a different way to Alana and the other women who knew nothing about the old ways. Now death meant an oak coffin sealed into a stone sarcophagus for preservation.

Nicholas reached for a step and climbed it so that he could touch Herden's coffin.

"Let me, Father. Please," said his son. "Go back upstairs and Richard and I will deal with this."

Nicholas glad of the excuse to be relieved of this gruesome task, left the men alone.

"What are we going to find?" asked Richard the younger.

"Not a clue," said his father and took the metal bar from its shelf and began to dislodge the mortar from around the lid. His son joined him using a pickaxe. In testament to the workmen who had constructed the sarcophagus, it took a long time to remove the lid. Laying bare the oak coffin released such a smell that they could not deny that a decomposing body lay inside.

They held their noses and tried to stop gagging.

"Shall I?" asked the younger.

"No, but catch me if I fall," said his father.

He prised the oak top and it broke free, breaking rather than coming off in one piece. It soon revealed the corpse of a man that was once his twin brother. He was wearing his black and gold tunic and his fur cloak. It was Herden.

"Who is on the cart then?"

"I have no clue," said his father. "Fetch Lord Nicholas."

Nicholas arrived with Alana hanging on to his arm, eyes wide with anticipation.

"Is your brother there, Richard?"

"Yes, Mother. Herden is in his tomb."

"I want to see," she said. Before they could stop her, she was on the step and peering into the coffin. She stepped off quietly and made her stately way upstairs to the chapel.

"Shall I close it now?" asked the younger.

"I suppose so. Whoever is in the cart, it's not my twin brother."

The younger Richard began repositioning the lid and pulling the stones back.

"I'll get the mason to fix it tomorrow."

They went upstairs and found the rest of the family.

"We are going to tell Alain and William to take it to the Priory tomorrow. Let them deal with it," Nicholas informed them.

"We thought we would let the masons finish clearing up in the crypt," said Richard.

"We should do another service for Herden," insisted Alana. "Help him rest."

Morgana nodded and the women huddled together collecting candles and incense,

"We need a monk," said Alana.

"We can manage without, Alana," said her daughter-in-law. Alana nodded, weakened by recent events.

Nicholas and the Richards followed their men outside, hoods up, the weather still raw and determined. They strode over to the cart.

"Better get it under cover," instructed Nicholas. "Perhaps the body could melt or dissolve in this weather."

Richard the elder lifted the sacking and dropped it again. He turned to look at the others and then turned back to the cart. He lifted the sacking and stared. There lay a dead pig. A pig that had been dead for a long time.

"It's a pig," said Nicholas.

"I don't understand," said the younger.

"We can't take it to the Priory," said the elder.

"No."

"We should burn it or the wolves will dig it up and I don't want them poisoned by this weird pig-man-devil thing," Nicholas insisted.

"There's a fire at Biscovey, lets tip it there tonight. I don't want it here any longer than I need to."

"Is the fire still going? In this rain?"

"It was a pretty big fire."

William jumped on the cart seat, "I will take it, my Lord."

"We will come with you."

That was the procession which moved quickly from Pridias, down the cliff path and south to Biscovey to the edge of the bay. Three Lords, two men servants and a cart carrying a decomposing pig, cantering through the torrential rain. As they arrived at the site of the fire, they found two men tending the blaze.

"We are burning the old bedding from the barns, my Lords. It was dry when we started but this storm blew up and we daren't stop tending it."

"We have something which will help it burn," said Alain and he and William took both ends of the sacking and threw the bundle on to the fire. Within a few minutes the spitting began and the group stood back a little to watch. As the fire glowed brighter and spat there was a general feeling that a problem had been solved. Asking no questions of their Lordships, the workmen promised to remain with the fire until all evidence was gone and so the Pridias group trotted homewards.

When they reached Landreath, they heard an explosion behind. They all turned and saw a huge pall of smoke and ball of flame shoot into the sky. The giant spirit image of Herden appeared in the air. Its mouth opened and screamed and then it vanished, leaving only a large bonfire.

"Don't tell the women," instructed Lord Nicholas.

The men rode home.

Lord Nicholas of the tired heart died in his bed the following day.

THE JOUSTING LORDS

Featuring Richard de Pridias (1160 - 1225)

Travelling around France with his horses and men was the best fun Richard had ever had. Guinevere coming along was interesting too. He would rather that had she remained at Pridias with the baby, but she had insisted that she accompany him, citing his wellbeing. Everyone knew that it was because she didn't want him enjoying himself with the women, beautiful young women, who liked to follow the knights and their entourage around the tournament circuit. That was a shame, as he was partial to young women. Guinevere was good company however and supported him in whatever he did.

Richard first got interested in the sport after his Royal sojourn with his father and the King. Until then, he hadn't realised that he could be so good at anything. He loved the sound of the cheers and the claps of the crowd. Richard had always been a good rider, excelling at the kind of paces that worked well with music. He often made one of the servants play while he rode at Pridias so that he could improve his timing. He was a great swordsman and archer and so he had only to master jousting. He had practised and practiced with his tutor and Herden and improved every time.

Herden was a different matter. He was quite a good rider, but weak at the sword and bow. He practised with Richard, taking on all the instruction and advice and ended up a poor second. When their soldiers joined in, Herden would move down the rankings - he was always last. They had never used a sparring partner who finished lower than Herden. But Herden seemed unaffected by his poor skills and was just happy to compete.

Therein lay the problem. They both went to France on the first tournament circuit and enjoyed it as much as each other. On their return home, they talked of their successes and fame and popularity and the money they had earned. They were equally proud of their achievements, although Richard had evidently earned the most. They returned for the seventh season and Herden was getting better and had been placed in several competitions. He had beaten Richard on a couple of occasions and Richard was beating some good knights. He really felt that he was beginning to make his mark. One more season should do it.

The instruction was then sent down from the Earl that Richard must remain in England and Herden would be allowed to go to France, Herden was excited. Handsome Herden would now be lauded instead of handsome Richard. Richard pouted, sulked, complained and finally left with his wife, horses and men on an early tide, giving Herden little choice in the matter.

Then the supposedly impartial Nicholas came up with the scheme of passing off Herden as Richard in order to avoid punishments and the ruination of their own good name. Herden eventually agreed, and only the closest personal servants were aware of the switch. Herden began to enjoy the role, not realising until this point that his brother was treated far better locally than he ever had been. It might be good to be Richard for a while.

Herden had two separate blow ups with his father, once when he was not allowed to make decisions on some horse purchases from a Spanish merchant and second when his father discovered that Herden had been using one of the young daughters of a woodsman in a most ungentlemanly way. She had been too frightened to tell and it was her mother who discovered the outrage and walked directly to Lord Nicholas and told him to do something about it. He published Herden financially, not wishing to report him to the Priory and paid the woodsman's family off. Both times, Herden complained to the Priory that Richard had gone to France and twice Nicholas was fined. The Earl of Cornwall was more irritated by Herden and his obnoxious ways than the transgressions of Nicholas, but had to be seen to punish Nicholas in some way. None of it helped the family dynamics.

Richard, currently in Rouen, had no knowledge of these domestic upsets and was getting ready to meet his next opponent, who if he beat would earn him enough money to finish the season. It was a funny thing recently, although he was having so much fun, home was calling. His son Richard, the sea, the woods - even his father.

Guinevere came skipping into the stable.

"Is Perseus ready? Oh, he is! Let me straighten everything, he looks so lovely!" Guinevere fussed over the grey stallion, beloved of everyone in the Pridias team. She straightened his coverings, polished his leather and kissed him on the nose. They had four horses with them now, all capable of winning, so long as their master could do his job properly. They were worth a good deal of money and Richard had been offered a King's ransom for Perseus, the best of them all. Richard intended breeding from him as soon as they were all home and that was one of the plans on his mind. Horses were hurt in this sport, some badly and he didn't want that fate for Perseus, or any of them for that matter.

"Don't baby him Gwen," he said.

"Baby him? I look after him so that he looks after you, my lovely husband," she laughed.

They kissed and Perseus pushed them with his nose. His squire ran in and said breathlessly,

"Lord Marshal has asked if there can be a delay, my Lord."

"No! If he is not ready, then he must take the forfeit!"

"His horse has been stolen, my Lord."

"That is the third one this week," said Guinevere.

"Yes, it is becoming a worry," admitted Richard. "Tell me John, does anyone have any idea of how this calamity happened?"

"It seems not, my Lord, but as sure as anything the thieves will take one too many and then they will pay for it."

"You must maintain a guard on all of the horses and particularly this one here," said Richard pointing to the grey.

"I would never let anything happen to the horses. I would die first, my Lord."

"I will guard them too," added Guinevere defiantly.

Richard smiled at his team, this was real brotherhood he thought. Working together, not in competition as he had been with his own brother.

"Tell Lord Marshal, I shall wait until he is ready. I presume he has other horses?"

"I do Lord Pridias. I have two other horses, but it will take a while to get one ready, perhaps 30 minutes. The organisers have given their permission so long as you agree. If you do not, you may take the win as my forfeit." Marshal had entered the stables with his squire and two men.

"It is no honour to me to take your forfeit, Lord Marshal."

"I might have taken it the other way about," he answered.

"I doubt it. I shall be out soon and then I shall beat you on the field."

Richard did beat Marshal. His second horse was neither so fast nor agile and was probably tired from his outings that morning. Richard felt the thrill as he always did when he galloped with his lance towards his opponent. At the first strike, he knew that Marshal was not as strong as he usually was and although the pass went to Richard, he did not go so hard on the second pass. It felt like he was taking advantage somehow. So, he won, but felt the cheers and the applause not quite as deserved as they might be.

As he rode back to the stables, Perseus still prancing under his body, he saw a face he recognised in the crowd. He couldn't remember where he had seen this man, but felt that he was not a good man.

"There is a man over there John. The one with the red beard and odd looking boots, standing by the pie seller. Can you see him?"

"Yes, my Lord."

"Do you recognise him?"

"I am sure he was at the last tour… in fact I am sure he is friends with Cholmondeley's squire. Shall I speak to him before you do?"

"No, no John, But I would be very interested in finding out what he has been up to lately."

"You think he is something to do with the thefts?"

"I do John and I couldn't tell you why I think it."

They got back to the stables and Guinevere was there, talking closely to one of their servants, James. They moved apart as Richard rode in and Guinevere said,

"James has something to tell you Richard."

"Oh yes?" said her husband, using the block to dismount.

"My Lord, I have been given some information about the people who are stealing horses."

"Not so much been given the information Richard, as he beat it out of him."

Handsome and blushing James bowed his head and then looked at his master. Richard saw that James was in love with his wife, but worried not. Guinevere would not be unfaithful to him, he could guarantee that.

"Tell me, James."

James told Richard of his visit to one of the taverns in town where he had been informed by a Frenchman that bets were being taken against the expected outcome of challenges. It seemed that some men were able to clean up with bets against the favourites and this phenomenon was being linked to the recent spate of sword and saddle thefts or similar. Now the horse thefts had added to the odds against a champion. Bets on the reliable constant winners were not resulting in a profit, they no longer had the edge.

"Do you know who is behind it?"

"Joachim of Aquitaine."

"Really?" Richard was surprised to hear this. Joachim was a well-known competitor, but not that successful.

"They say he began by sending his squires to steal so that he could sell and bring in some cash. His father will not release any more money to him and the servants needed to steal in order to eat. Then Aquitaine got bigger ideas and has now been selling the horses for breeding. It seems not everyone is worried about using stolen animals to improve their tournament stock. Then he soon realised that he could earn more money through betting scams. He's stupid though because he's crossing people who will kill him."

"I will kill him if he takes anything of ours," said Guinevere.

"He won't," said Richard and he instructed John to take care of the horses and he beckoned his wife to accompany him.

He walked with her directly to Joachim's tent and walked in. A servant followed them inside and asked what they were doing.

"Looking for my friend. Where is he?"

"My Lord, he is not here at the moment. Shall I tell him you called?"

"I will find him later," said Richard.

They were soon joined in the tent by the man Richard had noticed after his event. The man seemed surprised to see Richard there but soon recovered his composure and said,

"You did well today, my Lord."

"Thank you, thank you."

"Your horse is a wonderful beast, are you intending to use him for breeding? I would be interested in using him."

Richard squeezed Guinevere's hand to keep her quiet.

"No, no. I don't think so."

"I understand, my Lord, and red beard bowed.

They left and Richard had a feeling he would be dealing with the man again. He certainly felt that he was being watched.

"We all stay with our stuff from now on. At least until we have the thieves sorted."

Two nights later, they had their chance. Joachim Aquitaine and the man with the beard and the odd boots, who they discovered was called Philippe la Garre, called late one evening and seemed surprised to find everyone at the stables. Not only were the Pridias team, but the Marshals and the Cholmondeleys, all of whom had suffered recent thefts, were working a shift pattern of guard duties. In fact, they were currently having a meeting about how to proceed and were amazed that Aquitaine had shown his hand so swiftly.

"Gentleman! Ah, I see my Lady Guinevere is also here!"

"Why are you here?" asked Marshal.

"I came only for a walk on a lovely night," he answered.

They had just been discussing how Joachim had apparently recently received news that there would be no money and that he was to be disinherited because of his debts. Once Marshal had discovered who had likely taken his horse, he was apoplectic. All the competitors loved their horses – really loved their horses.

"Do you know anything of the missing horses, Joachim?" Marshal asked him.

"Of course not William. How should I? You must be most upset that your lovely bay has gone. He was such a good ride."

"How would you know? No one has ridden him other than me or my squire?"

Joachim shifted his feet and the atmosphere in the room became tense. La Garre put his hand on his dagger in its sheath and the tension exploded. Marshal leapt across the stall and held his sword across Joachim's throat.

"Where is he?"

"Who?" he asked.

Before there were any more words, La Garre drew his own dagger and went for Marshal. Richard grabbed him around the neck and so La Garre turned on him. Within a few seconds the man was dead and Richard held the bloody dagger. Joachim Aquitaine began to cry out and Marshal stabbed him.

"Where is my horse, you bastard?"

"I do not know and if I did, I would not tell an English pig such as you."

Marshal slit Aquitaine's throat and the stunned vigilante group looked at the bodies. Squire John ripped sacking from the stall sides and threw it over the dead men. The action spurred the others on and soon the bodies were wrapped, tied and hidden on a cart. One of Marshal's men brought in a pig's carcass and threw it on top of the bodies.

"Now search his place and stables before anyone realises he is missing," instructed Richard.

"I will go too," said Guinevere.

Guinevere moved majestically between the tents and the men and the horses, accompanied by the squire John and William Marshal and two of his men. They couple chattered innocently between themselves as they made their way directly to Aquitaine's camp. When they arrived, there were only two boys looking after the horses.

"Is your master here?" asked Marshal.

"No, my Lord. He went to fetch another horse he has bought and then he is coming back."

"He must have great faith in you to leave you with his horses?"

"Yes, my Lady. He does."

"Have you been with him long?"

"Only a week, my Lady. His last servants went to work for another Knight."

"Well, we shall return later when your master is back. I am buying some horses from him and he was to let us ride them today," said Marshal. "It's a pity he is not here, as we may not all been able to see them until tomorrow."

"Perhaps you could let us look now? It would save us all time and I know my Lord Aquitaine is keen to sell the horses and we have money to buy them," asked Guinevere. Marshal rattled his money pouch for effect.

"We could give you some coins for your time and trouble?" said Guinevere brightly.

The servant children grinned and held out their hands. Satisfied, they led the group to the stables. Of the three horses there, Marshal went to the quiet animal at the back which was covered by a dull rug. The horse recognised him immediately and Marshal had to stop the tears which came to his eyes.

"We are going home now," he whispered in its ear and he quickly removed the rug. He flinched when he saw the whip marks on his flanks.

"My Lord?" said his own man. "These other horses belong to Cholmondeley and Mortimer. They have their markings."

"Saddle them, take them back to their owners," he instructed.

"Are you taking the horses now, my Lord?" asked the Aquitaine servant boys.

"Yes, tell your master we have taken them when he returns." He threw the boys extra coins and they vanished.

Once the horses were back with their owners and the bodies burned, Richard decided that he had had enough. His leg was really hurting him after the fight and the deaths had shaken him. He didn't feel guilty about the deaths, just that Guinevere had been involved. She seemed to have enjoyed herself however and was really pleased to have been part of retrieving the horses. Their fellow jousters and competitors and friends said nothing about the disappearance of Joachim Aquitaine and his lackeys, telling any enquirers that they knew he had been short of money and deeply in debt and had perhaps just vanished and begun a new life in Italy or somewhere. If they knew the truth, they weren't saying.

But it still seemed the right time to go home and his wife agreed. They all made their way to the coast where they rented a ship capable of carrying them and their horses and sailed home, eventually docking at Ponts Mill. Richard did not tell Guinevere or any of his men that he had seen two men following them on horses to the Brittany coast. On one of their overnight camps, he had left the group and gone in search of the men, but seen no one. He began to feel as though he were imagining it and assumed that God punished differently when He considered a death murder, rather than a battle death. Was dying in battle somehow nobler? He hadn't thought so until recently.

Richard became more alarmed when they sailed across the sea to Cornwall and he thought he saw the two men in a boat a way behind. He chose to ignore them. When they arrived at Ponts Mill, he insisted that they moor on the eastern side of the river citing his desire to cross his grandfather's bridge and cleanse the whole group at the hermitage chapel. There were no arguments and no troubles as the tired men, woman and horses disembarked on the quay. He asked one of the men at the quayside to lend them a cart upon which they could load their possessions and the driver could haul them the short distance home. When the gatekeeper opened the bridge gate and bowed low, they entered and began to cross the bridge. Tenants who were home shouted greetings to Richard and Guinevere. Richard looked behind and noticed the guard allowing unseen travellers on to the bridge behind them.

By the time they reached the far side of the bridge, Richard only passed a short conversation with the guard and shooed his group through. The cart trundled behind. He could see no one at the hermitage and hoped that he would be able to make it home safely with the Disperkel stopping any demons following.

"Where is the hermit monk?" he asked the guard.

"He was called to the Priory, my Lord. Your Father and Mother will be very pleased to see you. Are you home for good now, my Lord?"

"We are," answered Guinevere.

So, the Disperkel monk was not there to save him from these spirit horsemen, that was not good news.

They made their way up the track and through the woods to the Hall. Richard looked behind as they went through the entrance gate in the walls and thought he caught the shape of two riders in the woods. He was brought back from his musings as soon as their return was announced to the family and they were overwhelmed with welcome.

When Herden galloped off into the woods in his huff after Richard's reinstatement as Lord in waiting, it had not been expected that he would kill himself. But suicide was the accepted verdict and he was buried in the family crypt.

Richard never saw the two shadow riders again after Herden's death and he resolutely put out of his mind that Herden in his gold and black tunic looked exactly the same as Richard did in his.

THE PRIESTESS

Featuring Richard de Pridias (1180 – 1250)

My dear Geoffrey,

I feel that I must explain my behaviour on your last visit and apologise. It was good to see you and Isabella and the boys, although they are no longer boys, are they? Roger 12 and Piers 9, time goes so quickly. We always say that as adults and yet it is such a true statement. I feel old lately and your brother tells me that I must get used to it. I still feel as though I am a young man and yet your brother has been taking over more of the responsibilities of the Manor, without informing me. Our income has gone down so much in recent years with these new mining laws and the sons of our workers would rather leave the land than farm it. I find it all so confusing and wonder how much longer I can put up with it. Baldwin tells me that the lands are safe in his hands but we both know how selfish he is. He likes spending money and has redecorated his own hall with such splendour I wonder where he imagines the money will come from. Reginald we never see now that he is such an important lawyer. I have heard tell that the Bishop is very impressed with him. He certainly gives him some favourable cases and I am not sure that Reginald is too interested in what is the best for the Cornish. He mentions Rome and the Church far too often for my liking. I want the old ways, but we are no longer able to mention them. People have forgotten. She has told me that soon those ways will vanish from our world.

Your father

Richard
Lord of Pridias

Father,

You do not need to apologise. However, you did not explain in the letter what the trouble was. Perhaps you can let me know more in your next letter. Isabella and I really enjoy our visits home, although I must say Orcherton seems so much warmer after rainy and misty Pridias. When Pridias is at its best with the hot sun and the beach and the clear sea, there is no better place on earth. But, Devon is so green and the rocks are so warm and red and I fell in love with it the first day I arrived. I want to visit Cornwall often and am sad that our parting was so very uncomfortable. Isabella and Roger and Piers send their love. By the way - Who is she?

Geoffrey

Baldwin,

I had a strange letter from Father by messenger today and have sent a reply separate to this letter. Is

he alright? You know how odd he was on my last
visit with my wife and the children, insisting that
they were foreigners and the like. He said he wanted
to explain and then he didn't and he mentioned
some woman. Perhaps I am making a fuss but I just
wanted to check. He is still going on about Reg and
his lawyering, I think he is worried the connection
with the Church and their interference at Pridias. Are
you and the family going to come over to Orcherton
soon? You will love it here.

Geoffrey and Isabella.

Brother dear,

Father is getting old, that's half the trouble and don't
worry about Reginald. He is learning what he can,
where he can and is making waves and lots of money
in the meantime. Reginald is not remotely religious
and cares little about Bishops and monks, he cares
only about money. That is not a bad thing, I could
certainly do with more money. Father says I spend
too much, when all I am trying to do is bring the
place up to the present day. Father does so live in
the 11th century and wants to tell me about
protecting spirits and relics buried in the grounds
and Melusine bloodlines. It's all nonsense of course,
all that matters is today. I don't know who this she
is, unless he's getting religious fever and is talking
about the Virgin Mary. I am not speaking out of turn,
but I think he has been around long enough and
should go and join his ancestors. We will come when

we have some spare time, my wife is currently awaiting another arrival.

Baldwin

Father,

I hope you got my last letter. It has been two months and I have heard nothing from you. I do worry and I cannot help it. Shall I come home for a while? Everyone is well here and send their love.

Geoffrey and Isabella.

Father,

Another month has passed and I think that I should come back to Pridias. I have written to Baldwin too and he has not replied. If you are not careful, I shall write to Reginald and then we shall all be in a pickle! Please write soon, I have asked this messenger to deliver this into your hands and insist you send me a reply.

Geoffrey

Geoffrey

The messenger delivered your letter to me, he having asked for Lord Pridias and the servant he met considers me as such. Father is so confused these days that most of the servants and villagers come to me for instruction. I am afraid that we keep him in his quarters as much as possible as he will wander into the woods and then follow the river down to the bridge and knock on the hermitage door or run across the bridge. It is most undignified and I am glad that our mother is no longer alive to witness it. The healers and doctors have told us that he is a victim of old age and will never get better. Come if you wish, but rushing will make no difference. We are looking after him and I am taking more duties from him.

Lord Baldwin of Pridias

Brother,

Thank you for the letter. I was rather hoping to hear from Father and am hoping that signing your letter to me as Lord Baldwin was a mistake. I am your brother and not your servant. I will come and visit and make sure everything is alright. I expect you have managed to take over control of the family money and I would like to speak to Reginald about that. I have seen evidence of spirits on our land and I am proud of our lineage - apparently, you are not.

Sir Geoffrey of Orcherton

Geoffrey,

I hope this letter reaches you safely. The messenger
is my most trusted servant. Sad to say, there are few
here at Pridias Hall I can trust. All these years I have
ruled them well and they now obey your brother
rather than me. I am neither senile nor suffering
from mental decay and yet I am kept under lock and
key in the south tower at the Hall while Baldwin
swaggers about spending our money on himself
rather than our estates and there is a danger our
people could starve. The lady I speak to is a Priestess
of ancient times. I am not hallucinating nor making
this up. She is an immortal soul who knew Tristan
and Iseult and King Mark and all our ancestors. I first
saw her at Golant standing at the water's edge with
her pale blue dress floating on the tide and her long
pale red hair blowing behind her. I thought she was
the most beautiful creature I have ever seen. Even
more than your mother and she was very lovely as
you know. I say creature because she was
otherworldly – is otherworldly and has become my
confidante. I used to love talking to you about the
old ways and the family secrets and the magic and
since you left us to take over those lands at Devon
which I still want to visit, I have no ally here. The
Priestess has told me such stories and explained the
mysteries of the world to me. I would like to pass
them on to you, but not by message. I will tell you
when you come and come you must. Your brother
has taken hold of the purse strings and is keeping my
friends away, telling them that I am too ill to be
seen. I have a spare key which he does not know
about and let myself out and ride to Golant when I

can. The guards at the bridge allow me across and I believe that I have their silence.

Richard, your father.

Reginald,

I have been receiving strange correspondence from Father and Baldwin and wonder if you have the time to travel from Truro to Pridias and find out what is going on. Father tells me he is being locked in his room and Baldwin tells me Father is incapable of running the estates and has taken control of the money. If necessary I shall travel down from Orcherton, but am in the middle of some deals involving my own estates and may well be going into politics. Do let me know as soon as you can and tread carefully with Baldwin, we both know what he is like. The family send their love.

Geoffrey and Isabella

Geoffrey and Isabella,

I am at Pridias, having left Truro directly after I received you message. You worried me and in some ways, you were quite correct so to do. Father is definitely not as he was, rambling constantly about ghost women, well one woman, some priestess he believes that she is. I suspect it is all in his imagination. Unless it is a village woman trying to obtain money or worse – a marriage proposal. That would upset Baldwin I have no doubt. I asked Father's attendants and they believe that he is suffering from some kind of brain inflammation, some sort of delayed shock reaction following Mother's death. I am currently waiting for the doctor to arrive as I write and see what he says. Father says that he has nothing more to tell me, but wishes I would remain at the Hall. I explained that I have my own life to live and that he must rely on the good graces of Baldwin and his family. He is to inherit after all and you and I must make our own way. I have told Baldwin that he has no legal right to take over the finances, although from what I have seen so far, I don't think he is doing anything rash. He is neither a drinker nor a gambler and wishes to keep the estate together, so there is scant reason for him to gamble with his own inheritance. You and Isabella will be made welcome here, I have no doubt. I shall come to Orcherton soon in order that I can through the leases and properties for you and Isabella. I am cheaper and more reliable than any of those Devon men!

Best wishes to my nephews.

Reginald

My dear interfering Sir Geoffrey,

How dare you send for Reginald and ask him to investigate the way I am running estates here at Pridias? Hoping to have me convicted of some form of fraud and then you two can inherit instead of me? Well, he couldn't find anything wrong and my doctor has confirmed that Father is suffering from senile decay and that it is a good job I have taken more control as the estate could fail and the people starve under his command. The Prior has also expressed concern at Father's ramblings. He is worried about income to the Priory and the upkeep of the bridge and success of the harvests. I am more than capable of taking care of that. If you were here on a regular basis you would see that Father is old and sick, but you are not. You are in your secure Devon estates with a rich wife and plenty of money. I must say that you are no longer welcome here at Pridias until I receive a full apology and acknowledgment that Father is sick and I am in no way caring for him incorrectly.

Baldwin, Lord of Pridias.

Baldwin,

I don't know why you are making such a fuss. I worry about my Father and Reginald lives nearer and was able to call and see him easier than I. I shall call whenever I wish, the estate is still under Father's name and as a Pridias you cannot ban me nor my family. I don't think our ancestors would approve, do you? Now, let us behave like gentlemen and not argue. I would be greatly obliged if you could keep me informed as to his health.

Geoffrey

Father,

I have heard back from Reginald about his visit and he tells me that you are quite well, but fears that there is a woman who is trying to bewitch you. I am sure that this is nonsense and I am quite willing to believe in your Priestess. What is it that she requires of you? I agree that there are supernatural forces at work everywhere in our world and I have many memories of the stories you told us of the woodland spirits and the Disbobmajig who lives under the bridge. You told us of Jehanne and Tristen and their magical ability to keep the Pridias land under our control and I have believed you despite never seeing any evidence myself. Baldwin is telling me that I am banned from seeing you and coming home but I am paying no attention to that stupidity. Shall I come?

Best love Geoffrey

My dearest son,

I am so pleased to hear from you. Reginald did come, but seemed to spend more time arguing with Baldwin about who was right about the finances. I am sad that none of my boys have the same love for this magical and special place that your ancestors did. Our ancestors lived and ruled here before the Saxons and the Romans and can be traced back to Lyonesse and they all loved and protected these lands. The Priestess tells me that a spell has been cast over my children and I must do my best to break it. The Disperkel and other spirits cannot protect us when we do not acknowledge their existence. Nothing can exist if denied. Nothing. She has taught me a lot. I speak to her on many occasions, but shall not tell you how, as you may tell your brothers and they will stop that avenue of escape if they can. I hope the family are well and I would visit your Devon lands if the Priestess did not advise against it.

Your only father

Richard

My dear wife,

I hope you are having an excellent visit with your sister and have to tell you that I miss you very much. The boys play with their friends and are very well and happy and you must not worry about them. I hope that our brother-in-law will return to health soon and I understand that you must take care of your sister during her troubles. I want to ask your advice on the ongoing saga of our father Richard. I

do not know who to believe, my brothers or my
Father. Both seem very set on their side of the story.
I do not know if this Priestess is a conniving woman,
a figment of his imagination or worse – a real
phantom! Perhaps when you have returned, I shall
visit him. You may come too and the boys are
excited at the thought of a visit there. I should hate
Father to die when I haven't said goodbye and I have
to admit only to you, my dearest Isabella, that I am
concerned about Baldwin and his actions in spite of
his statements to the contrary. Please do keep
yourself well and do not overtire yourself looking
after others. We both know what you are like.

Your loving husband Joffrey

Husband,

I am quite well and am taking quite as much rest as I
need. My thought is that you and the boys must go
to Pridias immediately and see what is happening.
Perhaps do not announce your arrival. And my
dearest dear – we both know that there are many
unusual happenings in this world. My father often
spoke of the people who live under the sea and his
father would speak of men and women who knew
magic and my family do not lie. Go to Pridias and
write from there. My best love.

Isabella

Isabella,

We are at Pridias and I have to say that our welcome was unusual. Baldwin had instructed the guards at the bridge to not allow us through. Can you believe it? The guards obeyed his orders and then went back into their towers while (accidentally) leaving the bridge gates opened. I stopped at Golant on the way to Baldwin's Bridge and I must say that I had almost forgotten how beautiful it is there. The little church and the small harbour with the colourful fishing boats moored on the jetty were imaged in paintings by Mother. I must find those again, I think they were put in one of the towers. The cottagers, mainly fishing people, seemed surprised to see us but pleased nonetheless. I asked about Father and they said they often see him. He rides there and sits on the jetty and looks over the water and talks to himself, they told me. There was no hermit nor monk at the chapel and I do believe the door was locked. I could not gain access anyway. By the time, we arrived at the Hall, we were very tired and I was in no mood for an argument. Baldwin's servants answered the door and told me to wait! Eventually Baldwin arrived and told me that I should have informed him of my visit. I am afraid I told a lie and said that I had sent a message which he obviously hadn't received. We were allowed in and he passed off the original entry refusal and said that we were welcome and asked most prettily after your welfare. His wife has become very fat since we last saw her and I do not believe that she is with child again, but I did not ask. She was also very miserable and appeared angry that we were here. They do have full residence as Lord and Lady with nothing in view that shows Father is still alive. We ate and drank well and were not able to see Father before we retired.

However, in the night he appeared in my quarters and I was shocked to see how much he had aged. He would not tell me how he got to my room without the servants stopping him, but his tale was worth listening to. I must begin by saying that he did not seem mentally unwell, just anxious and over excited. He told me that the Priestess is related to Jehanne and has the interests of the Pridias lands at heart. I asked if I could meet her and he said yes, to my astonishment. And meet her I did! The boys were asked to come but only Roger wanted to as Piers had arranged to go sailing with Baldwin and Baldwin assumed that we were only exploring the woods. He let Father come with us and we went to the woods north of Luxulyan. Father rode as though he was meeting his maker and we struggled to keep up. In a clearing, which I swear I have never seen before, was a hut built from stone with an oak roof. In some ways, the building was very similar to the hermitage by Baldwin's Bridge. There was a white horse who roamed freely and wolves, white and blue wolves, reminiscent of the wolves our ancestors kept as guardians. I don't know why we let the habit go, they are beautiful beasts. Father jumped from his horse and ran into the little cottage and then came out followed by the most ethereal woman I have ever seen. You are beautiful my love, but she! There was a rainbowed aura surrounding her. She wore pale blue with a white over tunic. Her hair was blonde-red and flowed free and was long and jewelled. She opened her arms to us in welcome and we dismounted and went to her and bowed. She took us to a table which sat under an ancient oak tree and was laden with food. We sat and talked for hours and I don't think that I can remember a small portion of what was said. What I do know is that Baldwin has been bewitched by his wife's family who want the lands for their own. They want Richard dead and then they will work on Baldwin and then claim the lands. She told us how it can be stopped and yet I cannot remember what she said. There was just a feeling that we had somehow agreed the right thing to do. As we rode away I was convinced that the family was to be saved and Father was happier than before. When we arrived back at the Hall, Baldwin and his wife were very upset and had the servants take Father directly to his rooms. We are to stay for two more days and I shall write again.

My deepest love Joffrey

My dear sister Isabella,

I write to let you know that your husband and sons are sick with fever here at Pridias. Our dear Father is ill too. They are in my own Hall at Landreath and are in the good hands of my servants there. We do not want the children infected and so for now we shall keep apart. They are not in danger and so you must not worry. You must not attend them if you are to keep yourself well.

Your loving brother
Baldwin, Lord of Pridias

Joffrey,

This letter is short as it is my third and I have received no reply from you or Baldwin. I am very worried, please write to me. I am returned to Orcherton and will send soldiers if I hear nothing soon.

Isabella

Mother,

I have escaped the Hall and am at the hermitage - safe. The Priestess helped me and left me here. We were to go the Priory, but that is not now deemed safe. Father and Grandfather are locked in the tower at Pridias, but we have set in motion a plan to free them. She knows spells and soon they will be free.

Roger

My dear wife,

We are all free! Your soldiers arrived as the Priestess cast the spell. It was a binding spell and the soldiers – the mercenary soldiers of Baldwin - were killed. They all had a sudden fever and became paralysed for long enough for us to be freed. The Priestess was magnificent as she opened her arms, this time not in welcome but with power. She grew Isabella! To the size of a giant! We were all free and Father was as happy as he ever has been. Baldwin fainted and did not recover consciousness for two days. His wife immediately died of the fever (she was just fat and not with child) and the Priestess said that Pridias is now free and her work is done. It was so wonderful my love. Roger and I shall be back at Orcherton soon. I am sending the soldiers back with Piers and this letter and a few items which have been given to me by my Father. (Including Mother's paintings – aren't they wonderful?) Baldwin now accepts that he has been under the curse of his wife and her devilish family and the Prior and the monks have been here to cleanse the Halls and the lands. Reginald is ensuring that legal safeguards are in place and Baldwin has given the Priory a little land to sweeten their resolve towards our family.

Our best love to you.

Joffrey and Roger.

My Dear Geoffrey,

I know I thanked you when you were here, but I want to again. To have the lands restored as they were and my heir Baldwin back within the fold and no longer under the influence of that dreadful wife of his, is heaven to me. Priestess is with me less often but I can still call at her cottage in the woods. Although I do admit that I am not always able to find it. She did tell us though that there are many versions of our world existing alongside each other and we can choose which one in which to reside at any moment. Do you remember? There is so much that she told us and I think I must write it down and hide it somewhere. I do know that if I say any of this publicly, the Prior will tell the Bishop and he will tell the Earl and I do also know that Reginald will suddenly become more Church than Pridias and judge me badly. I have revived the walled garden. I have planted lavender, roses, all the herbs and medicinal plants and trees. The colours and scents are marvellous and renewing. On some days, I ride to the old fort which was at one time King Mark's Palace and watch the monks working with the broom and indigo and rubia and woad. I wanted to reclaim Carnubelbanathel between that castle and Golant, but it is still leased to the Priory as agreed by our Pridias ancestors and Baldwin wants to honour the contract. The monks are very skilled and have helped me re-establish the garden. They have grown so many plants at the Priory and purchase cuttings and seedlings from the merchants when they arrive by sea. When I am finally gone to our ancestors, I ask that many of my flowers are on display at the chapel. Yes, I shall write about the truths she told us, such a different interpretation of the Christian teachings. This Rome looks after itself and has put ridiculously costumed nincompoops between man and God. Man can find salvation without the Church but there is no money, power nor control in that truth. Rome will never let the truth be told. I shall hide the writings where you alone know they can be found. The weather has been glorious here recently, the woods and meadows and beach and sea are so wonderful. These lands have always been and will always be Pridias lands.

Your loving father Richard.

My dear Roger,

I found them. I found the writings and I shall return with them and we shall hide them. Baldwin and Reginald will never know, for I fear that neither of my brothers will carry on any of the old ways. Now that my beloved father is laid to rest in our chapel and Baldwin has remarried a very religious woman and if the writings were to be discovered, they will be destroyed. I went to the cottage of the Priestess and she told me that she is leaving now to join Richard and our ancestors. She prophecies a time when the Pridias lands will be far from the sea and the Priory will crumble. She says the remaining lands will remain in Pridias hands for hundreds of years and then into other hands for 280 years until they are recovered by a blood Pridias. Then the spirits and witches and guardians will return. The Priestess will return then too. You will be part of this secret Roger, as will your son and his son and so on. I went to the walled garden and sat for many hours where I meditated and heard Father speak to me. He is happy and I am happy. I shall be home soon my boy.

Your loving father.

Geoffrey.

I AM RICH

Featuring Geoffrey de Pridias (1200 – 1270)

"That is a wonderful painting Baldwin. I assume it is of our Priestess as it captures her likeness so, but who painted it?"

"Our latest monk at the hermitage chapel. He was in her presence before Father died."

"The setting is the clearing I see," said Geoffrey.

"It is, have you had time to visit it yet?"

"No, but I shall. When we were here for the funeral, there was no time for visiting with all the arrangements and the grief."

"And your need to be alone with your new and very young bride!"

"Nicholaa would never take me away from my family!"

"Calm yourself Geoffrey! I jest only! She is a beautiful young woman and I am pleased, as is our brother Reginald to have such a lovely sister. The match has helped us greatly here at Pridias."

"Because her father has such political connections? It is a good job, as she brought no money to the match," said Geoffrey.

"But she did bring a 20-year-old body to it!"

"Your new wife is not much older Baldwin!"

"I know. Isn't it amazing that these young women and their fathers find eligible and filthy- rich, titled, old men attractive?"

"It is a mystery!"

"Your boys are married now Geoffrey. We are getting old."

"It seems ridiculous that Roger has two children and another on the way and even Piers is now expecting. I am still playing on the Pridias beach and sailing out to sea with old John in my mind."

"John, he was a kind old man. You know his grandson now lives in his old cottage? He doesn't fish, he is frightened of the sea he says, but he helped Father with the garden."

"You will keep the garden? Father was so proud of it."

"Of course and it will be tended as lovingly as when he was here. I feel as though he is still there, perhaps all our people are there and not in the crypt. It would be nice to think so."

Baldwin took another drink of wine. The brothers were eating and drinking in the dining hall. The furniture in this room had changed little in over a hundred years. The table, chairs and side tables were all English oak. The tapestries and paintings were exquisite and ancient and kept in first class condition by the servants. The candlesticks and plate were gold and silver and the carpets woven and embroidered in silk and wool. Many of the decorations and trinkets had been bought from foreign merchants over the years. The glassware, expensive and gold rimmed, reflected the candlelight. Here, they had hosted many banquets sealing marriage and business deals.

"I know that you are going away tomorrow and I wish to ask a favour Baldwin."

"Anything Geoffrey."

"I would like to remain at Pridias Hall in your absence and remember the time I was a child. I am fifty-one years old and may never have the chance to amuse myself in my old home in this way again."

"And yet you and all of your family will always be welcome here."

"I know and I am grateful, but…"

"Of course, Geoffrey, I think I understand. Yes, yes. We shall be at St Ives for one week and you may stay for the entire time and beyond if it, if you desire. I shall instruct the servants and the soldiers of this

and you, my brother shall be free of any
interference."

When Geoffrey came down the following morning,
Baldwin and his family had already left. The
maidservant brought his breakfast into the dining
room and dropped an embarrassed curtsey as she
did so. Geoffrey ate leisurely before he went out to
the walls and looked out to sea. The tide was coming
in and appeared to be bringing a storm with it. The
boats bobbed and tacked on the waves, hoping to
make safe harbour before the storm landed. He saw
the herdsmen ushering their stock towards shelter
and had an urge to help them. He was a young boy,
free to run about the estates. He laughed to himself
in the memory.

He hadn't lied to Baldwin, he wanted the time at
Pridias alone. He owned and ruled huge estates in
Devon but Pridias was home. He was also glad to be
free of his young wife for a time. She was relentless
in her nagging about – everything. Her desire for a
child and her desire for jewellery and clothes was
insatiable and she literally never shut up. It had
seemed such a good idea to marry a beautiful young
woman, but it became exhausting after only a few
months.

Geoffrey had yesterday sent her a letter saying that
it was imperative he remain at Pridias for the time
being and he would return shortly. What Geoffrey
really wanted, was to find the writings of his father.
Richard had told him by letter during those final
years that he would write down all the spiritual and
magical teachings he had learned from the lips of the

Priestess. He had said that he would hide it in a place that only Geoffrey could find and despite many hours of thought, Geoffrey could not remember any such place. He decided that he would search the estates until he found the prize. Geoffrey hoped that being home would prompt his memory and being alone would deter questions from his brothers.

He decided that he would clear the ground beneath his feet first and that meant checking the Hall and then the garden, followed by the grounds. If no luck there, he must spread his search to the clearing and the hermitage and bridge and then perhaps Golant and the rest of the estate. Suddenly he recognised the enormity of such a task to be undertaken by one man. He would have to rethink. He went outside and walked to the cliff edge. His first intention was to go to the beach until he saw that the tide was coming in and would soon cut off his exit. So, he trudged further south until he arrived at the Pridias chapel.

So recently he has been here with his wife, sons and their families joining the line of surviving Pridias and their soldiers and servants behind the body of his father. The sun had been streaming across the land that day and the light wind had been strong enough to move the many flags and banners which depicted the Pridias colours. The garlands of flowers which lined the route had come not only from the Hall gardens, but from the cottages and farmers and the Priory and other Manors. Not one bouquet or offering had come under duress, everyone wanted to honour Richard, Lord of Pridias Manor. What a day that had been, there had been as much joy as sorrow. Geoffrey wished that Isabella had been by his side rather than the beautiful and self-absorbed Nicholaa.

Isabella was such a Lady in all senses and he still had not got over the shock of her sudden death. She died on her seat at Orcherton overlooking the estuary and the sea. The doctor told them all that it was a quick end and that her heart had given out. Geoffrey soon married Nicholaa for two reasons, one, he thought she might be a younger version of Isabella and two, it was supposed to be a good political connection for his family and his own political ambitions. It hadn't quite worked out like that and now he missed Isabella more than ever.

He opened the chapel door and entered just as the storm arrived and slammed the door closed behind him. The change in pressure blew out some of the candles and left most of the chapel in darkness.

"Hello!" he called out. "Anyone here?"

There was no answer and Geoffrey walked to the altar. He picked up a taper and began lighting the candles, all of which seemed determined to blow out as quickly as they were lit. He turned around quickly when he heard the main door open again, but it was closed.

"Hello?" he asked.

Apart from a shuffling sound which Geoffrey decided to put down to the blowing wind, there was no one else in the chapel with him. So, why did he feel so anxious, with goose pimples all over his body?

The extra candle light shone into a few corners and Geoffrey's spirits lifted. He moved about the chapel, lifting this and looking in that, wondering where the documents could be. Or was it in the form of a book? He knew that the monks could do that but surely, they would have been alarmed at the content? Unless Richard had paid the monk well, they always liked money. But, there was nothing to be found up here and he knew he must go down to the crypt. He lit a torch and opened the door at the top of the stairs. A musty and decaying smell hit his nostrils which he knew would clear the longer the door was open. As he took the top step, the last thing he saw from the chapel was a flash of lightning and he heard the sound of thunder and wind. It almost put him off descending, instead he shook the feeling and walked quickly down to the crypt.

Once down there, he wondered what on earth he had been thinking. His hands shook as he tried to use his taper to light the large candles on the sconces and candle stands. They wouldn't light immediately and he stopped himself from looking behind or at any corner of the crypt when he heard a scuffle or a whisper.

"I am too old to be in here on my own," he said.

Even being surrounded by all his family could not help his anxious feeling. There was an almost overpowering smell of decomposition and he made a mental note to call back the stonemason who clearly had done a poor job of sealing his father's tomb.

"I am rich," said a voice.

"So am I!" answered Geoffrey, chuckling at his witticism and trying not to become hysterical.

The dust on the stone floor swirled and Geoffrey felt a cold breeze about his body. He tried to ignore it, instead busying himself by looking amongst the coffins for the notes. He was finding nothing except butterflies in his stomach and a desire to evacuate his bladder. He had no intention to do that in this place, not unless he were to be locked in for any reason. That thought was enough to make him trot up the steps to the door. He lifted the latch and pushed, but there was resistance. Geoffrey's heart almost stopped as he pulled and pushed. He was sure there was something behind him, watching him.

"I am rich," something said and Geoffrey wondered why a demon would want to brag in such a way.

He remembered to lift the latch and was soon in the chapel and he immediately thought about the candles he had left lighted down below. He decided that he would wander about the chapel a little longer and regain Lordly composure, before he went down to blow them out. The storm was now at its height and the electric tension could be felt in the chapel. As the lightning flashed, Geoffrey went to the stained-glass window to look out. If there was anyone there, he could not see them. The rain was so heavy and the sky so dark, that an army could be marching past and be invisible. The constant thunder and lightning indicated that the storm was overhead and Geoffrey knew he would be stupid to leave the chapel now.

At least he had more time to search here. He sat on one of the solid oak benches and stared at the altar. This was distinctly Christian, with a crucifix, incense and prayer books. Geoffrey knew that this had been done for the benefit of the Priory and the increasingly conformative neighbours. He knew that in the oak chest in the small room behind the altar lay some personalised Pridias items for – he should say worship, but perhaps magic would be more appropriate. On the walls were several likenesses of his ancestors, the Lords anyway, made from their death masks. The women were represented on wall paintings and each of them looked beautiful. He thought about the Lords prior to Richard, the father of Paganus who were not immortalised here, but elsewhere under quoits on the estates. He also realised that there would never be a death mask of him or his sons in this crypt. Baldwin and his descendants would be represented here. He felt disappointed and decided there and then that he would have a crypt built at Orcherton. He would keep it separate to the Orcherton tombs for purity, he thought. Even though he was now the owner of hundreds of acres of Devon lands and many Devon properties, Geoffrey considered himself firmly Cornish. And a Pridias. He wondered if his descendants would feel the same.

An almighty crack of thunder made him jump up and look around just as the front door swung open with a gust of wind. He ran to it and looked out. There was no chance of him leaving just yet. His view was still obliterated by the rain, but he had a few glimpses of the huge waves and he said a silent prayer for anyone caught at sea or on land in this frightening weather. He was glad that he had not brought his horse as he would have been sorely tempted to bring him into the chapel for shelter.

"I am rich," came the voice.

"Who is this?" asked Geoffrey and the statement was repeated. This time he was sure that the voice had come from the crypt. He was going to have to go and check.

He put a large candle into the hurricane lamp he found by the door and made sure that it was securely fastened. He put two candles in his tunic pocket and two tapers. As an afterthought, he unsheathed his dagger. He mused that he did not prepare this much for a hunt. He opened the crypt door and jammed it open with one of the oak benches. The smell hit him again and he put his hand to his mouth, almost cutting his nose with the dagger. The lights from downstairs flickered and he knew he must go and blow them out if he did not want to remove all evidence of his forebears in one giant explosion.

Geoffrey was so nervous that he could scarcely keep his balance as he stepped down into the crypt. He pondered that he should only feel secure when his lamp lit the corners of the room, as if that made it alright. He reached the far end of the crypt where the candles were and blew them out. His hurricane lamp left enough light to see by – until it went out and the crypt door slammed shut. He guessed the outside chapel door had blown open again.

"I am rich."

"Who are you? If you are trying to scare me, you are doing a great job."

Well that should get the spirits properly rattled, Geoffrey thought. The smell was becoming stronger and he found that he was breathless, whether with fear or decay he could not say. Each breath took three short attempts to come in and he couldn't work out how he was breathing out. He put his hand behind him and felt around the candles and their holders hoping for a flint or some way of lighting the candles. He did not turn around, fearing being grabbed or poked or being touched. He managed to control his breathing a little better and tried to listen. If he was to be murdered by a demon of some sort at least he wanted a chance of knowing when it would occur.

He could hear nothing and so shuffled forward through the thick darkness with one hand moving across the tombs at the side of the crypt so that he could be sure he was heading towards the stairs. The tombs felt cool and the mortar flaked against his hand and Geoffrey hoped that he would not accidentally pull out a stone or knock off a lid. Blood relatives they may be - but hell no.

He could smell that the strongest scent came from the end tomb, which he knew was that of his father.

"I am rich."

Geoffrey was sure that the sound was next to his ear. Could it be coming from a tomb?

"Hello?"

He had responded too many times now and not had a reply, so he vowed not to answer again. Instead he walked forward, eager to get out and determined not to be side-tracked. He quickened his step as he guessed he must be almost at the bottom step by now. He walked in an exaggerated way hoping that his foot would soon touch the raised stone which represented his escape.

"Ooooo!" he squealed as he felt something move down his neck. He put his hand up to his hairline and turned around and moved his arm from side to side and thankfully contacted nothing but the wall and tombs.

Oh no! He heard the sliding of stone against stone followed by rocks landing on the floor. The smell was stronger now and he thought he heard someone trying to get out of a tomb. He stopped breathing when he heard someone or something, jump down on the floor.

"I am rich," it said.

"Not sure that you are sir," Geoffrey said. "If you are a demon, then you are not rich, are you?"

Geoffrey heard more creaking and crumbling and the sliding and crunching of stone against stone. He hoped against forlorn hope that this did not signal more demons climbing out of their tombs. With each sliding there came a renewed smell of decay. The sound of feet hitting the floor and hands against the walls made his heart beat too fast and then stop as it if it was trying to regulate itself. The atmosphere was thick with the smell and the shrinking space inside the crypt and Geoffrey thought that he might be dying right here, right now. This must be how it felt. The Roman Church had promised that the process of death was to be a horrendous experience and one which every sinner deserved.

No, not me.

"What is this?" he shouted and as he did he felt his power rise within him again. If he was dying, he was going down fighting.

"This is my life and my eternity!" he said fiercely. "Stop trying to frighten me. I say again, who are you?"

"I am rich."

"I am rich." Another voice.

"I am rich." And another.

Geoffrey said, "Stop!"

"I am rich." A fourth voice.

"I am Pagan."

"I am Baldwin."

"I am Nicholas."

Geoffrey fell to his knees and began to cry.

"So, I am dead?"

"No, my son. You came here to find the teachings and I have been trying to tell you where they are."

As he spoke, the dark in the crypt brightened a little and Geoffrey could see the pale silver features of his ancestors smiling and nodding behind his father.

"Where are the teachings? And are you all alright?"

"Haha! I see where your priorities lie Geoffrey! The documents are in my tomb, I asked your brother to bury the container with me and I knew it would be safe there until you came alone. Just reach in, it won't be too sticky!"

"We are all quite well, my darling." It was Morgana and she looked as she had when Geoffrey last saw her. She was cloaked in a misty blue and white haze and reminded Geoffrey of the descriptions of ghosts he had heard over the years. So, it was true.

"I am not ready to join you," he said.

"No, no, no my boy. You have a lot to do yet. You will be quite an old man before you join us but don't despair! It's really nice here! Quickly now!"

Geoffrey reached in and felt around the tomb. The light from his long dead, glowing and amiable ancestors assisted his search and soon his hand rested against a gold cylinder. He took it out and held it to his chest. There was a round of applause which Geoffrey considered unusual but accepted nonetheless.

"Goodnight, sleep tight, Joffrey," said Morgana.

"Don't rush to join us yet," added his father and began to climb back into his tomb. Geoffrey watched as each ancestor, male and female returned to their stone coffins and slid their lids back. As they did so, the dark crept in a little more with each closure until Geoffrey stood in the dark, all alone. This time he was not afraid and he wondered if he ever would be again.

"My Lord!"

The crypt door had opened and a servant with a lantern stood at the top of the stairs.

"Yes John, I am here."

"Oh, my Lord! We were so worried about you with this storm and all. We have been looking for you. Were you locked in?"

"No, John. I am quite safe. I was just visiting the family."

"Of course, my Lord, only it has been such a long time and supper has long been ready at the Hall."

Geoffrey walked upstairs and saw that it was dark outside. They left together out of the chapel door and Geoffrey noticed that the weather was calm and warm and the sea peaceful.

"Were you not frightened in the dark all alone, my Lord?" asked John with genuine concern.

"Not at all John. They are my family after all."

John nodded but did not seem convinced. He had been frightened enough just searching for his master.

Geoffrey enjoyed the return walk along the coast path and looked from the view across the bay to the twinkling lights of Tywardreath and the Priory and back to the dark shadow of the walled Pridias Hall atop of which hung bright flaming lanterns to mark their destination.

The following day he went to the clearing and met with the Priestess for one last time. Following the meeting he wrote to his son.

My dear Roger,

I found them. I found the writings and I shall return with them and we shall hide them. Baldwin and Reginald will never know, for I fear that neither of my brothers will carry on any of the old ways. Now that my beloved father is laid to rest in our chapel and Baldwin has remarried a very religious woman, if the writings were to be discovered, they will be destroyed. I went to the cottage of the Priestess and she told me that she is leaving now to join Richard and our ancestors. She prophecies a time when the Pridias lands will be far from the sea and the Priory will crumble. She says the remaining lands will remain in Pridias hands for hundreds of years and then into other hands for 280 years until they are recovered by a blood Pridias. Then the spirits and witches and guardians will return. The Priestess will return then too. You will be part of this secret Roger, as will your son and his son and so on. I went to the walled garden and sat for many hours where I meditated and heard Father speak to me. He is happy and I am happy. I shall be home soon my boy.

Your loving father.

Geoffrey.

THE SHERIFF OF DEVON

Featuring Roger de Pridias (1224 - 1291)

It's one thing to know that children are involved in coven meetings, but quite another to do something about it.

Roger was serving his third year as High Sheriff of Devon, a role given to him originally by Richard, Earl of Cornwall because of his close friendship and trust in Roger. His service in that role continued following Richard's death which had been caused by grief following the murder of his son Henry, by the de Montforts.

Roger was good friends with Edmund, Richard's second son who was to inherit titles previously destined for Henry, one of which was 2nd Earl of Cornwall. Edmund continued his associations with the Pridias family both in Cornwall and Devon after his father's death, even though the family had always been more friends with Richard than Edmund.

Edmund was often in London as he pursued his goals, but travelled back to the South West, mainly by ship. He docked at Orcherton, Ponts Mill or Helston and other small ports, dependent upon his aims at the time. He spent much of his time at Restormel, a little north of Pridias Hall and regularly went to Trematon and Tintagel, both being castles that he loved. **Edmund's father** Richard, the King of Almain and first Earl of Cornwall, had acquired these properties during his lifetime. He had successfully persuaded Gervase de Hornicote to exchange Tintagel Castle for some manors around Haylesford. Richard in 1236, then added the curtain wall and the great ward on the mainland which was linked to the island by a bridge. This move was to help ingratiate himself with the Cornish by affirming and accepting the Cornish link with King Arthur as had been written by Geoffrey of Monmouth. Richard also obtained Restormel and all lands on the east of the road between Bodmin and Lostwithiel from the heiress, Isolda de Cardinham.

Edmund loved Restormel so much that he made **Lostwithiel** the capital of his county. It became his seat of government where tinners came with their blocks of metal and was the site of the goal where many transgressors suffered the ultimate penalty of hanging. Edmund however would not help the poverty stricken and already tumbledown Tywardreath Priory. Instead he relied on the hermits who were spiritual descendants of the early saints, for his own spiritual progress.

The Cornish branch of the Pridias family had been party to and witnesses of, these contracts. They had their feet firmly under the table.

The Knights of Cornwall and Devon disliked Edmund, mistrusted him and resented him. Many would have preferred Henry, but he was dead and his murderers punished with only excommunication. Roger, perceived by many to being in league with Edmund, was not popular among his neighbours. He was unfazed because the affiliation was making him richer by the day. He had even offered to buy back the Pridias lands in Cornwall, but had his offer refused even though his kin were in dire need of financial injection.

Roger sat many times in the Shire courts and unable to be swayed by bribes, often ruled against his own countrymen. He raised more tax for the Crown than was considered acceptable locally and he made many enemies. He considered himself to be a fair man, believing in the rights of all men and women. He played a great part in helping in establishing the borough of **Modbury** which now had a weekly market and two annual fairs. Roger also encouraged development by granting charters to peasants who were able to extend their holdings field by field as they colonised waste land. He wanted each man to have the opportunity to better himself. But he had many arguments and litigation battles and it began to wear him down.

His parents Geoffrey and Isabella, had given him a great deal of land on his marriage to Gilda, a kinswoman of the Reskymer family of Haylesford. Roger had only to pay for this privilege with one pair of white gloves or one penny if he found it impossible to find the white gloves, to Isabella. Roger also took control of land and property around Haylesford, which had been bequeathed to his wife. They not only ensured that all their children were born at Haylesford, but conceived in Cornwall.

Roger and Gilda considered themselves Cornish and not Devonian. Geoffrey had told Roger that he and his brother were conceived and born in Cornwall too and Roger hoped to persuade his own children to consider themselves Cornishmen who owned owning Devon lands, rather than the other way about.

Edmund cared not about Cornishmen and their urge to remain as such, but he did care about the magical abilities of some people and knew quite well of the Melusine blood which flowed through their veins. It was said that the golden-haired Gilda was of this blood and this fact had encouraged Roger to marry her, upon Richard the first Earl of Cornwall's, recommendation. Gilda for her part knew of her bloodline but had no conscious knowledge of her abilities and Roger hoped that these would rise to the surface before long.

He knew that it was only a matter of time before he would be dismissed from his role and felt that he wanted it to be on his own terms and no one else's. Gilda and her friends could help him in this goal. Roger had begun to make plans in that regard but Edmund again stood in his way.

Edmund had obtained several items and relics said to be connected to Jesus. In a pendant reminiscent of the one once owned by Charlemagne, Edmund had a blood relic of Jesus which he had purloined on his Crusading skirmishes. He had been envious of Charlemagne's talisman and so had a jeweller envelop his own relic with gold and jewels. Edmund had shown it to Roger and Gilda and they had agreed with him that they should use the skills of the Mothecombe coven in order to establish its authenticity.

Edmund was ecstatic with the suggestion and promised Roger that he would let him have another of his minor relics in return for this service. A few shreds of the shroud fashioned into a ring which could be worn on a man's little finger, he said. Roger remembered the conversation he had the previous night with Gilda.

"That cross and shroud must have been massive, the number of relics that have come from them. And the blood of Jesus? Enough to fill a lake."

Roger had laughed with his wife but he had no intention of laughing with Edmund. He was notoriously emotionally unpredictable and Roger lived on a knife edge during each conversation with him. They had agreed to have him meet the coven because to refuse would have meant consequences. Gilda was a member and while they helped some women find partners or get pregnant, they also helped men with their business dealings and political ambitions. This coven was accepted in the locality and consulted by many. Their identities were secret in order to prevent repercussions and this was facilitated by the gowns and hoods they wore.

They weren't that harmless though. Gilda had read the documents that her father-in-law had left and had understood their meaning, suddenly, on the thirtieth reading. She now knew how life worked and how it was not only possible, but necessary that any person living could control their own life and the lives of others.

Did she have Melusine blood? Her family said so and Roger hoped so. Whenever she returned home to Helford to give birth, the old women and maids who attended her births confirmed that the new baby did what all Melusine children did – they opened their eyes as soon as they took their first breath. None of her babies behaved like a vulnerable creature, but as a small adult awaiting its maturity.

Gilda now considered her family complete with Piers, Reginald, Thomas, Alice and Lucy. Roger agreed and accepted her instructions that he must no longer bother her in that regard and that he was quite welcome to take a mistress. Roger didn't, preferring to remain true to Gilda and he was also finding that he was constantly stressed about his knife-edge friendship with Edmund.

The night that Edmund was allowed to enter the coven interior was kept secret from all but coven members and Edmund's personal guards. Edmund had been sworn to secrecy and had been told and believed that the witches would be able to tell if he had told about the meeting.

The coven met in the copious woods at Mothecombe which spread along the coastline and the estuary sides inland to Ermington and beyond. These woods were matched in their density and confusion on the opposite side of the banks of the River Erme. It was said that only the witches could find the stone archway which marked their own chapel. Others had tried and failed and worse, had become hopelessly lost in the process. Seekers ended up on the beaches beneath the banks at low tide, hailing passing boats and begging for rescue.

Edmund arrived on horseback to the edge of the woodland and was met by twenty hooded and cloaked beings. It was impossible to tell whether they were male or female and he shivered with excitement. His guards had their hands on the sword hilts, ready to draw them at a moment's notice, but

Edmund told them to desist. Roger clapped his hands and asked that they all leave their horses where they were and his men would take care of them.

The gold-robed figures turned in unison and moved into the darkness of the woods. Although it was a darkly cloudy night the glimmer of the moon reflected off the cloaks, seemingly lighting the way. Roger was excited, he loved these nights. He was proud of his wife and her abilities and the results she obtained from her practices. Edmund and his men would not know that she was the figure with the silver Celtic cross embroidered on the back of her cloak which would only become visible when lighted at certain angles by moon, lamp or fire.

One figure lightly beat a skin drum in time to their steps and no words were spoken. They moved deeper and deeper into the darkness and even Roger, accustomed as he was to the ceremony, felt himself jump when strange noises echoed through the trees.

It was 30 minutes before the group arrived at the stone archway and the drumming stopped.

Edmund asked, "Is this it Roger? Are we here?"

"Ssssh Sir," instructed one of the figures and Edmund obeyed.

There was a glow from the chapel window and the group moved towards it and entered one by one. Roger indicated the way to Edmund who clutched his talisman to his breast as he entered the room. The door was closed behind him and Roger pointed out the wall hangings of heavy blue cloth, woven with threads of gold, silver and many other colours, depicting scenes of sorcery. Or this was how it appeared to Edmund when he saw the enchanted creatures and the wise men and women standing by monuments. At the far end was a large oak table upon which sat items of gold and silver and where candles and incense burned. A small man was attending to the table and its contents. He checked and rechecked the order in which the items were set out and Edmund wondered why that was so important.

In front of the table were three thrones, the middle throne larger than the other two and three robed figures sat upon them. This was a signal to the other figures who sat on the benches lining the walls. Roger beckoned Edmund to walk through the centre of the group and had him place his talisman on the table on a blue silken cloth. This, Roger neatly arranged and then covered it with another piece of blue silk. Edmund looked alarmed at its apparent disappearance but Roger raised his hand in demonstration of there being no need to worry. Edmund was allocated a covered seat in the corner of the chapel between the head three and the rest of the coven.

Roger sat in another corner and watched as the coven stood before moving towards the centre of the room and then turning to face the still seated three. They bowed in unison and the three dipped their heads in acknowledgement. The small man lifted the gold plate containing the silk and the talisman and brought it to the throned three and dropped to his knees while offering the plate to them. The centre figure took the plate from him and placed it on the wide arm of his own throne. Roger glanced across at Edmund to see if he was upset about the process, him being a minor part of it, but Edmund seemed perfectly happy and focussed.

The middle figure stood and raised the covered plate to the ceiling, which Edmund had only just realised was painted as a night sky with stars, planets and chariots carrying God-like men and women. As the figure chanted in unison with the group, one of the painted figures leaned down from his place in the ceiling painting and turned into a coloured mist as he fell to the ground. He reformed as a life-sized man dressed in Biblical robes and soon he was joined by his counterparts from the ceiling.

Roger never ceased to be amazed by this and noticed that Edmund had his mouth wide open and his eyes goggled as he turned to Roger. Roger put his finger to his lips and smiled at his Royal superior and Edmund obeyed by snapping his mouth shut and returning his gaze to the strange scene.

The spirits, for they must have been spirits, clicked their fingers and another line of hooded figures entered the chapel. Roger had never seen these before and from their movement and their high-pitched whimpering, it was clear that these were children. He couldn't stop himself saying,

"What is this? Why are there children here? Who ordered this?"

His answer came in the form of a sharp thump in his back and his arms were pulled behind him.

"Silence now, Sir Roger. We must all do as we are told within these walls."

"I most certainly do not," Roger answered. "This is my chapel and my ceremony. You cannot frighten me."

"You should be frightened Sir. They seem impressed with this talisman you have brought us."

The grip grew tighter and Roger stifled the cry he felt, for he had no idea who this robed coven member was, nor could he identify his own wife amongst the others. This meeting was different to before and he knew not why. He was dragged roughly back to the wall and tied to a chair.

The spirits took the talisman from the platter and the first spirit put it around his neck. Roger could not see how Edmund was taking this, but he could hear no complaints. The robed figures began to move in a clockwise direction around the centre group, who knelt at the feet of the talisman wearer as he turned his face and hands to the ceiling and began a chant. This was taken up by the rest and as the noise became a vibration, the walls of the chapel disappeared and the painted sky and stars became part of the experience. The trees in the woods were faintly visible in the background with no chapel walls between. And all were now standing, then dancing in mid-air, with stars and planets surrounding them.

Roger had seen similar before but he was still worried. This experience was stronger and it felt as though they were the visitors in an unknown place instead of visitor Gods granting their silly questions and requests. And the children, that had never happened.

The children had already been ushered to the centre and the talisman-wearing God instructed that they surround him in a tight group. The children were crying now, no longer whimpering.

Roger said, "You cannot harm them! Leave the children!"

The children were frightened even further by this shout and some were trying to run away. There was no door and so their struggles were met by laughs and grabs before they were returned to the talisman God. After ten minutes of this fruitless effort, the children began to quieten and stay where they had been put.

The talisman-God raised his arms aloft and Roger saw that he now carried a glittering sword. As Roger shouted, "No!" the sword was brought to the God's waist and he span around quickly, mowing down each child as he did so.

When Roger woke, he found Gilda sitting next to him, cradling his head in her hands.

"Roger! My dear Roger! Are you alright? You were so strange tonight."

"The children. What about the children?"

"Our children? They are at home or at their own homes."

"I mean tonight's children. The ones that were killed."

"Killed? No one was killed. Why would children be killed here?"

Gilda was genuinely concerned and beckoned to another to help her with her husband.

Edmund had enjoyed himself, Roger was told. He had received confirmation that his talisman was genuine and could bring him nothing but good luck and so had ridden away to Restormel with his guards. He had expressed his thanks to Gilda and asked that she inform the seemingly unwell Roger that his assistance would be rewarded. He had handed her an ornate ring and Gilda promised to give it to her husband when he recovered. This she now did and placed it on Roger's little finger.

Roger sat up and saw that he was lying between the archway and the chapel. The coven members had all but gone, leaving only Gilda, the small man and William Abbott, his own man.

"I need to go back inside the chapel," said Roger.

"Why my love? Let us go home now. Everything has been cleaned up and you know as well as I do that to return will mean that I have to go through the whole process of cleansing again."

Roger did know this to be true for it was the spells that protected the area and kept it from prying eyes. Gilda would not want her work undone, she was tired enough.

"We all did well tonight, Roger," she said to him. "Edmund will make sure that we never want for money or assistance and he will consider himself in your debt."

"You cast that one too then?"

"Of course I did. Times are too difficult not to have influential friends in very high places."

"And there was me thinking that it was my political skill and good company which kept him close."

"Don't be ridiculous Roger," she said.

"Fetch my horse my dear, while I go behind a tree."

She laughed and walked away from him as he struggled to his feet. Roger felt ill and dizzy and that worried him as he had never been this way at any other meeting. As he watered the tree he thought about what generally happened and this time, apart from Edmund being present it had only been the children that was different. Yet everyone else denied their presence there and yet he had seen them killed! Had he though? Had he been bewitched by the others?

Gilda was riding back to him and leading his horse. The servants had fetched them from the edge of the wood as they would now be able to navigate the trees without assistance. Mothecombe woods had changed again.

"Here you are my love," she said as she threw him the reins.

"I saw the children," he insisted.

"There are no dead children here Roger. Look around you."

He did and could see nothing.

"You were happy with the talisman?"

"Oh, yes we were. It seems a shame that a stupid man such as Edmund should have ownership of such an important and powerful item."

"It has power?"

"It has a great deal of power Roger and I don't believe that Edmund is a fit man to have it."

"But he has it nevertheless."

"So it would appear."

And that was still his problem. He knew, he just knew that children had been there and if that were so, they must have been killed. Or perhaps they had been sent to another dimension, many existed he was fully aware of that. He knew that death did not happen as almost everyone believed it would. We are all dead already and choose how to spend our long journey while we wait to wake up. That was the essence of the teachings Richard had left the family. To understand it was to believe it and to use all day, every day and yet these words, written in plain sight were unbelievable to most and therefore useless.

Following this night, Edmund had kept to his word and helped Roger's appointments and his career and Gilda had become head of the Mothecombe coven and was powerful. Roger was benefiting in her wake. Property deals and land acquisition were already falling into his lap. And he liked it.

Roger had just had a meeting with three local women, famous for their do-gooding about the neighbourhood and they had told him that an alarming number of children had been going missing recently.

"Granted my Lord, they are the children of vagabonds and thieves and dirty gypsies. But it does not mean that they should be stolen."

"I have heard tell that witches and devil worshippers want children because it furthers their powers," said her friend.

"I doubt that is true," answered Roger.

"Well perhaps you don't see what goes on, hidden here in your big house, Sir Roger. But I am telling you something funny is happening."

"Do you have any idea of who may be involved?"

"No, my Lord. Shall I let you know if I find anything out?"

"Indeed yes. I should be most interested. In fact, you must inform me and no one else."

"Of course, my Lord." She bobbed a curtsey and they all left, happy that his Lordship would be taking care of the matter.

Any notion of following up on these thoughts was reduced sharply when he immediately received notice from his estate manager that Roger was now the new owner of some more Devon property.

The spells were working.

When they were undressing that night, Gilda had her jewellery chest open as she returned her ruby necklace to its container. Roger recognised a glint from another half-opened box and when Gilda left the room to visit her washroom, he looked inside.

It was the talisman.

If not it, then a jolly good replica of it. He picked it up and held it and knew that it was the original. He returned it swiftly and ran to his side of the bed before Gilda saw him.

"Gilda. That talisman of Edmund's. How powerful would it be if we had possession of it?"

"And a replica had been returned to Edmund during all the smoke and mirrors confusion, you mean?"

"Well, yes."

"We would be the most powerful family in the South West. In the country. Why do you ask?"

"No reason, my dear. Just curious."

He got into bed as Gilda snapped the chest shut and locked it.

THE MOTHECOMBE COVEN

Featuring Peter de Pridias (1260-1316)

Now that his father was dead, Peter felt that he had to get to the bottom of the conundrum. For it was surely that, in this year of 1299.

During the summer, Peter's father Roger had settled some of his Cornish property on Peter and if Peter were to die without heirs, then the inheritance would pass to his younger brother Reginald and if he died, the properties were to go to his then single daughter Marjery and her heirs before it would go to his other two daughters and their husbands. Roger had not known at his death that Marjery was being pursued by Richard Heligan and he would have heartily approved of their subsequent marriage and children. Perhaps she told him all about it when she died during the birth of her second child only a few years later.

Roger had wanted to ensure that his other son Thomas would be so far away from the money and properties that he and his family would never inherit. Roger would be receiving a fair income for this until he died and at that time his Devon and other Cornish properties were bequeathed in the same way.

Peter was given in trust, Brodoke and Redwall and the lands, woods, manor and tenements for a fee payable each Easter and in its entirety following his parents' deaths. These vast swathes of Cornwall were as dear to Peter as they had been to Roger and Geoffrey and he determined to keep them in his family in addition to the Devon properties. In some ways, the Cornish properties were dearer to him - he was still a strong blood Cornishman. It was understood that there would be nothing for Thomas, not upon his marriage to Isolda and not upon the death of his father.

Thomas had been told and told not to marry her. Isolda was the daughter of one of the coven members and she and Gilda did not get on. Isolda's mother Anastasia, was aiming for a better position within the membership and had tried some spells of her own to gain her wish. But she was a weakling, a junior compared to Gilda and all she achieved was Gilda's wrath and a binding spell. Thomas's marriage was forbidden, but he went ahead anyway and banished himself from his own family. No one sent him good wishes on the birth of his son whom he had named Roger, after his father.

His second brother Reginald, had been going to marry a wonderful Cornish girl called Marjery Chartery, a Prideaux cousin via her mother and yet another rumoured Melusine descendant. She was tiny and red haired and hailed from Luxulyan. Reginald had met her on one of his trips to Pridias with his father and Peter. They were making a visit to their lands and houses at Bradoc and their manor on the banks of the river opposite Golant. Roger had inherited these lands from Geoffrey along with several Cornish properties at Rodewell. When Reginald saw her standing on the riverbank that day, her hair blowing in the wind, he fell in love right there and then.

The whole family were ecstatic and Gilda took Marjery to her coven meetings which she seemed to enjoy. Then, two days before the wedding to Reginald, Marjery was found dead on the same river bank he first saw her. after having been lured from her house in the middle of the night. Reginald was inconsolable and despite his mother's begging, he joined the priesthood. Roger ensured that Reginald became the Rector of Bradoc in their Cornish manor so that he would always be near his beloved Marjery who was buried in the churchyard there. Reginald paid for a stone representation of her, arms folded aloft her tomb and spent as much time there as he could. Reginald gave his own lands and inheritance to Peter when he became a priest.

His sisters had married well, having better luck than two of their brothers. Alice married Richard Reskymer, a landowner and businessman of Helston, and Lucy married Benedict Reynward, a fabulously wealthy landowner and tin mine owner from Cornwall. His family had interests in Liskeard, St Minver, Bodmin and many more towns. Their youngest sister Marjery married Richard Heligan, another landed Cornishman who was to inherit the lands near Mevagissey.

They all helped each other out, unless business interests clashed and that happened more often than not. But blood was blood and it usually came out alright in the end. There were no long-term arguments and that was why no one had been really surprised when Roger announced that there had been a change in his mind and he now wanted to leave money and a manor to his previously estranged son, Thomas. He said that he wanted to bring him back into the family and included his children in that bequest. Peter's wife Clarice, mentioned that perhaps it was easier for Roger to do such a thing now that Isolda was so pious and determined to ingratiate herself back into the Pridias fold. Also, she had heard that they were running short of money.

Peter had agreed that some of the properties which had been previously going to Reginald, now firmly ensconced in his religious life, could pass to Thomas and his heirs. The deed was done on the 29th September 1291, two weeks prior to Roger's death and Roger was happy that he could leave his properties in good hands. Clarice told Peter that Isolda was positively wagging her tail with excitement and had quickly begun trying to get nominated to the Mothecombe coven. Three members must nominate her for her application to be considered. Then, four weeks after his father's death, Thomas insisted that his inheritance be returned to Peter and that he wanted nothing more to do with it.

"But your son and his children? They must have something to live on after you have gone? Lord knows you have little enough as it is!"

"We have the manor from Isolda and I have been told that there will be enough income from the farms and orchards."

"It isn't much Thomas. I have so much here and in Cornwall and now that Reginald is a God follower and all the girls gone to their husbands, I want you to share it with me."

Even Peter was surprised at how emotional he felt about it. Perhaps it was that only a few years ago, they had been six children playing and riding together. Often, they would be brought on display as beautifully well-dressed specimens at parties that their parents hosted. But, more often than not they were in the care of maids and teachers. Peter would remember the fun the siblings had had in so many beautiful houses of their own, or belonging to close family in both Devon and Cornwall. Drummed into their minds was the information that they were a Cornish family with rich Cornish blood and told that they must in the future marry only Cornish men and women and ensure that their children were born in Cornwall. They had all done as they were told, believing strongly in the Pridias line. All except Thomas. He had married the Devon woman who, although of good blood, was not of good Cornish blood.

"My son will never survive his illness and there will no line stretching on from my blood Peter. I don't want the lands to leave too. If I die before Isolda, she will leave it to her ridiculous nephews. You have it back, Isolda will go mental when she finds out but I really don't care about that. She has her affairs while I..."

"You are not happy, are you brother? I wish you could work with me."

"You will be fine Peter. Everyone brought you up for the role of Lord."

This was true and as Peter watched his brother leave, he thought about what he should do. Thomas and Reginald were both dear to him as was all his siblings, but the girls were happy and well married and beyond need of his help. But those two – how had it come to this?

The worry went from his mind for the next months as he took full control of the estates. The tenants and business men paid homage to the new Lord and Clarice could not have been happier. It was not until the following summer that she told him that she was now the head of the Mothecombe coven.

Peter had not been as involved as his father had in the coven. His mother Gilda was in her late sixties and in mourning. But, she was still agile and playing an active part in coven business. Gilda had been the head witch until Roger became ill a year prior and she had temporarily handed the reins over to

Anastasia Cwm, Isolda's mother, there being no one else suitable. This had not worked out well as Anastasia quickly made enemies and so a new leader had been sought.

Now Clarice had power and she asked that Peter come to a meeting and see just how she had progressed the coven. Peter was tempted to go but was a little frightened, though he would never have admitted the fact. He managed to put the meeting off for several months until Gilda took him to one side after the family had hosted a party one evening.

"I don't think I have long left on this earth Peter and I want to tell you a story before it is too late."

"Mother, you do not have to tell me anything that you don't want to," answered Peter, terrified that he was about to hear something he had managed to not know perfectly well to date.

"Sit here Peter," and Gilda patted the oak bench which gave them a great view of the moonlit rippled river which they both knew curled out of their sight through the willow branches before it reached the sea. It was a lovely warm night and the stocks smelled wonderful.

"Clarice tells me that she can't get you to see her at the meetings. She is very proud of her position and you should be too."

"I am proud of her, it's just that..."

"You are scared, I know baby. You were always scared of the dark and especially if I came home in my robes."

"I hardly remember that. I just know that some of the friends that you and father had and brought back to the house would frighten me sometimes."

"In what way?"

"Oh, I remember I would sneak out on to the landing and peep through the banister rails and look down, they would talk about the Devil and demons in the chapel in the woods and casting spells. I heard about mermaids and giant sea creatures and if I ever mentioned anything to Father he told me that I shouldn't have been listening."

"I see. It is all true you know. And that is what I want to talk to you about."

There was silence between them for a moment as they watched a merchant boat make its way back to sea. A sailor waved to them and they both waved back and Peter thought fondly of his childhood when they would all wait to wave to the boats and score points for each wave returned.

"I know that witchcraft works and that you can cast spells good or bad. What I don't understand is, why the need to get involved in the first place?"

"Silly boy. Power, influence, money and excitement."

She cuddled him and he let her.

"Now that Clarice has made it to the top of the tree, she will want to change the way the coven is run and you know why she wants to do that?"

"No."

"Because she doesn't understand any of it. She thinks spell craft is about chanting some words and beheading cockerels and mixing blood with frog's eyes."

"And it's not?"

"No. It's about having the knowledge and understanding it. Not many do and I want you to understand it before I leave here to join the rest of the family."

"Are you not feeling well? You aren't going anywhere yet, are you?"

"Not just yet, but I shall be one day and it is imperative that I pass on the understanding to you so that you can in turn."

"Is this something to do with Geoffrey?"

"He brought back the information from Richard who had secreted it in his tomb."

"How did Geoffrey find it then?"

"That has been written down too so that the stories cannot be forgotten."

"Where is all this stuff kept? I've never found it."

"It's all in the library. We can go and look now or tomorrow morning, but we need to do it soon. It will take you a while to learn and understand properly."

The sea had become very quiet, no boats, no early fishermen and they had not been disturbed by any person. It was very late and the moon was showing them that it was bedtime from self-respecting people.

"Why not now?" asked Peter. "We shall be pestered and bothered by everyone tomorrow and I would like to know these family secrets."

Gilda seemed pleased and held his arm tightly as they made their way back to the house across the dampening grass. They could see dim lights reflecting against the hall windows and knew that these had been left by the servants for their return. They also knew that there would be Thomas, an old retainer, sitting on the oak bench in the porch and waiting for them. It was also highly likely that he would be asleep.

They crept past the sleeping man and made their way to the kitchen for a hot drink to take to the library. Gilda brought out cake and then sent Peter ahead as she went back to nudge Thomas and tell him that it was now safe to lock up and go to bed.

Peter had riddled the fire - enough to get a blaze going and Gilda was glad of it.

"Thomas has gone up now. He was most disturbed that he hadn't noticed us coming in."

"Thomas is getting old. We need a younger man on the door."

"We will never find a more loyal man. Let him continue, the spells keep us safe."

"If the spells keep us so safe, how come Reginald lost his fiancée and we lose members of our family?" He riddled harder.

"Silly boy Peter. We never lose anyone, they only go into another place."

"Do we all go into the same place when we die? I mean whether we have chosen the 'correct' religion, or whether we just go about our business and never refer to God?"

"Yes, but it is a difficult question which requires a complicated answer..." she began.

"That is an easy way to say that you don't know the answer."

"No, that's not true. If your question was, will I be able to speak German one day, then I could answer in the same way. I would explain that although you know speaking German is possible and you know all the letters of the alphabet, you must still go through a process of practice and understanding before you succeed."

"I suppose," answered Peter, in a surprisingly sulky way.

"Sit down over there and I will bring you a book."

Peter did as he was told and watched his mother walk over to the wall and fiddle with one of the shelves. He loved this room and came here often when he wanted a break from his responsibilities. The walls were lined with books of all descriptions. There were record books of everything that had ever happened on the estate and details of every person who had ever lived there or dealt with the family. There were records from Orcherton and other Devon properties and the holdings and manors in Cornwall. Each tenant must give full details of their family and history in order to get a cottage or a job. Business dealings when recorded, also detailed the people involved and the family now had so much paperwork that one of the walls was completely occupied with them.

No one outside of their trusted staff knew about these. The documents were hidden behind calf leather and oak bindings and were too numerous to be noticed individually. This was the wall along which Gilda was running her hand. As she came to one section, there was a flash and a glow and Gilda removed the books from that particular section and laid them on the table. Peter left his chair and took hold of the books, bringing them all back carefully to the low table by the fire, which already held their refreshments.

When Gilda settled opposite him, she pointed to the top book and Peter obediently took hold of it and opened it carefully.

"Read it," instructed Gilda.

Peter began reading and Gilda leaned across and tapped his hand.

"Out loud Peter. You will understand it better then."

Peter grumbled but obeyed.

This is a true account of the teachings given to me by The Priestess at her cottage in the Pridias woods. I recommend that these teachings be read over and over again and thought about when going about your daily business. You may find that other people will not understand what these teachings refer to and so for that and many other reasons, I suggest that you do not discuss their content with anyone else.

"How much of this do I have to read?"

"More than you have so far. I will tell you when to stop." Gilda was leaning back in her chair, eyes closed and a smile on her face.

"Hmmm."

She has told me so many things that I find it difficult to put them in order. I don't think that it is necessary to practice the teachings in any particular order. I certainly didn't. I think that it is a matter of practicing and dedicating time to understanding and eventually it is just that. The understanding brings belief and belief brings conscious results rather than unconscious results.

He looked up and recognised that his mother was asleep and so he got up and covered her with a large fur blanket. She stirred slightly and snuggled down in the chair. Peter returned to his own chair, now interested in his book. He whispered the words, not wanting to upset his dear mother.

It seems that the only thing we must understand is that we are all God. He is not separate to us nor above us. He is not to be worshipped from afar, but to be acknowledged as the whole of which we are a part. If we want to possess something and encounter an experience, God already knows it and is willing to grant it. Praying is nothing more than an instruction to God to grant your desire and never, I repeat never, an incantation that must be said in the right order and at the right time before God decides whether or not He will answer your prayer. It is impossible to have a desire that cannot be granted. Impossible to have a thought that will not come true. But, be aware that God does not care whether you wish for evil or good, He will grant it regardless.

Firstly – Be careful and conscious of your thoughts

Secondly – Be aware that you can affect the actions and thoughts of another with your own thoughts.

Thirdly – Remain focussed at all times.

Fourthly – What you are doing to others, you are doing to yourself.

Fifthly – Nothing exists outside of yourself

Sixthly – If you want something, believe you already have it and never direct your thoughts in an opposite direction to your fulfilled wish.

Seventhly – All wishes come true.

Peter stopped reading. There were many more pages to go yet and an initial flick through showed him that these contained detailed instructions on how to achieve the focus. Was this how his mother achieved her notoriety and success in spell craft? Were all spells nothing more than concentrated thought? He leant back in his own chair, pulled a fur rug over his body and drifted into sleep.

He woke with a start and noticed that Gilda had already gone to bed. The fire was out, but Gilda had apparently lit some candles and by the light of these, Peter could see that the books were still on the table. He reached for them and turning the pages of the three he had not read, he noticed that the contents had been written by other hands than the original. The books contained spells and the results of spells and there were illustrations on many pages.

Peter looked back at the first book and saw that the pages had originally been part of long rolls which had been cut and bound in the oak and leather in which it sat. He felt the silver ornate corner pieces and read the name Lord Richard de Pridias on the front which had been embossed in gold leaf. It was beautiful and he hugged it to him as he suddenly remembered the story of its discovery as told to him by his late father.

It was the knocking at the library door which took him out of his musings. He slowly got up and moved to the door and was strangely nervous. The knocking was so insistent and unusual – that was the problem, he suddenly realised. He didn't recognise the knocking and if it was a stranger, how had he got as far as the library door?

The light from the hallway reflected feet moving, very large feet with odd, long toed shoes such as he had never seen. He put out his hand to open the door and realised that the handle was too high up. He could reach it, but now he had to reach up and not down as he had earlier that evening. He looked down and saw that he was dressed as a boy and a boy ready for bed. He scurried over to the ornate mirror hanging opposite the windows and saw that he was no taller than three and a half feet, perhaps less. He was carrying the Richard de Pridias book and it covered the whole of his torso and suddenly felt very heavy. He dropped it and the crashing noise it made as it hit the floor stopped the knocking and the feet ceased their shuffling.

Peter held his breath and when the door began to open, he ran behind it, ensuring that he would be hidden from whatever monster might be about to enter the room. The creature man shuffled in, bent over and his right arm crooked and holding on to his lower back. He swung each leg to the side before he moved it forward, making his progress slow and menacing. He grumbled and grunted and looked about him. The light from the hallway spread behind the creature, exaggerating and elongating his shadow across the room. He turned and Peter shrank back into the darkness as the creature's head pointed full on his direction. Peter saw dark, shiny eyes, huge and almond shaped, flicking from side to side. There appeared to be no whites in those dreadful eyes. The nose was thin and pointed and the mouth thin and large. It opened his mouth, drawing grey lips over ugly, short and sharp teeth.

It seemed that Peter was safe from his gaze, with the hallway light in the creature's eyes and Peter in the dark shadow. When the creature turned back to the room, Peter slipped out of the doorway and ran along the hallway. He must find his mother and have her help him.

He ran up the stairs and along the corridor to his parents' room. He didn't knock as he would usually have done, instead bursting in and running towards the bed. He drew back the curtain and shouted,

"Mama, Mama! A monster in the library!"

There was no answer. The bed was empty and still made up and Peter began to cry. This must be a dream – he could clearly remember being an adult not very long ago.

There were voices on the landing and Peter jumped on to the bed and drew the curtains, breathing erratically. This feeling of fear felt familiar and he half remembered being here before. He pushed himself under the blankets and shivered.

"How did it manage to find its way here?" A woman was talking as she entered the bedroom.

"My dear, my dear, I do not know. But I suspect it is something to do with Anastasia."

"Yes, she has always used the teachings for ill. I am glad that she doesn't know them in their entirety."

"Perhaps, but she is doing enough damage only knowing a part. I hadn't realised that she was conjuring a monster in her own woods. The stupid, stupid cow."

The woman threw a cloak on an oak chest and turned to the man accompanying her. Peter saw that is was his father and he let out a cry.

"Papa! Oh Papa!"

"Did you hear that noise?" asked Roger of his wife.

"I did. It sounded as though it was coming from the next room."

"I thought it came from in here. I thought that it sounded like little Peter."

"No, he should be abed with the other children. The maids would know if he was missing."

"They would."

"Mama! Papa! I am here!"

"I heard it again!"

"So did I, Roger."

Peter struggled with the curtains, desperately trying to open them, but they would not.

"Mama! Papa!" he cried.

"Why are the bed curtains moving so?" asked Roger.

Gilda took a sharp inward breath and rushed to her bed. She drew the curtains back and cried,

"Nothing here."

"We must be imagining it," said Roger.

"No, we are not. This is all part of the conjuring. Anastasia has bewitched us all."

"Even the children?"

"Peter anyway. He is the heir after all," added Gilda.

"And you think she wants to hurt him?"

"Confuse him, then she can control him later. We both know it has happened before."

Peter listened and drew back the curtains and ran towards his parents. It soon became obvious that he was invisible to them and he stood by the door, sobbing. How was he to save himself from this sorry state? Gilda had said that he was bewitched and he dreaded living through his childhood again.

"Listen," said Gilda sharply.

There were shuffling noises on the stairs and all three rushed to the landing. The creature was making its slow and swinging way up the stairs. Peter was terrified, he now knew that his parents were unable to help him. The dark, cloaked shape made its slow way through the gloom of the candlelight. Peter ran in front of his mother and stood at the head of the stairs.

The creature stopped too and stared at Peter.

"He can see something, Roger," said Gilda.

"Yes. Perhaps its Peter."

The creature had a quicker turn of speed and made it to the top before anyone expected. It stood in front of Peter and raised his arms. The cloak sleeves dropped back and the claw like hands lunged for him. Gilda sprung from her position by the banister rail and stood between Peter and the creature.

"Go back from whence you came," she snarled at the creature. "Leave my family alone and find comfort in the family of your creator!"

She closed her eyes and stood still.

"Stop the world," she said. "Change it. Now move on."

The creature dropped his arms and stood still.

"Leave us," added Gilda.

The creature turned and made his lumbering way down the stairs.

"Well done, my dear," praised Roger.

"Peter is here," said Gilda.

Peter turned to Gilda and threw his arms around her waist.

"I love you my boy," she said.

Roger and Gilda moved towards their room and Peter watched them go. He knew instinctively that he must return to the library if he was to return to his adult life. He sprinted down the stairs and towards the library door. From the corner of his eye, he saw the creature lumbering towards the front door and a younger Thomas shooing him out with a long broom.

Peter ran into the library and towards the chair. Then he got up, picked up Richard's book and shut the door before returning to his chair. He closed his eyes and waited.

He must have waited a long time, for he fell asleep and was woken by Thomas.

"You alright Sir? You must be cold sitting here all night."

"No, I'm not cold. I am fine." Peter patted himself down, relieved to see that he was now an adult again.

He stood up as Gilda came into the room.

"Mama!" he said without thinking.

"Ah! You have remembered Peter," said Gilda. "Fetch us refreshment Thomas, would you?"

"Yes, my Lady," answered Thomas and he left the room.

"I was a boy again."

"The spell is broken now Peter. Anastasia can no longer affect the family. So many deaths and misfortune just recently. She killed young Marjery, but never tell Reginald. He will see her again. And she bewitched Thomas to marry that hag of a daughter of hers. I had to cast an emergency spell on Thomas after your father left him property, she would have used it against us. But we are safe now that we have come full circle."

"I read some of the book, Mama."

"And you must read more and learn. These teachings can be used for good or ill, but you must be prepared for it to come back to you as creator. The ill was sent back to Anastasia and will have reached her today. The harvest is upon her now that you have been back in your mind and remembered."

Thomas came back into the room carrying a tray filled with a jug, goblets and plates of food.

"Thank you, Thomas," said Peter. "Thomas, I wanted to say how much we recognise the care you bestow on our family. It is very much appreciated."

Thomas blushed and said, "No more than I want to do, my Lord. The Pridias family have always been very good to me and mine."

Peter nodded and Gilda smiled.

"Oh, I almost forgot!" said Thomas.

"What's that?" asked Gilda.

"Anastasia Cwm died in the night. It came as quite a shock to the family it seems, as she had not been unwell. Came out of the blue, they say. Apparently, she woke in the night screaming that a creature was banging on her bedroom door. When the maid went in, Mrs Cwm dropped down dead."

"Oh, that is dreadful," said Peter.

"Hmmm," said Gilda. "She shouldn't have planted seeds in the world that she was not prepared to see bloom."

"Do we have no control over what blooms from another's seed, Mama?"

"No, but we can choose our reaction and that overcomes and changes that which we wish had not been planted. Come to a coven meeting with Clarice and I, you will learn more there. And read the teachings and tell no one of them except your first born. Not Clarice. She will not understand."

"Yes Mama."

"Listen to your Mama," added Thomas. "I have seen what she can do."

ICE DAY AT SEQUERS BRIDGE

Featuring Sir Roger de Pridias (1294-1347)

Winter has begun early and is achingly cold.

This was the first diary entry I read which seems relevant to the events that followed. Such strange events, the result of which I have neither seen nor heard the like before or since.

I am Sir John Pridias, son of Sir Roger de Pridias and Elizabeth Treverbyn of Cornwall. We are Cornish men and women, although we own more lands now in Devon than in Cornwall. My elder brother Sir Roger the heir inherited…. Well, I am running ahead of myself here. There is a lot to say before I get there. My wife Joan is the daughter and heir of Gilbert Adeston and I have upon my marriage three years ago become heir to two large properties south of Modbury which join with the lands of my family and if my brother. Now, I must continue with the diary entries of my father in order that the story will make sense to you. It doesn't make sense to me and so I am asking for your help.

Monday: I noticed the brook icing up when I rode across Sequers Bridge today. That is a very unusual occurrence and I mentioned it to a man carrying sacks of something or other as we passed on the bridge. He said that it was a sign that this winter would one of the worst we would see. I thanked him for his cheerful forecast and he clicked his pony on, not understanding my wit. I stood there for a few minutes and watched as the ice crackled in from the banks towards the centre of the stream. I thought that it would soon become difficult for the boats to come up and down and bring much needed products along the Erme and from the sea or Ermington.

Wednesday: I rode down to the bridge again today and the ice was moving in further. The trees are covered in a thick hoarfrost this morning and the birds are struggling to find food. There are still berries about the bushes, but seem too frozen for them to peck at. As I stand, my horse becomes impatient and cold I suspect. He paws at the ground and chips at the ice with his hooves. I did wonder whether I should ride on the road in case we should slip, but have stuck to the verge where I can. A rabbit runs out from the hedge and I watch it scurry away. Philip, one of my gamekeepers tells me that the poachers are becoming braver and less discreet as they became hungry. Some poachers are selling because they need money and others because their families are hungry. I must judge them when they are brought to court and I find it difficult to be cruel. Then a young fox ran across the bridge and caught the rabbit and I heard it squeal so dreadfully. I felt ill for the rest of the day.

Sunday: There has not even been the reprieve of snow. We are quite warm at the Hall and so are the servants, but there are some homeless and poor cottagers who are finding it very difficult to manage.

I was told about a man who had been found frozen to death on the road and they couldn't move him because of the ice. So, they had to chip at him with an axe until he moved. Horrible.

Tuesday: It was a moonlit night last night and when I looked out of my window at the garden the view was that of a dream. Everywhere was white and black, softened by grey. A large owl, a Tawny, flew from an elm and landed on something, a mouse or a weasel perhaps and ate it whole. I looked back at Elizabeth sleeping solidly` in the bed. The wine she drinks before she retires every night helps her sleep. I know many do not sleep together when they have been married for so many years, but even after 25 years together I cannot sleep unless her body is beside me. I put on my coat and went downstairs and outside. No one saw me leave. The cold that hit me as I left the front porchway almost stopped my breath and I pulled my fur scarf over my face. I was going to fetch my horse, but decided that would be too much fuss and walked along the trackway instead. I could see Sequers Bridge across the fields and it looked white against the dark sky. I suspect it was the reflection of the moon. The owl screamed and flew past my ear in search of further titbits. It made me feel peculiar and I carried on with my walk with a heightened sensation of – anxiety – I think it was. I could see the ice on the brook as I neared it and as the wind picked up, the ice collected and blew towards me in such a strange way that I stopped in my tracks. Then there came a bright light in the sky, a huge light and I felt so sick and my head banged.

Saturday: I wrote Tuesday's entry just now as today's entry will make no sense without it. They tell me that I have been missing since Wednesday morning, when Elizabeth did not find me abed with her. All I can remember is the bright light and the owl and then waking up on the bridge. A man from the village found me and brought me home and they think I am suffering from some sort of mental decay because I don't know where I have been. I am now in bed with a hot pan and broth and ale on a tray until I recover. My son is here too. Roger that is. He is with his second wife Joan who is a Clifford and a cousin of his first wife. They have five children to add to his three from Elizabeth, but she died after birthing the last child, Edith. Peter and John are his boys from her and Peter is his heir. Then he has Alice, Johan, Elizabeth, Anne and Agnes with Joan. They are all under five years old and I don't know how his wife manages. Although I must admit that the maids look after them all and Elizabeth spends her day laying on a couch in her room whether with child or without. But, the women have brought to the family great areas of land adjacent to ours and we must be thankful for that. John is not currently here, he has business with his wife's family, the Adestons. That girl has brought to the family lands which are adjacent to ours too. The wives are not Cornish and I am not terribly happy about that, but they have brought wealth and property and in this modern world we cannot have everything it seems. I will stop now so that I may sleep. I am so very tired and the weather is still so very cold.

Wednesday: I have slept so much and had such terrible dreams. I am still abed and not allowed up until the weekend. My servant John, washes me with a cloth and changes my bedding while rolling me from side to side. I am not sure why, although I do feel so weak and my heart rattles and speeds at such speeds. I see frost on the windows and sometimes on the inside too. John scrapes the ice off telling me that there never has been such a winter and its only November! It makes me anxious to see the ice and I go back to my nightmares. I dream of flying chariots which come from - I don't know where – and take me back to their lair where they would – and there I cannot remember what happens next. I started to tell Elizabeth and she had such a shocked look on her face and talked about the Devil and his demons and how I was describing things which God would not approve. It has not been pursued with me as to where I was for those days though. No one has asked me nor mentioned it and that is odd in itself.

Sunday: Roger has accompanied me on a visit to Sequers Bridge. Both of our wives had begged that we should not go, but I insisted. As my mind cleared, I was adamant that I had done nothing other than go for a night-time walk in the ice and yes – I remembered the ice as it blew froth-like towards me and then the owl and the bright light. Roger says that I must have mistaken the moon for the light and even when I explained how the light had made it impossible to see anything other than the light, they did not believe me. The horses took us down the drive to the road and then turned southwards towards the bridge. We passed the gatekeeper at the front door of his cottage and he shouted that we should take great care on the roads because of the thick ice. Roger dutifully slowed the horses down and we ambled to the bridge. I pulled my rug tighter and higher as the ice was so terrible we could hardly breathe. When we stopped at the bridge crown, I pointed out where I had seen the light, halfway between the bridge and the hall. Now, the brook is frozen across and white. The trees overhanging is solid with ice and the overhanging branches are frozen into the water. Ducks stagger along the surface and stare hopelessly at the shadows of frozen fish beneath the surface. My son tells me that the boats are no longer able to come upstream from above Mothecombe with even the river current being stopped by the thick ice. The ice from the River Erme was blowing out to the sea on the outgoing tide and even the mermaids were stuck in their undersea homes. We should come at night, I told him. Perhaps we would see the white light then. Roger seems disappointed that I have not remembered what happened to me during those days and I expect he thinks I was laid up in some cottage with a comely woman. I was not.

Tuesday: I have persuaded Roger to come out with me after supper to see if there would be any sign. He was reluctant in front of his wife, but excited and interested I believe. Peter, my grandson wanted to come too and with promises to look after him, Peter was wrapped up and added to the mission. The night was darker than before and the thick clouds held a promise of snow. Peter was excited at the prospect while Roger said that his hunting would be upset if it did snow. We arrived at the bank of the brook and waited. The ice was thicker than before and it is very strange. Peter suddenly screamed that he could see a huge white object in the sky – much bigger than an owl or a bird. We looked and gracious me! A round building hovering in the sky and we could not work out whether it was over the land or the sea. We stared at it and noticed a light streaming downwards from it which proved that it was further away from us than we thought. The horses were impatient and we decided to return to the Hall. There was the most peculiar feeling in the air, like just before a big thunderstorm and yet the weather is completely wrong for that to be the case. When we arrived home, both Peter and Roger were nervous, I could tell.

I have refrained from transcribing several of Roger's entries as I can summarise without breaking momentum. The weather became worse and the snow fell, lying feet thick in some places. Roger and his son and grandson became ill and were sent to their beds to recover. It was assumed that they had some kind of paralysis from their ventures on a cold night. They were delirious and talked of gods and chariots in the sky. They were not believed. There was also much discussion about the number of animals that were going missing, considered the result of poachers in this difficult winter. Horses and cattle were gone and also a family who rented a cottage on the edge of the Orcherton estate and a couple near Bigbury. They had left their four children who were taken to the church and placed with their aunt and uncle until their parents returned. So far, no one had returned and there had been no word and so the poaching was laid at their door. I have transcribed again from 9th February 1347 when the weather was still atrocious.

Thursday: There is no longer anytime for laying in our beds. This is the weather of doom with the constant ice and thick snow. People and animals are starving and there are more and more sightings of the strange chariot in the sky. Sometimes it appears in the daylight in addition to the night and more people are seeing it. Ships at sea have watched it swoop along the waves and then below the sea and vanishing. It has also to be said that in addition to families vanishing and a great deal of people dying, I do not and cannot believe, that it is solely to do with the bad weather. Unless of course, the chariot has something to do with this bad weather. Our family has been ill and I have insisted that my other son, John and his family do not visit us because Roger and his younger daughters especially, have not been well of late.

Monday: I have just been visited today by some of my neighbours. The rich and landed ones naturally. It is not considered appropriate for me, a Knight of the County to be announcing the second coming of Christ or angels. Members of the clergy have said that is what I am about, although I know for a fact that two of my neighbours and one of the Rectors who was mentioned to me have seen the chariot for themselves. I suspect that I am being used as a scapegoat in case everything turns out to be an illusion. I explained again what I saw and said that I will only ever speak the truth and answer to my Maker accordingly. There was a much harrumphing, but they left in a good mood. I haven't told them that my memory has been coming back and I have an inkling that I have been on board the chariot. I am remembering some very strange sights of men and women dressed in a way I do not recognise and them speaking in our language, but with some differences. They were kind to me and told me about life travelling around space and time, I believe they said, although that made no sense to me. I remember talking about my family and they said I could go home. That is all I remember.

Friday: I remembered more today. They told me that I was going back with them to Lyonesse. Is Lyonesse the land of my ancestors? I think so. I must ask my son Roger. Still very cold and even we are getting hungry now.

Sunday: At church, I talked to more neighbours and the gossip is all about the harsh weather. It was so cold in the church that the font has frozen solid and there is ice inside the windows and on the inside of the doors. We all shivered and shook as the Rector babbled on about – I know not what – I was too busy thinking about that chariot. Perhaps that has come from God? Its mentioned in the Bible certainly. Old Bigbury told me that he has seen something in the sky, sending down to the sea a huge light which illuminated under the water and he said he thought that he saw a wrecked ship there. I don't know if that is true and yet I have never heard him lie. There were more people attending the service than usual today and I see a rise in anxiety in the congregation.

Thursday: My son Roger called to fetch me and took me to Sir William Bigbury's Hall as apparently, he wanted to show me something. We had an excellent dinner and when the women had left us, Sir William ordered his carriage and the three of us set off for the coastline, which is very close to his Hall. We took the lane which leads to the beach from where one can reach the island at low tide. That was to be at 2 am and so as we began our walk across the beach at midnight, we would have four safe hours in which to cross to the island and return. The three of us set off across the beach and soon reached the inn and cottages at the base of the island. Lights flickered inside, but saw no one apart from a man quickly opening the door and peering round. Upon seeing his master walking with his friends, he nodded and went back inside and dropped the bar on his door. Sir William hurried us along, informing us that after midnight was the best time to see. To see what, we asked? Hurry along, he insisted and hurry we did. We were all quite breathless as we crowned the hill and looked out to sea. We saw nothing unusual other than ships sailing silently westwards and the dim lights of coastal cottages perched aloft the cliffs. We sat down on a bench there, huddled against the icy wind and drinking the wine brought by my son Roger. Just as we were about to begin our return, there was the most dreadful screeching sound and something huge passed above our heads and out to sea. When I say huge, I mean we could not see the sky at all as it passed over. The speed it went out to the horizon and then back to centre stage, I cannot describe adequately. We did not speak as we watched and I don't know how I shall ever explain what we saw to anyone else. It seems like a lie. I saw a huge white and grey carriage or chariot, the like of which I have never seen. Perhaps a sky-going ship without the sails – I think I will try and draw it. We could not take our eyes away from it and when a light came down from it into the sea, it was as though Heaven had opened and was beckoning souls to return. We wondered if that is what it is – the way we return to our Lord at the end of our life. I felt a strange energy in my stomach. Like when a carriage goes over a bridge too fast and there is a tickling sensation. I told Roger and Sir William of my memory of being told I was to return and go to my ancestors and Roger said that would be exciting and Sir William said it was a Devil's trick. Anyway, the light revealed shipwrecks and sea creatures before it suddenly switched off and then the chariot vanished. I thought it vanished, but Sir William said he was sure it just moved very quickly away. We had much to discuss on the journey home and were very surprised when the servants at Bigbury insisted that we had been gone for a night and a day. Roger said he felt very sick as did I and Sir William said he was going to go directly to his son's Hall in the north of the County as he had never felt so disorientated in his life.

And that was all. My father never made another entry in his journal as he sickened after that night and eventually died three months later. My brother Roger lasted a further month, but succumbed to the same wasting disease. The surgeons cannot decide whether it is because of the severe weather or an unknown sickness. We have heard that plague is moving up through Europe and perhaps some ship or merchant has brought it to our shores. Currently, the five younger children of Roger are very sick and Peter, his heir, is being made a ward of Walter de Wodeland, a man of dubious honour. I have not shown the journal to anyone, feeling that it will only confuse the matter and will keep it instead in the oak chest in which many personal Pridias documents are kept.

Perhaps it was the chariot of our Lord.

I hope it was not the chariot of the Devil.

BIG, BLACK RATS

Featuring Sir John Pridias (1320-1357)

"No one likes rats."

"I think it is fair to take that as a given John," said Joan.

"I heard of one man in the village who keeps them as pets and trains them to fetch him food," answered her husband.

"Why would anyone want to eat food that a rat had fetched?"

"I have no idea," John said.

John and Joan had been married for thirteen years and had a twelve year old son, Giles. Joan's father Gilbert Adeston, owned huge tracts of land south of Modbury and as husband of his co heir, John was immensely rich. This situation was fortunate but had been planned. He was the second son of Roger de Pridias, who had died a few weeks following the death of his heir and John's elder brother Roger. In the weeks following, the deceased heir lost his youngest five children. Now, Roger's son and John's eldest nephew Peter, was under the wardship of Walter de Wodeland and the ancestral Pridias lands would be lost to John forever. Walter now wanted to wed his own daughter to Peter and as Walter had already married a female ward of his and gained her properties, he knew the game.

One of the servants, Alan, had recently entered the room and informed them that there were now so many rats around the stables and outbuildings, that they could not kill them quickly enough. The known rat catcher in the village was busy in the villages killing the unusually high number living in the church, cottages, woods and everywhere else.

"So, my Lord and my Lady, he won't be coming here to help us."

"That is such a nuisance," said Joan. "I said that they should not have killed so many cats and then we would not have the rats."

"Nor the plague and the Sweating Sickness. These rats carry it all."

"I am sure that something, a merchant ship or a foreign traveller, brought the infected rats with them and caused the deaths of so many of your family, John."

"Perhaps, perhaps. It is certain that we must kill more rats and kill them quicker if we want to rid our country of these dreadful diseases." He was thinking about the stories his father and brother had told him about the flying chariot.

Joan rose from her chair to stem the anxiety she felt. Rats, big ones in grey, black and brown roamed freely around. It was terrifying to take a walk when the ground could be carpeted at any time by the horrid creatures who had no hint of fear. They had no enemies other than terrier dogs or men with great clubs and these enemies appeared to constantly busy elsewhere. When she was a girl, Joan knew that rats mooched and nested about the barns and stables, but the cats and the men had kept them at bay. Now one never saw a cat and men who were willing to kill the rats.

"At least we don't have so many witches," commented John.

"Not in plain sight," answered his wife. She knew of the coven history of John's family, but said nothing.

"What shall I do now, my Lord?"

"Oh Alan, I do not know. We may have to lure them into a barn and sacrifice that to fire."

"Yes, my Lord," and he bowed.

"Off you go, I shall let you know."

The next afternoon, Joan was walking across the long meadow which led to Sequers Bridge. She was alone today and was wondering why she had not managed to conceive another child since Peter. She knew that neither she nor John had a problem – Peter was testament to that. She was wondering whether to visit the Mothecombe coven and ask there. She was sure that John's family had been involved in it but as it was a secret group, had no real confirmation of such. There must be an introduction in order to a have a question answered or a spell cast by them and she daren't ask John. No, he would not approve.

Her musings were disturbed by a scurrying noise in the reeds to her left.

"My Lady! Move yourself! Quick now!"

Move herself she did and with her heart beating fast, Joan Pridias leapt on to the cart from where her rescuer screamed. The ground upon which she had previously stood was coated with rats. Unbeknownst to her, rats had been following her steps as she meandered down the bank path and were being joined forward and back by their friends and family. The carter had noticed this as he moved at a distance behind her and had cantered his pony in order to reach her before the rats did. As Joan hurled herself into the seat alongside the driver, he grabbed her skirts and legs and threw her safely into the well of the cart. Then he whipped the air above his frightened pony and cantered across the meadow until they reached the driveway to the Hall.

Joan had held tightly on to the rails around the cart and managed to turn herself in spite of the bouncing. The driver pulled up on the drive and leant down to comfort his sweating, terrified pony.

"I apologise my Lady. I did not mean to frighten you and manhandle you in such a disrespectful way. But…"

"It was necessary and I am grateful that you rescued me. I shall see that you are rewarded well by my husband."

"I did not do it for that, my Lady. I did not want you hurt like the people in the village and cottages. Have you heard that rats are now killing babies which have been left unattended and that they are biting and attacking anyone?"

"No! No, I have not and I am alarmed to hear about such a dreadful thing! Why do we have so many just now?" Joan was brushing her skirts with her gloved hands and realised that she had an urge for a pee, but naturally was unable to tell this stranger.

"I think that it is a mixture of things, my Lady. People have died from the plague, no cats about and more men going to work in the mines. There's more money there than working for rich families as servants."

Joan smiled, expecting the carter to realise his faux pas and apologise, but he did not.

"I will take you back home, my Lady and don't come out without a manservant and in a carriage until this problem has been sorted."

"Do you know how the problem must be solved?" she asked.

"Kill the damned lot of them! There is no use for a rat as far as I can see, other than food."

"Do people eat rats?" she asked, horrified.

The carter looked at her bemused, "Starving people do, my Lady. Starving people do."

Joan remained quiet until she was at the door of the Hall. Her rescuer insisted that she stay aboard until he had fetched help. He knocked sharply at the front door and ignored the scowling look from Alan, when he saw him.

"I have your Lady here. She has had a shock and I brought her home. I wish to see his Lordship while I am here," he insisted.

"I do not know if my Lord is at home," sniffed Alan.

"Yes, you do and he is. I need to see him."

"It is alright Alan," said Joan. "Help me down and then fetch my husband."

John listened to the morning's events and sighed heavily.

"Something must be done," he said. "And quickly."

Joan listened quietly and when the carter, Thomas Black, had left, said to her husband,

"Can the coven help?"

He looked at her and answered,

"I am going to ask."

It was not until the following day, that John told her as they ate breakfast,

"I have spoken to the coven. I shall not upset you with the details, my dear, but they are to do something and I have promised to help."

"Will it be dangerous?" Joan asked.

"There is always an element of danger Joan. But we must accept that to allow these rats to roam free, is hugely dangerous. I cannot bear to imagine what could have happened to you if that carter had not rescued you."

"I cannot bear to think of it myself John. I am not sure that I dare go out alone now."

"You must not go out alone and do not allow Giles to either."

"Not even with his dog?"

"Not at all. We shall send servants for anything needed and no one will go out alone."

Joan shivered as she looked out of the huge windows and saw packs of rats moving together, unaffected by the servant who was throwing stones at them. She did not want her breakfast now.

The household was raised in the middle of the night by the banging of the door and the ringing of the bell. As John and Joan lifted their heads from their pillows, they tensed against the terrible screams they heard. John jumped from his bed and covered himself with his cloak. He picked up the lamp and hissed to his wife,

"Make sure Giles is safe and then lock yourselves in his room," before he left the bedchamber.

Joan cloaked her body and ran across the landing, then up the stairs to Giles room. He was awake and white-faced.

"Mama! What's happening?"

"I don't know, Giles. Your father and the servants are dealing with it. We are to remain locked in here."

Giles stood straight and said,

"I will protect you Mama."

He double bolted both doors and opened the curtains so that he could check the window locks.

"Look Mama," he said.

Joan climbed onto the window seat and looked out. There were several people running about the drive way and in the trap, was a woman holding two children close to her. The lamps hanging from the trap illuminated two rearing horses and a servant trying to calm them.

"There are things running under the horses' feet," squealed Joan.

"They are rats!"

"Oh, my Lord! They are running up the horses' legs and the trap!"

Suddenly the servant could no longer hold the horses and they kicked and galloped back up the driveway, lamps swinging and rats being flung right and left. The screams of the woman and children could be heard even through the locked windows until the noise dimmed as they went from view.

"There is Papa! Oh, do be careful Papa!"

John was on the drive way with the visitors and they saw Alan and other servants. They were dancing and smashing the ground with their sticks and the rats were running towards them and filling in the ground where they had been dancing. Rats always ran away! But these rats were not!

"John! Get inside!" screamed Joan as she began to rattle the window and open it.

"No Mama! Don't!"

Giles pulled at his mother and slammed the window shut just as a large black rat plopped onto the outside sill from the little gable roof above the window. He was joined by another and another and as Joan screamed, they stood on their hind legs and tried to smash the glass with their pointed scratchy paws. Giles imagined how those pointy nails would feel upon his body and almost fainted.

"Mama, stop making such a noise. They are attracted to it."

Joan shut her mouth and put her hand over it to prevent a recurrence.

"I am sorry Giles. I am a little in shock I think."

He kissed her and then set about reinforcing the window with the heavy wooden shutters generally only closed on the coldest of evenings. He lit more lamps and candles and instructed,

"Make sure there are no weaknesses in the room Mama."

This task busied their bodies and their minds and it seemed that no weakness could be found.

"I have been hearing rats scratching at the panels the past few nights, Mama!" confessed Giles.

"Did you tell the servants? Your father?"

"I told Papa and he said that he was dealing with it and that I was not to worry."

Their whisperings were stopped when they heard John outside the door.

"My dears!"

"Oh John, what is happening?"

"It's the rats. They are attacking the houses. Not just ours, everyone's house."

"Who was that? In the trap with the children?"

"They are the Bigbury's. William Bigbury is still here, but the trap horses ran away with his wife and children. We are getting a party together to rescue them."

"Papa, rats have been trying to get in through the windows."

"Giles, I need your help. Make sure your mother is safe and then ensure the whole Hall is safe from rat intrusions. The coven is sorting something out as we speak and hopefully the problem will be finished by morning."

"Yes Papa. Please take care of yourself." He began unlocking the door and John shouted,

"Keep your mother safe!"

The door opened and Joan ran out and hugged her husband.

"I have a bad feeling John. I wish you would stay here with us."

He held her arms and answered,

"I must do my duty Joan. You know that."

"We should be your duty father, not the Bigburys."

A look passed between them and John clicked his heels together and bowed to the pair of them before he turned and ran down the stairs. As the front door slammed Giles stood at the stop of the stairs and said,

"Mama, you lock yourself back in and I shall secure the Hall."

"I will not Giles. You go downstairs and begin there. Make sure all doors and windows are secure and I shall do up here after I make sure the servants are busy too. Do not worry, the Hall is built solidly and rats have only entered before through an opening and not the wall or foundations."

They busied themselves, locking doors and windows, bolting shutters and boosting the fires in all the chimneys. The remaining servants, mainly women, helped and they were soon done. Joan and her son went back upstairs and placed themselves behind shutters in the largest window.

The could see a lamplit group making their way down the driveway and another larger group, also lamplit, coming towards them from the direction of the driveway gatehouse.

"It's the Mothecombe coven," said Joan.

When John shut the front door behind him, he also had a bad feeling. He wondered if he would be coming home again and so he swiftly shook the thought from his mind. The tousled group in front of him consisted of Sir William Bigbury, his servants and John's own servants. Bigbury was hysterical and pleading for help with his family.

"Why did you bring them here on such a night?" asked John.

"Because man, we were travelling home from Modbury and when the bridge was blocked with rats and such, I decided to bring them to your Hall for safety!"

"Yes, yes, I see. We will go and find them and bring them back here. I have reinforcements coming over at midnight."

"Who?" asked Bigbury.

"The coven."

The rats had been temporarily spooked by the runaway trap, but were now gaining confidence and returning to the group. John had the servants hand out flaming torches and they began to try and set fire to the rats. Apparently, rats are not terribly flammable and the torches only served to move them further away.

They decided against horses and instead walked down the drive in the direction of the horse and trap. John could soon see that the lit coven was moving towards them from the drive entrance. There was a faint chanting and melodic singing and in response to this, the group walked faster.

The rats were closing in on them again and surrounded their feet and scampered over the top of their boots and began running up their legs. Grown men screamed and squealed as they smashed torches and sticks against their own bodies. The rats reached shoulders and heads and the men grappled with them, throwing one or two to the floor which were replaced by another two or three. They were being overrun and overpowered.

The singing became louder as the coven almost reached them and the rats stopped moving. They suddenly fell from the men like wasps who had been sprayed with vinegar and lay curled on their backs and squealed and screamed. It was horrible.

The chanting and singing continued and the rats on the driveway and the meadow ran towards them and as they neared, they fell on their backs and died a terrible death. Rats came from the house and the stables and the river and fell and died. It took half an hour before the rats stopped coming and there was a carpet, several rats high as far as they could see. To move was to walk across still squirming, furry bodies which squeaked and cried as they were trodden on.

"My family?" asked Bigbury.

The hooded coven leader, slowly shook her head and Bigbury fell to the ground sobbing. But he soon rose again when he touched the squirming rats.

"Are you going to kill them all?" enquired John.

She nodded and turned and the coven moved away, chanting and singing.

"Alan, let us check on Sir William's family."

Alan nodded and they made their way to the upturned trap, still lit by lamps but missing the horses who had run well out of danger. It took a while, as they first must lift one foot above the corpses and then the other. The family were bloodied and rat covered and Alan knocked them away with his torch. John went forward and lifted the family up, one by one.

"The children are still breathing," he shouted and Sir William arrived to assist. He tried to raise the trap from the ground but was stopped by John.

"William, even if we manage to move the trap, we will never get it past the rat bodies."

"We must carry the children back to the Hall. Gently now."

And they did. They carried the children between them, sometimes carrying one and then passing it over to another man so they could have a breather. They were struggling to clamber over the rats, some of which still did not appear to be totally dead. They squeaked and almost drowned out the screams of their dying cousins who were currently being killed on the boundaries of their land. The lamp lit coven were visible and then invisible as they made their way over Sequers Bridge and down the road to Bigbury.

John thought about his meeting with her last night and the discussion of the rats. They agreed that the fear of witches had resulted in a cull of cats and a rise in the number of rats. There was a thought running through his mind now that the number of rats seemed inconsistent with the lack of cats. What was now to result from this catastrophe was the allowing of as many cats as anyone wanted, small and large. There was to be no limit and John knew full well that the coven wanted their cats back. Had this been a plan? By the coven? Had they spread the plague? And the chariot?

She laughed when he asked her that.

John felt ill and faint. Perhaps it was the result of tonight's shocks and the effort of carrying two dying children over heaps of dead rats.

"There is blood pouring from your neck my Lord," said Alan.

John put his hand to his throat and realised that he was losing a lot of blood. In fact, it was running river-like down his tunic. He just made it to the front door as Joan and Giles ran out.

"Help the children!" shrieked Sir William.

John fell on the big, black rats piled on the drive.

And died.

GHOST SHIP

Featuring Giles Prideaux (1345-1410)

Twenty-eight-year-old Sir Giles handed the documents to one of King Edward III Customs Officers as they sat opposite each other in the cleanest of the harbour inns.

"I see you have signed it Giles Prideaux. Why have you decided to change from de Pridias?"

"I decided a few years ago, when I became Burgess and MP for Totnes. My stepfather and father-in-law had been trying to persuade me that my proper name was reminiscent of old times and if I wanted to get on, I needed a modern interpretation."

"According to Hawley, others in your clan have changed to Prideaux too."

"Yes. My father and his ancestors would not approve, but we must survive and maintain our lands, whatever it takes."

"And is that why you have joined forces with John Hawley to relieve merchants of their cargos?"

"No. We are not pirates, we are merchants and businessmen. It is all in the documentation you hold in your hand."

"Hmmm. My master King Edward, has had complaints from his continental friends that cargos are being pirated and that businessmen from Dartmouth are to blame."

"It is not true. We are respectable men here, not pirates."

The Customs Officer read quickly and said,

"You are still maintaining that this was a ghost ship?"

"It was a ghost ship. I don't know what else it could be called."

The men said nothing further until another man joined their table.

"Aaah John, your man here is still determined that we are pirates."

"I find it difficult to think of a way to tell my superiors and betters that a ghost ship has been sailing our waters," said Customs.

"Not just one, they are often seen hereabouts," added Hawley.

"You should write fiction my friends. There are enough ideas here for plays and plays."

"Perhaps you can use us as characters in your own work."

"My scribbles, you mean? I doubt that anyone will ever read them!"

"I have read them and they are not too bad Geoffrey!" answered John.

Geoffrey Chaucer laughed and sat back in his chair,

"Well, Sir Giles Prideaux, let me hear the tale from your own mouth."

"To make you understand the tale in its entirety, I have to take you back to my childhood...," began Giles.

"Oh Lord, not that Giles! Geoffrey doesn't have to hear all the trimmings, just the facts!"

"You are wrong John. I want to hear everything. I like background and foreground. It is the only way to understand. Then I can trim the story to suit." Geoffrey poured more wine and beckoned to Giles.

"My father died when I was twelve and as I was the heir to his properties and those of Mama's, I was made ward of Simon Longbrooke, a neighbour of ours. He was a good man and his family had suffered with the plague and the rats as had mine. My mother remained Lord of Adeston until she handed over the whole property to me last year."

"My parents died of the plague and an uncle brought me up. That was why I was so determined to become rich and never rely on another," said John.

"Did your father die of plague Giles?" asked Geoffrey.

"No. He was killed and partially eaten by the giant rats that roamed our neighbourhood for a time."

"Oh! I had not expected that. How dreadful. And your mother?"

"She married John de Moel, a family friend from Cadbury. He was a very good man and looked after her and our properties very well, along with my father in law."

"And his name?"

"He was Simon Longbrooke. I married his beautiful daughter Isabelle," confessed Giles.

"A clever boy with a clever father in law. He managed to get your lands into his family coffers," said John.

"The properties are all in my name and everything will go to our children. Unlike my cousins, descended from the heir to Orcherton."

"What happened to them?" asked Chaucer.

"Cousin John killed Sir William Bigbury at Sequers Bridge near our home. There was an argument about how my father died and about the treatment of Bigbury's daughter. It began as an argument over who killed a deer and ended up in death. The King confiscated most of the properties that had been in our family for generations, but cousin John did not die."

"I bet the family were pleased about losing all that."

"Not really. It's a good job I have a lot of property, I suppose. But it takes much money to keep it all going, servants aren't what they were," said Giles.

"So, he came into business with me and we got him elected as Burgess and MP and we do some profitable business together. We import fancy goods and export tin and wool, but we do not steal," said John Hawley.

"And as we deal a lot with France, they pronounce my name as we say it now. Anyway, Mama became ill last year and handed all properties over to me. She sadly died a few months ago and is buried at home with the other members of my family."

"I am sorry to hear that. It is a terrible thing to lose your mother," said Chaucer.

"We none of us have living mothers I fear," added John. "Let us drink to them!"

And they did.

Giles continued.

"Now I am left with keeping the Houses of Adeston and Longbrooke running and paying all the bills. Hence my aforementioned diversion into business. Hawley and I have a usefully profitable business between us and ships are coming in and out all the time. It has been said that Hawley can take advantage of the wind, for he will always have a ship somewhere where the wind is favourable."

"I do, I do," agreed John.

"Then this one night a ship docked and told us of a ship they had seen drifting just outside the harbour. There appeared to be no one aboard and it was surrounded by a very unusual mist."

"Unusual? How?"

"They said that when they tried to tack over to the shop, they felt the same sensation as when a storm was about to occur. But there was no storm, it was a peaceful night, warm and calm. The crew did not attempt to board her, just came and told us. We organised a boat and took some men and sailed to where it had been seen. And we saw nothing."

Chaucer said, "No ship?"

"And no evidence. We thought the sailors must have been hysterical or drunk," added Hawley.

"Until the next time. It only took three days before two separate captains told us about a drifting ship with no crew. Both mentioned the peculiar mist and the feeling it gave them when they approached. Another week and five more sightings, yet no one had boarded and when the ship was specifically sought out, it was not to be seen."

"I am enjoying your story Giles Prideaux," said Chaucer. "I am taking mental notes."

"It is a tale of the truth Mr Chaucer and I hope that you are convinced by the time I have finished it," said Giles.

"If it is the truth, then I have no reason to stop listening."

"I hope not. Now, these sightings continued for more than two months and we left Spring and went into Summer. The light nights meant that locals could, during their leisure, take coast walks and as a result, the sightings increased. The ship was seen by many and the descriptions were all the same. A tall ship with flapping sails which was surrounded by a greenish mist that swirled and thickened as the ship moved. It sailed aimlessly across the sea and John and I were determined to board her and see what was there."

"So, we let it be known that we must be told as soon as the ship was spotted. I had a small schooner ready for immediate sail and stocked with necessities. We had no shortage of volunteers to jump when word was given," added John.

"And then one evening we were off! A family were having an evening picnic on the beach and they spotted the ship. They sent their lad back to the harbour and he ran into this very inn and told us the ghost ship was in view. We sprang into action and within minutes were on our way. The tide was with us and off we set. It was still light, although the orange sun was beginning to sink. The ghost ship was there, shrouded in a mist and we looked back to home to see that the coast line was becoming covered by sailors and locals and merchants as the news spread. It was very exciting and the wind brought us near to our goal and we chattered and got ready to snare the ship with our ropes and anchors. The mist, which had been thin, was now thickening again and spread its cold fingers on our direction. I felt almost over excited, drunk with anticipation until the fear came over me and I realised that fear was what I had been feeling all along."

"We all felt fear, it was the most bizarre thing. We sailed around the ship in a large circle in order to get nearer and as we lost contact with the mist, the fear went," interrupted John Hawley.

"But we continued. We had a short conversation amongst our crew about the danger, but we could see no one on board and curiosity had the better of us."

"I wish it was tonight, for I would sail with you," said Geoffrey Chaucer.

"I shall give you as much detail as possible and see if that is enough for you," said Giles. "Now I shall continue with my tale swiftly, for I have told my wife I shall be home at Adeston tonight. As we neared the ship, a rope with a large hook attached to the end was thrown over the side. It caught and we were able to throw on three more and secure it to our own ship. The mist still surrounded us and we all were fearful. I noticed that the ship was called *Borja* and I shouted its name as we climbed over the rails, but there was no answer. We left two men on our own ship and eight of us went aboard *Borja*. We held daggers and swords and split in twos so that we could explore quickly."

Hawley, listening intently, lifted the dagger which he had around his neck on a cord and Chaucer smiled and nodded. Giles continued,

"The mist was still surrounding us, but it was doing just that. Surrounding the ship and there was no sign of it aboard. I could no longer see the people along the coastline and the setting sun looked green. Whether that was the mist I do not know, for the sun has a tendency to turn into a green ball just before it falls off the horizon. We shouted and looked about, but saw nothing on the deck and so Hawley and I beckoned the others to go into the cabin and the hold. The tables were laid with food and there were plates and beakers about as though a meal had just been eaten. I am quite aware that ships such as this have been seen before, with talk that the crew perhaps fell ill or overboard. But it did not feel like that. It was as though the crew were still there and we could not see them. There were noises and mutterings but we could see no one. There was a shout from below and we went to see what had been found there. There were no people and no cargo. I didn't know then what was supposed to be aboard, but I am telling you that there was no cargo when we first went aboard. We went through the whole ship three times and found nothing that would intimate a person was or had recently been, on board. So, we went back on deck chattering amongst ourselves and agreeing to tow the ship to port. We could keep it until its owners were found."

"And perhaps claim it if they weren't," noted Chaucer.

"Perhaps, but it wasn't to be that simple. When we looked over the side, our own ship had gone, sailed back to port to catch the tide, we assumed. However, one of our men pointed out that it was now daylight and that the coastline looked 'a bit funny'. It certainly did. There were more people on the beaches and many seemed to have colourful tents or flags of some kind. There were people in the water and then we noticed the boats! Small ones with a colourful sail which carried a standing person dressed in black, swaying to and fro. Some large boats had sails too and some had no sails at all, but were steered by handles and cut through the waves very quickly. We shouted out and a couple came over to us and laughed and joked when we asked their names. They seemed to think that we were actors or jokers and they said that we were very good. We could get nothing more from them and I am afraid I did not ask too much as I was quite shocked at how little these people were wearing. The men wore nothing more than big pants and the women were practically naked. Two little bits of fancy string about their loins and breasts and no one seemed bothered! Some of those women were beautiful..."

"And some not so much..." added Hawley.

"We tried to leave the ship by throwing a boat over, intending to climb into it, but as soon as it hit the water it vanished. We were in magical realm we thought and decided that the only way out, was to collect the sails together and steer *Borja* back to port. We tried, oh we tried and it wouldn't work. We would set our course with all hands on deck and although we appeared to cross waves and tack towards the harbour, the coast remained the same distance away. Suddenly the mist dropped again and our new sights and sounds became blurred through it. My anxiety was rising and the crew began shouting at each other. Then a man who none of us knew suddenly appeared on the deck before us. He spoke Italian, I think it was and he seemed most agitated. We tried to get him to let us know what had happened to the rest of his crew and he pointed his palms to the air as if he couldn't understand and then began praying and crying. Then he vanished into the mist which swirled around him and the deck. I have to tell you that we were all very frightened by now because none of it made sense. The new peculiar scene had now vanished and we could see only the almost set sun through the mist. Then a shout of 'Ahoy!' made us look to the rails and there was our own ship with its skeleton crew asking us where in the hell we had been? We couldn't answer satisfactorily and they told us that we had vanished too. The ship had still been there but there had been no sign of us and they were about to leave and fetch help. We towed the ***Borja*** back to port and had it thoroughly looked over. There was definitely no cargo, no crew and no obvious explanation. If the Genoa friends of the King are saying that we stole the cargo and killed the crew, then they are mistaken."

"Do you seriously think that if I tell them this story, they will believe it?"

"I don't suppose they will, but we would have to lie in order to have you believe us and that does not sit well with me. Everything we send out comes back to us and so I am very careful about what I say. My brother in law, John Longbrooke is the Vicar at Ermington and a very holy man he is. Always telling me about right and wrong, although I have just sold him and his brother a house and land at Ermington for only 100 marks of silver, so he should shut up for a while."

"Noble sentiments Giles, I shall make notes."

"Thanks. I can also tell you that we have no knowledge of how the ***Borja*** left the harbour for no one saw it leave. It is an impossible thing to happen without people noticing."

"It just vanished?"

"Yes, but it has been seen further out to sea, still surrounded by the mist and still with no crew."

"Tell me, how I am supposed to explain all of this?"

"Use what I have written there. As Burgess and MP, I should be listened to. My word is good and I have come to the conclusion that the crew of the *Borja* stole the cargo, took it away and let the ship drift to its own destiny. A ship is harder to hide than a cargo. I expect they unloaded it in Cornwall where there are many creeks in which to hide. If someone there had knowledge of it, then theft and smuggling would be easy to achieve. Or, Mr Geoffrey Chaucer, I can write down the truth and see which gaol we end up in."

Chaucer rolled up the papers and tapped his mouth with them.

"I expect they are more likely to believe that the crew are thieves than you lot had a weird adventure in some ghostly green mist. Look, I will do what you say, if you allow me to use your story and write it up at some point in the future? It will make a great poem or play."

"As you please, but I don't really think of it as an adventure. Wherever we were for those hours, I had an awful feeling that we could have been stuck there and I believe that the crew and the cargo are stuck somewhere too. Whether it is in another time or place, I know not. It is not the only ship that has gone missing on this coastline with no explanation."

Hawley interrupted, "It was the strangest experience of my life and I don't want it to happen again. And the next time I see a ghost ship, I am leaving it alone."

"Fine, but buy me supper tonight," said Chaucer.

BURIAL GROUND

Featuring Sir John Prideaux (1380-1443)

Sir John Prideaux used to have a lot of problems falling asleep but now it seemed that waking up was becoming the problem.

He had been going to sleep at around midnight and then waking up a couple of hours later remembering. He had much to remember, Agincourt, Joan of Arc, both events still sickened him to the core. Recently John, his eldest son and heir had died and that meant that all the Horilake properties had gone to his daughter Joan and so to her husband Robert Stretchley. Effectively those lands were now out of John's control and the income with it. But he still had Adeston and his businesses in Totnes and Dartmouth begun by his father Giles, now long dead.

Financially this branch of the family was sound, it was the guilt and the deaths which ran around and around his mind incessantly. He had refused to take any part in the shameful slaughter of those noble French prisoners at Agincourt, but had been forced by King Henry to watch the murder – not execution as it had been sold back home. John had considered it murder and he had known some of those French noblemen. Not for them the glorious death in battle, but the slow swipe of the dagger or the badly aimed arrow. John had thought that bad enough to not be sorry when he heard of Henry's death from dysentery at the same battle field John had been on. Then having to be present with the Duke of Bedford and Sir John Robeassart, the Captain of the Castle of Saint Sauvieur le Viscount when they killed that young French girl because they had no other way to deal with her, was almost too traumatic. The screams of all of those dying souls, invaded his mind every time he tried to relax.

Sir John's coping mechanisms had become ridiculous. He had been washing his hands and body over and over, never feeling that the blood was washed away. Then he discovered that his own eyes would cloud over with flashing lights accompanied by a terrible headache, which could not be relaxed with rest or potion. He assumed he was trying to unsee all he had seen.

Now, following that evening visiting what he had been told was an ancient burial ground at the southern edge of his lands and banked on the River Erme, he had been unable to wake up without a servant shaking him vigorously. The supposed burial ground looked nothing more than a copse in a riverside meadow, grazed by cattle and ponies, although John had to admit that this was an area, covered by willow, hazel and elm trees, where no bird flew nor nested. When they hunted that spot, the horses would rear and refuse to enter and the dogs ran in any direction other than into the copse.

It was Richard Wodeland who had taken him. They dealt with each other in business and a few years ago, John had bought some land from him between Dartmouth and Torre. John was also trying to recoup land which had been taken from them by the Crown in order to save the skin of an ancestor cousin who had killed a Bigbury, but was only able to buy back field by field whenever the Bigbury's needed money.

That night, Wodeland rode with him, saying that he had known about this place since a child. Some Prideaux ancestor had told a Wodeland ancestor – Peter Prideaux had once been a ward of the Wodelands – after he had heard it from a coven which used to operate around here. Or perhaps still did, Wodeland didn't know. John Prideaux knew. His grandmother had been part of the coven and his current, living wife, was also a member. John knew about them and their practices, but had not known of the burial ground. He was eager to see it.

The horses would not go too near and so the men left them on a long tether to graze and they walked to the copse. It did look different in moonlight, but that was to be expected. A cloudless night with a full moon and a quiet river did not feel safe. Somehow a wailing wind or lashing rain was something to work against or run from. This sneaky peacefulness meant John thought of a dastardly shape hiding behind that tree, or a sea monster hiding on the bank waiting for him to pass so that it could creep behind him as he walked. John shivered and Richard looked at him,

"You alright John? I told you it was creepy here."

"You did. But I have been in such terrible places in my life and not felt as I do here, tonight."

"Come on, let's hurry into the copse. I want us to be ready for when it happens."

"When what happens?" asked John, shocked. His anxiety had been rising since they left the horses and as his level of anxiety was often too high, for no outward reason, the current shocks were almost paralysing him.

"When the spirits from the graves walk. I told you, didn't I? Or did I forget? It's a very interesting experience and one that very few have seen."

"You told me no such thing Wodeland and I wouldn't have come, had I known."

"Don't be such a baby. You have seen more than this on those battle fields."

"Perhaps, but I am not eager to see any more horrors."

"You will find it all very interesting. Come on, stop wasting time."

The resulting episode would not leave John's mind. They reached the centre of the copse, John with leaden legs until he drank a large swig of the proffered wine, and they both sat on a fallen tree, now covered in furry moss. Richard placed his finger on his lips, signalling silence and John tried to keep his mind in check. It was telling him to leave, right now before he fainted or passed out or died. However, he was used to these feelings and so did nothing.

Then they heard a whispering of men's voices, although they could not understand what was being said. They jumped from the stump and moved silently behind a large elm tree from behind which, they peeped. The men were dressed in tunics and leggings similar to that which men from 300-400 years ago had worn. These clothes must have been blue or grey in colour as the men seemed almost invisible. They carried swords, unsheathed. One spirit turned his head in the men's direction and John was horrified to see that it was nothing but a skull with hair. John gasped and Richard slapped his hand across John's mouth.

The spirit moved its head from side to side trying to locate the sound. Unable to tune in, it walked forward with its associates. A mist rose and John thought of a tale his father had told him once of a ghost ship. Giles had told him that he thought he might have travelled in time and John considered the possibility that he and Richard had too.

The spirit men looked from side to side and moved on through the trees and out of sight.

"It's not over yet!" said Richard with glee.

A line of monks passed through, heads bowed and chanting. The last monk carried a small child which whimpered and shouted for his mama. John tried to get up to rescue it, but Richard held him back.

"Phantoms," he reminded him.

Then arrived twenty, thirty men dragging other men and forcing them to kneel facing John and Richard.

"Haven't seen this lot before," muttered Richard.

"I have," said John. "Agincourt."

The spirits reinacted the scene he had watched twenty years ago, horrific, bloody and pathetically noisy. John wretched and tears welled in his eyes as the executioners re-sheathed their swords and daggers and the dead fell to the ground.

"Oh, my Lord God," gasped Richard. "That wasn't very jolly." He took another swig from the bottle.

"I never wanted to see that again. Henry was a barbarian."

When a group of men spirits arrived next, surrounding a praying and very small woman to the centre of the trees and some began raising a pole, John got up and said,

"No, no, no, no. I'm going!"

He ran to his horse, untethered it and mounted as Richard arrived puffing and wheezing.

"Do you know what they did?"

"Yes, I do. I don't know what is happening here or if it is your idea of a joke, but I'm not having it."

"It's not me John! I told you the copse is haunted!"

John kicked his horse on and did not stop galloping until he brought the sweating, panting animal to the stables at Adeston and handed over the reins to a very cross and disapproving servant.

That was last week and now when John went to bed, he fell asleep too quickly and could not be woken. He spent his days at the cemetery where his two previous wives, Isabelle Bromford and Maude French and he and Isabelle's son John, were buried. He felt guilty and responsible and apologised to them for spending so much time abroad fighting and working for the King. Then he would visit his daughters Elizabeth and Julian and their husbands', William and Adam Somaster at Old Port and Jane and her husband William Drew at their own manor. He would tell them how much he loved them and they told him that they loved him and was he feeling well?

Every evening Sir John ate scantily and then went to bed to fall unconscious, sometimes before he properly undressed. Twice Richard Wodeland took him back to the copse to see if it had all been a trick of the light and twice nothing happened. John was becoming weaker in mind and body and his wife and children were all very concerned. His heir William, began asking him about the estates and how he should best run them and John realised that he had to get a grip of himself. He must get out of this depression and anxiety that was making him a nuisance.

He became conscious that his body was being shaken and opened his eyes.

"My Lord! My Lord! You are asleep again! Wake up Sir John!"

He dreamily came around and sat up in bed. His wife Anne, bustled in and told the servant to open the shutters and windows.

"John, this has to stop! It is the middle of the day and men have been awaiting your instructions for the day's work. William has instructed them and sent them on their way. Thank God that he knows his duty!"

She went to the bed and said,

"Read this book. It was written by your ancestor Richard and offers some explanation of your life. Do not come down until it has been read."

John got up and relieved himself in the bucket behind the curtain in his room. He swilled his hands and face in the bowl of cold water previously brought in by the servant and went back to bed. He reached over to the food and drink placed on his bedside table and opened the book. He had been made to read it by his father and then tested on its contents many times. He had found it boring and forgotten most of it. He realised he had also forgotten that he must pass on its contents to his own son and felt ashamed.

He read,

You are dreaming your life and will not be free until you wake. In order to wake, you must first discover where you are sleeping.

That seemed familiar. He remembered the discussions on the actual reality of life and how we are unconsciously creating all that happens to us. Once we create consciously, we are beginning to free ourselves.

He heard,

"Wake up! Sir John wake up!" He must have fallen asleep again, how annoying.

He opened his eyes and stared disbelieving into the face of his son in law, William Somaster. Standing next to him was his brother Adam.

"Oh, thank the Lord. You are alive!"

"I don't understand," he whimpered. John felt cold and wet.

"You were washed ashore, Sir John. Were you out in a boat? We saw lights at the old copse across the river there and came to investigate."

"We thought there was a fire, the flames were so high! There is nothing there now though. Were you there, Sir John?"

John sat up and looked across to the copse and saw Richard Wodeland. The sun was rising and it was quite easy to see him. Richard waved.

"Look there!" Adam pointed across the river.

"Ah, I see. A line of soldiers, is it? Where are they going?"

"Am I awake or asleep?" asked John.

"Ill and in shock, I should say Sir. Here, let us help you onto the cart and we shall take you home where your daughters may care for you."

John shivered and shook as the fur cloak was placed around his shoulders, but he realised that his anxiety had left him. He felt confident and relaxed.

"I am awake now and I have been asleep for so long. It has all been a dream We are all dreaming this. I can't die, you can't die, no one dies, because we are already dead."

William and Adam Somaster looked at each other and pulled faces.

"I hope the old boy isn't going senile," said William.

"Such a shame," agreed Adam.

IT IS DIFFICULT TO RECOGNISE A GHOST

Featuring William Prideaux (1422-1472)

When I was first introduced to Rose, I thought I would never want another woman. It wasn't the fact that she was Cornish, itself a great bonus, it was that she was just so pretty and nice. Her mother told mine, when they met at Pridias Hall on a visit once, that their family had Pridias blood in their line and my mother agreed that we would make a good match. So that was how we ended up married – our mothers decided. We married at Treffrey would you believe, for Rose's sister Elizabeth had married into that family and they were nicely ensconced in the magnificent property overlooking the harbour. I loved watching the chain being raised at the harbour mouth when invasion or attack was feared from pirates, or worse, Bretons.

But she died trying to give birth to our son William, who also died. God had chosen to leave them both in agonies and blood-covered terror for three days. It was terrible and I could not bear to view either of them as they lay in a joint coffin. I cannot remember much of the funeral, but I have been to so many over the years.

Mother said that I must marry again and get an heir and so I married little Joan Fortescue. The Fortescues of Fallapit, Allington and our family have been friends for ever and Joan and I used to play and ride together when we were small. I know that she was upset when I married Rose, but it was out of my hands. She was happy that she had me next and I tried very hard to love her. I could only think of her as a sister and found it difficult to perform, my marital duties. However, I managed to get her pregnant quite early on and so did not have to worry about that side of things until at least after the birth.

It was another son, born alive and a huge boy! He ripped apart little Joan and she died the next day from blood loss. My boy William, died an hour after he was born and they were buried together in another oak coffin. Her parents were devastated and I saw her mother glaring at me from behind her veil as though it were my fault somehow. I could not attend the funeral, I don't attend funerals any longer. Too morbid and final.

My third wife Alice, was the daughter and heir of Stephen Gifford of Theuborough. She inherited a huge house, estates and manors, which naturally were under my control as were my own estates. It became difficult to run the two, Theuborough being north of Dartmoor, but I was ready for the challenge. I spend a lot of time travelling between my properties aswell as Dartford and Totnes and spent little time at home. We have lots and lots of money, however.

Alice knew her job and set about it immediately. John arrived within a year of our marriage, Fulke a year later and after a few mishaps, Joan appeared in 1468. I decided early on that John would have my estates south of the moor and Fulke all properties north. My wife and I played cards to decide that problem. Joan married an Acland, so that was all very tidy.

I must say that I have been quite upset lately with that dreadful William Wollacombe being at Theuborough all the time. Now, he has always been a friend of mine, we have hunted and dined on many occasions. Indeed, my wife and I were most solicitous to him when his own wife died. I just feel that he has been taking advantage of our hospitality and spending too much time at Theuborough. On many occasions, I have seen him with my dear Alice even when I am out of the house. Only yesterday I arrived back from an errand to find him eating in the dining hall with Alice as though he was Master! I went in and remonstrated with them, but both got up and left the room without speaking to me.

Another peculiar thing happened last week, I believe it was. I was walking along the beach at Bude. It was early morning and no one was about. I jumped onto the sand and as the sea was quite a way out, I thought I should take a good long walk from the estuary northwards. It was very bracing and I was glad of my cloak. I became aware of someone following me after around ten minutes. Although I couldn't possible say that he was actually following, he may have merely been walking in the same direction as me, with similar intentions. That of wasting a morning in exercise.

It is a common trait amongst men to look behind at various intervals and gauge the distance of another walker. I certainly did and noted that he was gaining on me. Only slightly, but gaining nonetheless. I walked a little quicker trying to lose him, but this man, no doubt fitter than I, was still gaining ground on me.

I don't really know why, but it made me feel uncomfortable. As he neared I swore that I could hear muttering or perhaps the squealing of a suckling pig. I did not like it and so at the earliest opportunity I left the beach via a low cliff and stood on the meadow there. Now, I intended to walk back to Bude along the cliff and not the beach. This was a shame, but I felt more comfortable doing so.

The man had stopped moving northwards and stood facing me from the beach as I stood on the clifftop. He had his hands on his hips and was staring at me. I waved and the man turned and ran, ran mark you, back southwards to Bude. I made up my mind to walk back across country to Theuborough, in case the man meant me harm.

I muttered to myself on the walk, firstly that I wished that I had ridden to Bude, but I hadn't, so there it was. Then I began to wonder if, and soon became firmly convinced that, Woolacombe was something to do with the strange man. By the time I had reached Launcells Cross and saw a man swinging from a gibbet there, I was sure. I stopped to look at the blackened corpse and fancied that I heard him say,

"You too then?"

I answered, "What do you mean?" before I realised that it was ridiculous to talk to a corpse and I scurried away.

When I walked up the driveway to Theuborough Hall, I was surprised to see another man staring at me, but not addressing me. This time it was the Rector. Now this man knows me very well and yet he says nothing to me? I chose to begin a conversation.

"Hello Rector. Is there a problem at the house? Is Alice alright?"

He nodded to me, said, "No Sir, no, there is no problem. Alice, Lady Prideaux, is fine." He clutched his Bible to his breast and ran towards the gate.

Now I was sure. There was a problem and he doesn't want to tell me. Why not? Well, he feels guilty, not upset and there was only one thing to feel guilty about. Woolacombe! I ran up the drive and saw Woolacombe climbing onto his horse and being assisted by my very own servant. I rushed towards them shouting,

"Woolacombe! What are you doing here again?"

I must have startled his horse with my shrieking, for it reared straight up and Woolacombe fell roughly to the ground. He moaned and groaned and his leg was bent in a horrible way. I felt guilty and said,

"Will, I am sorry."

He did not answer me and when my darling Alice ran out, I apologised to her for my display. She must have been very cross with me, for she pushed me out of the way and fell next to Woolacombe, crying!

For his part, Will Woolacombe pointed at me and said, "You devil you! Keep away from me! You are trying to kill me!"

Alice turned to face me and she screamed too!

"William! What are you doing? Why are you trying to kill Will!"

The servants were becoming restless and panicky and the horse ran down the drive.

"What is the matter with you all?" I shouted.

They were all crying and screaming and wailing and Woolacombe held his leg and shouted for help. The noise was so dreadful that my son Fulke came out of the house.

"Father! I don't understand!"

He was white faced and looked shocked.

"Fulke, I have only been for a walk and come back to this. Why is Will Woolacombe being treated as though he lives here?"

"Because he does Father! He and Mother married last year. After you died! You fell from you horse and broke your neck, don't you remember?"

There was still much whimpering, some of it coming from me. I ran into Theuborough Hall and up the stairs to my own rooms, where I looked out from the window. From there I heard,

"Mother, I told you I had seen Father's spirit. He doesn't seem to understand that he is dead."

"Fetch the Rector. He must bless the house again. It isn't your father, it is the Devil!"

Later that evening, Fulke came into my rooms and walked over to my chair.

"You are not visible to me now Father and ask your indulgence over this. I know you are here somewhere in this room and I know that you are not the Devil. But really, if you wish to carry on living here, you must stop scaring people and accept that you must not walk about the neighbourhood in the daylight. Be like other ghosts and stick to the night hours."

So that is what I do. I only come out at night, when people find it difficult to recognise a ghost.

THE TERROR OF THE THUNDERSTORM

Featuring John Prideaux (1461 – 1523)

John loved owning property and he loved being rich. He had inherited all the Prideaux properties in the South Hams from his father William and would also inherit the huge properties in North Devon should his brother Fulke die childless. Fulke had married Sir Richard Edgecombe's daughter Jane and she had died in childbirth. Depressed Fulke confirmed their father's wish that John and his heirs would inherit everything upon Fulke's death. However, Fulke had his libido roused by Katherine, the clever daughter of Sir Humphrey Poyntz. During the following fifteen years, Fulke and Katherine had driven home with a mallet, that John would not be inheriting any of the properties north of the moor, by producing 13 children.

However, John married Sybil Luson who was heiress of lands and manors adjacent to John's properties at Orcherton and Adeston. They were relatively happy together and produced four sons, Hugh, John, Henry and Thomas. The boys were a joy to their parents, full of life and competing with each other at every opportunity. John and Sybil would have liked to share the inheritance between the boys, but understood that to split the properties too much could result in their eventual loss. But, to give the eldest everything in this day and age, put him at risk of losing it anyway, because of the expenses.

The matter was settled by willing Orcherton and Adeston to Hugh, Woodland, Stowford and land round Ermington and the Ivy Bridge to John and the remaining lands between Henry and Thomas. The two youngest naturally had less land and a smaller share in the Dartmouth and Totnes businesses.

Their life was happy and privileged and there were no issues, except perhaps the marked increase in severe thunderstorms over the years. None of them really minded a storm, in fact it was quite exciting to watch the sky, either sea side or moor side, flashing and crashing as the storm raged. They felt sorry for the sailors or the shepherds, knowing that neither would be able to escape the hot and wet dramas. The boys would count the time lag between the flash and the bang and tease each other how long they dare stay outside.

John and Sybil remembered their experience of childhood storms. Storms had been few and far between but exciting nonetheless. This year, storms during the summer were occurring two or three times a month. The storm would announce its arrival early, with the air becoming more humid followed by a strange silence among the birds. The sky darkened and a low grumbling in the distance signalled the direction from which the storm would appear. Then the rain, often so heavy you could be drenched in seconds, was followed dramatically by thunder and lightning.

It was terrific when the storm swirled around the property and scary as it neared. If the dark also accompanied the event, then extra excitement was enjoyed or endured, depending upon your feelings.

Of course, that was the usual way a storm occurred. The pattern had however, begun to alter of late. The increasing regularity was the first thing that was noticed.

"There were three last week," said Sybil's maid, Netta.

"And the week before," agreed Sybil.

"My father told me that it was the Devil throwing burning rocks at God," Netta informed her mistress.

"I thought it was God moving his furniture around?" said Sybil.

"But why? If that was the case, then we would hear him stomping about or moving his chair from his table," said Netta reasonably.

"I have a feeling that it is really unusual weather systems," noted Sybil with finality.

A few weeks later, young Jonny came into his mother's rooms and said,

"Mama, when we had that horrible storm last night, I looked out of the window. I know I shouldn't, but I did. And I saw something very horrible in the garden by the sundial when the lightning flashed."

Sybil hugged him and asked, "What did you see Jonny?"

"I saw a very tall man and he was dressed like a monk. He had a black robe and a big hood which was pulled up against the rain, I suppose. There was a rope around his waist with something dangling from it, probably prayer beads. His head was bowed and as I was watching him, he suddenly raised his head and he could see inside his hood! It was a skull!"

"Oh dear, you must have been very scared. What happened next?"

"The next flash of lightning came and he was gone, so I suppose he went into the trees. I hope he didn't get into the Hall, because he didn't look very nice."

"Perhaps it was the lightning that made a small tree or a statue look like a monk. There are plenty there," pointed out Sybil.

"I knew you would say that Mama, so I made sure. It was a monk and he was horrible."

Sybil kissed him and sent him on his way, but when she told John later, she said,

"Jonny doesn't lie, nor does he make mistakes. Make sure the servants keep a look out. Some of these monks are not so nice."

"No, but he may have been a hermit, they are often seen after travelling from Ireland or Wales to Cornwall."

"I know and I don't mind that. I don't mind when you provide them with food and shelter, I know how much all this magical nonsense means to your family, but I don't want to be murdered in my bed by a crazy foreigner pretending to be a holy man."

"Nonsense? It's not nonsense, but I have to admit that the stories are being forgotten. I keep losing that old book of Richard de Pridias. I go and look for it in the library, just to check and I can't find it and then another time, I can. I wonder if..."

"John, don't ramble. Make sure there are no intruders, will you?"

John huffed out of the room and went downstairs. He instructed Philip to post a man at the door each night as there had been sightings of a strange man outside.

"Is it the monk?"

John stopped.

"Yes, have you seen him?"

"No Sir. Quite a few people have though. They say he comes with the storms and is a sign of danger."

"I doubt that. Let's make sure he cannot get into the house. If the man is in need, feed him, give him a few coins and send him on his way. My wife and children are becoming alarmed."

"Yes Sir."

The following week, there was a heavy storm every day. Even though it was now midsummer, the days never really got properly light. As soon as the sun came out, the air became leaden and humid. The women fanned themselves and wore fewer clothes under their tunics and found excuses to splash themselves with water. Many were breathless with heat, which by midday was almost unbearable and some people had died as a result. By around mid-afternoon, the rain came and then the black and dreadful storm.

Cattle and sheep were getting hit by the lightning and killed. People, instead of joking and keeping away from trees and open spaces, fearfully ran for their houses and barns as the jagged lightning cracked across the sky. After the storms, which would often carry on rumbling through the evening and night, jobs were caught up on and visits done quickly.

On one of these days, Sybil shouted to John as he returned from an early morning trip to another part of the estate.

"John! Jonny is missing! He went to look for his dog and I don't know where he is. I don't want him hurt!"

John remounted and he and his servant rode towards the coast, in the direction pointed out by his wife. The clouds were thickening and both men were conscious that the storm could not be far away. The horses were not as forward going as they had been and John needed to squeeze encouragement to his mount. Cottagers and workmen raised their arms or hats, depending on their sex, then went for shelter remarking how stupid John Prideaux was to be out in this weather.

The rain began to fall and they pulled their cloaks tighter. They had to slow to a walk by the time they arrived at Mothecombe, for the incoming tide was raising the river levels quite high and they didn't want to slip. The thunder had begun now and looking out to sea, they saw ships, over and under whelming as they tried to gain control. John had never liked the sea and was glad that he had never been forced to travel abroad by an Earl or King.

"Jonny! Jonny!" they shouted and received no answer.

The lightning had come and it cracked on the horizon. As the shore lit up, John saw what he thought was a cloaked man standing a distance away from them. A minute more and another flash, nearer this time and he thought the man was nearer also, although he hadn't seen him move.

"Sir, we should find shelter."

"Yes, but my son may not be in shelter and I can't bear that. We must find him." This plea could not be ignored by Philip and he pushed his horse forward towards the man.

"I say! You! Have you seen a boy? A ten-year-old boy?"

There was no answer and another flash of lightning lit up the scene. The cloaked man was now within throwing distance, although nothing was thrown.

"Perhaps he doesn't understand. Perhaps he only speaks Gaelic?" said John.

"He shouldn't be here then," answered Philip. "What is beginning to bother me Sir, is that lightning is coming in a direct line towards us. If it does not divert, one of those flashes is going to hit us."

John shouted to the man.

"We are looking for my son. He is possibly with a small dog. Please, have you seen him?"

The monk walked towards the men and another lightning strike hit the coastline. He held out his hands towards a tree just in front of John and Philip. The next strike they didn't see, just heard. An echoing crack and blackness all around.

"We are dead," John said out loud.

"I think we are Sir," answered Philip.

The monk stood in front of them and handed them a parchment.

"A prayer, John Prideaux. Read it, repeat it and make sure your family uses it always. It works particularly well in times of strife. Such as when your boy and his dog are missing in a thunderstorm. It was sent by the Disperkel."

He bowed and vanished into the blackness.

"Should I read it now, do you think?" asked John.

"Yes Sir."

John read,

O God, That knowest us to bee set in the midst of so many and great dangers, that for Mans frailenesse we cannot always stand uprightly, guard to us the health of Body and Soul, that all those things which we suffer for sinne, by thy holy wee may well passe and overcome, through Jesus Christ our Lord.

It was light and the storm had passed. The ground on all sides of the two men was blackened and burnt and there was a dreadful smell of singeing. The ships were settled on the sea and birds had begun their songs.

"Papa! Papa!"

Running towards them was Jonny and his dog.

"I was lost Papa! I went to a strange place full of people who said they knew me. And there were wolves! But everything is alright now. Can we go home?"

John pulled his son up onto his horse and they rode slowly back home, the dog trotting behind.

"What is the Disperkel?" asked Philip.

"He is something to do with our lands in Cornwall. From hundreds of years ago."

John resolved to find that old book when he got home and keep it properly safe.

That was the last storm of the season, but not the last time the monk was seen by a Prideaux.

A GHOST STORY

Featuring John Prideaux (1505 – 1568)

John Prideaux bent down in front of the fire and stabbed at it vigorously with a beautiful brass and iron poker. After a few moments, he was rewarded with yellow and orange flames crackling towards the chimney so he threw several more logs upon the fire. The cheerful blaze finally sent heat and light into the room.

"That's much better, now we can all be a little warmer at last," said Ann Prideaux, relaxing visibly.

The Prideauxs were hosting a dinner party for their friends and family which involved a meal of several courses and expensive brandy and wine. It was their turn this Tuesday. The group took turns each week to entertain on this otherwise uneventful evening.

The dining room had become colder as the meal progressed. When Ann instructed her servants to bring life back into the fire, the obedient Arthur had tried in vain to please his mistress and only succeeded in making the room smokier and darker.

Everyone was pleased when the meal finished and Ann asked the guests to move en-masse into the drawing room. She knew that the fire in this room would warm them quickly, without the danger of being suffocated. It is very upsetting to see your guests unable to appreciate the good food put in front of them because they were quietly pulling cloaks and furs about their arms against the cold.

"I apologise for the coldness of the dining room," said Ann to her guests.

"Ann, you are not to worry. The weather at the moment is beyond understanding. I am positive that the winters are getting colder each year. We seem to have more snow now than when I was a boy."

Thomas Rogers lived further along the Kings Highway and was a very good friend to the Prideaux family.

"I agree. The snow was falling quite quickly when we arrived. I am glad we do not need to go home in the carriage tonight," said his wife Joan.

"Are we still hunting tomorrow John, if this weather continues?" Thomas did not like to miss any days hunting.

"We can always go shooting if the horses are not able to get onto the moor," answered John.

Another cousin of John's was a guest that night. He was a regular visitor and confidante of the Prideaux family and the other guests. Parson William Hele was one of the Hele business men.

The servants poured more drinks for the guests as Adam Williams walked over to the wooden screens and partly opened them.

"Adam! Shut those screens! Goodness man, we have only just got ourselves warm, I thought I would catch my death of cold tonight!" Robert Fox spoke loudly, but then had the decency to look embarrassed as he realized his hosts were still actually in the room and could hear him. The Prideauxs chose to ignore their cousin and John went over to join Adam at the window.

Adam Williams was married to Alice Prideaux, yet another cousin of John's. Adam lived at Stowford Manor and was responsible for acres of land which bordered the River Erme and stretched from the Highway to Dartmoor. Alice was the daughter of Thomas Prideaux, a landowner and respected churchwarden at Ashburton and related to John Prideaux through their grandfather.

Their children Thomas and Katherine were their pride and joy. Thomas had been admitted to the Inner Temple when he was only 24 and he currently had aims to enter Parliament. Katherine was married to a wealthy and naturally, suitable gentleman.

It was Alice who had ensured that John Prideaux bought this large house and lands from her husband. These lands led directly to the hunting grounds on Dartmoor and bordered land owned by the King. They were part of the lands that had originally come to the Prideaux family from the Wodelands many years previous.

It was a bonus that all the families got on so well with each other.

"The snow is coming down thick and fast. It is lying too. I expect we shall have drifts by the morning." John said.

"I have to congratulate you on your garden. The moon on the snow makes the place look like a painting! What a pity we cannot capture the scene," noted Adam.

The garden was covered in white. Snow hung around the sundial and gave the statues snow hats. The tree branches and clipped box hedges wore snowy cloaks.

"I love the snow," said Ann Prideaux. "I shall walk onto the moors tomorrow if I cannot ride."

John looked across at his wife, proud of her bravery and determination.

"Will you take Johnny and William?" he asked.

"Of course!"

Ann was very fond of her sons. They were the only children they had managed to produce. John knew that Ann was severely disappointed that no girls would be born to them, but the doctor had been quite emphatic after their last child.

"Another pregnancy will likely kill your wife, John. No more children I am afraid."

John took the news well. Some of his contemporaries had taken mistresses at similar news, but so far John had not felt the need.

They closed the wooden screens on the lovely scene and came back into the room.

"Why don't we have dinner with you next week Parson?"

This was a long running joke among the group of friends. Although everyone took turns to serve dinner, Hele never did. The others had decided that he was too mean to entertain them and they let no opportunity pass without mentioning it.

Parson Hele was a big man and took no offence.

"Perhaps one day, soon," he said.

"Tell us a story. John!" asked Sybil.

John Prideaux was famous for his stories.

"What kind of a story?" he asked his friends.

"A murder story."

"A love story."

"A love story? After dinner on a snowy night with people lost on the moor as we speak? Don't be a stupid woman," Robert shouted at his romantic wife.

The others knew, however, that the only romance his little wife experienced came from this type of romantic storytelling or from books. Her boorish husband covered his romance with a thick layer of infidelity.

She was an unhappy woman.

Suddenly a small voice disturbed the general chatter of the party. It was young Johnny Prideaux who stood in front of the fire, rubbing his eyes.

"Now, Johnny what is the meaning of this?" John senior tried to sound cross, but found it impossible with his boys. Everyone knew that Johnny and his father were particularly close.

"I could not sleep father. I looked out of the window and saw the snow and thought that I should go for a walk on the moor with mother."

"We cannot go now John," said Ann. "We have guests and it is nighttime."

"Father used to travel the moor at night, didn't you father?"

"Yes, I did," answered John. He picked up his six-year-old son and sat him next to Joan on the seat nearest to the fire. Joan put her arms and a fur cloak around the boy and handed him some of her wine and a sweet pastry. Johnny snuggled up to his Aunt Joan happily. Now there was a jolly good chance that he would not be sent back to bed.

"I know what tale I shall tell you all. It is a mystery story and even I do not know how the story ends."

"Well that will be no good. Are we to guess the ending?" asked Thomas.

"Perhaps you could just draw your own conclusions," John answered.

Everyone made themselves comfortable around the fireplace and John sat in his chair in the circle.

Small tables were placed in the middle of the group and housed drinks and food. Little John snuggled closer to Aunt Joan and wisely kept quiet.

"The story I have to tell you is a mystery as I have said. However, it is also a true story. I know that because it happened to me."

The audience fell silent and John began.

"My story begins two years ago in 1545. It was a winter's night, very much like this one. The snow was falling heavily and the night quiet and subdued. As the large flakes fell to earth, all the sound from the place vanished. The animals, apart from a hungry fox, had retired into the trees or burrows early in the storm. They were waiting until the daylight brought some respite and they could safely scurry and fly out looking for food. As the evening wore on, the wind died down but the snow kept on falling.

The only reason I was out on this winter's night was to help a friend of mine. He had asked me to meet him as a matter of life and death. I set off at five in the afternoon, complete with lamp and walking stick. I wrapped myself in a heavy wool cloak, a scarf and hat. I was a lonely figure as I trudged from Stowford towards Dartmoor.

"Don't go out in this weather sir," the housekeeper had said to me. "You could come to harm and none of us would know until it was too late. Your wife would not be pleased if I reported that I had let you out on a night like this."

"Not to worry about me Mrs. Tamm. I shall be back before midnight. Keep the fires burning for me and leave me some food out and I shall be happy."

Ann was away at her parents with the boys and so I had no other explanations to make.

I went out into the snow, turning back to look at my house once or twice. I noticed the lights in the window for a little while, but I was surprised just how quickly I lost sight of the house as the snow fell. I kept my mind on the journey in hand and continued head down, following my feet along the track I knew by heart, even though it was covered in deep snow.

You will all know that, when it is snowing very heavily and although the snow is fresh and white, the effect is of complete and utter darkness. Those narrow lanes and the high hedges made me feel as though I was walking along a tunnel to heaven or to hell. I'm not sure which. I found it lonely and other worldly that evening and began to imagine all kinds of strange things.

I found my mind running to the stories I had heard over the years about beasts and phantoms and witches. As I wiped the snow from my face, I stopped to look and listen. There was nothing, no sound, no movement around me and I started to lose my bearings.

I was becoming a little anxious and thought about what would happen if I died of cold and could not be found until the spring. I could not see myself, so how would anyone see me?

"John, you are a silly person." I told myself.

I was going to meet my friend Matthew. You may ask what sort of a friend wants you to meet him on Dartmoor, late at night in the middle of a snow storm? Well he was quite a good one actually.

I met Matthew Prowse while out riding one summer day on Ugborough Moor. It was in the 30's. I was on my own, except for my hounds and my horse and was just enjoying the day. Suddenly, my horse spooked at a bird flying from the bracken, I was thrown and hit the ground with some force. I must have been knocked out for a time, because when I opened my eyes a strange man was looking at me in a concerned way.

"Are you alright sir?" he asked.

"Well yes I think so. What happened?"

"You were thrown from your horse and hit your head."

"Oh. Is my horse alright? Where are my hounds?"

"Don't worry, they are all fine." The man seemed amused at my questions.

I sat up and took stock of the situation. My animals may be fine, but I felt very queasy. The man helped me to my feet and upon seeing how wobbly I was, insisted that I accompanied him to his house. I did not feel like arguing and followed him to his black carriage which stood nearby. I cannot remember much about the journey, but very soon we were arriving at the front door of a large stone property which had ivy growing up the front of the house, almost covering the windows.

Inside the house it was dark, even though the sun shone brightly on this August day. We had left a bright moor, almost scorched from the long drought we had been experiencing. But standing in the hallway, I felt cold and shivery. Perhaps it was the shock setting in.

Matthew Prowse, for we had now been introduced, insisted I go into the library, where a large fire had been lit. I sat in front of it and accepted gratefully the sustenance he offered.

It seems that Matthew had lived here on his own, with only a few servants, ever since his wife died in childbirth five years prior. He had not felt the need to find another wife, preferring his own company and that of his two hounds.

"Are you not lonely here?" I asked him.

"No, I have my faith and know that the Lord will assist me to carry out whatever purpose he has for me," was the strange reply.

Now, I was as well aware then as I am today, that to talk of one's religious beliefs in front of a stranger is a very dangerous thing to do. So, I kept my peace and asked no more.

I spent the next hour or two admiring the books in his library and the fine furniture and tapestries in his house. We talked about many things and found that we got on famously. I wondered how much religion did feature in his life as I noticed an altar in the corner of the library with candles, seemingly constantly lit. There was a Latin Bible which Matthew saw me examining, but he said nothing, merely smiled.

After supper, I was loaded onto the carriage and my horse tied to the back. My hounds were allowed to travel in the carriage with me. The coachman drove me home as Matthew waved to me from his driveway. I had accepted an invitation to supper the following evening, before leaving.

I did join him for supper the next evening and for several evenings after that. Matthew never came to my house nor accompanied me anywhere else. I enjoyed his company and we laughed and had great fun together. I was not married then and I often found the time hanging heavy unless I spent it with Matthew. Both my parents were dead and my brother Hugh busy with his inheritance at Luson. Henry and Thomas my other two brothers also found that their lands kept them busy. I have to admit that until I met Matthew, I was also constantly busy with my own properties. Suddenly these responsibilities were taking a back seat.

We spent time riding, hunting and playing cards. We also discussed religion and his upset at the reforms of King Henry and his marriage to 'that harlot'. I soon realized he was not a fan of hers.

"It is not right that so many good people are losing their lives in such terrible ways. I personally find the King's unpredictable explosions quite unnerving. I have been present for a few of them and so have removed myself here, far away from his ravings and his presence."

I learnt that Matthew had made his feelings known to the King and suffered his temper and his disapproval. Matthew had been able to leave the Court with little fuss even though other influences at court had made him nervous. He felt that some wanted to be rid of him permanently. I liked the man and did not want anything to happen to him.

Perhaps if I am honest, I was also impressed with the names he mentioned. The fact that our family had long been involved in the same circles as Matthew made the stories so very interesting.

I did not see him quite as much once I married and he was often busy, in London, he said.

Once he told me something that has stayed with me to this very day.

"There are really more things in heaven and earth that are not understood. The King has started to make people believe that all relics and rituals are dangerous and evil and that they don't work. There are also many who know that this is not true and will do whatever is necessary to preserve the good old ways. I would like to show you how we can have an amazing influence on our own life if only we knew what to do."

I listened to him and kept an open mind. For it has to be said, my grandfather had similar beliefs. Grandfather told me that none of our family needs to rely on others for our salvation. It rests completely with us.

Matthew continued, "I have some books here in my library and some relics hidden well away that will explain how this can be done. On no account must you mention this to anyone else John. For if you do I may not be able to stay here and I must ask you to promise me something."

"I will if I can Matthew."

"Thank you John. Soon Christmas will be here and I must travel to London in disguise. There, I shall meet a friend and will return home in the New Year. I must ask you to meet me here on the 28th January no matter what else is occurring in your life. No matter what else!" He emphasized the point firstly, by repetition and secondly, by leaning into my face.

"Why? What is going to happen on that night?" I was becoming a little worried by my friend's demeanor.

"You only need to know that the date is important. I should also tell you that it might not be next January."

I promised him that I would and also said that I would make sure that I returned each and every 28th January until I saw him again.

"Don't make rash promises you have no intention of keeping," Matthew answered.

"I just promised you, did I not? Now are you going to let me see these relics? I would be very much interested in them."

Matthew looked at me and I could see that he was wondering whether or not to let me in on his secret. I was interested, but if honest I was also more than a little skeptical about the things he told me. I would be a fool not to admit that relics were around the country and I had heard tales of their magical properties. There were tales of eternal life, flying, travelling to other worlds in addition to the more mundane tales of wart curing and love potions.

"Follow me," he said eventually and got up from his chair. I followed him out of the room and across the hall to the library. He walked over to a bookcase which heaved with books, manuscripts and old papers. I had leafed through these documents on many occasions during my visits to him and found nothing more exotic than history books, personal papers and some court documents.

He looked at me again and said,

"You promise never to talk about what you are about to see?" I gave him my promise and thus appeased, he hit a small gargoyle on the central pillar and a door opened in the shelves. I stood amazed for a moment but soon followed my friend into the darkness.

Matthew carried a torch and I could see what lay in the small space beyond the library shelves. I was shocked and saddened and overcome with an overwhelming emotional release and I cried.

"You see why I made you promise?" he asked.

"Yes," was all I could answer.

"What was it? What did you see?" asked my audience.

"I made a promise and I intend to keep it." John told them.

"You can't do that!" said Robert.

"If I may be allowed to continue with my tale?"

John was met with nods from everyone. He was happy to see that he had their complete and utter attention. More wood was put on the fire, more food and drink handed around and John continued.

"As soon as I saw the contents of the room, I understood why Matthew was so protective and why others would kill him in order to possess the items.

"Matthew, how long have you known about these?"

"I learnt about them at Oxford. I met academics who knew and I eventually was entrusted with some of the things when our great and glorious King fell for this whore. They were insisting that all relics must be destroyed."

"Because these things prove the existence of other worlds and our ability to reach them?"

"Exactly."

"May I touch?"

Upon receiving a positive answer, I entered the room and touched and held the items. It felt as though I had come home.

I departed my friend's house that night feeling like a different person. I waved goodbye to him and repeated my promise to return on the 28th of the following month.

That brings me back to the night I was telling you about. The journey to Matthew's house took over four hours by the time I made my way through the high drifts. Immediately I noticed that there were very few signs of life at the house. Well, none in fact. There were no lamps at the window and no evidence of smoke from the chimneys. Although to be honest I would have had difficulty seeing that in the snow. But there is always a smell of smoke is there not? There was no smell, but I knocked at the door nevertheless. There was no answer, so I pulled the huge knocker further away from the door and dropped it heavily against the oak. The noise made me jump, never mind anyone in the house and I waited for a time. There was still no answer. So, I made the decision to open the door.

I did not expect it to be locked. Matthew never had his door locked as the servants were always present. The door opened quite easily and I made my way inside. The hall was deserted and felt freezing cold. I had the same feeling any normal person has when they enter a house without invitation, one of guilt. It is as if the spirit of the house is giving all of the attention to you as an uninvited guest.

I shivered involuntarily and made my way to the kitchen in the hope of finding a lamp and fire of some sort.

The kitchen was almost as cold as the rest of the house, but I saw that a fire had been lit and although it now only held smouldering logs, there was hope there. I rattled away with a poker after adding some more kindling and dry straw. The fire began to show more life and I used the flame to light a lamp. I filled up a kettle with water and put this onto a hook which hung over the flames. I intended to fill a warming bottle and if I was lucky enough to find some wine, would warm that too.

I looked around the room and saw that everything appeared to be in order. But there was not the fresh food about I had been used to seeing during my visits to Matthew. It was very odd. I soon had to accept that Matthew was not at home and perhaps there was a servant only coming rarely to check the place. I rummaged around and found some biscuits and ate a few. The wine helped warm my body which was almost frozen solid. My mind must have been frozen too as I was beginning to think more logically as I warmed up.

This was odd. Where was my friend and why had he not returned? Where were the servants?

I put more logs on the fire and took the lamp with me as I went to explore the rest of the house. I started with the kitchen and the rooms off that. All the windows were closed firmly, but the back door was unlocked. I opened it and saw Matthew's two large hounds standing at the back door. They looked thin and pitiful and jumped at me wagging their tails in recognition. Being a dog lover, my heart went out to these poor beasts that seemed to have had to fend for themselves for a considerable time. I brought them in to the warm kitchen and opened the biscuit box and shared out the remains between the dogs. They helped me in the pantry as we found some salted beef which they ate hungrily. I decided there and then to take them home with me.

They walked with me around the house and I felt much braver being accompanied by these two huge dogs sniffing ahead of me. The result of the search proved only that no one was living here and had not for some time. Matthew's bedchamber was cold and dusty and I still found it a little creepy with only the lamplight casting shadows ahead of me and the wind howling against the windows. I was sure that the feeling of a haunted house would be similar to this.

As I stood at the top of the stairs, now having explored everywhere, I thought of the little room in the library which Matthew had shown me on my last visit. I thought that I should check that.

I called the dogs and went to the library. I had a sudden desire to light a second lamp in case I lost the light from the first one. I did not think that I could stand for that to happen. Thus prepared I went to the shelves and touched the same gargoyle I had seen Matthew touch but nothing happened. I tried again and still nothing. I looked along the shelves in case there was another gargoyle I had missed, but there wasn't.

I went over to Matthew's desk and decided to have a look in the drawers. There I found a document addressed to 'My friend John Prideaux.' I opened it and read.

John,

If you are reading this, it is January 28th and I am not here. Don't give up on me and return every 28th January until you find me again.

I am putting my faith in you.

Matthew

I reread it and found nothing that could be construed as a hidden secret message. So, I went back to the kitchen and stoked up the fire again. I don't really know why I did this, but had thoughts about other travelers who may need warmth. I blew out the lamps and went out of the back door with the dogs following closely.

Looking back over my shoulder, I thought I saw a light upstairs, but it must have been a trick of my eyes because it was not there now.

I pulled my cloak tighter about me and trudged back to my own house. When I came back in through my own front door over three hours later, I was greeted with a warm feeling.   I saw the fires and lamps lit and there was a wonderful smell of hot food. What a difference to the house I had visited so recently.

My own hounds met me ecstatically and greeted Matthew's hounds with equal enthusiasm. We all trouped into the kitchen and found soup and pasties warming on the iron plate over the fire. A meal has never been more welcome before or since."

John Prideaux stopped speaking and looked at his audience who had not uttered a word. The spell was broken and Alice Williams said,

"So, what happened next?"

"I said it was a mystery, I have never found out what happened to this day."

"You cannot leave us with a story half told John! That is not fair!"

"Well, perhaps if you ask me some questions we can work out what happened that night," said John.

"Did you go back to the house again?" asked Adam.

"I did and each year the house has become colder and felt more haunted. A servant goes there and cleans up and lights fires when necessary, he says that his master intends to return one day. He has been paid to work there and work there he will."

"Who pays him then?" persisted Adam.

"Some lawyer, I believe. These lawyers keep the place maintained, but will say nothing about their client's whereabouts or intentions."

"What happened to the dogs?" asked Joan, ever the animal lover.

"We still have them. Bat and Spangle live with us here in the house and we have given the pups from them and my own dogs to some of you," said Ann.

"We have had two ourselves. I hadn't realized where they came from," said Adam.

"As long as they have a happy life. I was worried about them having nothing to eat and being cold and lonely out there in the snow," Joan said timidly.

Her husband Thomas raised his eyes to the heavens in despair.

"Ann just told you that they are here in this house and they have puppies and everything!"

"Oh! I thought she meant just John's own dogs!"

The gathering giggled a little and then continued with their questions.

"So, can you tell us know what you saw in the little room?"

"No."

"I have never heard of you going about with this Matthew chap, when did that happen?" asked Thomas.

"We do not live in each other's pockets, Thomas. We all have friends the others do not know about," said Parson Hele.

Alice suddenly said, "Forgive me, but is it not the 28th January tonight?"

Everyone turned to look at her, and began talking all at once.

"So, it is!"

"There is nothing for it, we must go out tonight."

"In this snow?"

"John has travelled there before in the snow. Come on John. Show us the way!"

If this outcome had been John's intention, then it was going accordingly to plan. Perhaps he was tired of travelling to the house in the woods on his own and wanted some help. As it was, only half an hour had passed before the men were well wrapped up and had collected lamps and food and wine. They carried sticks and had several hounds spinning about their heels, excited about the late-night adventure.

The women waved them off at the door and immediately settled themselves by the fire talking of the silliness of men, while all quietly wishing they could go too.

"The men are so brave," said Joan.

"Not really, they have all the excitement, never us," answered Ann.

The women set about taking Johnny upstairs, as he had fallen fast asleep in Joan's arms.

"It's a pity he won't have a sister Ann," said Joan without thinking.

Ann patted her stomach. "I am with child now Joan, But John does not know, so don't tell him."

"I thought the doctor told you that would be too dangerous?" asked Alice in horror.

"I am sure it will be fine. I feel so well."

The other ladies looked at each other, they knew that the doctor's warning had been serious and were worried for their friend.

The men set off in the thick snow, tramping the virgin whiteness with their leather boots and carrying heavy hazel sticks. Their outward appearances changed as the snow covered their clothing.

John Prideaux looked at his friends, thinking how different this trip was to his other adventures. No lonely trudge through the snow now. Everyone laughed and joked and pushed each other about. They were not acting like the gentleman of Stowford and Ermington, more like schoolboys on a mystery tour.

"We should be very thankful that we do not have to cross the river. Now that would be a battle," said Adam.

The four men followed John along the Harford road and after an hour the talking and joking subsided. They were using all of their energy just lifting their legs high out of the snow. They saw no one else on their travels except an old fox which had braved the storm to look for food.

"I have just had a thought," said Robert Fox after two hours of trudging.

"We should drink to that!" Adam quipped. Adam, although 57 years old, was as fit as any man there and had a razor-sharp mind.

"Oh ha-ha! But I am being serious, I have never seen a house where you described and my father has never mentioned one."

The others began murmuring their agreement.

John carried on walking, but for the first time in the ten years he had known Matthew, considered the fact that he had never heard of a house there before either.

They walked past Harford Church, where they spent part of their Sundays and attended weddings and christenings. The few cottages on the lane were well shuttered and closed to the snowy outside world they were walking through.

Parson Hele said, "My little church looks so lonely tonight."

"Don't worry Parson, its only asleep," said John comfortingly.

They passed the parsonage, also in darkness, save for one lamp at a downstairs window and within a hundred steps, were on the moor. They struggled as they trudged slowly through the deepening snow. The blizzarding storm ensured they kept their heads well down and it would have been easy to forget which way the track headed. The strong wind howled and screamed as it travelled from one sea to another.

"We must be the only fools out on the moor," shouted Adam, for now the noise of the wind was increasing dramatically as they climbed higher. There was almost nothing stopping in its path as it flew across the moor.

"We are not fools!" answered Adam. "We are adventurers!"

He was unable to hear any answer because the snow hit their faces and bodies with such force that it was becoming difficult to stand upright against it.

Eventually they reached a familiar row of ancient standing stones and walked for another half an hour beyond them. It was here that John expected to see the house. He stopped in his tracks.

"It's not there!" he said.

"Perhaps you have taken a wrong turning," said Robert.

"I can't have done, I have made this journey many times. I have walked it and ridden it. I don't understand this." John was truly confused.

"Well, my friend, you need to find the place soon. The weather is not improving and I for one am getting a little tired." said Adam.

John looked around and said to his friends.

"But, I do not understand this. The house should be here, right here!"

"It isn't here though, is it?" said his parson cousin gently. "Follow me back to the church and we can shelter and have a think."

"Why not your house Hele?" asked Adam reasonably.

Parson Hele only said, "We cannot disturb my servants this late. We shall be safe at the church."

"Safe? From what?" asked Robert.

"Come on John. I am not happy about being on the moor any longer than I have to be."

By now, the swirls of snow appeared to be going back up to the heavens as fast as they were coming down. It created a spinning tunnel effect and was starting to look menacing, rather than beautiful.

John nodded without speaking, but did turn around and the others followed. There were all now trying to find their previous footsteps before they were obliterated.

It was another hour before he led the men and hounds past the parsonage and through the door of St Petrocs. The door banged shut and Thomas dropped the latch.

"You see, I knew where the church was and this place is just as difficult to find as Matthew's house. Why can I not see the house?"

"Don't worry yourself John. Use your energy on keeping warm and not on thinking about things you can do nothing about."

"I will, William. It's certainly cold enough in here."

"It is cold in here. Your church is bad enough on a Sunday morning, but apparently on a Tuesday night it is even worse," complained Adam. "Why can't we go into your house Parson?"

William Hele said nothing, but the look on his face quelled any further questions.

"At least we are out of that rotten wind and snow for a while," said Robert.

"But when we were moving I felt warmer than I do now. I think I am wet through my cloak." Adam took it off and shook the snow from it. He hung the dark cloak over the back of a pew.

"John, is this a joke? Part of your mystery story? If so I am very impressed that you brought us out here under false pretences. Very clever, but now can we go home?" Robert was becoming annoyed.

"No, it is not a joke! I don't understand what is happening here. It is all a bit mad." John sat on a pew holding his face in his heads as though in desolate prayer.

"We should try and get some heat and light going, before we all catch our deaths," said Thomas.

Robert found a taper in a jar by the altar and used it to begin lighting the candles around the church. The others followed his lead, glad to have their minds taken away from their cold limbs. Soon the place looked much more cheerful as the lanterns sent a glow around the beautiful small church.

"Someone may see what is happening here and walk over," said Robert. "One of your servants Parson?"

"Not likely, not in this weather. I wager that they won't even be able to see the lights at the windows, especially if they have their own screens closed," reasoned Adam.

Robert Fox looked out of the window, cupping his hands around his eyes in order to eliminate the light from inside the church.

"It looks creepy out there now," he observed. "Mark you, its creepy in here too."

The others nodded their heads. There was a collective feeling of waiting for their fate among the group. A grim fate.

The candles and lanterns did not reach the dark corners and even the pulpit had a shadow across it.

"We should stay here for a while until we get warmer and have a better idea of what is going on," said John. Inwardly, he was becoming concerned for his own sanity. He was feeling confused and more than a little stupid.

"Was this Matthew man a ghost, do you think?" asked Robert.

"No such thing as ghosts," said Adam. He was becoming concerned about the way the night was going and was trying very hard, not to think about ghosts.

"What is your view on ghosts Parson?" asked Adam, who was still feeling peeved that they were not sitting in the parsonage in front of the fire there. He had no doubt it would be roaring and there would be food and wine.

Parson Hele was quiet for a time, but then beckoned them all to sit. He went over to the altar and opened a chest. Reaching in, he produced wine, beakers and a large cake.

"A cake? William, a cake?" asked Robert.

"Some of my ladies like to give me things," he answered. "And my servants do not want these gifts in the house."

"You mean that witch of a housekeeper you have doesn't allow it," said John. "You should get rid of the woman."

"Or marry her," laughed Adam.

Parson Hele sat down and said, "I have a tale of my own if you want to hear it."

"We might as well listen to your tale," said Adam. "While we wait for the weather to improve."

Everyone agreed and fell silent.

"I am constantly asked why people are rarely allowed at my home and never after dark. Perhaps now would be a good time to let you all know why that is. I have been parson here since 1521, when I took over from Parson John Teake…"

"My God!" exclaimed Robert. "Is it really that long? Well, I hope you last as long as that old boy did, he was quite ancient when he finally went off to meet his employer!"

"Yes, although the problem seems to be, that he never actually left."

"Ah, I see. Is this to be a ghost story to match John's?" asked Adam.

"I don't know whether it matches, but it is a ghost story," answered Parson Hele.

"Oh excellent," said John. He was feeling brighter now.

"My family thought I should take up a local benefice and was employed soon after Parson Teake was buried. You were instrumental in that Adam. Teake had taken most of the services, in spite of his great age, until he was too ill to continue. I assisted with the duties until he took his last breath and took over completely after that. I took his funeral service and have never had a day off since. It has to be said however, that Teake was not pleased with me. It was not so much me, as anyone taking over from him. St Petrocs was his and he told me that he never wanted to leave. The church had been known as St George the Martyr, but the tinners didn't want that and have always referred to it as St Petrocs. He wanted to call it St George, but I have always said St Petrocs."

"Partly my fault," said Adam. "Thought I could hide our church and keep the workers happy at the same time. Teake always was a fool."

"I like St Petroc," said John.

Parson Hele smiled in respect to their mutual Cornish roots and continued.

"Even when he was quite ill, he did not appreciate the help I gave him, instead choosing to criticise. I was not permitted to stay at the Parsonage, but boarded instead at Lukesland. Even in his last days I would arrive at the church to find him taking the services, at the wrong times. He would be at the pulpit, half dressed and with straggled hair, preaching that we were all doomed to hell."

"I remember that," said Adam. "We used to think that you weren't helping him much as it appeared that he had to preach even though he was so ill. Then we soon realized that his erratic behavior was due to his failing mind and after he died, we forgot about it."

"Well it seems that he didn't forget about it. His last words to me were. 'You bastard. You are killing me so you can steal my home and my church! I won't ever leave!'

And he didn't. After he was buried, I moved to the Parsonage and took his old rooms changing little save for adding my possessions. That first night I was woken by him standing at the bottom of my bed, staring at me in the most alarming way. I told him to leave and he did. Sadly, he continued to return night after night. Soon there came talk of lights in the church during the early hours. I went to check and saw my predecessor standing at the pulpit, dressed shoddily and preaching his hell fire to the empty pews. He could see me however and he would stare and point his finger in my direction, cursing me all the while."

"Why have you never told us?" asked Robert.

"In case you thought I was mad, but apparently I am not the only mad one in our group! Now we have John. But my visitations have happened almost every night since Teake's death. Teake preaches from the pulpit through the night hours and interspersed with these sermons, will spend time at the Parsonage. He frightens the few servants who will stay. Mrs. Morton is one of those few who will remain with me. But even she will lock herself into her rooms soon after seven, saying that is the only way she feels safe. I can have no guests when there is a white-haired spirit roaming around the corridors, shouting and swearing. I do not know how to get rid of him and am limited to what can be done to a supposed holy man."

"So, is he here tonight? I mean, are we in the presence of ghosts? I thought we were safe in a church," cried Adam.

"You are safe in the church," he answered.

"Tonight got me thinking in a different way after you told your relic story John. I hope I can trust you all, but during my time here I have found relics and texts, which I should have relinquished during these recent troubles. There is also some plate and silver crosses which would be taxable if I had ever told of their existence."

Adam Williams said,

"I am not so sure I should be hearing about this. My position requires that I tell the authorities."

"But you are not going to, are you? We want no more interference in our lives here than is necessary." Robert said.

"No, no I am not. I am not interested in our selfish King and his taxations. He gets enough contribution from me for his wars and weddings. Are we allowed to see these relics of yours, as we are not allowed to see the ones belonging to your Matthew friend?"

"Sadly, they are not here in the church. I have them hidden in the cellars at the house. I will show them to you another time. In the daylight, when we shall not be interrupted. I don't think my predecessor approved of these Petroc relics. He kept them well hidden even though he was the person who showed me where they were. I wonder if he regrets doing that?"

"Well I hope he doesn't turn up tonight to give us a stern sermon," noted Robert.

There was a loud knock at the church door.

A knock at a door in normal circumstances means nothing more than a welcome or an unwelcome guest, either was possible.

But, in the middle of the night at a lonely church door on Dartmoor, in a snow storm?

The five nervous men stood like statues.

The knock came again.

"God above! What can this mean?" whispered Adam.

"If it is a ghost or a phantom rector or a monster of any kind, I shall drop dead on the spot," whispered Robert.

John realized that the dogs were not barking or whimpering, but instead were sniffing at the door.

Emboldened by this, he said, "I shall answer the door, you cowards!"

He went over to the door, lifted the latch and his jaw dropped as soon as he saw the owner of the knock.

"Who is it?" hissed Adam.

John opened the door fully and stepping aside, beckoned in the visitor.

"My friends, let me introduce Matthew Prowse!"

Matthew Prowse walked confidently into the church, hand outstretched.

"I am very pleased to meet you all. John, I am honored that you returned to help me as instructed. You are a true friend indeed. But here, I must introduce you all to a companion of mine. Henry, do come in."

A very fat man followed Matthew into the church. He was red bearded and had one of the roundest faces John had ever seen in his life. The man looked confused and asked them all if they were monks.

"I have been plagued by monks recently," he informed them.

"No, we are not monks. We are men on an adventure, which has turned out rather differently than the one we expected." Adam answered. He felt that this man was familiar to him, but could not work out why.

"My day has turned out differently too. Why, earlier this day I was lying in my bed contemplating the sins

I have committed in my life and regretting most of them. I hope Edward makes a better job of it than I did," said Henry.

The others looked confused but decided to say nothing. The man did not look very well.

"Come inside sir and warm yourself. Close the door John, the snow is coming in," Adam. He thought that the man looked as though he could drop down dead at any moment.

"Have some cake and wine. You look as though you need it."

"Thank you, you are very kind. I have not been a kind man, but I have been brave."

The friends pulled faces to each other and made room for the man who they considered was probably simple minded.

"Matthew, you have some explaining to do, I think," John said to his old friend.

"All in good time John."

"How is it that I cannot find your house?"

"I don't know what you are talking about John." Matthew smiled broadly. "My house is exactly where I left it."

John took Matthew to one side and said,

"Now look here, I have come back here every 28th January since we spoke last and several times during the year too. The least you can do is offer me some sort of explanation. And who is this man? He seems ill."

"Perhaps he is known to you in some small way John."

John looked at Matthew and began to think that his friend was going peculiar.

William Hele walked over to the visitors and stared into the face of Henry.

"Do I know you sir?" he asked.

"I don't think so. Are you a monk? The monks have been pestering me for a long time. Telling me about hell and such. There is one of them over there!" he said, pointing to the pulpit. "I must apologise to you sir!"

Everyone looked towards the pulpit, but they saw no one.

"Come along Henry, we must make tracks. We need to arrive before dawn," said Matthew.

"What time is it now?" asked Henry.

"It is after four in the morning."

"So, tomorrow already. They will remember the 28th as the end for me. It is over."

Henry got up from his chair and took Adam's hand.

"I thank you again for your kindness sir. I think that one day soon, your son Thomas will meet my daughter Elizabeth. He must tell her the whereabouts of some belongings of mine and give her this ring. She will reward him with an excellent job and other assets. Tell her I am sorry and I love her. I will speak to her when she is older. Remember, I am talking about Elizabeth and not Mary. I cannot speak to Mary, she is scarred and poisoned by her mother's words."

Henry whispered something in the ear of Adam and shook the hands of everyone else present. He had tears in his eyes as he preceded Matthew out of the door.

Suddenly Henry stopped and said to John, "Mr. Prideaux, take my staff and use it well. I am grateful for your help."

John did as he was bid and took the oak and gold staff. It had a royal crest carved into the gold.

"Matthew!" hissed John, aware that he sounded like a cross wife.

"John! Yes, you deserve an explanation of sorts. I know that you have not told anyone of the contents of the room I showed you. They would not believe you anyway and probably not what I am about to tell you. But, here goes. I have a specific job in this world. You remember how we first met?"

"Of course, you found me after I fell from my horse."

"I did. Consider this, if you had died that day and not been knocked out, your children would not have been born nor their children nor their...... You get the point. Descendants of yours will have important tasks to complete and so it was imperative that you lived and had heirs. Dying prematurely would have made this impossible. So, if my specific job were to collect the dead and guide them on their journey, I would no doubt be allowed certain discretions in the few occasions I consider necessary. Perhaps your fall was one of those times."

Matthew stopped and watched his audience. John still seemed confused. The other men assumed it was some sort of personal matter in which they should not interfere; they certainly didn't understand what was being said. Parson Hele was the only one who appeared to understand.

"What about all the things you told me and showed me?"

"All true. But, you will never find the house again in this life. Not in this life," he repeated.

"What about all the things in the library?"

"One day you may see them again." Matthew said mysteriously.

"Why was I supposed to keep coming on the 28th January?"

"Because I knew the date was important and I had to have someone I trusted to open this church for me. This church is a sainted gateway to the next world and I needed to travel through Dartmoor with this man. I took his father through Cadair Idris in Wales, but this Henry had to come to Dartmoor. It's to do with Arthur."

"Arthur Tresidda from Theuborough?" asked Adam.

"No, not that one, a much older man. He has been dead years," answered Matthew, looking amused.

"I don't understand what all this had been about," said Robert.

"No, I don't expect you do Robert. But John, thank you for being my friend and for your kindness to me. Goodnight all! I guarantee that we shall all meet again one day!"

On that cheery note, he left the church.

"The man is mad!" said Robert.

The wind was still howling against the church walls and the snow beat against its old windows as though it would smash them.

"Let's go home," said John and began to put out the candles.

"Agreed! Who do you think they were really? I don't think anyone will believe us about tonight." Robert was very confused and unhappy.

"I am having a great time!" said Adam. "I don't see how I can beat this at my dinner party next week! Although you were a close second to John with your scary rector story Hele!"

Once the candles and lamps had been extinguished, St Petrocs Church regained its lonely spirit.

"Why are churches so grim and frightening?" asked Adam.

"I know, there is nothing welcoming about an empty church," agreed John.

"Especially when it is dark," said Parson Hele.

John made sure his friends were outside on the path before he shut the heavy door. As he was about to latch it, he heard someone talking inside. He opened the door quietly and saw the old rector preaching from the pulpit. He turned towards John, pointing ominously with his outstretched fingers.

"Death is on its way to your house John Prideaux!"

John slammed the door and turned back to the others.

"Are you quite well John? You look as though you have seen a ghost!" said Adam cheerily.

"I fear we have all seen ghosts tonight," muttered Robert. No one felt the need to answer him and they walked down the path to the gate.

Parson Hele smiled and told his friends that he would return, quietly, to his house and go straight to bed. There had been a lot of excitement tonight.

Taking their leave, the rest of the band began their return journey down to Stowford. The snow had stopped and the wind had quietened down. It was a beautiful night and the men felt their energies rise as they made the trip home. They began to joke around and laugh again.

"Look over there!" said John suddenly.

They all stopped and looked across the moor. A very bright light with a rainbow aura appeared in the sky. It was as if a bonfire had been lit and fireworks set off.

"What was that?" asked Robert.

"Probably another ghost," said Adam.

It didn't generally take as long to return to Stowford as the other way about, it being downhill. But tonight, the deep snowdrifts meant that every step involved lifting their legs as high as they could in an effort to clear the snow.

It was dawn by the time they arrived back home. They were met by the wives who were anxious to hear their news. The women had slept in turns by the fire and now instructed the waking servants to serve an early breakfast. The women listened in awe and would not have believed the story had not all four men stuck to the same theme.

Young John Prideaux listened to all from his hidey hole on the balcony and thought he would never forget this night.

It was a day later when Ann Prideaux ran into her husband's study and said,

"Guess what I have just heard in the town?"

"I cannot imagine." John answered drily.

"The King is dead! He died two days ago and Edward is our new King. What about that!"

John put down his book and looked out of his window at the moor.

"What about that indeed," he answered.

THE DARTMOOR WITCH

Featuring John Prideaux (1540 – 1620)

This Stowford party had been anticipated for weeks.

Following years of religious uncertainty and persecution, recently there had been a period of peace in the country. Emlyn Williams told those who would listen that it was because Queen Elizabeth had been getting rid of anyone whom she considered to be her enemy. Emlyn's father-in-law Thomas Williams had been a Speaker of the House of Commons until his tragic and sudden death. With this familial backing she considered herself an oracle on all things political. She probably was, she knew enough of the 'right' people.

"As soon as that Scottish woman is dead, the Queen will feel safe and the rest of us will be able to get on with our own lives," Great Aunt Alice Williams announced to her Devonian niece, Agnes.

"I don't like all this killing and the constant executions under the pretence of treason and crimes against God," Agnes answered forcefully.

"I should keep that opinion to yourself, my dear," advised her aunt.

Agnes bobbed a dutiful curtsey in acknowledgement and skipped off to her friends. At 18 years old, Agnes was feeling the need to marry quickly before she lost her looks. She was used to living with privilege and had no intention of marrying out of it. This wonderful party at Stowford Hall was a treat and she was going to take full advantage. Her Great Aunt, Alice Williams had promised the women several eligible men and she had promised the men several beautiful and well-connected women.

Both Emlyn and Alice Williams were good at throwing parties when they felt the time was right and everyone who was anyone would attend.

The young women stood together collectively giggling and gossiping, albeit in full view of their chaperones, who casually sat in nearby chairs.

"Who is that?" asked Agnes of her friend Johanna.

"That is John Prideaux. He is related to your Aunt Emlyn, so I suppose he must be related to you somehow," her friend answered. "He lives very near to us in Stowford."

"Who is the girl making eyes at him?"

"That is Anna Fortescue. I think she has quite a bit of money coming to her. Why? Do you like the look of him?"

"Liking the look and going to get him."

Agnes had the determined expression on her face with which Johanna was so familiar.

"Bad luck Miss Fortescue, you just lost a competition you did not even know you were in," said Johanna, grabbing hold of her friend's arm.

The girls laughed out loud, causing some of the women at the gathering to tut-tut their disapproval. John Prideaux looked across at them and smiled at Agnes.

"Round one to moi," she said.

"I can tell you some things about that young lady that she would not expect anyone here to know," whispered Johanna.

"Tell me, tell me!" squealed Agnes.

Agnes Williams was a well-heeled cousin of the Williams family of Devon. It was her Aunt Emlyn Williams, a wealthy landowner with acres of property in Stowford, who was throwing this party for her neighbours.

Emlyn had been married to Thomas Williams. Recently widowed and often bored, she enjoyed her matchmaking and socialising. Thomas's father Adam had bought up large tracts of land following the dissolution of the monasteries. Thomas Williams then purchased more land to become an even wealthier man than his father.

Adam Williams married Alice Prideaux who turned out to be a great financial advisor and knew how to make money. When Thomas their son, became a favourite of Queen Elizabeth in his role as Speaker, he was rewarded with the demesne lands between Stowford Manor and Prideaux House to the south of Dartmoor. The Queen gave these 100 acres of former royal hunting ground to him and his heirs forever.

The farms and properties which accompanied these lands were now the responsibility of Thomas to manage. During his many absences in London, he left the management in the capable hands of his mother Alice and his wife Emlyn. When Thomas died in 1566, two years prior to this party following a fall from his horse while out hunting. Emlyn Williams continued her management and looked after the tenants and the lands, working as hard as she ever had.

Parties such as the one these young people attended happened often around the County and were an excellent place for the young and the widowed to meet the right sort of person. The Williams family often used them as fundraisers, either in cash or in kind. They were very successful social and charitable occasions. The son and heir of Thomas and Emlyn was still a teenager but allowed to attend this party. Although Thomas had not approved of his son or his raucous behavior, Thomas's will revealed that he had nevertheless ensured in law that his son John was his heir. John, even after learning of his new responsibilities was still a wastrel and cared little about Stowford and the family inheritance. Alice and Emlyn needed to keep a constant eye upon him.

Agnes Williams had spent much of her teenage years in Exeter and Bath with extended family and through the friends she met there and the connections she made had learnt behaviours that were not familiar to the inhabitants of the South Hams. Agnes did not intend to let these skills go to waste.

"Agnes my dear, you are looking very thoughtful."

"Aunt Alice! Yes, I have seen the man I intend to marry and was just wondering how to go about getting him."

"I see. Am I allowed to know the name of this man?"

"Yes, John Prideaux. I only just found out his name myself."

"One of my own family! I shall have to see how I can help you, I know his parents well. Thomas was very good friends with his father John. They used to have such fine adventures together. There was this one time when they travelled onto the moor during a snowstorm... But I am sure that would not interest you." The smile on the old lady's face began to falter as she thought of her son. But she rallied and asked,

"Where is he Agnes?"

Agnes pointed to the handsome young man talking to Miss Fortescue.

"I see that he is already occupied. She should not present too much trouble for you, young lady. That girl does not look as though she has much fight in her."

Agnes stared at the quiet girl in the beige dress standing next to John Prideaux. Her face was pale and her fair hair and brown eyes were not lighting the room. She compared the girl's image with that of John Prideaux. He was a tall man with dark wavy hair, grown long enough to touch the top of his collar. His complexion was dark and his eyes hazel. The full lips and huge grin which seemed to be permanently fixed showed white teeth which gave the impression of trouble.

"He is just the kind of man I want," Agnes unconsciously said out loud.

"He has made an impression on you darling. Come on, let's get a proper introduction," whispered Great Aunt Alice. She had managed to catch rich Adam Williams and so instantly recognised the determined look in her niece's eyes. It would be fun to help her. There wasn't much fun at 80 years old.

"John. John! Come over here this instant!" Shouting at her grandson was a guaranteed way to get his attention. In spite of the young man's wealth, influence and careless attitude to life, he came meekly over to his grandmother's side. She still had some control over his allowance.

"Yes grandmother, what can I do for you? Do you want another drink? Hello Agnes, are you enjoying yourself?" John said with the attractive charm he used on everyone.

"Don't fuss so John. Now listen to me, you see John Prideaux over there, by the fireplace? I want you to introduce him to Agnes."

John knew better than to ask his grandmother why and so walked towards his guest, returning with him less than a minute later.

"Grandmother, John Prideaux wants to say hello."

"Hello John."

John Prideaux bowed and took the hand of his hostess and kissed it lightly.

"A pleasure as always, Mrs. Williams. You are looking beautiful."

Agnes listened to the deep tones of the attractive man and felt her cheeks flush.

"You are very charming Mr. Prideaux but are welcome here nonetheless." She nudged her grandson and John Williams did his duty.

"John, do you know my cousin, Miss Agnes Williams?"

John Prideaux turned his attention to the pretty girl standing next to Alice and rewarded her with his smile.

"I am honoured to meet you, Miss Williams."

Agnes gave a curtsey and lowered her eyes. Then she rose and looked John straight in the eye and smiled back.

John was a little taken aback as he generally expected his close presence to overcome the women he met and make them nervous. He knew he was handsome and that was enough to get him, well – anything he wanted. This girl was different.

"Mr. Prideaux, I understand you are a good rider, perhaps you will be accompanying my cousin at his hunting tomorrow?"

Now why had she asked him that? It sounded too forward and yet she didn't care.

"We often hunt together Miss Williams but I don't suppose you realize that. Agnes is an accomplished rider, John. She also rides far too fast," said her cousin.

John Williams looked at his two friends and then quizzically at his grandmother, who merely smiled. What had his grandmother dragged him into? If John Prideaux thought he was being set up, he would not let him forget it in a hurry.

"Then we shall see you at the meet tomorrow Mr. Prideaux," Agnes said.

"I sincerely hope so," answered John.

"Hello Mrs. Williams!"

Anna Fortescue had used her feminine sixth sense and moved swiftly over to the small gathering, where her potential beau was being snared.

"What a wonderful party this is, Mrs. Williams. John and I were just saying how much we were enjoying ourselves."

Agnes turned to her rival and said,

"Miss Fortescue, it is a pleasure to finally meet you. I have heard so much about you from my dear friend Johanna Fiennes. You have a mutual friend in Mr. Giles Abson, I believe?"

Anna Fortescue went white but regained her composure quickly.

"I think that Miss Fiennes was a closer friend of his than I was."

"Apparently, he still speaks fondly of the times you two spent together. He was most disappointed when you left town so suddenly."

"I cannot think why," she answered shortly. "John, I am feeling rather warm, perhaps we could take some air?" She looked plaintively at John Prideaux.

"Of course Anna, I would not want you to faint in front of everyone. Perhaps you would like to join us Miss Williams? Mrs. Williams what about you? John, please join us. It is a wonderful evening and I saw some stocks in the garden, they should smell sweetly in this warm evening air." John apparently wanted a crowd.

"Thank you Mr. Prideaux, but my stock smelling days are behind me now. You go Agnes and John and show John Prideaux and of course, Miss Fortescue around the gardens," said the old lady, trying and failing to hide a smile.

"Yes Aunt, I shall."

The four of them moved in the direction of the terrace doors but John Prideaux excused himself as they went through the doorway.

"I must just pop somewhere before we walk ladies," he informed them. He winked at his namesake and the two men went to fetch another drink.

The girls carried on into the warm, moonlit night.

"You seem very interested in my John," said Anna.

"I was not aware that he was your John!" Agnes said in a mock surprised tone.

"He is, or soon will be. I prefer that you accept that information and move on to someone else."

Agnes laughed.

"I am sure that Mr. Prideaux is quite capable making up his own mind."

"Perhaps, but I can also make it up for him." Anna
looked at Agnes trying to understand what was
going on.

"Does he know about the baby?" Agnes swiftly
delivered the arrow to her rival's heart.

"No! How do you know about that?" Anna stopped
in her tracks.

"Gossip I am afraid. None of us are safe from that.
That is why we women must keep ourselves tidy."
Agnes suddenly felt guilty. Perhaps she had gone too
far and she certainly had no intentions of passing on
the gossip.

"I am lost if that becomes public knowledge. Mother
is bringing up the boy as her own. Father knows, but
wants to keep it secret."

"No one will hear it from me," said Agnes quietly.

They looked each other, so what now?

John Prideaux came out to join them.

"Ladies, ladies. Let's walk to the walled garden, I
hear it is beautiful! But what is the matter with you
both? The gaiety has gone!"

The two ladies laughed and accompanied their eager
companion as he led them to the gardens.

Two days later a maid announced to Agnes that she
was required downstairs to attend her aunt. Agnes

had been dressing her most recent homemade doll with a lock of her hair and some she had managed to steal from the collar of John Prideaux. She kissed it and lay it down on her pillow next to her nightgown. She finished dressing in her new pale blue gown and made her way into the library where she expected to see Aunt Emlyn.

As Agnes walked into the room, she caught her breath when she saw who was there. It was her Great Aunt Alice sitting grandly by the fireplace and she was accompanied by John Prideaux. Agnes thought her heart would stop, as he turned to face her when she came into the room.

"John has come to ask if you would like to accompany him on a ride Agnes," said the old lady.

"That would be wonderful," Agnes said, deciding immediately not to hide her joy.

"Change your clothes, Agnes and have your maid go with you. I am not having two young people go out with no other companion!"

John smiled at her during the whole conversation and winked as she was dismissed by her aunt. Agnes walked gracefully out of the room but as soon as she was out of sight, she ran back to her own quarters.

"Mary, Mary!" she shouted to her maid. "Get my new riding clothes, we ride out today!"

The two girls were downstairs in fifteen minutes. Instructions had been given to the stables earlier and the horses were outside, ready and waiting. Agnes was to ride her favourite, a beautiful grey horse and her maid a bay. John was already seated on his black stallion and after much chattering and excitement they were all making their way to the moor.

"Not with Miss Fortescue today Mr. Prideaux?" asked Agnes. She was genuinely curious to know how the girl was, as she still felt guilty about letting Anna know that her secret was out in the open.

"She has left the county I am sorry to tell you, Miss Williams. She has gone back to her parents in Cornwall on some urgent family business. I don't think that she will be returning here."

"That is bad news. I enjoyed her company," Agnes answered.

"Let us see if you can enjoy my company as much," he said.

She noticed that even his eyes smiled and his voice was deep and consequently very attractive to Agnes. Dolly was working her charm back in the bedroom.

She suddenly galloped away from him and was pleased when she saw that he was chasing her. John was surprised to see that catching Agnes was not as easy as he had imagined. Mary the maid, remembering her instructions, wisely held back her pony in a jogtrot.

The two raced onto Dartmoor and made their way towards the highest peaks, passing the ancient stone monuments on the way. John always felt that the vibrations coming from these stones seemed to give them a life of their own.

Today the weather was excellent with a cloudless sky and views for miles. They both knew that this place could become treacherous within minutes if the mist rolled in and the unsuspecting rider or walker became lost. Deaths had occurred in such a way on many occasions in the past.

"Look over there!" shouted John. The two eased up their horses and saw a lone wolf on top of a rocky crag looking back at them. The horses had disturbed partridge which squawked their protest as they flew towards the wolf.

"I wonder why he is out in the daylight without any cover?" asked Agnes, though with no hint of nerves.

"I should imagine that he is hunting food for his cubs. He will ignore us. He has more than enough to eat without attacking us." John said.

They watched for a few minutes, their horses pawing the ground. In their current view were the wolf, partridge, buzzards, sheep, ponies, cattle, and boars. The flora too in this supposedly bleak place was manifold and beautiful.

"I love this place," said Agnes. "We are so lucky to be here. I want to live here forever."

John looked at her lovely profile appreciating the scenery he had loved from a boy and thought that he would not mind spending a lot of time with this girl.

"We are very lucky," he answered.

They rode further into the moors going north when suddenly they came upon an old cottage which stood completely alone. The cottage was stone built and surrounded by several dilapidated stone outbuildings which appeared to be used as storehouses and shelters for animals. Smoke spiraled from the chimney showing that the cottage was occupied. A small dog came out to greet them, barking a couple of times, but it soon stopped and began to wag its little tail.

"Hello! Is there anyone there?" shouted John.

There was no answer and so interest aroused, he dismounted and went to the door.

"Hello!" he shouted again. Then turning to Agnes, he said, "I haven't noticed this place before."

Agnes watched him walk in and after a few moments come out again.

"Jump down Agnes, the lady who lives here has kindly offered us some refreshment."

"How kind," she said and jumped from her horse. Neither thought it unusual that she should do this without assistance. Both instinctively realized how independent the other one was. They moved their horses into a walled area which had water and grazing and Agnes followed John into the cottage.

Inside it was very dark and warm, almost stuffy. The table was covered in jars and bottles filled with herbs and flowers while pots and pans hung from the ceiling. There was a large fireplace surrounded by oak shelves. These shelves were also covered by small jars and pots.

It was this fire which provided the only light and the heat in the room. As she started to feel a little overcome, Agnes became aware of a very small woman seated on of the settles which were at right angles to the fireplace. She wore a red dress and her long grey hair was arranged loosely about her shoulders. Although obviously very old, she was nevertheless quite an attractive woman.

"Hello Miss., Would you like to sit by me here?" She patted the seat next to her.

Agnes looked at John who smiled and she took up the offer. It was strange how comfortable she felt sitting next to this woman.

"It is very kind of you to let us into your home. Do you have many visitors?" Agnes said as she removed her gloves.

"I have all the visitors I am meant to," the woman answered, still smiling.

"Oh, I see." Although Agnes didn't see at all.

"Take some of the cakes from the oven Sir and then pour us all something to drink. You will find some lovely wine in the jug on the table. Go on, don't be shy."

John did as he was bid and brought over the refreshments to the women. They both felt surprisingly happy and at home in the cottage and found that they could not stop smiling.

"Now then, you two young people, shall I read your fortunes?"

"Oh, yes please!" said Agnes with rather more enthusiasm than she might have done when more guarded.

"I wouldn't mind," said John.

The old woman got up from her chair and made some room on the table. She asked John to pass her a large box from its place on a shelf by the fire place. He was obedient to the request and upon receipt she opened the box and took out some cards and placed them on a table.

They both moved over to the table while pulling up stools and Agnes took the hand painted cards and shuffled them as requested. The old lady took them from her and laid them out in a pattern on the table. She asked John to give her a ring he wore and she held this as she spoke to them.

"Now my dears, this is very interesting, shall I tell you everything I can see here?" Her accent was as broad Devonian as it was possible to be.

"Yes, yes please," they answered together.

"I see marriage and children. Ten children I think. One of the boys will be well known and influential. He will advise one Queen and three Kings and will know great highs and lows in his life. You will remain rich and landed."

"Which of us are you reading for now?" asked Agnes.

"I'm reading for the two of you together. You will marry each other this year and be very happy for many years."

Agnes blushed deeply, but inside her heart was singing.

John said nothing, just stared at the cards.

"Any questions?" she said.

"That all seems very nice ..." began Agnes.

The old woman turned over another card. It was of a hooded man.

"Beware the hooded man," said Agnes facetiously.

The old woman glared and said, "Indeed yes. You must protect yourself against the Devil. He walks all of our boundaries, trying to find a way in."

Agnes and John looked at each other and grinned.

The old woman did not grin.

"I have a gentleman with me. He has the same name as you Sir."

"I don't see him," said John, suddenly nervous.

"That's because he is not alive. I believe him to be your father. Yes, he is your father. He said to tell you that he has seen King Henry again and is laughing. He had quite an adventure at Harford Church one night. The moor is full of surprises and mysterious places."

"Yes, he told me lots about his adventures and took me on some. Err – is he alright?"

"He is very happy and is with his father and the rest of the clan. Apparently, they travel to France and Spain and Syria, so he tells me."

"He always wanted to travel," said John uncertainly.

"I am sorry John. I didn't know that your father had passed. Was it recent?" asked Agnes.

"This summer Miss Williams, I miss him very much."

"He tells me that you shouldn't miss him too much John. He will see you eventually and you don't want to die too soon," said the old woman.

"I suppose not, although I would love to see him again. We didn't say goodbye because I was in Fowey when he died," said John.

"What would you be willing to do to see him again?"

John was taken aback with the question and answered, "I'm not sure but nothing against God!"

The woman laughed and Agnes said, "What are you saying? Is there a way he can see his father?"

The woman laid out the cards and they looked at a picture of the Devil and a bearded King.

"What does that mean?" asked Agnes.

"Do you have any gold with you?"

"Well yes, I do. Do I have to pay to see my father?"

"It will help the connection," the old woman intimated.

Agnes imagined this to be a confidence trick of some sort but John looked more hopeful. He handed over two gold sovereigns and the old woman grabbed them and put them – somewhere. She stared at the two young people, who stared back. Outside it was becoming dark and there was a rumbling across the moor.

"A storm is coming. We should go home John, the horses will spook," Agnes said, shivering.

John rose from his chair and took her hand.

"Yes, we should. I don't want to be in trouble with Great Aunt Alice or Aunt Emlyn for that matter."

They laughed.

"John." A voice neither of them recognised was calling his name.

They both turned to the old woman and were shocked to see that she was no longer sitting at the table. Instead there was a tall man dressed in a shroud standing next to the fire. He had a greenish white face, so thin it was almost skull like. He had grey hair pasted down on his head and a glow around his person which was separate to the firelight.

"Father?" asked John in a tremulous voice.

"Are you a ghost?" asked Agnes in a less anxious tone. She had been raised in a house where disembodied voices and misty figures were common during the night.

"John," said the ghoul.

Agnes walked towards the mirage and reached out to touch him.

"Don't Agnes!" shouted John. "You might make him vanish!"

Agnes withdrew her hand and the spirit, for that is what it was, walked towards them. Or perhaps it was more of a glide as its movement caused John and Agnes to move backwards.

"John," said the spirit.

"Where is the old woman?" whispered Agnes.

"She has vanished; perhaps she has left us alone here?"

"Perhaps she was dressed herself as your father's ghost to warrant the two gold pieces," said Agnes and giggled.

John looked at her as if the idea had only just occurred to him too and their eyes locked.

"John!" roared the spirit.

They jumped and Agnes squealed, for the spirit was now standing next to them and the smell and freezing temperature they were experiencing was paralysing them.

"What do you want spirit?" asked Agnes, for now she knew it to be so.

"John!" it repeated.

"Are you really the spirit of my father?"

"Yes!" it shouted.

"Why must you shout so?" asked Agnes. "If you speak quietly, then we can understand you just the same."

The spirit looked at her and nodded gently.

"I am happy John. Death is not a doorway which cannot be crossed both ways. There are many such doorways on Dartmoor and elsewhere."

"I don't want to go through any doorways just yet father. I have things to do here."

"Good. Then you must cheer up and get on with those things."

"What's being dead like?" asked Agnes with genuine interest.

"It's better than being here and alive. I don't like being back in this painful body."

"Why have you come back then? For the money?"

The spirit looked confused – a state surprisingly easy to recognise.

"No girl. My son here has responsibilities and I have returned to remind him that he must take on those responsibilities. I can't do it and too many people depend upon him. So, get married John and get working."

"Father, I am not ready for marriage. Why do I need to become responsible when I am so young?

The spirit opened his mouth wider and wider and leant towards the couple as he roared his answer. The room vibrated and the noise and smell became overpowering and Agnes was near to tears.

"Our tenants and their families!"

The spirit appeared spent by this effort and shrank away from them and back towards the fire.

"Look after them all John, they cannot manage without your help."

He looked as small and vulnerable and sad now as John had seen him in the weeks prior to his death.

"I will father. I want you to be proud of me."

The spirit began to dissolve and with another flash of lightning was gone. The atmosphere in the room was heavy and musty and the young couple felt weak and light headed. A voice from the doorway said,

"That was worth the money Sir. I expect you are pleased with that."

"Yes, I expect I am. I'm not sure if I believe what just happened. Was that really my father's spirit?"

"Did it look like him? Did it sound like him? Did he know you?"

"All of that. I just didn't expect to see him. I didn't expect to see a ghost."

"And yet, see a ghost is what you did," she answered.

The lady took up her cards and put them back in the box and returned the ring to John, folding it into the palm of his hand.

"You are a special person Sir, don't throw that away easily."

"I won't," he said.

She went back to her chair by the fire, looking now quite old and tired.

"What do I owe you for the food and the advice?" asked John.

"Nothing Sir, nothing, I am happy to help. This is not the only time we shall meet."

Agnes nodded to him and he put two pennies onto the table. They left after saying their goodbyes and thanking her, but she appeared to have gone to sleep and did not respond.

"Come on John," said Agnes and they went out into the sunlight. It seemed very strange to be outside again, as though they had been in the cottage for hours.

"The sun has got quite low," John said. "We should be getting back."

They climbed onto their horses and rode back the way they had arrived. There was no sign of the maid and Agnes felt a stab of guilt knowing that Mary would have been very bored and probably hungry and thirsty while covering for her mistress.

"What do you think about that episode John?"

He was quiet for a moment, but it was a comfortable silence as they both now felt connected to each other.

"I think we shall get married," he said and looked at Agnes.

She smiled back at him and answered, "I think you are right. The life she promised seems too good to miss." They stopped their horses in a woodland glade and leant across to each other and kissed.

Now that felt very nice, thought Agnes. Creating ten children with this man did not seem like a problem at all.

"Grrrrr."

"Oh, my Lord!" exclaimed Agnes in genuine surprise. Standing in front of them was the wolf from earlier. It was a huge beast with lips curled up over his teeth.

"Stay perfectly still," said John in the time honoured way a man feels he must deal with a dangerous situation, as he began to draw his sword.

The wolf took two steps towards them and placed his nose on Agnes's dress.

"It's alright John, he is friendly," she said and bent to stroke the wolf on his neck.

The wolf nuzzled her hand and opened his mouth. John Prideaux took his sword and jumped from his horse. Neither horse appeared perturbed by the wolf's presence.

The wolf dropped something into Agnes's hand, nuzzled her again before turning and loping away.

"Are you alright Agnes?"

"Of course I am. But look what he gave me!" She opened her small hand to reveal two gold pieces. The very coins John had given the old woman before the spirit appeared. Agnes handed them to John who took them and folded them into his hand.

"I shall have them made into our wedding rings," he said.

When they arrived back at Stowford they discovered Mary had spent the day soaking her feet in a stream and sleeping. There was much clucking and feigned disapproval from the Aunts Alice and Emlyn when they returned to the Hall.

"I humbly beg your pardon for keeping your niece out so long ladies. However, during today we have come to an understanding and I should like to marry her."

Agnes smiled at her aunt, who said,

"Well done, you are happy Agnes?"

"Yes Aunt."

 "Clever girl Agnes, clever girl."

*

The couple were to live at the Prideaux family house now that both John's parents were dead.

This Prideaux property at Stowford was a beautiful estate with cottages for workers, stables and land running down to the Kings Highway. There were tracks leading directly onto the moor and John and Agnes and their planned children would make these moors their second home. The woodland groves and mock temples in the style of the Phoenicians who were said to have dwelt there at one point and the manicured Tudor gardens were the envy of the neighbourhood.

The wedding was arranged at the little church at Harford where the Prideaux and Williams families had always worshipped their God. As Agnes arrived for her wedding in a carriage from her uncle's house, she breathed in the beautiful day. The carriage and horses had been trimmed with flowers and ribbons and she knew that the church would be bedecked in a similar manner. The progress of the wedding procession was slow as the very narrow roads with high hedges made it difficult for the small carriage to travel without hitting the sides. Luckily the weather was dry and so although the rutted road was hard going for the horses, there was no mud in which the carriage wheels could come to grief. Many had used sedan chairs in the past, which progressed much more easily but Agnes wanted a fashionable arrival.

Walking in front and dressed in Sunday clothes, were the tenants and locals. Children giggled and threw flowers at Agnes and she tried to catch them. She stood up to reach a particularly lovely bunch of cornflowers and looked across the fields as she did so. She noticed a dark figure standing at the tree line. It was hooded and caped and stood motionless. Agnes felt as though time was standing still and everyone faded into a fuzzy background as the hooded man held her focus.

"Miss! Miss!" shouted one of the girls as she threw more flowers. Agnes looked round and caught the lilies.

"Thank you Hannah," she answered. Agnes added the lilies to her bouquet on the seat and she looked back to the tree line.

The figure had gone and before Agnes could consider the conundrum any further, they had arrived at Harford Church. The sight of flowers covering the gate and her family waiting and waving to her made her cry.

She alighted from the steps onto the pathway leading to the church door and took hold of her father's arm.

"You really do look lovely Agnes," he told her with pride evidenced on his large face.

"I know!" she answered and they both laughed at her modesty.

John was shuffling from foot to foot inside the church. Rector John Priest stood by the altar, alternately looking between the soon to be husband and the door. John had two of his good friends with him, John Williams and Giles Fox. They were telling him jokes about Agnes not turning up and him having to do a walk of shame back to his horse. He joined in but was feeling a little worried that she might. He went into his mind in order to quell panic.

He had begun seeing the figure shortly after the visit to the moor and the phantom visitation from his father. The first time he saw the figure was from his bedroom window two days later. The man, he firmly believed him to be such, wore a cloak with a hood which covered his face. He just stood immobile against the stone wall surrounding the yard. When one of the men came into the yard pushing a barrow, he didn't appear to see him. When John averted his eyes back to the figure – he was gone. John thought it must have been a trick of the light.

The next time was against the trees surrounding the property and the third and fourth times against the barn. The figure appeared during the daytime, remained immobile and vanished after a while.

The fifth and sixth times he saw the figure at the far end of the stables while he was getting ready to ride out. This time he went so far as to ask the lad if he could see him and the answer was no. But the lad said that there were often strangers coming looking for food and he always sent them away.

"Unless he's a ghost," he added.

"Ghost? You see ghosts William?" asked John.

"Sometimes Sir. Ghosts from the past and from the moor. Everyone does, do you?"

"Not sure William. Perhaps."

This continued over the weeks leading to the wedding. John told no one, because he didn't want to be thought of as deranged. He put it down to his anxieties following his father's death and the further responsibilities which were coming his way.

Then only a week ago, he had been in the house on his own. That was highly unusual, because even when the family was away, there were servants around. But this day was different. His sister and cousins were away in Cornwall and one of the maids was marrying the stonemason. John had attended the ceremony at Harford as was his duty as landowner and he had given the servants time off until midnight. He had supplied food and drinks for the tenants and then returned to the house in order that they may enjoy themselves without the Master present.

He realised shortly after his arrival back at Stowford House that it was the first time he had been there alone. He wasn't sure that he liked it very much. He went inside and quickly bolted the door behind him. He didn't really know why. Then, even though this made him feel a little stupid he still walked slowly around the ground floor, fastening windows and battening doors. He wanted the house safe by the time it got dark.

John went into the kitchen and poured some wine into a goblet favoured by his father. The container gave him comfort and lately he had been holding it more tightly than usual. What the hell had that been at the witch's house? Was it his father? It certainly seemed so, but he had also been so odd. Perhaps that was what death did to you.

There was a noise upstairs and John froze, with the goblet to his lips. He listened with everything he had and heard it again. Footsteps and yes, something being knocked over. He put down the wine and moved stealthily towards the hallway. He wasn't breathing and so had to begin with tiny breaths in order that he didn't faint. He felt a nudge on his leg and almost screamed. Looking round he saw his dogs, two small terriers, mother and daughter. They were scratching his leg and begging to be picked up. This he did, for he could hear the noises upstairs again.

He made sure that his dagger was at his belt and crept towards the stairs. He ought to shout and see who was there, but somehow, he couldn't. The dogs would generally wiggle in his arms, but this evening they were not. They were calm, almost subdued.

John hoped they weren't getting ill, he couldn't stand losing these dogs. They were like his children.

John stood on the bottom step, looking up. He could see the stained-glass window at the head of the stairs and the small landing there, where the stairs split again left and right. He couldn't see around there - obviously. He was wondering whether to go up and look when a noise from behind him made his body shoot fear through his soul. He turned around slowly, so very slowly and saw what he dreaded. The hooded man was standing in the hall, backed against the front door. The head was lowered so that the hood hid his face, showing only a dark shadow.

John didn't think he had ever been so scared. His dogs whimpered and John's thoughts went directly to protecting them.

"Who are you?" he asked.

There was no answer, apparently not all ghosts speak.

"Why are you doing this? I'm not afraid of you."

The hooded head began to rise, revealing more of the dark shadow space beneath. The creature began to move quietly across the stone floor towards John.

"Stop!" shouted John.

It didn't. It walked slowly and appeared to cover more ground than if he had run. John should move or the creature would be in front of him soon - too soon. His dogs barked and John thawed and turned to run up the stairs. At the small landing, he went left and ran again. He was aware that he seemed to be losing his strength and so tried to breathe deeper. He felt like an old man as he tried to get some distance between that thing and him. Although John refused to look, it never seemed to be too far behind him and John was trying to think where he could hide.

It was pointless going into a bedroom he thought. He must go to the attic and reach the hidden room at the far end. The feeling of fear in his middle and around his heart was stifling and he guessed that today was the day he would die. Dying could not feel any worse than this. This must be a heart attack or a brain explosion. John kept hold of the dogs as he scrabbled through the attic door. He shut the door behind him and locked it and he put the dogs on the floor.

John and his two best dogs ran up the attic steps and already he could hear the thing banging against the door, trying to get to them. The dogs were one with him now and he whispered,

"Puppies, puppies - come on girls. Come with me. We must hide." He must protect them at all costs. Their lives and safety seemed more important than his own, especially if he was to die right here, right now. He couldn't leave them to the mercy of this monster.

He moved some cabinets and opened the supposedly invisible door in the wall where John scooched the dogs in and he followed quickly. As he closed the door and barred it, he heard the attic door at the stair bottom give way. He thought he would cry. He put his fingers to his lips and said,

"Ssssh my little babies. Don't make any noise, we don't want him to hear us." The dogs understood him and hid under a small bed in the corner. John moved some small boxes in front of their hidey hole.

"There girls, you are safe so long as you don't make a noise and show your faces. Please, please, please stay safe."

John turned and heard the thing banging against his door. Then the wood began to crack and splinter and John saw a hand peep through the ragged hole. The leather gloved fingers broke the wood until the demon's hooded face could fit through. Now John could see the dark skeletal face and hollow eyes staring at him. There was no noise coming from it, not even as it smashed the door down.

"Why are you doing this? Are you the Devil? Please stop!"

The head was pushing through now and the demon's shoulders were showing. John felt inside his shirt and pulled out the crucifix given to him by his mother. He thrust it into the face of this devil man. The action achieved nothing.

"Please," said John- he had never felt so weak in his life. He thrust the crucifix wildly from side to side, trying to touch the thing in its face and – stop it somehow. The fear in his soul that he didn't think could get any worse – was getting infinitely worse. He was going to die, he knew that he was dying right there and then as he felt his heart cease and the blood stop circulating. The fear was leaving him, he was moving away and he heard a voice saying,

"John. Stop it. Stop the world."

It was his father. John slumped back against the bed and reached under it for his dogs.

"The world has stopped John. Your world has stopped. Look around you."

John did look. The demon had stopped - its face and hood and shoulders half in, half out of the broken door. It appeared dead. John looked under the bed and the puppies were snuggled together and he touched them. His hand went through their bodies. His father pointed to the round attic window and John looked outside. He saw the scene he recognised, the horses in the field and the farm and the trees. Everything had stopped and it was as a painting, flatly spread out in front of him.

"Am I dead, Father?" he asked.

His father laughed and John awaited his fate.

"We are all dead, my son."

"Did I have a heart attack? Was it my brain? What happens now? Do I get to see Jesus?"

"No John. We are all alive and dead at the same time."

"I don't understand."

"See all of this? Everything is flat, lifeless. Can you see?"

"I thought that was because I was dead? I am talking to you, that's proof enough I should say."

"You are recognising that we create our life. We can start it and stop it if we don't like it."

"I still don't understand."

"You saw that demon following you. You created it. It is there because you are full of fears and anxieties and you think they are closing in on you. You try and run away from them and they keep coming and then you fight them and they are still there."

"I don't see, Father."

"You have just stopped your unpleasant creation. Now you can see that it isn't as real as you believe it to be. Nothing is as real as you think it is. You give it life with your thoughts and you can take its life away."

"What should I do now?"

"For a start, I should get rid of that demon there and have something much nicer. A happy life, a happy marriage, anything you want."

"And where will the demon go? Will he be hiding back in the house?"

"He only exists because you allow him to. Decide you don't want it in your life. Decide what you want in your life."

"But, the Devil?"

"The Devil only exists when you recognise him. So, don't. The Devil is only doubt personified. Ignore him as you would ignore a person you no longer want to have contact with. Pay him no attention. Trust in yourself."

"Alright Father."

John felt the tension leave him and his fear went the same way. His shoulders dropped and he saw that he was in control. The demon vanished, the door fixed and his dogs yapped and scrabbled at the boxes in front of the bed. John moved them and the dogs ran to him and sat wagging on his lap, licking and nuzzling him.

"If you want to keep the Devil away, then only imagine the things you want. Don't give him the chance to sneak back into your life."

"Should I go to church more?" asked John, who was not a big churchgoer.

"Not necessarily, nor try and be really good. Just be aware that you are going to get what you think and the Devil is part of that."

"Are you sure about this? And are you really my father?"

"I am."

The spirit disappeared.

John went downstairs and the dogs happily followed him as if nothing had happened. He felt nothing out of the ordinary. He felt no fear that a demon would appear because he saw that he was causing it to come.

As he took some bread and meat, throwing some down to the dogs and thought about what had just happened, he felt light hearted and somehow free. He thought about his estate and his dogs and Agnes and how life without any of them would be unbearable. Then he stopped.

"I should be careful how I think," he said to his dogs.

He had been fine and managed to correct his wayward fears until just now at the church. The old feelings of, 'what if this was the wrong thing to do' and 'this marriage with Agnes is until I die.' He stopped his world and readjusted his thoughts. He wasn't sure how his thoughts affected other people and he didn't want Agnes scared or hurt. He didn't want to project his fears and his monsters on to her.

John smiled as broadly as any man could do when he saw his bride walking towards him. He reminded her on many occasions during their life together, of how he felt at that moment. Telling her about it meant he could calm her down when she was worried or upset and cheer her up when she was cross with him.

The witch on the moor was right - they were meant for each other.

"We are meant for each other," said Agnes.

"What is that my dear?"

Agnes opened her eyes and saw a woman in a cap looking at her and smiling.

"What are you saying my dear? Do you need a drink or something?"

"No, I don't. Where is my family? Where are my girls and my boys?"

"Thomas and Blanche are coming this afternoon and John will be here later."

"Good. I won't be around for much longer so I need to see them all during this week."

"Now we don't want any talk like that. You are just being a silly girl."

"Don't talk to me as though I am an idiot, my mind is perfectly sharp, I have decided to join my husband in Heaven. He is expecting me."

"That's right my dear, whatever you say. I shall just go and organise your lunch."

The nurse scuttled out of the room and Agnes sat herself up in bed. Although she was determined to die as soon as she had sorted out her estate, she was not as ill as she let the others believe. Agnes was quite sure that she would be dying this summer and that was fine.

She thought of the witch on the moors.

Everything she said had come true. Neither she nor John had ever told anyone else that they consulted Grace Trelawney on many occasions and her advice had always been good. She had finally died at well over 100 years old many years ago after telling Agnes that she would see them both soon. Each time she saw the hooded figure, she would speak to John. He told her that the rings would keep them safe,

"We must never take off the rings," he told her.

Her beloved John died peacefully on the second day of the New Year 1616 and devastated Agnes. The weather had been freezing cold. Snow began to fall during the middle of December 1615 and had continued through to March 1616. It meant that the grave they dug for John had taken days because the ground was too solid.

The funeral had to be held up until the work was finished. The children kept trying to tell their mother that the delay was caused by something else as they did not want to upset her. Agnes was seeing the hooded figure almost all of the time and she would close her eyes tightly, praying to John to come and save her. Every time she opened her eyes he was gone again.

"Don't be silly my children, this is not the first year that it has taken a long time to dig a grave. I expect your father does not want to go into the ground before me."

"Mother, please don't say such things, it scares me!" said Johan.

"Your father was almost eighty years old and I am seventy. We have had our time and a very happy time it has been. I consider myself to be a very lucky woman. I have had money and happiness and best of all ten wonderful, clever, handsome children. What more could I ask for?"

"You have paid back any good fortune you have had. Father and you have been generous and kind to your family and also to your neighbours. You have been welcome in all the big houses and good families hereabouts but have never failed in your duty to those worse off. We are all very proud of you both," said Thomas, her eldest son. He was to inherit the entire properties and estate but Agnes knew he would look after his brothers and sisters.

Once her husband was buried, Agnes retired to Churchland at the corner of the lands which overlooked the Ivy Bridge. Previously there had been an alehouse and prior to that a chapel on this spot. The older buildings were now incorporated in the outhouses. She took two maids with her whom she knew would look after her every need.

Thomas sent a man down most days to deal with any heavy or outside work. Agnes walked over to the main house most days and supervised work being done there too, much to the indignation of Blanche, Thomas's wife but who wisely kept her tongue.

Agnes rang the bell which had been left on her night table for that very purpose. After a few seconds the maid came into the room.

"Yes Mrs. Prideaux, what can I do for you?"

"Inform my children that we shall be having a picnic on the moor this Sunday. They must all attend and you must organize all the food and drink. We shall go by Harford Church on the way and attend service together. See to it Mary."

The maid looked at her mistress and guessed what was on her mind. She had seen this before - gathering the family together and setting everything to rights.

The end was near.

Mary smiled and said, "Of course Mrs. Prideaux, consider it done. You shall have a great day, the best day of your life."

"Not the best, Mary. That was the day I married my John."

On the following Sunday, a long line of Prideauxs riding in traps and riding horses, set off early towards Harford Church. Rector Andrew Helyer watched them all arrive from the church door. He had been forewarned about the event and he wanted to ensure that his great benefactor Agnes Prideaux was looked after properly. He made sure that her pew had a blanket upon it. The church was incredibly damp and many parishioners believed that bad chests were inevitable if the parson preached for too long.

Agnes was dressed in a beautiful gown of pale blue and white. Her husband loved her in these colours, they suited her so well.

Her hair still lustrous and shiny although now grey was styled carefully. Agnes had no need of a wig and as she stepped down from the carriage, was still a head turner. The family bustled around her and walked slowly with her up the path to the church.

They walked the very same steps to the church door that she had walked thousands of times before. The trees swayed in the light breeze and the flowers on the grassy banks and around the graveyard, dazzled the eye and threw out their scent in the glorious early sunshine. The old stone cross by the gate was covered with lilies and cornflowers on the instruction of her son Thomas.

"Good morning Mrs. Prideaux. It is an absolute pleasure to see you looking so well. I have heard such bad news about your health of late."

"I shall call you to the house when I am ready to go, have no fear. But today I am enjoying a day out with my family."

"It is wonderful to see all your children and grandchildren with you. There will be some squashing to fit them all in today."

Agnes glided into the church followed by her family. The local people, who turned out in numbers this morning were rewarded with a great spectacle of Prideaux finery.

"I would rather they all gathered for me while I lived than after my death," she whispered to Thomas.

"You are very naughty Mother," was his answer.

Later that morning, the party made their way up to the moor and the women set out chairs and the picnic.

"There is so much food here Blanche, I wonder whether it will all be eaten."

"Never fear mother, we shall eat all of this before we return. The men and the children are always hungry!"

A canopy was raised over the chair and table which Agnes was to use. Other canopies were placed round the same area and soon the whole area looked very promising.

"This is beautiful," said Agnes. "But this is not as sparse as when your father and I used to come here on our own. We only brought a little food and drank water from the stream. But I have to say that the water did not taste as nice as this wine. I do miss John and coming to see the old lady in the cottage."

Agnes smiled as she began to nod off.

The rest of the Prideaux clan watched her carefully and the hearts of her children were collectively filled with a mixture of love and nostalgia. They knew instinctively that Agnes was not long for this world, even though she could quite easily live another ten years if she put her mind to it. But it was not to be, for Agnes was determined to join her husband.

"He will be lonely without me," she said, whenever asked why.

Birds circled overhead and every so often a rabbit or a wild cat could be seen. The grandchildren enjoyed pointing out any wildlife and having it identified by the adults. The Prideauxs encouraged education at every opportunity and they expected their offspring to know the names of all flora and fauna and learn about the history of Devon and Cornwall, in addition to their own family history.

Agnes opened her eyes and watched her large brood playing and resting in the sun. Some sat in chairs under canopies and some lay flat on their backs enjoying the sun on their faces.

Her eyes wandered over to the line of ancient stones to her right. John and she had spent many hours around these old monuments and if she were to tell the truth to her families, four of them had been conceived there.

There it was - the lone wolf. He looked over at the group and then fixed Agnes with a stare of recognition. Agnes laughed and shouted,

"Hello John!"

The wolf stayed for a few minutes and then turned away from the stones and vanished.

"Time to head for home now, mother," said Francis. Henry followed his brother as he always did. Henry her fourth child had a learning difficulty, but was clever nonetheless.

"Mother when you die, you will be living here won't you?"

"Yes Henry, I shall be here with your father."

"I shall visit you here when I want to speak to you then."

They hugged.

Soon everyone was loaded back onto the traps and making their way down from the moors. Agnes was happy and tired in equal measure. The sun was now low in the sky but still radiated heat and light which made their journey a very pleasant one. The further down the valley they travelled, the more flies, bees and butterflies came to join them. Agnes listened to the birdsong and watched the wildflowers waving in the light breeze. By the time they arrived back at the large house she had known from being a young girl, she felt about 20 years old.

Agnes was so relaxed that her sons were able to carry her carefully into her bedroom. After being undressed by her maids, she asked that they bring her children into her room.

As they were all assembled Agnes said,

"I want you all to know that I love you all equally and I have enjoyed my life with you and particularly today, more than I can ever say. I must leave the property to Thomas as that is the way things are done. However, the rest of you have either made good marriages or have enough money of your own."

"Mother, why are you talking like this? It is upsetting me," said Richard.

"Because she wants everything sorted out so that she can fly with the birds tomorrow," explained Henry.

"That is correct, Henry. I just want you to know that you must enjoy and make the best of every moment of your life, because our life here is very short. I heard that time and time again from my elders and I thought that they were just jealous because I was younger and they had made a mess of their own lives. There are the early days when you are feeling superior because of your youth and then, when not expecting it, someone tells you that you are too old to understand and you cannot work out what day everything changed. So, goodnight all and God bless."

The family trooped out of her room and when they sat downstairs a little later on, the mood was somber. The women still wore their finery from their day out and the men were tanned and glowing from the sun. All the children were now in bed back at the main house in the care of the maids.

"I hope Mother is alright," said Thomas.

"She will do as she pleases, as always," said Blanche.

The nurse discovered Agnes had died in her sleep when she went to draw the curtains the following morning. She reached to close the curtains of the room in preparation for laying out the little body of her mistress. The room felt full of people, although they were the only two present. The nurse ignored this familiar feeling which she experienced every time she dealt with the recently passed.

"She looked so peaceful and happy," she commented later.

The funeral was held at Harford Church and Agnes was buried next to her beloved husband for eternity. It was only Thomas who saw two hooded black shapes standing behind the altar. He thought they were moving towards the coffin and stood up with a scream frozen in his mouth, pointing. He was pulled back down to the pew by Blanche, who imagined that he had some sort of funny turn with the stress of it all.

When Thomas and Henry were riding out on the moor a week later, they travelled to their last picnic place. As they rested for a moment and remembered quietly that last Sunday, Henry spoke,

"Look over there Thomas! Mother and Father together again!"

Thomas looked in the direction Henry pointed, but all he could see were a pair of wolves standing together by the ancient stones. The four of them looked at each other for a time before the wolves turned and walked off to be lost in the mists of the moor. Thomas reached for the two rings he had hanging from a leather thong around his neck. The ones their parents had worn. Thomas had taken the rings from their parents' bodies. Thomas never told anyone in the family that he had taken them. He also didn't know how much he was now protected.

"Wolves mate for life you know, Thomas," said Henry. "Just like Mother and Father."

STOWFORD DEMONS

Featuring Thomas Prideaux (1571 - 1641)

1588

"Oh Mother! It was so exciting! I have definitely decided that I want to be a sailor!"

Thomas Prideaux was sixteen years old and full of wonder and awe ever since he had accompanied his father to Plymouth and seen the might of the English Navy docked there and awaiting a battle with the Spanish Armada.

"There were hundreds of ships in the harbour and sailors all over the town. They are waiting for the Spanish fleet."

"That sounds a little worrying," said his mother. These skirmishes had been going on for years now and Agnes was scared that one day these dreadful foreign people would land at Plymouth and invade their county.

As if reading her thoughts, Thomas continued,

"There is talk that the Spanish are coming to invade England via Plymouth. They say that they will land there and march through the countryside towards London and kill the Queen."

"Don't frighten your brothers and sisters with talk like that, Thomas," warned his father John.

"But your cousin Captain Prideaux is sailing with the fleet and he told me what was happening. He would not lie to me, would he?"

"It is not a question of lying - it is a matter of what we talk about in front of the family," said his father carefully.

"What is happening John? This talk worries me," said Agnes.

"I will tell you later, there is nothing to worry about. The Navy is sorting out the problem."

The children carried on with their meal. In other large houses such as theirs, the children would generally eat with the maids but not in this Prideaux household. The whole family sat down and ate their meals together. This ensured that the family was not only close but also that there were very few secrets to be kept.

Thomas, Johan, Agnes, Henry, John, Hugh, Christopher, Richard, Elizabeth and Francis sat around the large oak table on chairs of varying heights, while their parents John and Agnes sat at either end of the table. The family lived in a large granite house and farmed land in Stowford. They were great friends with the Williams family, their nearest neighbours.

The Williams' ancestors along with the inhabitants of Harford and Cornwood looked to the moor for their income through tin mining and farming. John's Great Aunt Alice Prideaux had married Adam Williams, his wife's great uncle and the families remained connected through blood lines and friendship.

Food was passed down the table and Agnes continued her lecture.

"Our Queen will have the whole situation in hand. She knows better than any of the men under her control about Philip and the Spanish threat. She is the greatest monarch this country has ever known and I am convinced that so long as she draws breath, there will never be another invasion on the shores of England. So, do not be concerned my children. We are safe."

John gave a round of applause.

"Well said my love, although I am sure that Philip would be less content to invade us if privateers from this country did not constantly steal from his ships!"

"They are only getting back that which is rightfully ours." Agnes could always be relied upon to stand up for a woman. She taught her children the same beliefs and her husband John, a man with great regard and respect for his own mother would never try and alter those teachings.

"Anyway, the beacons worked well and the Fleet knew when the Armada appeared off St Michaels Mount in Cornwall."

"How did they do that?" asked young John, always a questioning child. At nine years old he told anyone who would listen, that he intended to make his way in the larger world. His family was quite used to his questioning attitude and his mother encouraged him whenever she could.

"Because a fire is kept ready to light on all high places along a chain from Lands End to London and beyond. As soon as those Devil ships were sighted off Cornwall, the first fire was lit and as soon as that fire was seen by the people manning the next one, then that fire was lit," answered Thomas, always happy to show that he knew more than his younger siblings.

"I hear that Prideaux Castle was one of the beacons."

"You are right about that Mother," said Thomas.

"The Navy left Plymouth and chased the Spanish up the Channel. Mark my words, our Queen will have them defeated before the end of the month," announced Father.

"Let us raise our glasses to our great and glorious Queen Elizabeth!" said Agnes and all at the table obeyed, with the exception of the babies who merely laughed and banged spoons at the general merriment.

The children worked around the farm as soon as they were old enough, but their parents also insisted they attended their education and in addition a local and retired Oxford man taught them. Their education added to the great confidence of a wealthy family. Harford Church was attended every Sunday, as religion featured strongly in the lives of the Prideauxs.

"It does not do any harm for our neighbours to see us attend church and show them our finery on a Sunday," said Agnes many times. To be truthful, Agnes and John felt very strongly about their connections to the Williams and other more affluent branches of the Prideaux family and enjoyed the social extension which church attendance offered. On more than one occasion a financial contribution had been made when pressed by the Rector. John had inherited all the properties and lands they occupied just before he married Agnes. They were responsible for tenants and house and farm servants. However, the cash flowed less easily while their glorious Queen fought her expensive political battles and so stretched her tax hikes as far as Devon and Cornwall.

In spite of all this, the couple ensured that all of their sons attended the Ashburton Grammar School. Thomas was always going to inherit the Stowford farm, but John and Agnes intended that the rest of the family should be set up in good careers or trades.

1594

John was proving to possess the greatest academic gifts and he applied for the post of parish clerk at Ugborough parish church when he was sixteen and due to leave the grammar school.

He attended an interview and although failed to obtain the post, Lady Fowell, yet another well connected cousin, heard him sing a psalm so beautifully that she immediately insisted that he attend further education at Ashburton under a scholarship from her in order to learn more Latin. John was ecstatic and his parents overjoyed. Thomas and the others were less interested in their brother's apparent good luck. They instead chose to dwell on the interview where there had been a singing competition between John and another in front of the entire congregation at Ugborough after the morning service. They listened to both singers and decided that the other boy was the best and therefore, apparently, a better bet for the role of parish clerk. There were many times in later years when John would call in at the church on his visits home in his envious finery, just to say hello.

"What are you going to do with all this learning John?" asked Henry.

"Go to London and meet the Queen," was his answer.

"Will you tell her about me, John?"

"Of course."

"What shall you tell her?"

"What a clever brother I have who is always kind to animals and can charm the wild creatures right out of their holes and onto his knee."

Henry laughed. It was of little concern to Henry that he was not quite as quick in the mind as the others and that schooling had been out of the question for him. He was happy exactly as he was and no one would argue with that.

Hugh was a boy full of mischief and devilment. He would hide when everyone else was ready for church and would only appear as the two carriages began to leave the drive ready to make the journey through the narrow lanes towards Harford.

One Sunday on the return journey he incurred the wrath of his elder brother Thomas.

"Tom has got a girlfriend! Tom has got a girlfriend!" Hugh had shouted over and over again. Thomas leant over and caught Hugh a good thump across the head.

"Thomas! What has got into you?"

"Nothing Mother," he answered.

"Then apologise to your brother. This is the Lord's day."

"I am sorry Hugh," Thomas said dutifully but insincerely. His eyes told Hugh that as soon as they were out of sight of their parents, he would clout him again.

Thomas had not had a good weekend. He was in love, madly in love with Blanche, the daughter of another gentleman farmer and who lived near Cornwood. Blanche loved Thomas too, but marriage was out of the question.

Blanche told anyone who enquired that her father needed her at home to keep him company now that her mother was dead. Because of his frail health, he would not countenance her marrying anyone. Blanche was a more than a little frightened of her father she said and felt duty bound to stay with him. Unfortunately, her mother had made her promise to look after her father and be obedient to him, while on her deathbed.

"Deathbed requests are not fair," reasoned Thomas. "After all, we change our minds constantly and to have something we said once apply forever, just does not make any sense. Your mother would want you to be happy and I will make you happy."

"Don't say that Thomas. I did promise Mother and perhaps as more time passes, Father will come round and we can marry."

"But you won't even let me ask him!"

"I don't want him upset. Things will work out for the best, you see."

"Well perhaps I don't want to wait until things work out Blanche. I can't wait around for you forever, I have needs too."

"Don't then," said Blanche and turned on her heel.

"I shall join the Navy then and you will never see me again!" he shouted at her.

"Good! Then your brother shall inherit the estates and I shall marry him instead!"

That was yesterday and Thomas had regretted what he said immediately. He watched her walk away from him and he climbed on his horse and began the ride back to Stowford. That afternoon had not gone as he planned. Then this morning at church, Blanche stayed close to her sister and did not look in his direction once. He felt terrible.

Agnes noticed all, but chose to say nothing. She would wait until she was on her own with her son and sort out his problems then. But due to their busy life, they did not have chance to talk until the following Thursday just after dinner. Agnes fulfilled her promise and told her son that she would see if she could persuade Blanche's father to accept a married daughter. Agnes liked Blanche and she wanted Thomas to be as happy as she and John had been.

"If we put our minds together, we shall work something out, you see," she told him. Thomas hugged his mother, he really loved her.

1596

Upon John Prideaux's successful graduation from Ashburton School, another opportunity for him came up. Lady Fowell had insisted that he should follow his fellow West Countrymen and attend Exeter College at Oxford University. She promised to sponsor him so long as he remained frugal.

John and Agnes discussed the matter at the meal table as usual. The family all listened intently.

"Oxford is a big step for any man John," his father informed him.

"I know father, but I am up to the task. I love learning and I find it easy to do. The only problems for me will be paying for the education and leaving you all in the lurch back here with regard to the farm. Lady Fowell has said she will help."

"We are coping easily with the work, John," said Thomas. "Hugh is old enough now and Richard works hard after school."

"I help too!" said Henry.

"Without your help and support, we should not be able to cope, Henry," answered his father with meaning.

"I think that you should go and make us all proud," said his mother.

"How shall I pay?" asked John. He desperately wanted to go to the great university and be one of the names who would be recorded forever. Lucky for him that Elizabethan Britain was a place where even the less well-off could be educated if they set their mind to it.

"We shall speak to our cousins and see what can be arranged," said Agnes, determined that her son should be an Oxford man. That would be something to boast about.

It was soon settled. Money was collected and put to one side for John's education. John decided that he would make his own way to Oxford and save money. Cousins from Devon would be awaiting his arrival and a job working in the kitchens at Exeter College had been arranged. He was to wait on as a servitor on his fellow sojourners and the Fellows of the college. In return he would receive board and lodging and pay only a small amount for tuition.

Exeter College had been founded in 1314 by Bishop Stapledon, the same worthy man who had founded Ashburton College. Many of the great and good West Countrymen attended both institutions.

John planned to walk to Oxford from Stowford, a total of 170 miles, in a pair of leather breeches which he kept hanging in his wardrobe for the rest of his days. They helped keep his mind out of the clouds, he said.

With numerous instructions from his mother, John set off early one morning in late September 1596 in order to make the life changing journey to Oxford University. He was given a lift to the Kings Highway by Thomas and hoped to get another lift from there on one of the many carts which made their way along that road.

Agnes insisted that he should not walk from their front door to the highway which ran along the edge of their land. John pointed out that he could quickly walk over the fields, over the gate and be on the road, but she would have none of it.

"It is bad enough that you must walk from there," she said.

A debate had opened about the possibility of finding a ship from Plymouth to London, but John was not as keen on this option as he would have little control should anything go wrong.

"I wish you all the luck in the world, John. I shall miss you greatly," his big brother Thomas said to him.

"I shall miss you too, big brother. I hope you are married to that girl of yours the next time I see you."

Thomas reddened and looked at the ground.

"I shall let you know brother."

They both felt embarrassed. Years of pushing each other around and arguing had prepared them badly for this goodbye.

"Got the prayer?" asked Thomas.

"In my bag," answered John, patting the leather satchel.

"You know it by heart though."

"We all do," answered John.

With no prompting, they both chanted,

"O God, That knowest us to bee set in the midst of so many and great dangers, that for Mans frailenesse we cannot always stand uprightly, guard to us the health of Body and Soul, that all those

things which we suffer for sinne, by thy holy wee may well passé and overcome, through Jesus Christ our Lord."

The prayer had been handed down through the Prideaux family and had been used particularly to ward off plague.

"We shall see each other many times Thomas, do not despair. I shall make my family proud."

"It does not matter. Even if you do not achieve what you set out to do, we shall always be proud of you." The brothers hugged and faced each other.

"Are you going to watch me walk away?" asked John sheepishly.

"No, ride away, here is another lift. You have your money and everything?"

"Yes Thomas, I will write to you all as soon as I am in Oxford." John leapt aboard the back of a cart, the driver of which the young men knew vaguely and John sat facing his brother and his home until they rounded the next corner.

John would never live at Stowford again.

The road was not a great deal wider than the back lanes. Only a cart and a horse could comfortably pass each other. The roads travelled up and down the hills and turned past every nook and cranny. There appeared to have been no attempt to make a straight road anywhere. It had once been said in Parliament when discussing the state of the Devonian highways, that they may as well be turned into canals, there was so much running water to be found upon them.

The day was a beautiful summer day with the green hedges and flowers reflected against the blue sky. Thomas watched until the cart rounded a corner and then he clicked at his horse and made his way back to the farm.

Thomas was surprised to realise that he was silently crying. The family was always together and now with John leaving so soon after both Johan and Agnes had announced their intentions of marrying local men - it felt as though the whole family were splitting up.

Thomas became deep in thought as he headed back to the house and then suddenly he turned the pony and trap around at the end of the lane and headed towards Cornwood.

Thomas arrived at the door of Blanche's home and knocked. A maid answered.

"Where is Miss Bigbury?" he asked.

"At the stables Sir," she answered. Her eyes were taking in the entire scene. She would have a lot to tell cook about Master Prideaux coming to the front door and looking all upset.

Thomas led his horse round to the stables and saw Blanche about to mount her horse.

"Blanche, I must talk to you!"

"Oh, Thomas, I didn't expect you. I am going riding now." Blanche's maid was also in attendance but nothing was going to stop Thomas now.

"Blanche, I want you to marry me and I don't want to wait."

"Is that so?" she answered and began to trot on.

"Blanche, will you stop and listen to me?"

Blanche waited until Thomas caught up with her and asked, "Has John left now?"

"Yes, he has, I have dropped him at the highway this morning. Blanche, I love you and want to marry you, may I please ask your father's permission?"

Blanche was impressed with his persistence. Today she was feeling saucy and said,

"Yes Thomas, you may."

Thomas thought he would burst, but instead of doing that, he allowed Blanche to ride away, giggling with her maid.

He drove the trap directly back to the house. A sulky maid answered the door this time and glared at the trap left in front of the house,

"The Master won't like that cart being left out there."

"Have a man move it then. I doubt I shall be long."

John was eventually led into the library by the scowling maid and he prepared to wait there until Philip Bigbury should appear.

He didn't have to wait long for after a few minutes the library door began to creak open and a face peered around it. In all the nine years he had courted Blanche, he had never met her father, as he was always ill and incapacitated. So, for that reason Thomas had no way of telling if the man who shuffled into the room with the aid of a heavy stick was Mr. Bigbury or not. Thomas quite naturally assumed that he was.

Thomas stood up as Bigbury came further into the room and held out his hand saying,

"It is a pleasure to meet you Sir. I am Thomas Prideaux of Stowford and I am here to ask for your daughter's hand in marriage."

Bigbury looked at him as though he were a tree talking. Thomas smiled, waiting for a response from his prospective father to be, but found it difficult to maintain when there was no response. He tried again,

"Sir, may I help you to your chair?"

As Thomas walked towards him, the man raised his stick in the air and brought it down hard on Thomas's arm. Thomas pulled it back and began rubbing it in order to ease the sting, puzzled and bemused.

"Sir, why did you do that? I have done you no harm!"

Bigbury did not answer and instead shuffled towards Thomas, waving the stick as though it was a sword and this was a battle. The stick landed heavily on Thomas's arm and it hurt. John tried to grab it but the old man hit him across the head, drawing blood. Thomas dodged past him and made for the library door. It should open easily but he still pulled the handle sharply, hoping for a quick escape and sanity returning. When this produced no positive result, he knocked on the door and shouted.

"Why do you shout?" asked the old man.

"Because you keep hitting me with your stick Sir and I don't want to retaliate and make things worse."

"I will kill you," he said.

"But why Sir? Because I wish to marry your daughter? I love her and have loved her for years and if we don't marry soon I shall have to marry someone else and provide heirs for the Prideaux estates. I don't want anyone else, I want your daughter and she wants me." Thomas realised he was sounded plaintive, but his heart was racing and his anxiety levels high.

"I like killing people, I have killed before and I will kill again. I must." Bigbury's face seemed to turn into a much younger image than before and he began to move in a jerky manner towards Thomas.

Thomas, for his part was feeling hot and sweaty. No one was coming to the door in response to his cries and he was now wedged against the corner of the door jam and the wall. He became properly scared when he discovered that he was losing control of his limbs and his senses. Bigbury was close to him now, his face upturned because he was at least a foot shorter than Thomas. His old arms were surprisingly strong and they grasped John like a vice. His breath smelt and Thomas was horrified to notice the teeth on the old man. They were long and looked so sharp and his tongue was licking the air, long and red and...

When Thomas woke, he noticed three people standing over him. He recognised the maid who had granted him access, a manservant of some kind and a gentleman.

"Prideaux, Prideaux, what's all this?" asked the gentleman.

"Err, mmm. The man, the old man. He did this."

The gentleman gave instructions for Thomas to be helped to the chair because of his very wobbly legs. Wine was brought and after drinking some, Thomas felt better and able to talk.

"Bigbury, he was trying to kill me I think. I don't know why."

"Bigbury?" asked the gentleman. "I am the only Bigbury here and I found you in a dead sleep and blocking my library doorway. We had to enter through the windows from outside."

"But the old man? With the stick and the teeth and the smell?"

The others looked at each other with concern.

"Please describe him to us Prideaux," instructed the gentleman.

This Thomas did and the gentleman sat down, shoulders slumped.

"It seems you have seen our ghost, Prideaux. He hasn't been about for a while."

"Ghost? What? Who is he? He was real, not a ghost!"

"He is a ghost. He is my great uncle and he used to live in the attic because he …" began the gentleman.

"He used to attack and kill people and they kept him locked up until he died. But he missed the place and won't leave. He doesn't generally make himself visible to strangers now and I'm not really sure why he chose you."

It was Blanche saying this and she came over to Thomas, knelt next to him and stroked his face. Thomas took her hand and kissed it.

"We can marry now, father. Thomas knows the truth and won't tell anyone, will you?"

"Tell anyone? About a ghost?"

"No, about the murders," said the real Mister Bigbury.

"I didn't get from what you told me that he actually used to murder people."

"He still does," said the maid.

"Leave us Anna and fetch more wine and perhaps some food," instructed Blanche.

"This is the real reason you could not marry. We are not so shamed about having a ghost, it is the fact he is a member of our family and a killer," Bigbury whispered.

"I want to marry Blanche and therefore I shall tell no one," said Thomas.

"Alright," agreed Bigbury as he leant back heavily in his chair. "My boy, I know your family very well and your parents are people of their word. I do not have the strength to look after my daughters for all of their lives. I want them to have husbands on whom I can rely."

Bigbury appeared beaten and spent - his face now much paler than when he had entered the room. The stress of the confessions appeared to be getting the better of him. Thomas sat on the chair opposite and both men heaved their breaths until they fell asleep.

1597

As it turned out, the marriage could not be arranged until the following summer because Blanche wanted a large affair at Harford Church and the celebrations afterwards to be held at Stowford.

A large and well attended wedding they did have and Blanche's only disappointment was that her father was too unwell to attend. He had allowed his house servants to go to Harford Church to see their mistress marry Thomas Prideaux and return for dinner and tell him all the news. Unfortunately, the servants became lost in the freedom and the merriment and forgot to go back home. It was during the early hours of the morning when many were drunkenly sleeping off their celebrations, when a rider came galloping into the Prideaux House yard.

He jumped from his horse and threw the reins at a tired looking man.

"Where is your Master?" he asked.

"I ain't got no Master," he answered back in a surly manner.

"Where is the Master of this house then? Mr. Prideaux?"

The farmhand pointed to the main door and the rider strode towards it. After some conversation with a maid he was allowed in. It took almost five minutes before shouting and screaming sounded from the upstairs windows and Thomas and his father John ran out of the front door.

Old man Bigbury was dead. An unexplained fire had begun in the library of the old house during the night and the place had swiftly burnt to the ground. A passing peddler, who had seen the fire start and reported it, had also seen an old man silhouetted against the library windows. He initially said that the man had been shouting for help but on reflection, considered that the old man was probably dancing.

"I didn't think that was possible at first," he related. "But, he seemed glad the fire was burning. It wasn't old Bigbury, it was a much older man."

"Did you recognise the man?" asked someone.

"No Sir, I never saw him before. He was still at the window when the whole place was aflame and he didn't seem bothered."

"Are you sure it wasn't Bigbury asking for help?"

"Can't have been Sir. I saw him slumped against his bedroom window at the front of the house. I saw them both at the same time."

Thomas Prideaux questioned him further about the strange old man at the library window and was aghast when he realised that the peddler was describing the spirit he had seen last year. When he told Blanche, she refused to listen and said that he shouldn't be trying to cause trouble. Her father was dead and the house razed to the ground. Now her brother would be able to build anew and have their family fortunes change.

John Prideaux, who had returned from Oxford for his brother's wedding, visited the site and performed some sort of prayer and the land was now apparently free of evil.

John had soon settled down at Oxford and wrote to his family often. He worked in the kitchens as promised and spent every spare minute studying and attending lectures. He was always to be found with a book in his hand. He spent little and impressed all with his piety and kindness. His academic dedication was surpassed by none. The family hoped that he knew what he was doing in regard to evil.

Thomas did not feel so confident.

Thomas and Blanche initially lived at Bridgend at the edge of the property and Thomas continued to assist his father run the farm. Johan and Agnes left to marry and the other children kept on with their schooling and various tasks.

Henry enjoyed every one of his days - always.

Thomas and Blanche were soon the parents to John and the busy kitchen at Prideaux House added another chair to the table on Sundays and celebration times, as each new member of the ever expanding Prideaux family arrived.

Thomas's brother Richard moved into Churchland, the house next door to Bridgend, so now both new Prideaux families could overlook the Ivy Bridge. Life was busy, but generally free from trouble and strife.

1615

Thomas would often see dark shapes which he would have identified as a man or a hooded demon, if he had been able to speak to a sympathetic soul. Instead he told himself that as he had only seen the shadow people from the corner of his eye, he could put it down to overwork.

Once he had been standing with his father in the Church Field, behind Churchland as they discussed the cattle and which were in calf and which should be sent to the market, when he saw the shadow against the stone wall. He gasped and stopped talking,

"What is the matter Thomas?" asked his father.

"I can see something over by the wall. Can you?"

"What can you see?"

"It is probably nothing but I thought it was an old man or – well – a monk?"

Thomas dreaded his father's ridicule and so was surprised when he answered,

"So, you can see him too?"

They sat upon the stone trough which was at the farm edge of the field and told each other of their ghostly experiences.

"It seems the whole place is haunted," noted Thomas.

"Or perhaps just the Prideaux family," answered his father.

The hooded man was standing stock still against the wall, head down and caped hands held in front, supported by a cane.

"He's back," said Thomas.

"So it would seem," acknowledged John. "I haven't seen him for a while. I wonder who he has come to fetch?"

"No one I hope," said Thomas.

"If it is me Thomas," John twirled the gold wedding ring on his finger. "I want you to take this ring before

I am buried. Don't tell the others why, but it will protect you from the worst."

"What about you Father?"

"I will no longer need it. I will be living a better life, just as we all will when we leave here. More fun and less stress."

Thomas looked at his father and then turned to the hooded man, still standing guard.

"And look after your mother," added John.

He put his arm around his son and walked him towards the gate on the Highway. As they climbed it, Thomas noticed that the man had now vanished.

1616

The intervening year had meant a lot of changes for the family.

By 1616 Thomas and Blanche were parents to John, Hugh, Susan, Richard and Thomas. Blanche was pregnant with what was to be another son, James. Thomas and his brothers Christopher and Francis all remained at home working on the farm.

But this year was also a very sad year for the family.

Grandfather John had died in the January while there was snow on the ground and Devon was colder than it had been for many winters. He was found dead in the Church Field after apparently suffering a stroke. He had gone out after breakfast and after kissing his wife as usual. It was snowing heavily and Agnes had begged him to be careful.

"You fuss about me too much Agnes. I am well wrapped up and perfectly healthy. I shall be home for lunch, so make sure there is something hot waiting for me."

Agnes held him extra tightly today although she could not explain why.

"Hey wife. What is the matter?"

"John I love you, I want you to know that."

"And I love you too little wife. What is this?"

"I saw the wolf yesterday. He came right up to me while I was walking in the gardens talking to the Goddess and touched my hand. I had such a peculiar feeling of connection. Then he vanished and I could trace no footsteps in the snow."

"You think it is an omen?"

"Perhaps. I don't know. Just be careful."

"And you be careful my wife. But if it means that I am leaving, know that I shall wait for you every day until you come to me. Don't hurry, come when you are ready."

He kissed her again, more slowly this time, and then cupped her chin before he left the house.

When she heard the terrible news later that morning, Agnes fell to her knees and sobbed as until she lost consciousness.

Rector John returned again from Oxford for the funeral. By now he was very famous in his field. He had been finally elected Rector of Exeter College just before his 35th birthday and became Canon of Christchurch, Regius Professor of Divinity and five times Vice Chancellor of Exeter College. It was as though royalty itself had arrived in Harford when

John came to take the funeral service of his father. Some in the family were trying not to resent their brother as he rolled in grandly to Stowford every time there was a family tragedy or celebration. But no one said anything to him. Agnes always made the best food for his visits and would say to the rest of the family,

"Don't touch that! It's for John when he gets here!"

Johan was in pieces and hardly able to cope after her father's death. She told the others,

"I am worried about mother. She and father were so in love that I am afraid she will not last long now. She keeps talking about father being in heaven and how she wants to be with him."

"I shall talk to her," promised John. He had brought his new wife Mary Grace to meet the family, although this was a very awkward first meeting for them all. Nevertheless, she was made welcome and the family remembered this one and only trip to her husband's birthplace fondly, for Mary never returned, dying a year after Agnes.

Once their father John was buried and things had returned to some sort of normality. Agnes's health declined considerably and she talked a lot about joining her husband in death because she missed him so much. Her sons talked to her about life and death and Agnes, promised she would do her best to stay around for a little longer.

Agnes would spend a lot of time in her garden talking to the Goddess there and feeding the wolf. The family paid little attention as they left her to her own devices and smiled when she brought in her basket of flowers and fruit. Agnes sitting in the sunshine or the snow on a bench under an archway of sweet smelling roses, meditated and mind travelled across the moor with her Goddess and wolf and John.

The Goddess was a tall stone statue of a beautiful woman. The statue had been there since before living memory and was often draped in flowers on special occasions. She was considered a good listener and some said she would impart advice. A secretly Catholic Agnes treated her like the Virgin Mary, but naturally kept that fact to herself.

1626

When Agnes finally left them all to begin her next journey, she was buried next to John in the churchyard where they had met, married and christened all their children and attended their weddings.

Her funeral at Harford Church was attended by so many people that some were forced to stand outside in the church yard. The weather that day was beautiful and Thomas felt surreal as he helped carry on his mother's little coffin. It was at this moment that he realised just what a tiny woman she was. She had been so strong and vital all her life and now it was as though they were carrying in a doll in a box.

Harford seemed more beautiful than ever that day. More so than the day he married his beloved Blanche at this little church sitting snugly under the trees. Surrounded by a stone wall, the lane moved past it on two sides, first coming from Stowford and then leading to Dartmoor and its ancient stones, cottages and mines. On the other side, the tiny track led to Cornwood, where the family of Blanche lived.

"I shall read the will as mother wrote it, it is fairly self-explanatory." Thomas informed them. He was standing at the head of the large oak dining table with the family seated around it. These days there were enough matching chairs for the entire family to be seated.

Rector John had managed to return for his mother's funeral and was allowed to take the service. He came alone as his wife was expecting a child and could not travel but he said he must return to Oxford almost immediately.

Thomas cleared his throat and began.

My body to be buried in the church of Harford.

To the poor of Harford 2s.

To my son Hugh 20s.

To my son Richard 20s.

To my son Christopher 20s

To my son Francis 20s and my greatest brasse panne.

To my son Henry 50s and my next greatest brasse panne.

To my daughter Johan 20s.

To my daughter Agnesse Dow my best chest and all my lynnen.

To John Prediaxe his sonne my best cuppe with a silver cover,

To Welmont Burt my little silver cupp.

To little Elizabeth Mychell my great brasse crocke.

To all my children's children 12d each.

To Susan Prediaxe one ewe sheep.

The rest to Thomas Prediaxe my son sole executor.

Also I give him all my rights in Stover as appears by a lease made by Richard Williams.

Sign of Agnes Predyaxe

John Bart of Wedenbury and John Shepherd overseers

Witnesses John Bart and John Shepherd

Inventory made by Richard Prideaux and John Scobble.

"I hope everyone is happy with the outcome," said Thomas to his wife when they were lying in bed later that night.

"It's too bad if they are not," she answered. Blanche at that moment had been planning the redecoration of Stowford. Agnes had been a wonderful woman and the two women got on well but Blanche had always been subtly discouraged from altering the place in any way. Now almost twenty years after her marriage, Blanche was free to do anything she wanted.

It had been difficult when Agnes called every day and still acted and was treated as the lady of the house. Tomorrow Blanche intended to walk around the house and gardens and write notes about her plan. She knew that Thomas would let her carry out the changes because Thomas only ever wanted a quiet life.

"That was a mean thing to say Blanche!" Thomas said to his wife.

"I know, I am sorry I did not mean it. It is just that we are very generous and kind to the rest of the family and we don't have to be. We are like that because it is the right way to be. They all know that we will help whatever goes on."

Thomas hugged Blanche. He knew exactly what she meant. Neither of them was ignorant of their responsibilities.

The couple were proud parents and enjoyed watching their own and their extended family grow. All of Thomas's brothers and sisters had married, with the exception of Henry who spent his time at the farm but lived with Francis his younger brother whom particularly got on with him. This move happened when Francis's first wife had died in childbirth and Henry went to stay with him. Even after Francis married again, the arrangement stood.

Thomas, Richard and Hugh formally signed over their claim to the administration of Henry's goods to Francis and as John had not been available added that,

This wee no doubt not, but that our brother the Doctor in Oxford will be ready and willing to do.

Poor Christopher also lost his wife, but this time as a result of being thrown from a horse. He never recovered from the shock and refused to marry again.

Thomas's son John could be secure in the knowledge that Stowford would belong to him on the death of his parents and the other children must either marry well or learn a trade in order to earn their living. Thomas and Blanche intended that their boys would also have a good property to live in and would not be allowing the extended family into any of the Stowford properties.

1639

The older generation remembered the style and majesty of Elizabeth's reign and so fell strongly behind the King. Others felt that taxation and law had become ridiculous and were for Parliament. Between 1629 and 1640 taxation levels were beyond a joke and despite the money raised, very little was being spent on the people of the land. In Devon and Cornwall the lack of investment in coastal defenses put the inhabitants under threat. Friends and neighbours were forced by their connection to government to collect default on taxes and confiscate their goods and livestock. These were then to be sold at auction, but no one would buy the goods in mutual allegiance and everything would be returned to their owners.

During this year, two siblings of Thomas Senior died. Aunt Agnes and Uncle Henry both died of a fever which ran through the community.

"What a ridiculous world we are living in," commented Thomas's eldest son John, now married and living at Bridgend with his wife Agnes. Hugh and Susan had married children of friends and lived locally. Thomas Junior was still living at home and becoming increasingly political in his beliefs. He had no intention of marrying, instead playing the field of willing local girls, who thought they might marry a Prideaux, should they manage to get 'caught.'

"Father is very upset that Professor John was not able to return from Oxford for their funerals. He is being kept under virtual house arrest and could not risk the journey," said Thomas.

"I think we should put up a plaque in the church in his honour and let the scoundrel Parliamentarians know whose side we are on. Then I am going to fight. Cousin Arthur is raising a troop for the King and I am going to join it. What about you John?"

"I may, but someone has to stay here and make sure that the farm keeps running. Mother and Father are not as well as they were."

Thomas was unimpressed with this attitude and told him that the women could manage on their own. Any fighting would not last for long and could possibly be over by Christmas. They argued for a time as the two often did. But they agreed on a plaque and worded it carefully. The commission was given to their brother Hugh, to be completed without anyone else's knowledge. They knew that the Rector William Hart of Harford would not object to its being put up in the church, if for no other reason than the huge financial contributions the Prideaux family had made to its upkeep over the years.

When the finished article was hung in the main body of the church a month later, many came to look and admire. Thomas and Blanche were pleased although they told their boys that they should have been informed. Their neighbours thought that the

Prideauxs were becoming more 'up' themselves by the day.

Here rest the bodies of John Prideaux of Stoford and Agnes his only wife. The parents of [7] sonnes and [3] daughters.

To Whom

John Prideaux their 4th sonne Doctor of Divinity and their Kings Majesties Professour thereof in the University of Oxford Rector of Exceter Colledge and Chaplain to Prince Henry King James the first and King Charles the first

Hath left this filiall remembrance

July 20 1639

1640

Thomas Prideaux Junior was becoming disillusioned with life 'at boring old Stowford' and informed his parents accordingly. He told his parents, Thomas and Blanche that he wanted to stay with his Uncle John and join him on his travels around Oxford and London.

"He has so much more fun than us down here. I mean, what was that with the witch trial? No one will tell me about it."

His mother changed the subject quickly. She accepted that for a man to be so high up in the Church as her brother in law was, he must deal with the dark side of life, the Devil included. But the rest of the family need not be involved. Everyone was well aware that Professor John had been chosen by King James to be chaplain and tutor to the heir apparent, Prince Henry and then Prince Charles. He had a wife and seven children and so many responsibilities and so much influence, that John Prideaux must be a safe advisor and companion for her precious son.

Blanche knew that she spoiled her petulant and argumentative son Thomas, but she thought she would lose him when he was born and felt responsible ever since. Her husband told her that she would 'turn him funny' the amount of time she spent with him and that she was the reason he still acted like a baby even though he was 31. Blanche ignored him, she had seen something in their son that reminded her of the ghostly old uncle who used to terrorise their home and worried that Thomas had somehow inherited his ghost. Naturally she told no one of this worry, for who would believe her?

Instead she kept a close eye on him ensuring that she could calm his more exuberant moods.

So, Thomas had written to his Uncle John asking for permission to send young Thomas and received a positive response. There was a good deal of high spirits while plans were made and spare money collected and clothes cleaned and mended.

"When my brother John went to Oxford, he walked there in leather breeches and only food and a prayer book to sustain him on the road," Thomas informed his son.

"I've heard that story many times father and while I admire his tenacity, I shall not be walking to my Uncle's house. I shall be riding to Oxford." Thomas folded his arms across his chest in petulant defiance. Knowing looks passed between his father and mother.

However, everything changed just before Thomas was about to leave, when a letter arrived at the house.

Thomas read it at the breakfast table.

"It seems that Uncle John has been accused of encouraging opposition in the University against the reforms of Archbishop Laud. His old pupil King Charles had to attend a hearing at Woodstock and apparently, John has received a good telling off. The King though has said that John should not lose his place as he has been an honest servant to the Crown. Uncle John told the King that no man can be honest all the time. They laughed and apparently, John was sent on his way. He says that although the King helped him out there and would ensure his safety, it is becoming increasingly apparent that there is trouble coming to this country and we must all be on our guard for spies. He thinks that there will come a time soon when brother shall be turned against brother."

"Well that all sounds very gloomy!" said Blanche, anxious to make light of the frightening letter.

"So, what about my trip to Oxford?" asked Thomas.

"My brother does not think that it will be safe for you just yet. He does not want to heighten the awareness of our family connections to Royalty. He says that soon allegiances will matter greatly. He said he will write only in an emergency as he cannot trust that his post is not being intercepted. He no longer tells people that he was born here, but in a different part of Devon altogether."

"Father, I am scared!" said Susan.

"Hush daughter, we shall be fine. We live too far from Parliament and the King. These politics shall not affect us, you'll see."

But Thomas was not nearly as sure as he sounded.

1641

Thomas Junior was conscious that his mother was becoming increasingly saddened and worried by the state of the county and the country as a whole. Arthur Prideaux at Ermington was raising a troop of horse for King Charles and the Stowford Prideauxs agreed to help finance it in whatever way they could afford. Now that he was not allowed to go to Oxford, Thomas was adamant about joining the troop and fighting alongside three of his brothers. Thomas had still not married, considering this a ridiculous world in which to bring up children. His parents also knew that a marriage for Thomas Junior must necessarily mean that he must earn a living for a wife and family but currently he was too lazy and inconsistent to do that. Even so, neither Thomas nor Blanche wanted any of their sons to fight.

"Please don't let them go!" begged Blanche of her husband.

"The boys are grown men Blanche, they must make their own choices. Times are becoming too difficult and perhaps they will need to fight to save us all from ruin."

Thomas did not know how to answer his wife with any comforting words. He heard some terrible stories from his friends which he did not share with Blanche. He was keeping the stress of it all deep within him and had taken to walking and working away from the house as much as he could.

A few days later he met some strangers walking along the Highway. They were dressed in the easily recognisable garb of the Puritans. These people he knew would be travelling from Plymouth in the hope they could get some more ears to listen to their version of the Word of God. Thomas avoided them as a rule when similar people called at the house, instead sending a servant to force them on their way. These past years however, it was becoming increasingly obvious that these door knockers were in the game of obtaining information by gossip and observation to give to their associates if they felt that the Protestant scum were behaving against the Lord in any way.

That activity had been laughable and gossip worthy a few years ago, but lately there had been some repercussions. The words 'witch' and 'traitor' were being bandied about too often. Thomas knew from the experience of his brother John what that could mean. He had spoken to him about it on the Doctor's last trip home. John had told him to keep his head down and claim allegiance to no one.

"It's not a good world to be in at the moment, Thomas. There are strange energies and I believe there is a civil war coming. I know Cromwell and he actually believes his own publicity especially when it comes from the mouths of his agenda writing lackeys. He is a dangerous man who will kill people."

Thomas could not get the statement out of his head and he feared for his family and his land and his responsibilities.

"Are you a believer Sir?" asked one of the men.

Thomas stared at them and did not answer.

"Sir, we asked you a question. Are you a believer or a sinner?"

Thomas began to back up and called his dog to heel.

"There is evil standing with you Sir. What is your name? What is its name?"

A man in the group was pointing to the stone wall at the edge of the field and Thomas turned slowly around. He saw what he presumed the group saw, a hooded man waving a cane. This old man was making his way towards them in the jerkiest fashion, alternatively waving the cane in the air and falling to the ground. For someone who could only make such unusual movements he was making rapid progress towards them.

They froze as the thing came nearer to them, for as it was clearer to view, it was much more like a hooded demon with glowing eyes. Thomas half recognised it as the spirit he had seen in the library so long ago. But surely, this demon was more devil like, less human.

"It is the Devil!" shrieked one of the be-capped women as she staggered backwards.

The men rallied together in voice saying, "It is a familiar. This man is a witch. What is your name Sir? Are you from the Prideaux House?"

Thomas did not know whether he was more frightened of the cloaked scampering man or the group of Puritan snitches. Deciding that escape from this scenario was the best idea, Thomas began to run back to the house, wishing that there were not quite so many high stone walls around his fields. He pushed the scampering man out of his way as he heard from the group, "We shall inform our brothers and sisters of this. You will have to face trial and you will lose your home!"

Thomas felt as though he was running through treacle and he was fast losing his strength. He didn't feel out of breath nor did his legs feel weak. He was feeling lighter and lighter and – unusual. He felt as though his head was moving in front of his body and escaping it. It reminded him of swimming in deep water and he could sense the creature swimming towards him.

"Stop the world," someone shouted. "Thomas! Stop your world!"

His family found him dead in the Church Field when they went looking for him later that evening. He was alone and unmarked and there was a strange silver topped cane next to his body. Thomas's eyes and mouth were wide open, but there was no obvious cause of death.

THE ERMINGTON CURSE

Featuring Thomas Prideaux (1610 – 1680)

One day during May 1641, when his brothers were making preparations to join Arthur Prideaux over at Ermington for a meeting, Thomas Junior burst in to the kitchen at Prideaux House and announced,

"There is a document we must all sign or be seen to sign and God knows what that means!"

"Thomas! Do not take the Lord's name in vain!" said his mother in a shocked voice. Since her husband's death, Blanche had had a visit from Puritan elders informing her that they believed her husband to be a Devil worshipper and that the Prideaux family must change their ways. Now it was certain that the family was being watched and their actions recorded.

"I apologise mother, but this is serious." Thomas threw one of the chairs across the kitchen in a flash of temper – he had been doing that a lot lately.

It seemed that they were all to sign a document which stated that they would be loyal to the King and the rights and privileges of Parliament and to uphold the true Protestant religion. Thomas was finding it difficult to take this constant pressure and worry and was recently veering from serious anger issues to total collapse.

Fearful that signing the documents would make them eligible for something for which they did not wish to be eligible and failing to sign and being branded a Catholic and losing their lands, made for tense times. The neighbourhood was forced to travel directly to Ivybridge on a summoned day in May and sign the Returns. The Prideaux men, Francis, Henry, Hugh, James, John, Richard, Simon and Thomas all signed along with their neighbours.

This done, there was a heightened sense of persecution. Thomas particularly became edgy and his already short temper became nastier. He was obsessing about his Uncle John and the news that his sons were fighting for the King. Thomas became enraged yet again and began smashing a shovel around the courtyard. His brother John had taken over the house since his father's death and was constantly encouraging Thomas to get married, get a job, do anything – just leave.

Thomas ignored him.

When a parliamentary rebellion began in South Devon, Hopton arrived to help crush it, much to the excitement of the Prideaux men and their cousins. This news inspired them to travel to Modbury with Arthur Prideaux to join the posse. The crowd excitement as they waited for the great Sir Ralph Hopton made the whole day seem more like a village fair than a posse. Friends joshed each other and pushed each other around and compared pikes and staffs.

The Prideaux men owned guns and were part of only twenty men so armed. They also owned riding horses and were able to ride to Modbury. Although they were equally excited by the general air of joviality, they were dismayed to see that there was no discipline amongst the men at all. The rabble drank and argued and would listen to nothing they were told in respect of planning for battle. They were keen on the idea of fighting and defending their neighbourhood, but once together in a group they only wanted to party.

Before the motley group was ready, an army of Parliament men quietly moved on the town of Modbury and the unarmed rustics fled for their lives. The Fortescues and Henry Champernowne were captured while all the Prideauxs managed to escape.

"This is dangerous," they said to each other as they galloped back to Stowford vowing not to tell the women just how bad things were becoming.

They kept their heads down for many months, working on the farm and engaging with only a few trusted souls. It was almost impossible to tell who was for the King and who for Cromwell. And it was too dangerous not to know.

Most of the Prideaux family was coping with this way of living, but Thomas found it stressful and difficult and was suffering from tense, angry outbursts interspersed with panic attacks. He was also suffering from bad dreams and hallucinations. Blanche was worried about her son, but then she always had been. Now he was telling her that he could see his father and his grandfather walking around the farm and that he had seen a tall hooded man beckoning to him with a cane. She told him to keep it to himself.

In spite of civil war breaking out all across the country, the men of the south west only came out to fight again in 1643, when there was another attack on the neighbourhood. This time there was hand to hand fighting in the streets of Modbury for many days and there were too many deaths on both sides. The Royalists eventually had to retreat under attack at all boundaries of the town by the Roundheads.

Thomas Prideaux was amongst the soldiers for the Royalist cause and one day he took a rest from the fighting by sitting on an oak bench hidden by shrubbery in the garden of a house just off the main street. Although most of the townspeople had fled, some were still hiding in their houses. As Thomas leant against the side of the house, he heard a voice from the window above him.

"Are you alright?"

Thomas looked up and saw the most beautiful girl he had ever seen, looking out of the window. He felt slightly foolish now that he was cowering behind a bush trying to drink some home whisky from a flask he held in his hand.

"Not really. I have just killed two men I know."

"Oh! What happened?"

"They killed my horse!"

"Well they deserved it," said the girl. "Had you had the horse long?"

"I reared him from a foal and I bred his mother and father and they just killed him and it took ages for him to die. I almost can't bear it." Thomas suddenly felt ashamed for declaring this weakness to a complete stranger. He got up quickly and made to leave.

"Please don't go just yet," she said. "Stay a moment and get your wits back. Would you like to come in and rest?" she added.

"No!" he answered horrified. To go inside a house and rest would be seen as cowardly. But his second thought was the acknowledgement that leaving the fight was exactly what he wanted to do and so he went into her cottage. Thomas was glad to sit down again.

"What is your name?" he asked.

"I am Joane Fox."

"Pleased to meet you Joane Fox, I am Thomas Prideaux of Stowford."

"I know of your family. I am pleased to meet you Thomas Prideaux."

Thomas stood up again and smiled at his new friend. He said with renewed confidence,

"I shall not forget your kindness to me Joane. I shall come back and find you when this fighting is over. Now go and make sure you keep yourself safe."

She rewarded him with a beautiful smile.

"Are you alone in the house?"

"My father is out fighting in the town somewhere. My mother and I are keeping everything safe here."

"Do you have brothers and sisters?"

"No, just father, mother and me."

Thomas was surprised to realise that although he was living amongst death and destruction, he was still pleased to hear that the owner of this lovely face was not married. Better than that, it appeared this lovely face, although a little manly but he liked manly, was sole heir to this house and land. She would do.

The war continued for too many more years and meant a great loss of fortune for the Stowford Prideauxs. Occupation of this area changed hands several times and in some cases people changed their names in order to stay safe. Neighbours were informing on their neighbours and everyone became very different people. Almost no conversations of substance took place and old arguments were surfacing and terrible revenges were being exacted.

It was almost impossible to make money when the men could not tend the stock and fields, leaving this work to the ever-capable womenfolk. The markets were often closed and food and animals were demanded by the armies, whichever army was occupying the farmland at the time. Blanche heard on more than one occasion,

"Mistress Prideaux. Who is the tall hooded man I have seen running through the woods? I fear he would attack me until I fired a shot in his direction."

"I know not Sir," she would answer. "He is not known to us."

Thomas no longer was ridiculed for his ghostly hallucinations as many were seeing spirits of the dead from both sides. It seemed that many recently killed sons and fathers were appearing back at their nearby homes informing their families that they were home for good, only for the same families to learn that at that exact moment he had taken a fatal blow of some sort and the family must go and fetch the body from a collection point in Modbury.

Thomas himself had seen the ghosts of the only two men he had killed. He was at root a coward, but he did love his horses. The ghosts he constantly saw, so recently and so long dead, were not helping his nerves and his excursions between temper and nerves were regular.

One morning he called round to see his brother John at Stowford.

The King had been executed and Thomas now had Woodlands Farm, due to some of the confiscations. He had acquired it from a Prideaux cousin whose branch of the family had occupied the property for three hundred years. Woodlands was situated on land to the south of the Highway and south west of the Ivy Bridge. As with the Stowford Manor and Prideaux land, the Ivy Bridge had a corner on all of their properties. The fourth corner was on land known as Pitt. If the Williams family and the two Prideauxs all stood in the corner of their lands, they could all touch the bridge. These landowners were under obligation to grind their corn at the mills owned by the Williams family which were situated on the Stowford bank.

"John," Thomas said as he entered the familiar kitchen. Although all the children had married and left home, they still treated Stowford as their own home and their brother John and his wife Agnes always made them welcome.

"Hello Thomas, come and sit down. Agnes, make Thomas some food and drink."

Agnes put down her baby and went over to the stove.

"How are Joane and little James?" she asked.

"Fine Agnes, fine. James is turning out to be a fat little baby and Joane spends all her time with him."

"So she should. After losing her mother and father in the fighting, she will want to keep hanging on to the baby."

"I know, that is why she wanted to call him James after her father. We will call the next one Thomas."

"But the property is coming to you though? To her?" John turned to glare at Agnes, the private conversations they had between them about Thomas marrying Joane for her money he did not want voicing outwardly.

Thomas looked at her and answered, "Of course the property and estate is mine. It is my right."

"It is hard to believe how many family and friends have died during the last few years," said Agnes, hoping to change the subject.

"Some from fighting and some from being worn out with worry," reminisced Thomas.

"Bishop John has fared the worst, losing all his five sons and his bishopric. They still consult him apparently, but he now has little fortune and lives with one of his daughters in a small parsonage in Bredon, I think."

"He wrote and said that he is trying to write down everything he has experienced in his life – it should be quite a tale. He is fading fast, what a way to end an important life."

"Leading that life put him in the firing line and perhaps us too, Thomas."

"What do you mean John?"

"You are to lose Woodland Farm, Thomas. The place has been confiscated again and sold and the new man is a Cromwell man who does not approve of us. Too many Royal connections he said."

"What about Joane's properties?"

"Those are currently safe and we must allow the lawyers to do their work."

"When did you find this out, brother of mine?" Thomas was standing now and menacing John with his fist.

John patted the air with his hands, trying to calm his volatile brother.

"I have spoken to Cousin Thomas at Ermington and he has found you a cottage there."

"But we have another baby on the way, Joane will be devastated!"

"There is nothing to be done, believe me I have tried very hard."

He watched Thomas shake and spill his drink. Ever since the fighting, Thomas had become harder to deal with. Seeing all the death and living under stress for so long had affected him badly. His temper was becoming worse and his family would tread carefully around him when he was particularly tense.

Thomas could not make decisions easily and John had kept the news of the loss from him until something had been sorted out, unacceptable as it might have been, at least it was something. It had been left to John to sort out most of the family's problems as heir and Thomas was not good at sorting out his own issues.

"I am sorry Thomas, I have done the best I can for your family. We are sorry that you are to lose your family home and it is heartbreaking. I am however trying to keep Prideaux family money and belongings together and I have a few schemes up my sleeve for that."

"But you are allowing them to take our home?"

"I am doing the best I can. Please don't criticise me."

Times were so difficult. When their Uncle Richard had died in 1645 and his wife Elizabeth a year later, the bulk of their property was left to Thomas Williams at Stowford in order to safeguard it from the government. So many neighbours helped each other out in order to protect lives and property. Sometimes John felt as though his head would explode while Thomas just seemed to ignore everything that was happening.

Agnes stood and watched the brothers carefully. She knew that Thomas may erupt explosively but she loved him as a brother who had experienced much and she considered his wife Joane a sister. She also knew that the Williams family appeared to be ignoring the safeguarding aspect of the Prideaux legacy and were refusing to return it to the family. This meant that the Williams now owned the land across the road and to the north west of their farm. The gardens had been landscaped in Elizabeth's time in her honour and were visited and enjoyed by local and visiting dignitaries alike. If Thomas learnt of that too, he would probably go to them and do something which would require a hanging.

John Prideaux must keep calm.

"You have to leave Thomas, for your family's safety."

Thomas dropped his fist and became almost rigid. John escorted him back to his horse which was tethered in the courtyard and patted his shoulders.

"It will work out fine Thomas, you see."

Thomas turned to him and said, "I shall never forgive you John, for this. Our ancestors will curse you and this property and haunt you to your death."

"Don't be silly Thomas," said Agnes.

As Thomas rode away towards Ivybridge John turned to his wife, "Better get the Rector Hart in to bless the place. Just in case."

Agnes nodded and walked back inside.

On a misty morning in May 1649, Thomas and Joane left Woodland for Ermington with baby James. Their cousin Thomas Prideaux from Ermington had found them a decent property which sat opposite the church and the rent from which would have to be paid to the church. James had been christened there rather than Modbury or Harford in order to confuse gossips.

Thomas slammed down his bag and walking stick in the new hallway and turned to his wife and said,

"I am ashamed to bring you to this place Joane. I never thought it would come to this."

"Not to worry Thomas, let's make the best of it, we shall be on our feet in no time, you see."

"I think I shall rest upstairs as soon as the bed has been laid out, you carry on organising the house my dear. I am feeling very shaky and tired."

Joane sighed. Really her husband was becoming most tiresome of late. Always nervy and cross and then tired and depressed. Why am I supposed to have more energy than him? He is only 39 and I have been through a lot too.

The walking stick was a new addition. Thomas said it made him feel secure as recently his legs were prone to giving way.

She shouted James into the kitchen and met the maids and set them about their work. As soon as the inheritance from her family property came through, she intended to invest in other property and secure a rental income from that. In the meantime, she would use the meagre savings she had kept from her lazy husband and keep the family safe.

But two years passed all too quickly, their second son Andrew had been born and another child on the way. Bishop John was dead and Cromwell was still in charge of the country.

"Any news about the money yet my dear?" she asked her husband at breakfast one morning. The lawyers were dealing with Thomas and not her, even though the inheritance was coming from her side of the family. He told her that the Parliamentarians were being shady and not allowing the money to change hands. This was not true and Thomas already had the quite substantial inheritance sitting in his own bank.

"Don't worry me about such things Joane. Get on with your responsibilities and leave me to mine. I have several plans in motion already. You are only a woman, you would not understand."

Joane said nothing, feeling the familiar heaviness of depression. This pregnancy was getting her down more than the other two and she vowed that this would be the last child she would produce for this family. She would make sure that she would keep her cool until the money came and then things would change. She was trying desperately not to hate the life growing inside her and holding her back from freedom.

Thomas felt a little giddy again.

I would have told her that the money had come through, he said to himself, but honestly, I do not have the strength to discuss it at the moment. I shall keep it in the bank and think about it later.

He got up from the breakfast table, taking up the cane he had rescued from beside the body of his father and went to the front door in order to go out for a walk.

He opened the door and the blast of cold air made him feel very jumpy.

I am still weak, he thought. I shall go back to bed and he turned and made his way upstairs.

Someone else will sort things out.

*

If I was actually going mad, would I know that I was? I don't really know what the rules are about that. I can't ask anyone about it because I could be locked up. Staring out of the window in my cottage in Ermington, I can see my boys running up the bank towards the church. They are laughing and joking and pushing each other over into the grass. Peter, the youngest boy looks as though he will cry sometimes but when Andrew and James pull him up and chase him again, he seems to forget about crying. I wish I could forget about crying. I feel so tired and ill. My legs are like lead weights and sometimes it is all I can do to walk across the room, let alone go out and work. But just lately things seem to have been getting worse.

"Mr. Prideaux," Ellen, the servant girl said as she entered the room. "What am I supposed to be making for supper?"

"Can't you sort that out yourself? I have enough on my mind."

"Well alright, but I just was wondering if you had any special thing you wanted. Not that there is much to choose from. I mean I am a good cook, but I think it would help if you gave me a bit more money so that I could buy more things from Mrs. Lane."

Does the woman not know how much I do not care about that? I am here with my mind going away from me, voices screaming, screaming, screaming and the stupid servant thinks that what she says is important.

"Make whatever the boys like best. I am not interested in eating today,"

Ellen screwed up her face, turned on her heel and stalked out of the room.

I return to my task of looking out of the window. I can only see two boys now and they are standing by the well next to the church. Annie Applecart is standing by them talking away. I don't think that is really her name, but that is what I shall call her.

Ellen stormed into the room again, causing the door to swing violently on its hinges.

"That witch is with the boys Mr. Prideaux. Shall I fetch them back?"

"You shouldn't call her a witch because that kind of talk gets innocent people into trouble."

"She is a witch, everyone knows that. I am not frightened to tell the truth! Anyway, am I to fetch the boys back or not?"

She had her hands on her hips and as I look at her I feel dizzy and peculiar. What on earth is the matter with me?

"The boys are fine. The truth is that I don't want the boys hanging around the house screaming and shouting. Their voices go through my brain, cutting it to shreds."

Now I think I shall put my papers in order again. I did it yesterday but I am not sure whether Ellen upset the order when she cleaned this morning. Although she calls it cleaning, I would not. I notice that there are cobwebs hanging from the beams.

"If we have spiders, we won't have flies," she told me.

I don't want either flies or spiders. Mice or rats for that matter will not be welcome as far as I am concerned. The crashing noise Ellen is making in the kitchen is driving me crackers. No not crackers, it is making me angry. Crash, bash and smash. Thank you for that. Oh not this, why should this be the letter which comes first in the pile? Now I will have to read it again three times and take away its power.

My dear new baby,

I am concerned that I may not be with you travelling the path of life. God has told me that I am needed with him earlier than I ever planned. I have reconciled myself to this, but am determined that I shall bring you into the world and allow you the chance to experience everything that this wonderful life has to offer. I have already grown to love you and never want you to feel that you will have missed out on knowing me. I shall ask Jesus to let me watch over you and help you on your way. I will watch over my Andrew and James too. Your father is a good man and will make sure that you will have all the love and support that you require. Your path in life can be short or long, good or bad but it is up to you to ensure that you are kind and loving whenever you can be.

Joane your loving Mother.

Yes, well done Joane, you got to go and live with Jesus and left me with the looking after them all. I think that was a very selfish thing for you to have done.

*"Give this letter to the new baby," I remember you
said. Well what good will that do? He can't read yet!*

"Mr. Prideaux, I think we should get those boys back
in here now. It is nearly suppertime and I don't like
them being near that woman."

*I go to the window again and can still see the two
eldest boys playing by the well. Annie is sitting on the
grass talking to them. Who is that standing behind
her? A man dressed in a long black coat and wearing
a tall black hat. I never saw anyone dressed like that
in my life. It is very odd.*

"I would be more worried about the man standing
with them," I answered. "I have never seen him
before."

"I don't know anything about a man. I didn't see a
man standing anywhere near them." Ellen was used
to her master's funny ways. "So, am I fetching the
boys back in?"

*I don't know why everything has to be so
complicated.*

"Yes, go and fetch them in." I instructed.

*I go back to the window and watch Ellen leave by the
gate and march over the lane and up the bank
towards the field. She seems undecided about
whether or not to walk up the church track or go
through the gate. Decision made, she tries the field
gate and finding it immovable, lifts up her skirts and
climbs over the wooden structure.*

*The two boys look up as Ellen strode up the field and
Annie stood up. Neither little Peter nor the odd-
looking man are anywhere to be seen. As Ellen
reaches the gathering she walks straight over to*

Annie and appears to punch her in the face. Annie fell to the ground whatever had happened. The boys run over to Annie to help but then stop and follow Ellen. She must have told them to leave the girl alone. I still can't see where Peter is. Now Ellen has her hands on her hips and is turning and shouting. After a while she moves over to the well, looks over the edge and then screams at the boys, who both now are running down the hill towards the cottage.

Transfixed, I watch them clamber over the gate and cross the road without looking. A man driving a pony and cart shouted at them to get out of his way. Ellen will not be pleased about that. Suddenly they are at my window jumping up and down and shouting.

"Father, Father! You must come quickly. Peter has fallen down the well!"

Really this is too much. What am I supposed to do about it? I can't climb down a well, or back up one for that matter. The boys have given up banging on the window and have come running into the house and up to my room.

"Father, did you not hear us? Peter has fallen down the well and Ellen says that you must come straight away!"

"Don't bother me now boys, I have such a headache. I am very tired and am sure that I could not make it up to the top of the hill. You must sort out your own problems."

"But father, he might die!" shouted James. At almost fifteen years old, James was grown up and he certainly was not shy about shouting at his father.

"Don't be so dramatic boy. I have to consider my health, your shouting has upset me you bad boy, I must go and lie down."

I only just made it to the chair by the fire. I don't know why they are still in the room. James and Andrew soon give up annoying me and leave. I feel so dizzy and my heart is racing. I can feel it banging against my chest. I can't decide whether or not I have a brain growth or am about to have a heart attack. I just know I can hardly lift my arms and have dark spots in front of my eyes. I must rest them now.

"Mr. Prideaux, wake up. Come on, wake up."

I open my eyes and see the doctor looking at me. He seems angry, not worried. Stupid man.

"So glad that you came to see me George. I have been feeling very poorly today."

"I am not interested in how you are feeling. We have put your son into his bed. He has a broken leg. I have set it as well as I can and we must watch him carefully over the next few weeks. He is lucky to be alive."

"Who has a broken leg?"

"Young Peter."

"How has that happened?"

I don't understand these people. Can't they see that I am the one who is ill?

"He fell down the well. Can you not remember?"

"I am tired. I need to sleep," I answer.

"You need to take hold of your responsibilities and look after your family properly," shouted the Doctor.

"We are all well aware of the troubles you have had in your life, but now you must move on. Your family needs you."

I close my eyes. I can still hear, but now the group in the room seems to be leaving me alone. This dark swirling which happens when I close my eyes is very unnerving. I lose my grip on the reality in which everyone else lives and feel as though I am falling down a deep dark hole, but spinning the entire time. It is so sickly and frightening. Joane my beautiful dead wife, I miss you so much. Perhaps if I reach out my hand I can touch you my darling. So nice of you to visit every time I have one of these spells. Does that mean I am dead too when this happens? Who knows? Who cares? When I see you, I remember how I got into this state. Shall I think about it again my love? Perhaps I shall improve when I do.

I feel as though I cannot take any more. When we arrived at this house, I was appalled. We now had a small front garden and two servants. There are only four rooms downstairs and four up. There is some land and buildings out the back, but really it is a disgrace.

Joane, you said that we must make the best of it and I really tried to settle in with the few possessions we had been allowed to take.

For a Prideaux to be in this position is wrong. My brothers have fared little better and it seems now that it will be down to our cousins to carry on the fame and fortune of our family name. It would not surprise me if they had not made advancement from the situation we find ourselves in.

We were only here for two weeks when Joane started with the baby. We had endured looks and comments from the new neighbors, who appeared to find it amusing that we were in this position. Joane took it all very well even though I wanted to cause some trouble.

I started to feel ill about this time. My heart raced and I felt peculiar when walking along the street. Nerves said my wife. I told her that was ridiculous. Nerves are a female trouble; it must be something more serious.

Her labour lasted for two days and Joane was in great distress. She was attended by Ellen and a woman from the village. Our own doctor could not of course come and see her and there was no doctor in the village at that time.

My lovely wife died and the boy survived. I know it was not Peter that killed her, but she died because of him all the same.

Ellen found a wet nurse for the boy and I buried my wife in the churchyard at Ermington. She should have been buried at Harford, along with my own parents and family, or at Modbury with her parents, but at least I can see her every time I look out of my windows at the front of the house.

From that point on, I often felt as though I could no longer cope. I knew that all the people in the village would look at me. Ellen said it was in sympathy, but I knew the truth. They thought that I had some hand in the death of my wife!

Peter, I have never felt close to. Andrew and James are not so bad, but Peter wants to annoy me at every opportunity. When the other boys were babies, they were well out of sight with their maids while we carried on with our lives. In fact, I suppose I hardly ever saw them except for bedtimes and playing in the garden. Now all the children are within my eyesight and earshot every moment of the day. I had not really been aware of the noise and smell involved with a new baby. I even caught the wet nurse feeding the boy on several occasions. Disgusting. When I was a child, all of this was carried on in the babies' nursery away from us all.

"Mr. Prideaux, Mr. Prideaux!"

I am being shaken about by Ellen.

"What on earth is the matter with you girl?"

I open my eyes and see that I am still lying on the sofa in the sitting room. It is daylight. I must have slept through the night.

"I thought you were dead Mr. Prideaux. You've slept all yesterday and today!" Ellen could not believe that anyone would sleep that long.

"I am ill, I keep telling you. Now go and get me some wine."

"Wine! We don't have wine. You are not in your big house now."

"Don't be so rude you dreadful girl, or I shall dismiss you!"

"You know you won't do any such thing. There is no one else that will put up with you. Anyway, I am not leaving those boys. You aren't fit to look after them." Ellen was nothing if not confident.

I lay back on my couch and then realise that I must visit the outside privy immediately. Oh, how the room spins and turns. The floor is moving and I am sure that I shall die.

"Ellen, Ellen! Come quickly and bring my po!"

"Mr. Prideaux, you are a disgrace. There is nothing wrong with you. The po is under the couch same as before. Now when you have done that, clean yourself up and go and visit your poor boy." She bustled back into the kitchen.

I did as I was told and was soon standing in the hallway looking up the stairs wondering if I could make it. It takes me such a long time, but on seeing my boy, I almost feel sorry for him.

"Hello Father," he said.

"Hello Peter. What happened to you?"

"I fell down the well. I don't know how Sir, I was talking to that man and next thing I knew I was down the well."

"You saw the man too? No one else seems to have done."

"I know, Andrew and James said they didn't see him either. He said he knew our family. But it was very odd because he would not say who he was."

I look down at my eleven-year-old son. He seems so much younger than his thirteen and fifteen-year-old brothers, more like a baby. I suppose that is because he is sick.

"I am sick too," I said out loud.

"Oh," answered Peter.

I know he finds me strange, we have never been close.

"So, tell me about this man," I asked.

"Better tell your father about that witch woman." Ellen had come into the room behind us.

"She's not really a witch Ellen. She's nice to me. She teaches me things," said Peter.

"What sort of things, may I ask? I can't see that she could teach you anything that will be any good to you in the long run. Pity you didn't pay as much attention to your tutor," answered Ellen curtly.

I know full well that Ellen has a crush on Mr. Grayling who comes to the house every day to teach the boys.

"She teaches me about plants and animals. You know, about herbs and things which can make people better," said Peter.

That was surprising as I had not been aware that Peter was learning anything from anyone. Certainly Mr. Grayling was not that pleased with the boy's progress.

"I don't know what use that could possibly be," I said.

Peter could be cheeky when he found his confidence.

"For example, Annie showed me a way we could help you with your nerves."

I gave Peter no chance to elaborate.

"You have been discussing my health with that witch! My illness is far too complicated for a pair of idiots such as you two to cure. Why, I have baffled greater brains than yours!"

As I leave the room, I notice Ellen standing in the hallway still. Peter has a crestfallen face and it serves him right. I gave him, a parting shot.

"Pity she didn't know a way to save your mother before you killed her!"

His face shows that this has hit home. He won't be giving me any of his ridiculous advice from now on.

"Mr. Prideaux! There was no call for that!" said Ellen.

I feel ill again. My legs are wobbling and the whole situation is too much for me. I shall retire to my bed.

*

I don't know why I have just been thinking about Peter and his broken leg. It must be 29 years since that happened.

"Now Mr. Prideaux, we need to get you washed and changed before your lawyer gets here."

Ellen left us years ago. She was followed by a long succession of housekeepers and maids and now I have this dragon of a woman to look after me. She does seem to understand how ill I am though, which is something. I don't know what the Lord is playing at, leaving me so poorly for so long. At one time, I could not travel far from the house and now I am unable to leave my bed. The best doctors are baffled and one gentleman wanted to study me saying that it would be a revelation to discover how a man who showed no outward or inward signs of illness could be so sick! I said to him, it is for you to discover that. I am too busy trying to keep my life together when so many things have been against me.

"That's right, move over so we can wash your face and trim your whiskers. Really you are so lucky to keep such a fine head of hair, when most men of your age have lost theirs!"

"Where are my children, Miss Traeth?"

"Well James is at his home, I should imagine. Remember he has married that nice Sarah Cope and they have the two babies, Sarah and Agnes?"

"Oh yes. It had slipped my mind just for the moment."

It is true to say that many things are easily forgotten by my poorly mind.

"Andrew is courting Joan Wake, but she will have a job getting him to the altar and Peter! Well I will be surprised if he ever marries! Too fond of himself that one."

"Peter has been trouble since the day he came into the world. He killed my beautiful Joane, just when I needed her to look after me. It really is too much."

"No need to talk about your flesh and blood like that, Mr. Prideaux. You are lucky to have such good healthy sons and grandchildren. I wish I had."

She busies herself nursing me and sorting out the bed and the room. I can hear some commotion downstairs and soon my lawyer, Mr. Kidling arrives.

"You are looking very well Thomas! You should be up and about today, the sun is glorious."

"No need for enforced joviality George. Have you prepared the documents?"

"Yes, I have and just as you asked. The boys will be very pleased with the amount of money and property you are leaving in your estate."

"I have never thought about spending much money, it was not necessary. I managed to come out of the disaster of Cromwell with more than anyone expected and have kept it invested since then."

"Indeed, you have. The will splits the money equally between the boys and if any die before you, then the balance shall be divided between the surviving sons."

"Exactly right."

"Now my clerk and Miss Traeth can witness your signature. There and there and there. I shall take this back to my office and keep it safe. Good day to you Thomas."

"Good day to you George."

"Hello Peter, I did not realize you were on the landing." The lawyer shook his hand.

"Neither did I Peter. What are you doing there? Trying to discover something which is of no concern of yours?"

"No indeed Father. I came to see if you wanted anything from Modbury. I am travelling there today."

"To see your gambling friends, I have no doubt. I am dismayed by the amount of money you waste in that game."

"I know I have been a constant disappointment to you Sir. I am sorry for that. Do you want anything then?"

"No I don't. I need to rest now."

*

"It's terrible sad about losing your brother and father within the same month, Peter."

"Yes, it is Miss Traeth."

"Just before Christmas too. I mean poor James dying of food poisoning and the same with your father."

"I don't think Father died of food poisoning. He has been ill for so long, it should be no surprise that he passed soon after James. He was his favorite son after all. The final shock I suppose."

Andrew came over to join them and Miss Traeth left to see to the other guests.

"It is rather odd though Peter. I have been used to father being ill all our life, I can't believe he is really dead."

"I know Andrew, but I am more amazed by James dying, than father. I worry for his poor wife and children. I hope that they will cope."

"We shall have to share some of our inheritance with them, so that they will be able to manage."

"You can if you like Andrew. Father insisted that the money was shared between his remaining sons. He never mentioned anything about providing for James's wife and children. It is father who is to blame for that little oversight."

"Peter, you can't possibly mean that! James would have looked after any family of ours."

"We don't have any family, that's the point."

"If you won't share yours, then I shall share mine with them!"

"That is up to you. My father has hated me since the day I was born and he let me know it almost every day. He hid his money from us all and let us live like paupers. With our background and history, that was awful. We could have lived well ever since Mother's old place had to be given up. I was very angry as soon as I heard about the money. Perhaps mother would even have lived if she had been attended by a proper doctor."

"You only heard about it the same time as me though, didn't you? At the reading of the will?"

"Oh, yes that's right, at the reading of the will. Anyway, I am going to finally enjoy my life and marry a rich woman and have sons. I will start another Prideaux dynasty and climb my way back up the ladder. We shall have our position back Andrew and that is not going to happen by giving our money away. After all, Sarah is only the daughter of a parson!"

"You didn't mind seeing the daughter of a stonemason last week. What happened to her?"

"That was just something to pass the time. I am aiming for bigger fish now."

"I am ashamed of you Peter."

"Do I look as though I care Andrew? We shall keep this house for you and I shall buy that new house at the end of the village and buy new clothes and horses. You can buy me out, I won't be coming back here. Soon I shall take my rightful place. You watch, Andrew, you watch!"

"Mother would be ashamed of you too!"

"Leave me now, I have to visit old Annie and give her a Christmas present. She has always been good to me."

*

"Oh, how pleased I am to see you Peter! Come on in."

"Thanks Annie." He sat by the fire and took the drink which Annie handed to him.

"Now do you want something to eat?"

"No thanks. I am content to sit here."

Annie sat opposite him and played with her cup, obviously wondering whether or not to say something to him. She decided to.

"I was worried you would not visit after the death of your father."

"Why would you think that?"

"Because of how he died."

Peter looked at her sharply.

"What do you mean by that?"

"It seems a mighty coincidence that your brother and father both died within a month of your learning about your father's will. They both died by poisoning too."

"James died from poisoning and Father died of shock."

"Stick to that story, it doesn't matter to me. It will never come from my lips that you know as much as me when it comes to herbs and plants and the effects they have on people."

Peter grabbed her by the arm,

"Don't ever let me hear you saying anything like that to anyone else."

Annie looked him in the eyes and smiled.

"Oh Peter, we have meant a lot to each other over the years, you know I never want you to be in trouble."

"I won't be in trouble, but you might if you don't leave me alone. Witches are still burnt you know. It would not take much for the village to be fired up, especially if I let them know about your spells and curses."

"Peter! Why would you do that?"

"Because you are a witch! And you are accusing me of harming my family. We still have a witch bottle in our fireplace. Ellen put it there years ago and I know quite a few others have them too. They believe your mother was a witch and that you are too."

"I can't believe you are saying this to me after all we have meant to each other."

Peter stood up and slapped the woman hard across the face.

"We are nothing to each other. I have money now and am going to make something of my life. You can't hurt me, our family has been too powerful for anything you say or do to affect us. A curse wouldn't even work on me."

Annie was slumped on the floor and crying.

"Don't bother me again. Don't come near me or I shall have you flogged and burned as a witch!"

Peter stared at her with his black eyes and then abruptly left her cottage.

"I know you were affected by your father's coldness, but you had every chance to remain good and not turn evil."

She turned over the little doll in her hand. She had made it years ago when Peter first kissed her because she knew this day would come.

"You will never have luck with money or love Peter Prideaux and your children and your children's' children will suffer the same unless the curse is broken. Not so clever, are you?"

She threw the doll on the fire and laughed.

"So, there you are fire, hold the secret."

Annie looked out of the doorway at the retreating Peter Prideaux.

"Bastard," she said.

THE BIGBURY BUTCHER

Featuring Peter Prideaux (1651 – 1725)

"To murder one wife is sin enough, but four wives is the work of a madman."

This statement was presented to me by the magistrate and I do not feel like answering him. What a stupid thing to say to me. I don't care about sin and I am certainly not mad. Indeed, a true madman would not be able to consider whether or not he was mad. I am considering it and coming to the rapid conclusion that I am not mad.

"I see." I decide to give the answer the magistrate seems to want. The answer however does not satisfy him and he grimaces and looks back at the papers on the table in front of him.

We are not in court, just at the Modbury home of Sir William Bigbury. He does not know that I know that he knows that one of my ancestors killed one of his.

Sir William would call it murder if asked, whereas our family called it a duel. And this duel was caused by the Bigburys and their appalling behaviour. This bad blood had been going on between the families for centuries and Sir William enjoyed seeing Peter Prideaux across the table from him under questioning. He wasn't acknowledging that my Grandmother Blanche was an aunt or a cousin of his.

I don't know which it is for we never spent any Christmases together. But I do know that the ghost of an ancestor of theirs and therefore mine burnt down their Hall in Cornwood. I decided not to bring it up here.

"Mr Baron, your father in law has advised me that your wife was killed by you using the same method it is generally believed you killed your previous three wives. He says that he has the evidence in the form of a letter from his daughter. There is also a similar accusation concerning the death of your two daughters."

"What method is that then?" I ask him.

This interview was becoming more surreal.

"We shall come to that later Mr Prideaux," he answers without looking up from his papers.

I expect that this way of dealing with me makes Sir William feel very important. Two can play at that game because I feel that I am quite important too.

"You don't have any right to keep me here, Sir William. There is no proof about any murder."

"What makes you so sure about that?"

"Because there were no murders," I say simply.

I have to stand – stand mark you – while these idiots fiddle about with papers and books for another ten minutes or so. Every so often there is a surly glance in my direction from Sir William and finally I announce,

"I am leaving now Bigbury. You have nothing on me and I have done nothing wrong. If you wish to speak to me about this again, then please deal with my solicitor at Modbury."

I walk out of the room and no one tries to stop me. A maid rushes towards me and hands me my hat and cane. Stupid girls always want an excuse to be near to me. I reward her with my best smile and she blushes and bobs a curtsey. She watches as I leave and untie my horse. I mount and ride away from the home of Sir William while pondering the interview which had just taken place.

As I glance back at the house, I notice a group of women standing on the stone steps. There are two children playing on the ground in front of them. I nod and the women place bony fingers upon their own lips, so I ride away swiftly.

Creepy servants Bigbury insists on employing.

I wave to one of my neighbours as I ride through the gate and trot back to the village. He does not wave back and I wonder why that should be. I kick my horse on and am soon outside my own property.

Although my house is larger than many in the village, most being cottages, it is still mortgaged via the Bigbury estate and I expect that this could now start to become a problem.

Walking in through the front door, I am met by my housekeeper, Mrs Thomas.

"Where is Peter?" I ask her.

"He is upstairs with that housekeeper woman, Miss Gardener," she answers.

Mrs Thomas does not approve of the pretty young woman who was employed by me after the death of my last wife. I personally could not care less about what Mrs Thomas thinks. She is employed as a cook and not my adviser.

"Bring me some food and I shall eat in the dining room. Go and ask Miss Gardener to come down and see me there now. I do not want to see the boy, just her."

That should give her plenty to think about - nosy old woman.

I wander into the dining room and sit at the table. Every so often in comes Mrs Thomas to set the table or bring in food and drink, but eventually in walks the delectable Miss Gardener.

"Sit down Miss Gardener," I tell her.

It is nice watching a young woman in my employ doing as she is told while refusing to look me in the eye. This is a more powerful feeling than marrying a young girl knowing that she would give in to me quickly and without question. I suppose that is because I am very good looking and charming when I want to be and all my little brides believed I was in love with them. It was too easy.

"Have you heard about my meeting with Sir William this morning?"

"I know you went there Sir, but I don't know why," she answers.

"You have not been listening to the talk then."

Her eyes were still downcast while she ate her soup and so gave nothing away to me. I know she is lying though. Everyone has heard the gossip even if they have not taken any part in it.

"No Sir."

We continue, eating in silence, she avoiding the touch of my hand when I reach for the bread at the same time as her. When I laugh at this, she blushes crimson. After the meal, I tell her to go back upstairs and look after the boy. She does so without question - of course.

I walk into the library in order to smoke and to think.

I met Elizabeth Saunders in Bigbury, where I moved almost immediately after I received my inheritance. . Elizabeth was quite a pretty girl and the daughter and heir of a gentleman, William Saunders from Aveton Gifford. Her mother and brother had died of a fever within two days of each other in 1681 - her mother Elizabeth on the 3rd and her brother and co heir Thomas on the 5th February. As Father and my brother James had died only a few months prior to her loss, we had a good deal in common.

My father and James died so close in time to each other, of poisoning the doctor said. And it is a terrible responsibility when your mother dies bringing you into the world. There is so much to prove, you see. I have to make my life count and therefore Mother's death need not be in vain.

Elizabeth's family on hearing that I had received a substantial inheritance opened their house and ultimately, their niece and her inheritance to me.

Aveton Gifford is a pretty village sitting at the head of the estuary and has a lovely church and bridge. I used to travel there by horse from Bigbury, through St Ann's Chapel and down a steep track to the tidal road which runs along the estuary. This road would be covered by the sea when the tide is high. It is a very pleasant drive and one which I have taken many times during my life.

At the dinner I attended when the Saunders family was first introduced to me, I decided that I must work fast on this girl in order to win her and her dowry. Being a sociable fellow, I had already wooed many local girls and the richer ones had been kept well away from me by their wary fathers. Being the great nephew of a Bishop and the grandson of a farmer of a large estate held little sway now that the Prideauxs had lost a good deal of ground and standing during Cromwell's time. It really was not right and I intended to live the life I should have been entitled to. When my father recently died, the money left to me and my brother was enough to set me on the right track again. And as my sights are set very high, I intend to use my considerable charms on the ladies with money and marry one of them. It seems fair enough to me.

I married Elizabeth Saunders on the 27th July 1684 in Aveton Gifford church at a ceremony attended by her family and my brother Andrew. The wedding was a great success which it had to be considering how much Elizabeth's father; William Saunders had spent on the event. He seemed to invite most of the village and in all it was a very gay affair. I have to say I enjoyed myself.

When we returned to our house for our wedding night at our new property in Aveton Gifford, courtesy of Saunders, I found Elizabeth to be totally inexperienced and shy. This was a good omen and I think that I made the whole event a pleasant one for my new bride - I enjoyed myself anyway.

We waited for the news of a pregnancy and were disappointed. I continued to be disappointed every month and spent a good deal of my time ensuring that I was giving all the correct attention was given to Elizabeth in order for a pregnancy to occur. I wanted a son, no daughters, just a son, or two. When I was not paying attention to my lovely wife I enjoyed the races, hunting and drinking and a lot of gambling. I was never as lucky with gambling as I should have been and money seemed to leave me much more easily than it ever arrived. Elizabeth felt that I was spending too much money on these pastimes and I told her that it was none of her business. All the money in our marriage was mine and no arguments.

She spent her days organising the house and gardens. She was very good at doing that and I allowed her to help out at the church sometimes. She was just absolutely useless at producing children and I was beginning to hope that I had not married a barren cow.

When the second Christmas of our union had passed with no blessing, I worried that I was never going to be a father. Elizabeth said that I was putting too much pressure on her, but I disagreed. She was young and perfectly capable of producing a son if she put her mind to it.

We spent Christmas with my Stowford family and I became angered by the constant referrals to our lack of issue. This was not seemly, so something would have to be done - there was no getting away from that.

With there being no baby by the time Easter arrived, I decided that a change of diet was called for and insisted that I supervised the preparation of my wife's food from now on.

Unfortunately poor Elizabeth died of food poisoning in April and we buried her on the 13th April 1687.

I was desolate naturally and could take comfort from no one, although I have to say that her family were less than sympathetic to my loss. As soon as Elizabeth's estate was finalised the large house in which we had been living at the time of her demise came to me entirely as her husband along with certain sums of money and so after a while, I was content.

Along came little Jane Boon. Now she was a precious young girl, as fair as Elizabeth had been dark and equally as pretty. I noticed Jane at the party which was attended by many of my friends at Bigbury towards Christmas the previous year. Elizabeth had been too sickly to attend. Jane was sweet and innocent and looked down at her pretty feet when I smiled at her. At 36 years old I still had good looks and the bearing of a gentleman and it was relatively easy to catch the eye of a shy and as luck would have it, rich young lady.

After discussing the matter with her parents and promising to sell my house in Aveton Gifford and move to Bigbury in order that their beloved daughter could be seen by her mother every day, a marriage was arranged for the 26th June 1687.

I bought a lovely house just outside the village, hired the servants recommended by my mother-in-law-to-be and set up home. The Boons were very happy with the match and settled a good sum on their daughter which I would of course be able to take charge of. They had no worries about this as I was quite evidently a rich man.

The wedding surpassed my first. Jane was not to be denied her day just because I was a widower and she my second wife. There were many guests and lots of food and flowers and the villagers turned out to wave and clap. What a day! I even noticed that one of my ancestors, Ralph Prideaux had once been Rector at the church.

Jane had promised me many children as she understood my disappointments to date. She said that she would say special prayers for a son to arrive nine months after our wedding. I performed my duty again and again. Jane did not always seem very receptive and told me that I was frightening her. I of course told her not to be so silly and carried on with my God given duty. She cried the first time and the second and the third. Girls are so manipulative with the little games they play. I don't think I shall ever understand them.

Her prayers came to nothing however. I asked her every month if we were to expect a son and she denied me each time. Really, this was too much.

Jane kept telling me that she was unwell and I did notice that's she was beginning to look pale and sad in a manner reminiscent of my dear Elizabeth. I told Jane so and reminded her that Elizabeth had eventually taken her dark depressions to the grave.

Jane spent a good deal of time visiting her mother or having her mother visit us, until I insisted that she cease. I told her mother that the visits were tiring

Jane. I began supervising her food, adding herbs here and there which I told her would make her feel much better. I wanted a son and not a sick and weak wife to drag me down.

This worked very well and Jane agreed to stop seeing her family quite so much. She understood that the contacts was interfering with her duties as a wife and she said that she was going to concentrate very hard on producing a son for our family.

Her friend Joan Stone was soon the only person visiting. Joan and I began a friendship almost as soon as we met. We had much in common including an interest in herbs and their properties. Often we would walk together seeking out special herbs and plants. In the early days of our marriage Jane would accompany us on these jaunts, but as time progressed she insisted that we walk while she rested in her own room. Joan was a very fit girl and so we often ventured further afield to the beach and over to the island to see the remains of the old monastery. I used to scare Joan when I told her about the ghost of smuggler Tom Crocker who haunted the inn and the island. Joan laughed and we fell together on the grass. Joan soon began to tell me of certain incantations which would compel a person to do as they were bid. She was very interesting.

I remember once that I met my father-in-law whilst out walking with Joan and he later told me that this was inappropriate. The upstart of a man telling me, Peter Prideaux, what should be done. I ignored him of course.

By the time Christmas 1688 arrived I was still not a father and most disappointed. Jane cried and apologised as usual and I was not feeling very pleased with her. I had hoped to be holding my son by that Christmas morning.

God obviously had other ideas for us as Jane died of some sort of food poisoning the next day. The doctor was most confused and her family distraught. I found that the event was not quite as upsetting as it might have been.

If I am honest with myself, Jane and I had grown apart in the eighteen months we were together and I had not felt as close to her as I might have done. I was left with the inconvenience of sorting out my affairs once again but found that my lawyer had ensured under my prior instructions that the business was concluded quickly and smoothly.

I married Joan Stone on the 28th May 1689.

This was not as unusual as the local shrews thought as we had so much in common and Joan had been a friend of Jane's and we both felt that it is something that she would have been happy with. We waited until May in order to prevent gossip, although this was not extended to Joan moving away until the wedding. She called at the house as often as she had before and the presence of my loyal staff at the same time gave the local women no cause for concern.

It does amaze me though how a woman becomes so different once she is married. She will literally change as soon as the ring is on her finger. The shy, demure and obedient woman with no view on any subject becomes a harridan who appears to believe that her own opinion matters. Women have so little experience of the world that it is ridiculous for them to imagine that this view could possibly be an informed one.

Joan for example, began to act as though we were in some kind of conspiracy together, asking for extra money for clothes and the like. I no longer felt as though I could go herb hunting with her and took to performing this task alone. I started riding out on my own to the inns of surrounding villages and towns. Modbury was particularly good for meeting fellow gamblers.

My finances were such that it was possible to attend certain clubs in Plymouth where more exciting gambling took place alongside wine and women. I also managed to buy some very fine horses. My life was good except that I was still not a father. Joan seemed less bothered about this than I and told me that a child would arrive soon enough. I however had a position to maintain. Three wives and no children were now beyond a joke and I insisted quite firmly that I should be expecting a child very soon.

I told Joan to take some herbs and she told me in return that her own ministrations to her health were good enough. I could not agree and was sorely disappointed that Joan should speak to me in this way.

I found myself spending more time with my male friends and it has to be said with some female friends while my wife spent a good deal of my money on herself and the house. I agree that the house looked wonderful with its modern furniture and I was never ashamed to bring anyone home and our parties were well attended, very gay and very expensive. I wanted to keep up with my friends and was pleased to be asked to invest in some of the mining ventures proposed.

I was married to Joan for five years until she died of a fall from a horse. She was not a good rider but insisted on riding the feisty mare that day when she accompanied me to visit a mine I had a financial interest in. I did not tell the doctor who attended her, but Joan had been convinced that I was using the rides as an excuse to visit a woman in secret. I challenged her to ride out with me, even choosing her horse and she fell while attempting to jump a hedge after I had already jumped it. She died almost immediately with few words and was buried on the 6th August 1694 in the same Bigbury church where we had been married.

The 20th November 1694 was another happy day, it being the day I married Anne Baron.

Anne was a young woman, sixteen years old, but ready and willing to marry. Her father seemed pleased with my income and property and ignored my age – 43 years old now, I can hardly believe it. Her father was a gentleman with a waning income and I was not adverse to a girl who could produce the son I wanted.

I paid a great deal of attention to Anne and let her have plenty of freedom. This was also to do with the fact I spent a lot of time in town. Three decent marriages had left me well off and I was still able to live the life of a gentleman.

And on the 17th September 1695 Anne produced my son and we named him Peter John.

I was so happy and Anne said that I deserved it after waiting all this time. I was pleased and celebrated so much with my friends that I almost forgot to thank Anne for her part.

Peter was a handsome little chap, but seemed much closer to his mother than to me.

Two years later Ann was born on the 17th May and following two born dead sons, in December 1701 Mary was born. These two daughters did not create the same celebration in the household as Peter had, as I was too busy and had little interest in girls.

Now outnumbered by women, I felt as if I was a stranger in my own house. I had enough of this.

God seemed to hear my complaints because within a month of Mary's birth, all three were dead. Baby Mary first succumbed to a fever, my wife found her dead in the morning. Then two days later four year old Mary was found dead in bed of the same fever. My wife seemed to sicken just after the girls' joint funeral and became depressed and inconsolable. I tried her with all sorts of tempting foods, but soon in mid-January, she too was in the ground on top of our daughters.

My son did not appear to be affected by the traumas and his new young nursemaid took good care of him. It was just after my wife's funeral that I began to notice that I was being treated differently by my friends and neighbours. Conversation stopped as I approached people at parties and some crossed the road and found some important task to take care of if I came anywhere near them.

Then I was summoned for the meeting with Sir William.

He would find no evidence against me as there was none to be found.

It could be asked why I stayed here in this county but the rolling Devon fields, cliffs and waterways are in my blood and I would miss them all if I went anywhere else.

I am startled from my thoughts when Miss Gardener once more enters the room.

"Sir, a note has arrived for you," she says and hands me an envelope. I open it, read it and see that I am summoned yet again to see Sir William. Damned insolence.

I arrive at the hall at twelve the next day. The note said ten, but I am not his servant.

"You are late," says Sir William.

"I am not under arrest. I shall arrive when I please, Sir William."

Sir William stares at me and I am glad that looks cannot kill. Standing next to him is John Potter, his clerk.

"What do you need to see me about today, Sir William? I do have a life apart from visiting you." I smile and this annoys him even more.

"Mr Baron will be here shortly to show me the letter he has which was written to him by your late wife. He has been checking other details which were referred to in the note and will bring all his findings. It seems as though today you shall lose your liberty."

"Is that the reason you have the men sitting in your entrance hall. Are they waiting to arrest me?" He can see I am not taking this seriously.

"Don't try to be so smart Prideaux. I shall have you behind bars by this ..."

We are interrupted by one of his men coming into the room carrying a letter.

Sir William opens it and as he reads, I see the colour drain from his face.

"Bad news?" I ask him.

"You are something to do with this aren't you?"

"With what?"

He waves the note in my face and drops it on the floor. Then he storms out of the room.

The clerk reaches it before the note hits the ground and reads it. He looks at me and says, "It appears that Mr Baron died last night."

"Oh that is terrible news," I answer. "How did that happen?"

"It seems that he was perfectly alright after his meal last night and then he went into the study to go through some papers. He was found dead there this morning. As yet they cannot confirm how he died, but initial reports suggest poisoning of some sort."

"Perhaps he has taken his own life. I know he has been very upset by the deaths of my wife and children. He has almost seemed a little unhinged," I say.

I know I must make my point carefully. After all the only reason I am standing here in this room with the clerk of Sir William is because of Baron.

"Yes," says the clerk. He felt quite uncomfortable because he did not know whether this Prideaux man was a mass murderer or a badly maligned person who had suffered dreadful tragedy in his life. The truth could go either way.

"Boo!" I say to the man and he looks startled and runs out of the room.

I look around the room and laugh out loud. Now there would be no further problems for me. A spot of luck my father-in-law dying like that.

When I visited him late last night in his study, my father-in-law had seemed pleased to see me. We talked through the whole situation and after a few drinks of the ale I brought with me; he seemed to come round to my way of thinking. He even started to understand that his daughter, my beloved wife, had been saying many strange things after the death of her daughters. After I tentatively asked to see the letter Anne had written, he was drunk enough to show me. When I read it through twice I realised that in the wrong hands, much could be made of its contents.

I had not known that Anne had spent so much of her time with me recoding all sorts of comments together with lists of herbs and the like.

Clever little Anne.

"I brought you some sweets too John," I said to him. John took and ate them all and soon began to doze peacefully in the armchair. I took my leave and went home.

I did not think that it would be a wise thing to tell anyone else of the visit. No one else had seen me, so I vowed to keep it to myself.

I walk out of the room and find Sir William, his clerk and several men talking in the hallway.

"I shall leave now William," I tell him. "I can't imagine you have any reason to talk to me again." I smile at him and leave by the front door. I can feel his eyes burning into me as I mount my horse.

As I ride home through the woods, I am conscious of a freezing mist which has suddenly dropped. My horse begins to spook and spin and I have to be quite firm with him until he calms down.

"Having trouble with him Sir? He is a fine looking animal."

I look to my left from where the voice comes. I have to say that my heart is racing and my body feels cold and tingly. I am looking at a parson of some sort, although I do not recognise him and I have had quite a bit to do with parsons and the like.

"He is. I think he was surprised to see you walking here. Are you lost?"

"We are all lost," answers the parson.

"Aaaah. You are not trapping me with that kind of talk Parson. I am asking if you are travelling somewhere in particular. I am riding back to my house if you need pointing in the right direction?"

"I know my way, Prideaux. I am wondering if you have any idea where you are going?"

"I just told you, I am going home." Peculiar little man.

"Now you are and yet if I were you, I would worry about where I was going when I die."

"You worry all you like friend. I believe that when you are dead, you are dead. Gone and never to be again."

"Oh no Prideaux. We carry on living and don't ever die and whatever we do causes something to be created in answer to what we have thought or done. Then we must continue another life in the same manner. That is what God does for us and with us."

"Spare me your sermons old man," I am feeling cross about his idiotic speech.

He laughs and throws his head back as he does so.

"Do you miss your mother Peter?"

"That witch left me as soon as she dumped me into this evil life. She left me with an idiot father who did nothing for me. You know Parson, like you I hate women and it started with her." I have no idea why I am telling him this.

"Aaaah, your confession and perhaps the first recognition of your causation."

I stop my horse. I don't need to speak to this man anymore. He is making me feel uncomfortable.

"On your way Parson," I instruct him.

He laughs.

And vanishes into the thick mist.

"Hey!" I shout.

There is no answer and so I assume the old Parson felt that he had warned me of the fate of my eternal soul and has now triumphantly continued his journey into the wood.

The mist is still surrounding us and I feel suddenly aware of mumblings and shadows and extreme ice cold. My horse is standing stock still and almost catatonic – as am I.

I see a group of women ahead of me on the track and shout out to them. The women stop their walk and turn to face me.

"Do you know where the Parson went to?"

They give me no answer and I must assume that they are plain rude. Probably common people.

"You women! Answer me now or I shall ride my horse through you!"

Two children came out from behind the skirts of the women and the dirty little wretches run towards me. The women did nothing to stop them.

"Papa! Papa!" they are saying.

"Where is your Papa?" I ask.

They stop in front of me and stroke my horse. Then in unison they look up to me and say,

"Papa! Why did you kill us all? We didn't harm you and we miss our brother. We miss Peter, we miss Peter!"

They chant and chant and the women join in, "We miss Peter!"

Surely not, surely not! Elizabeth, Jane, Joan, Anne, and little Ann and little Mary? That is not possible. I kick my horse on and ride through the group but they do not scatter as I might expect. They disperse, I mean their bodies disperse into the mist and as I look back from my galloping horse, their bodies reform! They are all holding fingers to their lips. I turn back to the front and do not stop until I reach my village.

When I arrive back home I am met by Miss Gardener.

"Everything alright Sir?" she asks.

"Fine," I answer, smiling at the trusting face.

"I hear Mr Baron was found dead this morning. Did he seem fine when you saw him last night?"

Oh dear. I had thought she was asleep when I left to make the visit. How did she know? I finger the letter and notes I have in my pocket. After considering briefly, I pull them out and give them to Miss Gardener to read.

"I think we should put that rubbish in the fire," she says as she glances over the contents. "Only harm will come from such ridiculous things."

I can see a long future with this girl.

THE RINGMORE WRAITH

Featuring Peter Prideaux (1695 – 1749)

The first time that Peter saw a ghost was in February 1702, just three weeks after the deaths of his mother and sisters. However, being six, he was not familiar with the concept of a ghost and therefore did not overreact.

He simply liked the young girls who came to his attic room to play with him and the beautiful lady who smelled of flowers and bread. This lady would come to him when he had been locked in his room by either his father or Miss Gardener. When his mother was alive, he had eaten with her and his sister Ann in the nursery until Mary was born. But Mary was so sick and his mother spent all her time with her and so the two elder children had to eat on their own. Then Ann was taken away to the room occupied by mother and baby Mary and Peter did not see any of them alive again.

He saw them once they were dead. His father thought it necessary that Peter should see his dead sisters lying in their shared coffin. He also thought it necessary that he should see his mother on her deathbed and then again in her coffin. When Peter asked his father why they smelled so funny and their faces were all wrinkled and scary, his father told him not to be a fool. They were dead and would soon be buried in the ground and have six feet of soil piled up on top of them and that meant that they could never climb out again because of the weight. He explained that that was why all of those bodies in the churchyard were buried so deep. He also said that if they were not buried with exactly six feet of soil on them, they could climb right out of their graves at night when no one was looking and come round to little boy's bedrooms if they had been naughty and disobeyed their fathers.

Young Peter did not get a proper night's sleep for the rest of his life following this informative lecture.

Miss Gardener was now in charge of his care and she became cruel and neglectful following his mother's death. He was locked in his attic more often than not, this cold, dark space now being used as his bedroom and playroom and dining room.

Miss Gardener and his father spent a great deal of time together during the troubles and for a long while afterwards. Then, gradually things began to change.

Young Peter noticed that as his father spent more time away from the house and away from Miss Gardener, the nastier she became.

Peter was forgotten about on several occasions. He often went without food and water and bathing. One of the maids would sneak up when she could and shout through the locked door,

"Master Peter! Master Peter!"

He would shuffle over to the door sniffling and whispering,

"I am so hungry. Where is Mama?"

The girl quickly unlocked the door and slipped inside.

"Ssssh. You must not say I have been here or I shall lose my place and then there will be no one to help you. Now Master Peter, eat and drink and wash yourself. I will get you some clean clothes from the chest here, but you must not say it is me. She will not notice that that you have been cleaned. I will wash these clothes and bring them back for you to put on again."

Six year old Peter did as he was told and ate and drank quickly. The girl, Matilda Stone, busied herself cleaning the bed and replacing the bedding with fresh from the linen cupboard at the far end of the attic and put all of the soiled garments and linen into a large cotton bag.

"I will wash these at home Master Peter. My mother has heard of the way you are being treated and she is disgusted. She told me to bring you home there, but of course your father will have the law against us."

"I won't say anything," said Peter. "Thank you Matilda."

Matilda smiled a teary smile and rubbed his head.

"I cannot tell you often enough not to tell anyone what I am doing. Just say nothing."

"I won't," he answered and chewed on the toffee she had given him. He felt full and comfortable for the first time in days.

"Cuddle," he said.

Matilda cuddled him and said, "Your mother will be turning in her grave."

Peter looked at with shock upon his face, "Will she climb out and come and save me? I wish she would Matty, I wish she would. I miss her and I want her to come and fetch me from that horrid woman. I want you to look after me."

"I will see what I can do," said Matilda.

It was two nights later when Peter saw his mother for the first time. She said,

"I came before with Ann and Mary, but you only saw us as shadows. We are here properly now."

Peter saw his sisters giggling on the floor as they played with his toy farmyard.

"Did you climb out Mama? Was there not enough soil on you?"

"Plenty of soil Peter my baby boy. Matilda and her mother know some little tricks that have helped me come and help you. But you must not tell anyone."

"No one wants me to tell anyone anything Mama. I don't speak to anyone."

"Does Papa come and see you?" she asked as she stroked his head, already knowing the answer.

"No Mama. I don't think he knows what Miss Gardener does. If he knew how cruel she was, he would save me wouldn't he?"

"Perhaps Peter. But in the meantime say nothing to anyone about anything."

"Never?"

"Never, my darling boy. Mama will always look after you."

His mother cuddled him closer and he slowly drifted off to sleep.

Miss Gardener had her suspicions about Peter Prideaux as soon as they first had sex. It wasn't the first time she had played this game - she had given herself to two previous employers, one in Plymouth and one in Launceston but neither relationship had come to anything. This time she felt that she had a chance of a married existence and a home in which she would be in charge.

In a differing role to the others who had no intention of getting rid of their families on her behalf, Peter appeared to have other ideas. Granted he did not kill his wife for her, but he had killed her nevertheless. Miss Gardener was not bothered over the death of the little girls who had given her several sleepless nights. Miss Gardener believed in the Ten Commandments and as she hadn't actually done the killings, she felt that she was probably safe from eternal damnation.

The little sod Peter, whom his father had told her to look after, was a personified reminder of Mistress Prideaux and the girls and so she did as little as she could for him. Giving instructions to the maids that no one was to attend to him other than herself, she felt as though she would be able to have some control over her destiny. She wasn't really sure how though.

When she did go to see the boy, he would run crying into the corner of the attic and so she slammed food and water on the table and told him to keep his mouth shut. His father never checked on him and rarely asked about him.

Peter Senior just satisfied his primal needs with Miss Gardener without speaking and when she asked about marriage, he answered,

"I am not getting married for the fifth time. They already think I murdered the others and I am not marrying a maid and giving the gossips something else to occupy their boring days."

"I know too much about you Peter. I could tell."

"You tell and you will be in the same place as the others. That is a promise."

So she kept quiet and took out her anger on the boy. Perhaps he too would soon die – perhaps from natural causes.

During the recent few days Miss Gardener had heard noises up in the attic. There was talking and singing and the sound of footsteps running across the floor. Not one set of steps, but several.

At first she had gone upstairs and told the boy off, threatening him with permanent imprisonment. He cried of course and said nothing.

That was another new thing. Peter had stopped speaking to her.

All of this was bad enough, but lately the noises had been continuing through the night. The attic was directly above her bedroom and so although she was not as aware during the day, she could not avoid the noises at night.

Tonight she lay still looking out of her window. It had been a bright night, not a full moon, but bright nonetheless. The clouds were now moving in from the coast and the rumbling in the distance signalled the arrival of a storm. It had been quiet in the attic and Miss Gardener was hoping that Peter would be quieter and quieter until he left the house permanently.

Yes, she could hear it – whispering and laughter. She sat up in bed with her heart beating loudly because she knew that he should be alone. She had checked on him before she retired and found him shivering and sobbing on his bed.

Good - horrible child.

And now there were these noises coming from the attic. She would like to send the maid but having shouted at and hit Matilda, banning her from visiting the child earlier that day - Miss Gardener did not want to back down.

She must go herself.

The night had become much darker and she knew the storm would begin soon. She shivered and drew her wool shawl tight around her shoulders. Her heart still raced with the noises and yet when they stopped she strained her ears to catch them again. It must be the atmosphere of the storm, like when the moon was full and could affect people. She was very jumpy and nervous.

She slapped herself lightly on the face and walked confidently out of the door and up the stairs. She wore slippers and so her traverse was silent. The chattering and squealing from the attic continued and increased and was soon interspersed with running feet and bangs.

As she approached the door, she saw that there were candles lit in the attic and light was dancing across the gap at the bottom. She could see shapes crossing in front of the light and there seemed to be more than one frail child creating them.

She gently opened the door, trying to avoid the creaking sound she knew it made. As she did so, the noises stopped and the lights extinguished. Miss Gardener pushed the door wide and heard whimpering in the room corner as she had when she left earlier.

"What are you doing boy? Waking up the house in the night and where did you get the candles?"

Now she could see that it had all been in her imagination, she stalked over to the bed with her arm raised and prepared to remind the child of who was the boss. The concentration this act required meant that she failed to see what was approaching her from behind.

The blow felled her and it was almost a minute before she felt that she could open her eyes. She was lying on the floor and as the lightning flashed she saw two, perhaps three children playing at the far end, dressed in nightclothes. Standing over her was a woman dressed in a dirty grey and green shroud and who wore long scraggly hair. Her face, reflected in the lightning strike was ghoulish and skeletal.

Miss Gardener whimpered.

"Frightened are you now? You didn't mind my little boy crying out in the dark on his own though, did you?"

"Mrs Prideaux? Is that you? I don't understand what is happening. Am I dead?"

"I am death brought back to life as are my children. Do you want to meet my sister wives? They are here too."

The ghoul seemed pleased with her work and poked Miss Gardener with her bare and dirty foot.

Miss Gardener tried to rise but was unable. The thunder rolled and the lightning struck and if she had had any control over her body at all she would have screamed.

"Come here Peter my boy," instructed Anne Prideaux to her son. This he did and as he crouched down he was joined by his sisters. They all had dark eyes and they moved their heads from side to side as they stared at Miss Gardener.

"What are you going to do to me?" she asked faintly.

"Shall we do what you did to us? Shall we poison you and treat you cruel?"

"I did not poison you, it was Peter. I only knew about it afterwards. And I am sorry about your son, I should have looked after him belter. I am so sorry."

Anne Prideaux answered, "I am not a cruel woman, so I shall not kill you. Instead, I shall …"

"Mama! I can hear Papa coming! He will beat me again!"

Mama held him closely and Miss Gardener saw her chance.

"He will not beat you ever again. I can see to that. You are dead Mrs Prideaux and unable to protect your son, but I am alive and I can."

This statement appeared to antagonise the phantom and it reared in the air, elongated and open mouthed. Miss Gardener screwed up her eyes and slammed her hands around her ears.

"I want to help, please let me help!" she shrieked. She heard a loud crash and felt suddenly extremely cold.

"What the hell is the matter with you woman?" asked the familiar voice of Peter.

Miss Gardner opened her eyes and answered,

"She was here. Your wife and your daughters. They were here."

She dropped her head on the floorboards sobbing. Peter dragged her upright using her braids.

"They are dead, you ridiculous woman. How can they have been here?" and he slapped her hard, whether from temper or to assist her in her hysterics, it could not be determined.

Miss Gardener rose, if a little unsteadily, to her feet and looked about the room. Young Peter was on the bed, sucking his thumb, but thankfully silent of sobs.

"They were here Peter, they have returned from the grave to protect your son, they said. Mrs Prideaux made me promise to protect him from your beatings or she will make you suffer."

Peter let go of her hair and strode over to his son.

"Is this true?" he asked him.

"Papa, they were here. My Mama and sisters were here with me and they are not buried in the churchyard. I don't think they were buried deep enough and I am so glad."

His father felt rage and fear rise within him, for he realised that if this were so, then there would be too many ghosts. It could not therefore be true.

"Do not speak of this to me or anyone else boy. This is the Devil's work and if you think you see spirits you could be burned as a witch. I would have to tell the parson that you are a witch and they would take you away immediately!"

Young Peter shut his mouth tightly to stop any more words escaping.

"Mr. Prideaux, do not speak to him so! I saw the spirits too and I am no witch!"

Peter ran back to Miss Gardener and kicked her in the stomach and she curled up. The room was silent and freezing and Peter suddenly became uneasy about the moving dark shadows he thought he could see in the attic room corners. His son sat motionless and speechless on the small cot and his housekeeper lay on the floor and was apparently bleeding through her skirt. He thought about dragging her downstairs and finishing her off. If that was a lost child coming from her, then there would be talk and he wanted no more talk.

"Get downstairs you whore and clean yourself up. Once you have done that, I want you to leave this house and never return."

She raised herself up and stared at him,

"But I promised your wife!"

"Promised her what?"

"That I would look after young Peter. If I don't she will attack me again."

"Don't be so ridiculous and get moving."

He ushered her downstairs, disgusted at the blood soaked clothes.

"I have lost the baby I think. It hurts."

He did not answer. He had no intention of producing a base born child in his line. Miss Gardener staggered to her room and shut the door. As she was removing her skirt, she saw the silhouette of Mrs Prideaux backed against the window.

"He is making me leave," Miss Gardener said.

"So I heard, but we are staying here."

"How?"

"You do not need to know how, I know how. The last thing I want you to do is remove the painting from my old room and take it to the attic and hang it over Peter's bed."

"Which painting?"

"I brought it here. It is from my home and is a picture of a stone house and surrounding parkland."

"I know the one, only your husband took it from your room when you died and it is now hidden behind a tapestry in the library."

"All the better, he won't notice it gone. Put it in the attic and tell the boy we are always with him."

The wraith vanished and Miss Gardener busied herself with her dress. Upon hearing a loud bang, she looked out of the window and saw Prideaux galloping away. She ran out of the room and downstairs to the back kitchen and quickly recovered the painting. She dragged it with difficulty until she met Matilda in the passage.

"We need to take this to Master Peter to keep him safe."

"You saw his mother? Did she punish you?"

Miss Gardener stopped her efforts and looked at the girl,

"Matty, I have just this last half hour miscarried my baby. I have been punished."

Matilda nodded and helped her former enemy with the painting and they soon had it installed on the attic wall. The still silent boy looked at it and cuddled his pillow.

"We should get him a dolly or a toy bear or something," said Matilda.

"You can, I have been told to leave today and never return."

"Why?"

"Because he is a coward and he doesn't want me here because I know..."

"You know what Miss?"

"I know what sort of a man he is and if I tell anyone, he will kill me."

Miss Gardener patted the boy on his head and said to Matilda,

"Look after him and keep the picture there and don't move it until Peter or his mother tells you to."

She swished out of the room and Matilda almost felt sorry for her. She examined the picture carefully as she dusted it. It was a very large oil painting of a stone mansion with lawns to the front and side and trees and shrubs circling it. It was a night scene and the full creamy moon had the edges of clouds surrounding it. The house windows were in darkness and the impression was one of sleep and comfort.

Matilda stroked Peter and said,

"I will look after you young man and I will fetch you food and clean clothes, now don't you worry."

Peter looked at the painting after Matilda left and surveyed the scene. He saw the house and the moon and the trees and the people standing in front of the house waving at him. There were lights at all the windows and the open front door revealed a warm and cosy hallway. A lady and two girls stood and waved and blew kisses and there, walking across the lawn were three more ladies who turned and waved too.

"You are safe Peter. We shall always watch over you!" they shouted.

He snuggled back under his blankets as Matilda returned with food.

"Eat this Peter and then go to sleep. You can have a bath and change your clothes in the morning."

Matilda glanced at the painting and muttered,

"Oh! I didn't see the people before. That's funny; they look like your mother and sisters."

The figures waved to Matilda and she stepped back at first shocked and then pleased.

"They are looking after you Peter," she said.

*

Peter never spoke a word again to a living soul. He relied on the picture to keep him sane and happy throughout his childhood and when he was finally allowed into a room of his own and had a tutor, he took the painting with him. His father did not notice as Matilda made the arrangements, ensuring that it was hung directly over his bed.

The tutor was brought in to help the boy learn as much as a mute could. Peter read most of the books in the library without commuting this fact to anyone other than Matilda and of course, the picture wraiths.

Initially Mama would climb out in order to rock him to sleep and his sisters would come and play with him and Matilda brought him his food and clean clothes. Later Mama helped him to read and study and learn how to behave like a gentleman. His sisters, who had remained a steady 10 years of age in direct conflict to the age they were when they died, taught him to dance and held competitions in many subjects. The previous wives, who visited the painting and therefore him, were a jolly trio who showered him with love and often gave aunt like assistance.

These women he did not need to speak to. They all understood through thought and Peter remained self-involved and ventured outside rarely.

His father rarely visited him, instead choosing to spend his time in ale houses and gambling. His fortune was diminishing and his investments bringing in little. He must bring in more income if he did not want to downsize his living standards in any way.

He decided that smuggling was to be his answer and agreed to allow hidden storage at their Ringmore home.

"I shall invest in the business if I make money from this involvement," he told a fellow gambling companion.

"You are doing this to pay off your debts and if I decide, you will be involved more. As soon as you have paid me off then we shall see about investment."

Peter Senior was finding it difficult to acknowledge the problems he was facing.

As the strange men arrived at their house during the night, bringing contraband which was to be stored in hidden cupboards and rooms latterly used during the Civil War, Peter and Matilda would leave the house and go down to the beach.

They would watch the men arrive in their boats and see the clippers far out to sea. They liked listening to the men panic or boast about their exploits. The beach was only minutes away from the house and no one noticed a mute boy and a tiny maid only five years older than he.

Mama had visited with them on a few occasions and the girls and his adopted aunts would come when they were sure the beach was empty. But it was too much of a picnic when they all attended and ran about.

And there was no swimming. The women would not enter the water.

"We can travel on the water in a boat," Mama informed her son.

"We would need a big boat," answered Peter.

"Not if you brought the picture," said Mama. "Then we could all row along the coast and see the sights."

So they chose a night when they could row between tides and stay in the shadows of a moonless night. Matilda put the painting in an old hand cart after wrapping it in a sack. She had added the usual food they liked to take, only for Peter and her, naturally. The run to the beach was all downhill and so the load easy. They were not thinking about the return journey.

Matty had chosen which boat they would take and they climbed into it, heaved the painting behind a seat and pushed the boat out of the shallows. The sound of the smooth calm incoming tide was relaxing. As Peter moved the oars in the dark water, he noticed how the sea seemed much thicker than stream water. He pondered the idea as they rowed further out to sea before heading west towards the mouth of the Erme.

"Let's go to Mothecombe and nose around there," said Mama from the lawn bench on which she sat in the front of the picture. The painting was propped up against a seat and secured by thin rope, to enable the women to view their night-time trip.

The water was so calm that they were able to see the lamps in cottage windows on the shore and the only sound from the sea was the waves slapping against the boat side. As they rowed around the headland, Peter noticed that the sea was becoming a little choppy but put it down to the changing tide.

They rowed across the estuary in order to reach the Mothecombe side and soon learned that this was a serious error when the rowing boat began rocking from side to side in a violent manner.

Matty said, "Peter, I think that this is getting a bit dangerous."

"Peter, you must not be alarmed but you must get us all to the shoreline. If you lose this painting, then we must stay here forever." His mother clearly trying to keep her family calm was failing miserably.

Peter was more than aware of the danger they were in. The idea of a row to Mothecombe, where he had visited with his aunt when he was younger had sounded so exciting. The thought that he could visit with his mother and sisters made it even better. Now the sea was frightening and the boat rocking and he really did not know what to do next.

White tops appeared on previously invisible waves and Matty and Peter had to hold tight onto both sides of the boat to save themselves from falling in. The oars had already dropped into the sea and the painting was wobbling dangerously from side to side. With the exception of his mother, the women were screaming in loud pitched voices.

Matty grabbed Peter's arm and pointed to the bobbing heads of seals surrounding the boat. He stared, unable to appreciate their beauty.

"Hello!" said a seal.

Peter stopped his panicking for a moment and watched the seal as she raised herself over the side of the boat. It was obvious she was a woman as her bare breasts were raised over the boat side as she held on, using her bent arms.

Matty squealed and said,

"You are a mermaid, aren't you? You are so pretty. I love mermaids!"

"Do you know many mermaids?"

"Well no! I have just heard the stories about you. I would love to be your friend."

"Funny little girl. I see that you have some spirit women who are in distress."

Peter put a protective arm over the painting as he saw his mother and sisters holding each other as they rocked and fell from the bench upon which they had been sat. His aunts were lying next to a large oak tree to which they held on for apparent dear life.

"You are a mute boy, aren't you? Many of us cannot speak where I live either, we don't need to."

The maid dragged herself higher onto the boat and Peter could see that she was naked from the waist up and was wearing some kind of pale green and blue shimmering garment below. Although still dark, he was surprised to note that he could still see the colours.

"Don't worry about the sea and the waves. We will look after you and your spirit family. It is they who drew us to you."

A giggling and splashing made them look behind the maid. There were several others, similar to their boat visitor and they were carrying seaweed which they began wrapping around the rowlocks.

Soon, the maids were pulling them towards the beach.

"Mothecombe Beach is very quiet. You can stay here until the tide turns and then paddle back to your own beach."

"I am Matilda and this is Peter Prideaux," said Matty, once they were safely ensconced with their boat on the dry sand. The mermaids had arranged themselves on the rocky outcrop at the beach edge and their tails splashed and kept contact with the water. They were beautiful creatures and their tails, much bigger than one might imagine, were covered in large rainbow coloured scales. They had tail fins, but these seemed to be intertwined with a floating rainbow like dress material.

They were naked, but their bodies were covered in long wavy hair and their laughter and graceful movements proved they were anything but ashamed or embarrassed of their undressed state.

Peter's mother, sisters and aunts were having the time of their lives running along the beach and squealing and shrieking.

"I wish we could stay here forever," said little Mary.

"You can if you wish," answered the mermaid.

"How?" asked Anne Prideaux.

"If you follow us into the sea, all you spirit people, down to where we live, you will be able to live in and by the sea forever."

"Will we not drown mother?" asked little Ann.

"No daughter, that is not possible. If we live by the sea and swim under the sea, we shall never be able to return to the picture. That is what it means Mistress Mermaid?"

"It is. We are all restless spirits under water, we cannot return to the land and spirits on land cannot go into the sea. It is your choice, but there will be no more living in a painting at the beck and call of only one person."

Peter looked up. The mermaid meant him.

"I wish to be near to my son and protect him from his murderous father."

"He is old enough to fend for himself now Anne. He will be forced to leave the family home soon when his father loses it."

Peter stood up and walked over to his mother. He was not able to hold back his tears, but he knew that he must release her from her prison and by letting her go, he would be able to leave too.

"We can all visit with each other anytime we want," said his mother. "The girls need to be able to get out and about now."

Peter nodded and after a few farewells, watched his erstwhile family walk happily into the sea. His mother turned and waved and blew him a kiss as she waded into the dark water. Matty reached for his hand and held it tightly as the spirits vanished into the water.

"Come on Peter. We have got to get back before it gets light again."

Peter helped push the boat back out to sea and jumped in after Matty. They began to row back across the river mouth towards the Red Cove side and encountered such rough water that they nearly lost the mermaid returned oars again. Before they were halfway across the estuary a head bobbed up and then another and then another.

"Peter! Look" We have tails! We can swim!"

And there they all were, swimming and splashing and happy.

"No one ever dies Peter. It is not possible!" And the laughing group pulled the rocking boat back to their launch site below Ringmore. There were two early fishermen busy at the water's edge.

"You youngsters better get back quick as you can. If Alf Pike finds you've had his boat out, he will clip your ears, Prideaux or no Prideaux," said one.

"Who is that in the water? One of your friends?" said his companion.

"Mermaids," answered Matty.

"Clear off or I will clip your ears," said the fisherman.

Peter and Matty ran up the hill away from the beach and when they looked back they could see the surface of the sea greatly disturbed with a patch moving south. Matty dragged Peter's arm and they began their homeward journey with hand trolley and half empty painting.

One of the fishermen said, "Pointless going out this morning now. Those damn mermaids will have taken the fish with them." And he bad temperedly threw his pots out of the boat.

*

In 1749 on a warm night in April, Peter took an early walk down to Aymer Cove using the track from his house. He enjoyed sitting on the pebbles and watching the sea.

He did this on as many mornings as he could and often in the early hours, as he had great difficulty sleeping.

He had five children, the eldest 20 and the youngest only 10. There had also been three dead babies and those losses had affected his wife very much. She was a difficult woman to live with and the fact that Peter never spoke and could only nod his head and offer mild pats in comfort, probably did not assist her recovery.

Peter hadn't married until his early thirties because he had needed to build a career as a carpenter when his father died shortly after losing their family home to his bankers. The only property they had left was a large house near Noddon Mill complete with land and orchards, for which his father had been given the 99 year lease on the 19th December 1698. Francis Kirkham the previous tenant, had died after falling into the mill pool late one night, apparently drunk and was found early the following morning. There had been rumours that Francis was owed a good deal of money by Peter Prideaux, but it could not be proven. Funnily enough it was this same pool where Miss Gardener was found dead, shortly after leaving her employ with the Prideauxs. It was said that she killed herself as there was evidence that she had recently lost a child and she knew that she would have been scorned.

Young Peter was 24 years old when his father finally died. He awoke after hearing screaming in the middle of the night and upon looking out of his bedroom window to the orchard, for this was from where the screaming came, saw his father in a nightshirt running towards the mill. Peter was sure that he could see a mist in pursuance of him. By the time Peter had run downstairs and found his father, he was face down in the stream, his legs in a fearsome animal trap.

He had such a look on his face that the women who laid him out and washed him said he must have died in dreadful fear.

Matty, her brother and his wife all worked for them and between them took care of the house, the animals and the land. The only money earned was that which was earned at market. John was also a carpenter and it was he who taught Peter his early carpentry skills, which Peter then elaborated upon throughout his life to eventually become a most sort after craftsman.

Peter had managed to stay in the house and smallholding and lived in comfort with his dogs and a few animals. There were plenty of young girls calling on him with pies and offers of help for a man could not manage alone, but these were all rejected. Peter had had enough of women.

It hadn't taken him long to put out of his mind the events of his childhood. The memories were terrible enough but the actions of his unhinged father gave Peter plenty to focus on. After his death, Peter had insisted that his father be buried one foot lower than usual so that he would never climb out. Rector

Thomas Heskett had wanted to have Peter Senior buried with his wife in order to save valuable space in the churchyard, but Peter paid extra to have him buried at the far end of the grounds.

He didn't climb back out and Peter had not been seen since. He had however seen many others walking around Ringmore and its narrow roads waving to him as they visited their old families and watched from the fence lines. Sometimes he would see them walk down to the beach on which he now sat. It was so much easier to see spirits when their glowing mist form was viewed against the dim and dark light of the night. Sunshine often cancels out the phantoms to the uninitiated.

The familiar splashing and high pitched squealing sounds carried across the water and Peter jumped up. He waved and his mother and sisters waved back.

"Come, come Peter! The night is wonderful!"

So he pushed a boat onto the water, now his own boat, and rowed over to his family.

This made him happy – being with them. Much more so than his own family which was an odd concept. He put it down to his unusual upbringing and his inability to feel love and affection for anything other than his dogs. He had been shown so little affection during his life that to give love to a person seemed strange. He was kind and helpful and aware of his responsibilities. His family had never gone without food and they enjoyed living in a decent house with an excellent reputation.

He wasn't enjoying his life lately though. He often felt as though a heavy black ceiling was above him and he couldn't raise his energies or enthusiasm high enough to move it. Over the years he had discovered that he used the least energy if he left the ceiling above his head until it moved of its own accord. Life was just too long and difficult and now his dog had died.

George had sickened suddenly over the past couple of weeks and he had done everything he could for him. He had stopped his work in order to care for him and sent his son instead. It seemed that his contractors were happy with the temporary replacement and so Peter was able to spend every waking minute with George - the most faithful dog a man could have.

Peter had initially been suspicious of his wife as she had no love of dogs and resented one in her home. Peter believed that she may have been poisoning him and it brought back too many memories. But Joan was genuinely upset about George's illness and looked after the dog while Peter slept.

Then last night George died. He licked his master's hand and howled as he fell back into his basket.

Peter didn't cry, because he never cried. And now his life was over.   He was 54 and didn't want to start again with another George.

He pushed the boat further out until he was waist deep in the water and then pulled himself into it. He had a surge of sadness as he thought of all the times George would have been waiting for him in the boat, wagging his tail and barking at his silly master.

Peter rowed towards the splashing and saw his mother and sisters swimming in the warm moonlight.

They looked as young as ever and welcomed him as they always had when he visited. He never brought his wife or his children to the beach and they left him to his night-time ramblings.

As he rowed nearer, he heard an almighty thunder crack which had been preceded by a lightning flash Then nothing.

Peter looked back to shore and noticed that a thick green mist obscured his view of the land. It would no doubt clear before long.

He reached for his oar and heard a bark.

It was George.

Peter reached out for his friend and George licked his hand and wagged his tail. His mother leaned over the side of the boat and stroked George as she always did. George jumped off the boat and swam along with the mermaids. Peter went to grab him, fearful of him drowning and then remembered that he had buried George only a few hours earlier.

Perhaps he hadn't buried him deep enough.

George swam away and then turned and barked at Peter and under the applause of his family, Peter jumped in too.

He now saw that the mist had moved seaward and covered his boat, but it didn't matter.

As Peter swam strongly towards Mothecombe with his family and his dog, he thought that his wife would not have to worry about how deep he was buried.

THE LANLIVERY LIGHTS

Featuring Peter Prideaux (1733 – 1810)

The document detailed below was written by Mary Prideaux, wife of Peter Prideaux following his death in 1810. It was discovered in her desk drawer by her son Thomas Peter Prideaux who became known as Teepee, for ease of address.

I have reproduced it word for word as I am able to read it – some of the pages have been spoiled over the years.

This is the life story of my husband Peter Prideaux and because of the years we have spent together is also my life story. Some of the facts I have taken from the questions I asked his and my family but most Peter told me or I already knew. Some of the story may appear to be in the form of a confession, but I want only to put my side of the story. I told him many times that he should record such an interesting life and he said he would do so when he had nothing better to do. He is now in the ground at Modbury church and so I have decided that before I join him, I shall write these stories down in case one of our ancestors may be interested.

Being fifteen when your father dies is very difficult for anyone and young Peter was no exception. He and his father had never been close but Peter thought of his childhood as happy and carefree.

His mother and father got on well together, although his father was a mute and only communicated by signal and written notes. The family only realised after his death that they knew little about his younger life apart from the gossip which persisted about his grandfather. I think that is also why I wanted to make sure that my Peter's personal history is known.

On the night his father died, he was noticed by an early fisherman climbing into his boat and rowing out to sea. Then he was seen jumping out of the boat and swimming away. The fisherman thought he saw dolphins or sharks splashing around him and it was assumed that he drowned while trying to escape from them. His body was never found, but that wasn't an uncommon occurrence on that coastline.

It had meant a deal of trouble for the young Prideaux family when it was certain that the breadwinner would not be returning home. There was very little money left and so my Peter had to actively pursue unpaid accounts. Most were paid immediately and more work given to him. The community did not want the family to starve and helped where they could.

"I promise I will complete the work that my father promised to do. I have finished my apprenticeship and will get in help if I need to," he pleaded with them.

 A few refused outright, not wishing to trust their jobs to such a young man, but some agreed to let him continue the jobs - at a reduced rate of course.

But he earned enough to keep the family fed and the youngest boy helped with the lighter and less complicated jobs. The eldest Joan went to work for a local farmer and his mother but was sent home when she became pregnant by him, although he denied touching her. The family suffered the shame of the arrival a base born son but the kind Rector Thomas Heskett, one of the longest serving holy men ever at All Hallows, did agree to baptise little John in order to insure him against a fiery eternity.

Peter made the errant seducer pay a few months later when he met him walking alone along the coast path by the cove one night and ensured he would not father another child.

After building up his new business for a couple of years, Peter was engaged to work on the house in which his father was born. This was the house which had been repossessed by his creditors.

"We should do well with this job mother," he said as he set off. "The house is very well built and the timber I have been given to work with is good oak. There is a porch to be built and carving to be done."

"Will you tell them who you are?" she asked.

"They already know mother. How could they not?"

"I gather that they are strangers from the north and may not yet have been told the history of the house."

"Somerset is hardly the north mother, but I take your point."

Peter had been practising on pieces of wood in his father's workshop. The feel of the wood and the tools with which he would make pictures on it, drew praise from anyone who saw it. He hoped he would make a great impression when he did the work.

He arrived at the house and walked directly to the front door. Young Peter had always loved the confident ability of his father to do this and be made welcome. It was not easy to get a master craftsman such as Peter Prideaux and so he was always looked after. My Peter hoped that he would have the same success as his father in this regard.

The current owner, Mr Fox, was aware that Peter's father and grandfather had once lived here. He was far too much of a gentleman to make comment however.

"Do you think you could have a look up there for me Peter? I have been thinking of getting carving along the timbers. What do you think? Go and have a look." said Mr Fox.

"I will sir. Though I am not sure how obvious any sort of carving would be. No one will see it."

"It would be visible from the balcony and I want this to be the most beautiful house in the neighbourhood!"

Peter moved the ladder over to the side of the house and made sure that it was safely in position.

"Shall I hold it for you Peter?" asked Mr Fox.

"No, I will be alright. You can go about your own work sir."

Mr Fox watched his young man move quickly up the ladder and begin to examine the timber above the attic floor windows. He moved away and walked towards the load of oak which was being delivered and addressed William Freeman.

"Hello William. I did not know that you were coming here today."

"I am just delivering some wood and stuff for all this building that is going on. I have to get back to town quickly though and bring back more. This job must be costing you a fortune!"

"Well don't complain. It is keeping you lot in work!"

"I won't. See you later Mr Fox."

William clicked to his pony and it trotted off, pulling the now empty cart around the corner of the house.

Edward Fox watched them trot off and he turned away. Suddenly he heard a tremendous crash followed by the sound of shouting and he saw men run towards the noise. He ran too, already dreading what may have happened. He came around the corner and saw a tangle of pony, cart and ladder.

The pony got up and stood still, apparently safe. Two men lay on the ground, neither moving. Mr Fox ran to the men and looked at the still body and staring eyes of William Freeman. Peter Prideaux was face down and unmoving.

"Come on sir. There is nothing you can do here," said one of the other men.

Fox pulled back and turned Peter over. Instinctively he thumped him in the chest and shouted, "Breathe!"

Two days later he attended the funeral of William Freeman and the sickbed of Peter Prideaux.

Edward Fox said that he was very sorry but he would have to get in another carpenter, now that my Peter was suffering from a broken leg and ribs. Peter could not be expected to take on the responsibility of such a big job on his own but he promised that he would recommend Peter for smaller jobs. He would also look out for some on his own estate.

This downturn in income affected the standing of the family greatly, especially when his mother and sister were forced to take in washing in order to meet the household bills while Peter recovered.

Peter wondered whether to mention to his mother about the sight which had met his eyes when he first climbed the ladder to reach the attic window. He never told her but did tell me one night when he was feeling a bit down.

He said he saw a little boy sobbing on a small cot in the corner of the attic. That did not seem right or appropriate and he determined to ask Mr Fox about him as soon as he was back on the ground.

He tapped on the window in order to get the boy's attention and give him comfort in some way. The boy looked at him and stopped sobbing for a while. Then he saw a woman dressed in grey seemingly jump from a painting on the wall and scoop the boy into her arms. Just as Peter was going to knock again, he noticed children jumping from the painting and land softly on the attic floor. Surely it must be a window – or a hatch?

As he pondered this conundrum he was utterly shocked when a woman's face appeared on the other side of his window. The face was ghoul like and green and the black eyes peering through the straggly hair burned into Peter's mind. He felt his senses smoke and his head spin. At the same moment he heard a crash and saw the ladder wobble and sway.

Before he fell, he saw more phantoms at the window laughing and pointing at him. Peter remembered nothing else until he looked into the eyes of Edward Fox as he came back from the dead.

His mother never recovered from the shock of his accident and the shame of their position and her health rapidly deteriorated until she could only sit in front of the fire and stare. Peter managed to get on his feet quite quickly and with the aid of a pair of crutches and strong will he disguised his serious pain and made chairs and tables in his workshop. These sold well and kept the bills paid until he was able to take on more serious jobs.

Joan finally died following years of poor health, on Peter's 23rd birthday and he arranged her burial within two days. He knew that she had died of a broken heart. I remember how sad the family was, but I was only five years old at the time. That seems odd when I think back although it has never mattered really.

Thomas, Peter's younger brother worked alongside Peter. Thomas was married but Peter did not bother with women. Responsibility was weighing heavy on him and he didn't want a wife and children for a while yet. That is what he told me years later, but I know for a fact that he had lots of girls.

Other local girls made plays for him and some he took up on their offers, but none were able to lead him to the altar. He saw Joan, Elizabeth, Ann and Thomas marry and begin families, but Peter was not tempted. He took girls to the nearby beach and into the woods, but never lost his heart.

He was plagued with dreams and fancies about the past. Work came in regularly and he could easily provide for a family now, but all he wanted to do was travel, not into unknown lands, but back to Cornwall where he felt very strongly that his roots lay.

Peter was well read and spent much of his time learning as much as possible. He asked questions of anyone whom he thought he might know and became quite an expert on the history of Devon and Cornish families.

He was quite sure that the Prideauxs could be traced prior to the Norman invasion, but had so far found it impossible to make the links. Some of his information had come from father to son and he felt that often this information was more reliable than that which was written by those who had no knowledge of the people about whom they were writing. Peter had been feeling this way since he had seen the phantoms in the attic.

Knowing a little of his recent ancestors, he was sure they were connected to him.

Sometimes he imagined that he had become more knowing since that day, when he nearly died. Or had died, if he paid any attention to what the other workmen were inclined to say.

His mother certainly thought that he was different after the accident, but would have been surprised to learn that since that day he often saw his dead family in addition to other friends and neighbours who had passed.

Peter would choose to visit Aymer Cove as he saw fewer people there than at Challaborough. He would often see large fish out at sea. If pressed he would have said mermaids, but felt more comfortable mentioning ghosts than mermaids. So he told no one.

My family - the Wills family were particular friends of the Prideauxs. We lived in one of the cottages between the Prideaux property by the mill and Ringmore village. They often talked to each other over a drink in the evening at the Inn.

My father Thomas, found Peter to be a very clever man and enjoyed spending time with him. My mother Annie had a serious crush on Peter before I was born and would try and seduce him whenever she could engineer that they were alone together. All that had come of it was a kiss and that he regretted especially as Annie reminded him of it whenever she saw him. He told me this story years later when he was a little drink sodden. I didn't mind but I had a horror that he was about to tell me that he had discovered that I was his daughter as well as his wife. Thankfully this was not so. It might seem a strange thing to say but I know of two – no three people who have the same father and grandfather and also marriages which have taken place between brother and sister when parental origins had not been completely brought into the open. I have been told that baptism wipes away all problems in this regard but I don't understand how that can be so.

When I was fifteen years old I began to take a shine to the dark haired, dashing Peter Prideaux. I was at the silly age that I have recognised in our own daughter. Because of the way I behaved, I looked after our girl too much and she resented me for it.

I went round one evening to see Peter and bring him a birthday present. An excuse of course, I had ensured that he would be on his own and that we were unlikely to be disturbed. His housekeeper was at her sister's and the other servants had finished work or gone to the inn. The night was dark and ideal for paying a visit to a friend which I did not want recorded. I clutched the embroidered waistcoat which I had been working on for months and was now wrapped in cream linen.

"Mary this must have cost you a fortune. I can't accept this."

"I was given the material by Mistress Stone; I just did the needlework myself. Do you like it?"

He told me later that my eyes had bewitched him and that night he could not see beyond those and forgot my age and innocence. I have come to see later that was his excuse to take advantage of me. But I was too young back then.

"Come on in the cottage silly and have a drink and a piece of cake. My sister brought me some food today."

"That is because you never bother for yourself. I would bother for you," I said in my practised shy voice. I followed him into the house and busied myself cutting cake and pouring ale, a task I had seen my mother perform for my father.

After performing a few more personal tasks for him, he said,

"Come on Mary. You had better get yourself home now."

I felt grown up, ashamed and conscious that I could never go back on what had just happened. It hadn't felt special or lovely or anything like that. I didn't even feel as close to him as I had when I first arrived at his door.

"Don't tell anyone about what we have just done," was all Peter said to me.

So I smiled, left his house and went home. In the weeks that followed, I hardly saw him, let alone spoke to him.

As I got fatter from what I thought was depression and overeating, Peter took himself off to Cornwall to take on a big job a friend had set up for him.

He told me all about a few years after we were married.

At The Crown Inn in Lanlivery, Peter stopped for sustenance and a bed.

"What is your business 'ere my lovely?" asked the bonny girl who served him.

"I am working locally for as few months and need board and lodging until I can find a cottage with a workshop."

"I can find you a bed 'ere. What is your name?"

"I am Peter Prideaux of South Devon."

"Well now!" she stopped pouring the cider and stood with her hand on her hip, as might be expected of a woman such as she.

"John, John come over here! We have one of your Devon relatives in tonight!"

This John Prideaux turned out to be a very friendly and influential man in Bodmin. Peter was made so welcome that he would normally have felt quite embarrassed about the attention.

"Now why have you come to visit us?" John asked.

Peter told him about the house on which he had been contracted to work and that he would be in the area until at least Christmas and needed a cottage to rent.

"You must meet my grandfather," he said and called over a very old man who had just entered the inn.

"Grandad, meet Peter Prideaux from Devon. He is working on the Old Manor and needs a place to stay for a few months."

William, the grandfather took Peter's hand and stared into his eyes.

"We have met before Peter," he said.

Peter suddenly felt very strange and wondered if it was the ale he had been drinking. He felt as though his head was swimming as he realised that the two of them were standing in a forest surrounded by men he did not recognise.

"Oh, have we?" he answered.

"I'll come with 'ee on the next part of your trip Peter. Come to my house tonight and we shall talk."

So Peter did as he was bid and was glad of it.

William showed Peter into the pretty cottage at Lanlivery after they had put the pony into a stable. It was warm inside but quite dark. William went over to the hearth and rattled the fire with a poker until he brought it back into life. He took the lamp, lit the wick and put it into the centre of the table.

"Sit down 'ere Peter and make yourself at home."

Peter sat on a wooden settle which was placed at right angles to the fire and leant forward towards the flames. He took the bowl which had been handed to him and sipped it. Hot soup was not quite what he expected, but he enjoyed it nonetheless.

"I will show you where you are sleeping in a minute Peter. Then tomorrow we shall talk about things."

William took Peter up the rickety steps and into a tiny room at the top of the stairs.

"I sleep here in the room on the right and you on the left," he said.

Peter lay on the small bed and wondered what age of small child it had been made for. He curled up his legs, covered himself with the patchwork covers and fell into a deep sleep. He was awakened by a noise which he initially assumed was his host calling him down for breakfast. It was still dark but Peter got up quickly not wishing to cause offence. He was downstairs before he realised that William was still in bed and it was only 2, according to the ticking clock.

Peter decided he would fetch some milk from the pitcher he had seen in the back kitchen and check on his pony. As he walked outside, the time was confirmed as he heard the hall clock chime twice. His pony was asleep, flat out on straw and perfectly content. Peter took a walk to the front of the cottage and stood in the lane watching contentedly the sleeping cottages.

He leant against the cottage and lit his pipe. He noticed flickering lamp lights over in the church yard initially and assumed that they belonged to early workers, possibly mine workers. The lights came across the cemetery and stopped at the wall which divided it from the lane. Peter looked forward to meeting the men as they passed through the lych-gate. But they never arrived. Peter saw the lamps reach the gate, the light hiding full detail of the shadows and then the lights extinguished.

Peter waited a moment and then his curiosity got the better of him. He went over to the gate and walked through it. He noticed an icy rain feeling which engulfed him as he did so but noticed nothing else. There was no one there.

Peter walked back to the cottage, nervously checking behind him every few steps.

The next morning dawned bright and clear and Peter came downstairs to find his host already making breakfast. Breakfast consisted of meat and egg and bread. Peter had not realised how hungry he was and ate quickly.

William ate also, but more slowly. He looked at Peter closely and said,

"You look just like the rest – handsome, strong and with those dark eyes. You are a seeker and look for information everywhere. You want to know it all in an instant. And you can see spirits."

Peter mentioned what he had seen in the night.

"Seen them already have you?" and he laughed.

"Seen who? Are you saying they were ghosts? And what do you mean by all the rest? Like whom?" asked Peter bewildered.

"We descend from a special people Peter and are always interacting with ghosts and phantoms and all sorts of strange things."

Peter said nothing. He felt uncomfortable about the content of William's speech.

"I will go with you to the Old Manor if you like. I could do with a trip out."

Peter agreed. He guessed that it might be useful to have a local man accompany him when he turned up for the job. This work had come from a recommendation from Mr Fox who still felt guilty about Peter's fall and sent work his way whenever he was able. The owner of the Old Manor, Mr Hele wanted panelling and carving in several rooms in the house including the grand staircase. Peter was nervous and he didn't mind saying so.

They tacked up William's pony and attached the cart, complete with his tools. They first pulled into the Crown Inn and spoke to the smith at the forge next to it.

William shouted over to him,

"Hello Tom, how are you? "

"Hello William. Who is the stranger with you?"

William brought Peter over to meet Tom who looked at him closely and said, "Oh I see, another one." And he went back to his work.

William went into the Crown to do whatever business he needed to do and Peter looked at the men and horses that were waiting for Tom the smith. One came over to talk to him.

"I used to work in the mine over at St Blazey but I lost my job there," he said after discovering that Peter was working locally.

"Oh dear why?"

"I complained about working conditions. No one does that. You don't need an assistant do you? I could do with some money."

"Are you a carpenter?"

"Twenty years man and boy down that pit sir. I am a very good and skilled carpenter if you need one."

"I will know better once I have seen the job. What is your name sir?"

"My name is Zeb Prowse. I live in the village and can be found quite easily."

"I will certainly keep you in mind. Are the conditions at the mine so bad?"

"There was a terrible accident there about twenty years ago. Six men from this village and surrounding area were killed including my father and two uncles."
"I am very sorry to hear about that Zeb."

Zeb touched his hat and walked away as William hobbled towards the cart.

"We need to get on our way William."

"Yes we do," he said and clambered aboard.

They travelled along the shaded byways. Peter guessed that these lanes were narrower than the lanes in Devon; they went past a small river running alongside the road.

"When the rain is falling during the winter, that stream is a torrent. The tinners used it to wash the ore and get the tin out, back in the day. Because of that practice, eventually the estuary silted up and now the sea does not come up so far. Not so very long ago, the water was right up to Pontsmill and different valleys around here had ships coming right up. Now it is only land and the ships can no longer get here," said William.

"Do you know, I was thinking that this place would have had more connection with the sea. I keep imagining that I will see someone I know, but I don't know how that is possible."

Warming to the theme, he added, "I really feel as though I have been here before."

"You have, in a manner of speaking. Wait until I show you the castle."

"Castle?"

William stopped talking now that he had Peter's full attention and stared straight ahead smiling. Every so often he gave instructions about which way to turn, up a lane, down a lane, all the time surrounded by woods and ferns, moss and bracken. They travelled through Luxulyan, a village which Peter promised himself that he would have a proper look at on the return journey. The valley out of Luxulyan was other worldly and Peter imagined he saw faces peering at him from behind trees and boulders.

"This is a beautiful place," remarked Peter.

"Aye it is. When I die, I shall come here and stay."

Peter thought that this was a peculiar remark to make, but on reflection he agreed. If there is a choice after death, then this would be a good place to spend eternity.

They continued up the steep, rock strewn path in silence and straight along when the road levelled until it began to drop down when suddenly, William told him to stop and down he jumped.

"Tie the pony up, we shall walk the rest of the way."

They had arrived by a track in the wood which led steeply uphill. First they crossed a stream by way of a log which had fallen conveniently over it. Peter thought he heard chanting or singing.

"Is there a monastery hereabouts?" he asked.

"Oh, hearing it already are you? No, there is no monastery here," laughed William and Peter asked nothing more. William was going to play with him today and Peter did not fancy being played with.

They climbed up the steep track further into the wood where the sky was only visible through the roof of the tree canopy and elsewhere the sun streamed through the trees intermittently. The track turned one way and then the other, all the time taking them skyward. There were small stone walls alongside the track which were covered in lichen and moss.

They scrambled over a wall and followed the track to where there were fewer trees and the land rose steeply. While Peter felt a little out of breath, William was not affected.

"See here and here. This is where the entrance would have been - well one of the entrances. Follow me and keep up!"

William seemed to climb faster and Peter caught up as William stood on yet another stone wall. Part of this wall was covered with grass and soil and was more than a little ramshackle.

"Up you get slowcoach. You a young man too!" William said laughingly.

Peter was not prepared for what he saw when he stood on the top of this wall. The wall was a large circle, no not a circle - an oval. It circumnavigated the summit save for two breaks where it was possible to enter and leave without climbing. Many of the stones were missing, removed no doubt by housebuilders and gardeners over the years.

His new companion said, "This was a stockade in years gone by, many years gone by. Inside there were wooden buildings were attached to the walls and the animals and men, women and children lived in them. This stone wall would have been a protection against invaders or pirates or enemies. I mean real pirates, not tradesman!"

In Peter's mind he could see the entire scene before it was described to him. He smelled the fires and the animals and saw people milling about and shouting. He felt like a ghost in someone else's time.

"Look out beyond Peter!"

It was astonishing.

He could see the sea! There on the left on the coastline he could see the Priory with its own landing stage and harbour. But what Priory? If it was Tywardreath, he knew it to be partly ruined and largely unoccupied, and yet there it was – intact and smoke rising from chimneys. There was sea at the bottom of the hill on which they stood. That could not be – for the sea now covered the lane on which they had left the trap. "Oh please let the pony be safe!"

"You are only seeing it as it was Peter just as your ancestors saw it. Tell me, what else do you see?"

"Ships, but I don't recognise the ships."

Peter was confused and he suddenly felt weak and helpless. He wobbled and leant against a tree.

"Affecting you a bit is it Peter?"

"I don't know if I am sickening for something. I've done a lot recently, but no more than I would normally do," answered Peter. If the truth were told he felt worried.

"It's only because you are not used to the power running through you at the moment. If you just accept it, you'll soon feel fine."

"Power?"

"When a true Prideaux stands on top of this place, then the power is magnified beyond imagination."

Peter had no idea what William was talking about and sat down on the grass covered stone wall. He closed his eyes and took some deep breaths. He felt giddy at first but that soon passed.

As he breathed deeply he became aware of the smell of the earth. He noticed that someone had lit a bonfire nearby - he could smell the smoke. He also heard men talking and shouting in the distance. They were to have company it seemed. Peter sat for a few minutes before opening his eyes.

The sight before him almost made him stop breathing. It was night time and the fort was ablaze with torches and there was a large fire in the middle of the camp. He saw a tall long wooden building which was filled with men who were eating and drinking.

Some women scurried about the site and in and out of small shed like buildings attached to the large stockade fence.

Peter could no longer see over the wall but as he looked up, he saw that there were men standing at the top of the fencing in a sort of crow's nest. They at least would have a good view of the sea or land dependent upon its current appearance. His current view was loud and smelly and frightening. A man lurched towards him. He was dirty and drunk and was accompanied by a huge hound dog. Peter tried to make himself appear smaller and the man did not notice him. The hound gave him a curious look and then began to bark.

"Come here you stupid dog, there is nothing there," said the drunk man.

Could the man not see him?

Peter got up and walked towards the large building in the centre. It soon became obvious that no one could see him and he quickly stopped questioning that fact.

A giggling woman pushed past him. She smelled of smoke and cooking fat. She also appeared to be drunk.

Peter walked inside the main building and looked around. Men were drinking and there was all manner of meat all over the tables and apples and bread. There was such noise as the men shouted and sang and congratulated each other. A dog came over to him and began licking his hand.

Peter bent down to stroke it and saw that it had turned into a sheep. He was standing in the middle of the empty and ruined stockade in modern 1768 feeling unsteady on his feet and his mind whirling. William came over to him and said,

"You see what I mean?"

"I went back in time didn't I?"

"No, you went back in your memory. Come on, we must go or we shall be late for our meeting. "

William, currently the stronger man, took Peter by the arm and helped him out of the hill fort and back through the wood.

The pony was waiting there as he had been left, quite dry and untroubled.

The Old Manor was situated just at the rear of the forty and William soon realised that the large and complicated job he had been offered was well within his capabilities. The men mounted and steadily returned to Lanlivery, foregoing the planned stop at Luxulyan until Peter felt better.

"I need a couple of extra hands to work with me. Do you know of anyone? Zeb Prowse said that he was interested – is he reliable?"

"He was sacked recently but he does have a family to feed."

"He said that he was sacked because he complained about safety."

"That's not surprising, considering his family were involved in a mine accident. I haven't heard anything bad about him."

"I will ask him later on this evening. At least he will be able to start quickly."

Zeb joined him on his job and Peter got another two assistants, both ex miners who were not as skilled as master carpenters but who were quite willing and capable of working hard.

Peter stayed in Lanlivery in a cottage opposite the smithy at the Crown, eager to leave William and his small bed but not his friendship. He had not been able to find lodgings nearer the job at St Blazey, but the trip was only 20 minutes or so and he enjoyed the journey. By the time December arrived he had finished the job at The Old Manor and got new jobs in Lanlivery, Luxulyan and Penpillick. They wanted him to go to Tywardreath too and he said that he would as soon as he had some time.

Peter was enjoying himself and that was why he never contacted me. My father had discovered his address when he intercepted a letter from Peter to his sister and sent several harshly worded notes about me and the baby which was due at Christmas.

Peter told me years later that he didn't get any letters but I am not inclined to believe him. I doubt he was happy knowing that his friend's fifteen year old daughter was about to give birth to his child and he had managed to reach 35 years old without a similar problem. Ironically it would disgust me to know that similar had happened to my daughter and it would to Peter too.

What was still happening to him however, were the continuous hauntings.

He had taken to going outside at around 2 in the morning on several nights in order to see the lanterns again. He soon discovered that the mysterious event only occurred on a Tuesday morning. It was always the same thing - he would see the line of lanterns moving across the churchyard and come to the lych-gate where they vanished. He asked various locals who made comments such as, "You must be imagining things" William smiled at his antics and Zeb said that he would come out with him to see.

It was Christmas Eve when Peter and Zeb were leaning against the wall which ran around the side of the Crown. They were smoking and drinking whisky while chatting about the work they had been doing and how much money was to be made with the extra jobs. They were firm friends now and Peter relied on Zeb. The assistants changed quite regularly, but that did not matter.

This Christmas Eve was cold and the moon almost full. The sky had been clear up to an hour before but it was beginning to cloud over and there was a threat of snow.

"So we will be starting this job in Luxulyan on the 7th January?" asked Zeb.

"We certainly will and then straight on to Tywardreath. Wait. There they are! Can you see them?"

Zeb peered into the churchyard.

"I can see them Peter. There are one, two three.......six!"

"Six lanterns, yes it's always six lanterns and no men."

"Well this time, let's not wait until they get to the gate," suggested Zeb.

"Right, let's go straight into the churchyard," Peter was braver with a pal.

They ran across the road, tightening coats against the snow which had suddenly begun to fall heavily and fiddled with the wooden gate until it opened. The hinges creaked as it swung, adding to the atmosphere. The lanterns were moving closer, obviously carried by men – or something which had once been men. Zeb and Peter stood on the path between the lanterns and the gate.

"They will have to come through us now," said Zeb.

"I hope to God they don't," answered Peter.

The lanterns were only a few steps from them and there was silence if you failed to count the heavy stilted breathing from the two men. Peter told me that he had never felt as scared as he did at that moment. The snow falling silently onto the graves highlighted the spookiness.

"I've got a baby due tomorrow," Peter told Zeb, suddenly confessional.

"You said before," answered Zeb.

The lanterns arrived in front of them and silhouetted against the snowy backdrop, shapes became visible. Murky shapes of men dressed for work.

"Who are you?" asked Peter.

The lantern-carrying men moved around until they formed a long line, army style. It was at this point that Peter realised that no footprints were being made in the snow and these men were not mortal.

"You can see them, can't you?" he asked Zeb.

"I recognise them," said Zeb. "Father, that's you isn't it?"

The man did not answer, but Peter felt that the change in Zeb was so palpable that he too must believe that this phantom was Zeb's father.

Zeb reached out to touch the man but it was as though he was suddenly out of reach of Zeb's hand and the phantoms had not moved. They stood in their line - with lanterns aloft, apparently not sure what they should do next.

"That is my father and he and he are my uncles. The other three I know to be the men who died alongside them in the mine accident all those years ago. They left early for their Tuesday shift and did not return home. Their bodies were never found because the accident was so catastrophic that they could not be recovered. It is highly unlikely that they knew what had happened."

"Perhaps you should tell them, a good man needs to know that a problem is not of his making."

Zeb began, "It was the manager's fault, not yours. He told you to blow the wrong wall because he had not properly checked the plans and you blew the dividing wall to the adjoining mine. There had been a flood in that mine and as soon as the wall fell, the water came torrenting through. None of you stood a chance."

"And their families?" interrupted Peter.

"The mine owners gave your families some money and that was it. But we all managed and the village pulled together and there is no need for you to walk to your shifts any more. That part of that mine is closed now."

The lantern men stood in front of them and the snow fell. Peter was shaking and whether from cold or fear it could not be confirmed. This impasse continued until the church bells sounded a peal so loud that they jumped, though not quite out of their skins. The lantern men turned on their heels and began walking towards the lych-gate as various villagers came out of their cottages to see what had happened which necessitated the church bells.

And so it was in this way that the six miners went to their last shift, trudging their way through the village and beyond, in front of their shocked and emotional friends and families.

They were never seen again Peter was reliably informed.

The event did not bring my Peter home however. Letter after letter was sent. My brother was sent and he returned to Ringmore with the message that Peter was earning a deal of money and would return when he had enough to expand his Ringmore business and would visit her then.

It took until the end of April before he did finally return, leaving Zeb running the Lanlivery Prideaux and Prowse Craftsman business and taking half the profits.

Peter would return to supervise some of the bigger jobs but eventually sold the whole business to Zeb, who immediately dropped the Prideaux part of the name. Peter heard years later that Zeb became lazy once Peter was no longer there to push him and eventually lost it all.

My father was more than furious with Peter, but he returned rich and with two businesses and he promised to marry me and so the fact that he had left me a young and unmarried mother was soon forgotten.

Thomas Peter was born in the early hours of 26th December 1768 and was a handsome lad with a powerful pair of lungs. Peter loved him the moment he picked him up. That seemed easier for him now that he was four months old and a little sweetheart. Peter called the baby Teepee, a nickname which stuck. He had no input into the names chosen for his son, not having been present at his arrival, but could not complain about Thomas or Peter.

We married on May 10th at Ringmore and Thomas Peter was baptised straight after. We went to live at the house in which Peter had been brought up and were happy.

We had Peter on 14th November 1770, Jenny on the 31st December 1775 and John on 23rd March 1779. John sadly died in 1784 and I was inconsolable for a time. It was during this recovery that Peter told me all about his Lanlivery adventures.

My Peter sold the business when he decided to retire as our Peter had gone to sea and Teepee had moved to Chudleigh with that awful girl we never got on with. Because of her my Peter did not want to leave him any inheritance, which was a shame. But we never saw him or any of their children and never had a letter from Teepee from the day he left Ringmore. Jenny stayed with us, unmarried and unable to catch a husband.

We bought a house and moved to Modbury when Peter was 70 years old.

On the 17th June 1810, Peter had been with me to Modbury church and said he felt wonderful. We had looked again at the effigy of his ancestor, Sir John Prideaux who rested next to his wife. Peter still had great attachment to his ancestors and had written a book about them. He told me to keep it safe after his death and I promised that I would. That afternoon as I busied myself in the kitchen making the Sunday meal to which we had invited some friends. Peter went into the small orchard we had in the back garden. He shouted that he thought he could see a glow by the trees and walked towards it. Then he shouted to me that he saw lights coming towards him. Peter made his way towards them and I ran out to find my husband dead under the apple tree wearing a huge smile on his face. I saw the lights too and I counted seven lanterns moving away towards the church.

I haven't got over the grief of losing my beloved husband and so wanted to write this epitaph before I join him in the coming months.

Postscript. Mary died in October that same year and was buried at Modbury with her Peter. The property was sold and the whole estate divided between Teepee and his awful wife, Peter the sailor and Jenny the daughter who never married.

THE CHUDLEIGH CHARITY

Featuring Thomas Peter Prideaux
(1768-1842)

"Mother," said Teepee.

"Yes dear."

"What does bastard mean?"

Mary looked at her son in shock.

"Where have you heard that word?"

"Some children said I was one."

"Which children?"

Mary's face was becoming pinched and white. How she had dreaded this day.

"It doesn't mean anything. Just ignore them and if they keep on, tell your father, he will sort them out."

Teepee left the kitchen and Mary put down the dough she was kneading and sat heavily on a chair by the fire. Her head dropped into her hands and she felt completely exhausted. Her life force seemed to drain from her.

She had put out of her mind long ago the thought that this day would come.

Ten years ago, when Mary was only fifteen years old, she became determinedly aware of the 35 year old Peter Prideaux. He was a master carpenter who had a house near to the Wills family home at Aymer

Cove, Ringmore. He was a fine, handsome man who had attracted many young women during his life. There had been several dalliances, but no marriages. There were also rumours that several children in the neighbourhood were being brought up by and unsuspecting men who believed their girls when they were told they were pregnant and must therefore marry.

She had got pregnant and given birth to Thomas Peter at Christmas 1768, but it took until May the following year to persuade Peter to marry and have the boy christened. That fact had been a source of gossip for the small minded of Ringmore and now apparently someone had passed on the information to their child.

Mary looked up from her crying as she felt an arm around her shoulder.

"I just found out what happened. I'll sort it," said her husband.

Peter went outside to find his son. He was playing with his horse and so Peter took him down to the cove in order to explain everything in as much detail as he thought Thomas could understand and left him in no doubt how loved he was.

The talk comforted Teepee but he was now niggled by the idea that his father had been forced to love him and that his mother had been taken advantage of by a much older man. The newly discovered knowledge drove a wedge between them that was never really removed.

Thomas nevertheless had a good life at home and learned his trade as a carpenter from his father.

Then, when he was twenty four he made friends with an older girl called Charity Strong. She was the daughter of Edwin Strong, a builder from Bishop Steignton and who often worked with Peter. One day he brought her to visit them at Ringmore and Teepee was immediately smitten.

He began to insist that he should now be called Thomas as Charity had said that Teepee was a baby's name. Mary disliked the girl from the first time she met her. Mary was only thirty nine to Charity's twenty nine and looked young for her age. Charity flounced and made negative little asides which women notice where men do not. She was five years older than Thomas and in need of a husband before it was too late.

Charity lodged with her aunt at St Ann's Chapel and acted as her companion. All the better to get near to my son, thought Mary. She dare not say anything, remembering perfectly well how she had laid a trap for her Peter.

"Don't get her with child Teepee," she said.

"Mother! Charity is not like that. She has more respect for herself and her family!"

There was an immediate silence as Thomas suddenly remembered his own start in life and Mary almost cried now that her son had thrown this insult in her face and both knew that it could never be taken back satisfactorily.

"I am so sorry mother. I did not mean to say that. I did not think."

But of course the damage was done.

When Thomas told his parents a few weeks later that Charity was pregnant and so of course he must marry her, Mary folded her arms, pursed her lips and walked away from her son.

Peter said,

"I will try and find you a cottage in the village son and you can stay here once you get married if we haven't found one by then."

"Thanks father but Charity wants to get married from home at her own church and her father has found me some work with a friend of his in Chudleigh."

"You will break your mother's heart," Peter said.

Thomas shrugged his shoulders, "I have to think of my own family now father."

"What about the business son? I've worked all this time for my family and wanted you and Peter to take over from me!"

"That is your dream and not mine. Anyway, Peter wants to go to sea, he's obsessed with it. Your life is not what we want. Ringmore is just too boring for the young - we want to live a bit father. I don't want to be like you, you tried to escape and then came back and bored yourself stupid for the rest of your life."

"I came back for you, you ungrateful boy. We never heard you speak in this way until that Charity Strong turned up. Now she will be happy if you never see us again."

"We want you to come to the wedding."

"I'm not going to your wedding to that woman and I doubt your mother will go without me."

And it was as simple as that. Thomas left home, his parents did not attend the wedding and neither did his brother or sister. Charity said that they were selfish people and Thomas was so smitten with his new wife, that he did not recognise the damage that had been caused until he was much older.

Thomas soon discovered that the Chudleigh work was not quite what had been promised and neither was the cottage. Thomas tentatively proposed to Charity that they return to Ringmore and make peace with his parents. Her hysterical and nasty reaction ensured that he never asked the question again.

After they married and had their son Thomas at Bishop Steignton, they moved to poor lodgings on Fore Street in Chudleigh. Edwin Strong blamed a sudden downturn in work and was very sorry – he said – that he must leave Thomas and Charity to fend for themselves.

The lodgings were disgraceful, with damp and leaks and rats. Thomas had never lived this way in his life although naturally had seen the poorer members of his community in South Devon suffer this way. They were paying sixteen guineas a year to William Burrel, Edwin Strong's friend, who said he had been told that Thomas would do all the work required at the property in order to bring it up to a decent living standard. Thomas constantly reminded his landlord that sixteen guineas was a rent payable on a far superior house and that it was the landlord's responsibility to repair. Burrel told him to find one then but to be aware that he was responsible for the rest of the lease.

One night Thomas put young Thomas to sleep in his crib which was in the corner of their room. There were three upstairs rooms, all of which were designated as bedrooms, but there was only one which overlooked Fore Street that was fit to sleep in.

"Just fix the place up!" nagged Charity.

"Why? It will cost us a fortune to get the place anything like it should be. I'm going to find us a better place instead."

Charity would stamp about the place, letting everyone know how she felt.

This night, Charity was not in the house. She had taken to meeting other ladies of the town every Tuesday where they discussed their businesses and how they could further their interests and social climb via trade. It had not always been like this, there being in the early days a hearing where Thomas had to prove his apprenticeship but also his birth. He was sure that Burrel and Edwin Strong had collaborated in order to – what – shame him? Embarrass him? Get rid of him? It worried him that he could not get to the bottom of it.

In 1794 Thomas Prideaux swore before two Justices of the Peace at Chudleigh that he was a fully qualified carpenter and that although his parents were not married at the time of his birth , they were married during the following May and he was duly baptised. It did mean that everyone who was interested in gossip in Chudleigh and its surrounds knew about his start in life. Charity said that it was a stain on their character and Thomas said nothing following the court hearing. He was allowed to live and work in Chudleigh and that was enough for now.

It did not affect the work he was given, but he knew full well that the name 'Tom the Base' was used in reference to him - behind his back of course.

Thomas sang to his son using a song he remembered his mother singing to him 25 years ago. He felt a tear come to his eye for he had not spoken to any of his family since he had left Ringmore to marry. He wished he could go back and show off this little boy.

The candle flickered in its sconce and the room became suddenly very cold. Thomas snuggled his boy in his blanket and made sure that he was comfortable before he went to check the candle. He lit another one in case this one went out. Little Tom liked a night light and Thomas recalled how scared he had been at night when he was a boy. That old mill at Aymer had made such dreadful creaks and he often saw the white figure of an old man running away at night. His brother said he had seen the ghost a blood soaked woman jump into the pond.

Thomas walked out onto the landing and went to have another look at the two upstairs rooms in case they looked any more habitable. They didn't and he mentally began to tick the work necessary. The room he was in currently overlooked Fore Street as did his own room. He opened the creaking window as far is it would go and looked out. He saw his wife run into the Hall with a couple of her friends and they were laughing and having more fun than she ever appeared to do with him. There was the baker's wife and the watchmaker's wife and the woman from the laundry. Most of the tradeswomen of the town seemed to attend the meetings these days. He pulled the window shut, conscious that spying never brought the spy satisfaction.

Thomas turned back to the door and was surprised to see an old man sitting on the bed. Thomas realised that he did not know who he was.

"Hello sir. Can I help you?"

"Your wife is a nasty piece of work. Do you know that she prevented my granddaughter from joining her stupid band of women?"

"No, no. Who is she?"

The man vanished and Thomas felt his legs wobble.

Thomas continued to have constant run-ins with Burrel who refused to reduce the rent or fix up the house. Thomas intended to leave the place as soon as he could find any other prominent house with an attached workshop. So far nothing had come available. And they were stuck with what they had.

Charity said that if he left the problem to her, she would sort it out. Thomas said no, he was the man, leave it to him.

"Charity begins at home," she said.

Thomas had seen the old man on several occasions but he always vanished after uttering some kind of warning such as,

"Beware the baker," or, "keep the water barrels full."

Thomas asked Charity one day if she had seen him and she looked at him as though he were mad.

Charity and her women now had several meetings a week and she wrote notes and kept files. Thomas looked at the once and was disappointed to see that records were being kept on townspeople, listing their perceived foibles and potential for blackmail.

He even saw his name there mentioning ghosts. The row they had that night when she returned was memorable.

What had increased in intensity around the house and workshop was the sound of scratching and the impression of tiny feet wearing clogs scampering around the house and workshop. Thomas would try and focus his hearing to check where the noises were originating. The children mentioned the noises and he told them that it was the sound of squirrels running across the roof. He promised to leave poison about and remove them and the children slept a little sounder. Charity said that she could not hear anything.

As the new century dawned Thomas began to have more trouble with Burrel and luckily it coincided with the chance of a larger property further along Fore Street which had a bigger workshop and more land. Thomas took the lease and told Burrell that he could not expect the balance of the rolling one year lease which Burrel was insisting upon. As a result Thomas had to present himself in front of two Justices of the Peace for a second time to put forward his case as a defendant.

He explained that Burrell had done no work at the property which was partly unusable thanks to the deterioration. He said he had taken new premises for the health and safety of his family. Thomas added that not only was the property overpriced by two guineas a year, but that the past five months had been particularly intolerable. 16 guineas was the equivalent of a hard working man's yearly income. The property was infested by rats and other vermin which kept his family awake at night. He declared that it was not fit for human inhabitation and asked to be relieved of the contract. William Burrell insisted that it was perfectly reasonable to expect Thomas to pay 16 guineas and do all the necessary repairs to the property. He denied vermin infestation, saying that he had seen no evidence of such. They ruled in Thomas's favour telling him that he could withdraw from the lease so long as he paid for the time he had lived there and all other charges were to be waived.

Burrell was furious and Thomas vowed to make him pay by stealing some of his business. Charity told him that their Honours were particular friends of hers and had helped Thomas win his case.

The new property was only 12 guineas a year with an option to buy after five years residency. The new house suited the Prideaux family well and trade increased and the children went to school and Charity would do her housework and then go to her meetings. She kept her files meticulously up to date and locked them in the cellar where they could not be accessed. It had been suggested that they should be kept somewhere else by her women followers, but Charity refused.

Thomas soon recognised that Charity had an uncanny knack of guessing what was going to happen in the town.

"It is easy to work out," she told him.

The only problem Thomas now experienced was the continuance of the vermin problem. The scampering increased as time went on. During dark nights and ignorant of lamps lit or not, the invaders took charge of their domain. The tap tapping of tiny feet wearing hobnail boots was heard at random and frightened the children. Thomas could not find the nests or the entrance points or even their pathways. He laid traps and poison and caught nothing.

Charity told them that they were all mad.

They had bought their Fore Street property and now Charity had her eye on an out of town farm and land.

"We can't afford that yet Charity," Thomas said.

"We have insurance and if anything were to happen to Fore Street, we would get a tidy sum."

"Like what?" Thomas asked her. He knew that they were paying a ridiculous sum every year against disaster. Charity's ladies had arranged a bulk deal with some new Insurance Society.

"Well there was the Great Fire of London, for an example."

Thomas ignored her then as he did many times.

Chudleigh was a very pretty town with buildings made from stone and wood. The other cottages were made from cob and wore thatched roofs. The houses in the central street had been built higgledy-piggledy as buildings were added on through the years. There were still several fields and orchards sitting between the houses. The houses off the main street and up the lanes which led to and away from the town were particularly pretty to look at. They now knew every person in the town and all would recognise a traveller as such. There were many who either travelled to Cornwall or used the town as a stopping point between Plymouth and Exeter. The war against Napoleon increased the volume of traffic and soldiers wandering through the town and some of them were quite scary as they fell drunkenly from the inns.

But Thomas loved it there and wished his family would come and see it. They had never visited and never seen his children. He wrote a letter each time a baby arrived, but had never received a reply. He never discovered that his family had in fact replied, asking for a truce and Charity had intercepted every letter and destroyed them before he ever saw them.

From early 1807 he saw the old man in too many places. Work, home, the inn, the stable, on walks. Everywhere. He would raise his fingers and point to his eyes and ears. Thomas assumed he meant he should keep them open, but in what regard he knew not. The scampering still happened on a regular basis, but apart from establishing that it must somehow be centred on the cellar, Thomas found nothing. The family were mostly used to the noises and rarely mentioned them.

Charity continued to plan their move to the farm and Thomas continued to remind her that they could not afford it.

"Wait and see," she would answer.

In May 1807 Chudleigh was looking its best. There had been a drought and the roads were dusty. Even the heavy through traffic of coaches and their passengers and the passing tradesmen did not affect the unusual cleanliness of the town.

Thomas and Charity were taking a walk one Thursday evening in May. They were so well established in business and society that they knew almost everyone in Chudleigh. They walked arm in arm down the main street smiling and waving to their neighbours. Determined to enjoy the lovely evening a little longer, they turned down Mill Lane and walked out towards Ugbrooke. They walked over a little bridge and looked at the water for a time.

"Chudleigh is a lovely place," said Charity.

"I love it," answered Thomas.

"It won't be long before we move," she said.

"I don't know how. We haven't any spare money."

"Soon, you see. Then I won't have to worry that someone might kidnap one of my children."

Thomas told her she was ridiculous, although this was one of the few towns in Devon where so many strangers passed through and there could be no mistaking the fact that children were being kidnapped from around the country to satisfy, God knows what desire.

They stopped in front of one cottage where their friend George lived. The couple were out on the front tending the garden which was already ablaze with colour. It was difficult to tell where the plants ended and the thatch began.

"May is the best month," said George. "My vegetables are coming up well and the wife is pleased because she has managed to get everything in the cottage clean and dry!"

Charity understood the last comment. The winter made the place so dirty no matter how hard a woman worked to clean up. It was lovely to have the sun shining in through clean windows onto spotless floors and fresh linen around the house. She breathed in deeply and smiled.

"I do love it here," she repeated.

"You already said!"

They wandered on for another hour leaving the lane and walking across the fields to the woods and spent an hour quietly there. This wood was next to the farm where Charity was adamant they would be living in very soon. It was late when they got back home in the soft dark. The babies were being looked after by a neighbour who had fallen asleep in the kitchen.

Charity gently nudged her and after apologies and a drink, every one made their way to bed. Before he fell asleep, Thomas saw the old man standing shimmering in the corner of their room. He held up his hands to his face and they set on fire. Soon the spirit was ablaze and the room became orange and yellow. Unaffected by the flames were dreadful black and hairy creatures which ran all over the man and made him scream in complaint. They chewed on him and ran up and down his body with their many legs, too many legs. Thomas couldn't decide if they had eight or more.

"No!" he shouted and the noise woke Charity.

"What on earth is the matter with you?" she asked, sitting bolt upright in bed.

The flaming spook and the little spiky creatures had vanished. They were alone in the dark night reflecting only the lights from the houses in the street. There was complete silence.

In the morning after seeing Thomas to work and the children to school, Charity set about cleaning up and moving belongings around. She was excited about today. It felt different.

It was nearly lunchtime before she thought she smelt smoke.

It was almost at the same time that Thomas, working in his workshop at the rear of the property thought the same thing. They met in the yard as they left their respective workstations.

"Something is on fire," Thomas said with great understatement.

"Look, there is smoke over there," Charity said, trying to suppress the panic she was beginning to feel inside. She had seen farm buildings go up in smoke when she was a little girl and the speed of the destruction still scared her. Now this was all too real.

"Pack up your important tools Thomas and move them to the cellar. Quickly!"

This he did and was surprised to see so many boxes already down there. He closed the lid.

"Make sure both doors are closed," insisted Charity.

They ran onto Fore Street and noticed many of their neighbours either running to or away from the smoke and flames which were now becoming obvious. There was a terrifying crackling and fizzing sound carried upon the air.

"What has happened?" asked Thomas of a neighbour who was running towards them.

"The bakery caught fire and now it is spreading, very fast Tom, look after your house and family!"

Charity felt as though she was rooted to the spot - just as she had been as a child. Even on this very hot May morning, she could feel the heat from the distant fire.

Emboldened, she ran back inside and picked up little Peter. The children at school should be safe as they were further away from the fire than the house was. Charity put Peter in the little cart they owned and Thomas got the pony ready to pull it. They both loaded food and clothes on the cart and got ready to move away south of the fire. The flames and heat were galloping towards their home, skipping from one roof to the next. There was a constant cracking sound as fresh thatch and wood caught fire.

The wind was blowing little arrows of lighted thatch further along the street and setting fire to houses which were not directly in the path of the fire. This was a very frightening place to be. They could hear screaming and the crashing of buildings and Thomas just wanted to save his family.

"Please Lord, save my family," he repeated over and over again. He knew there was a family prayer that he should repeat, but he couldn't remember it. He should have listened to his father more carefully.

Just as Thomas was about to say that they should go to the school, they saw John running towards them.

He was white faced and looked as though he had been crying.

Charity opened her arms wide and John ran into them and hugged her close. She asked about his brother and sister.

"They are still at school mother," he answered.

She let John go and find his friend and told him to keep away from the fire. John was a loner and quite capable of taking care of himself. He would be quite safe.

Thomas told his wife to get to the cart and start the pony moving away towards the church.

"Pick up the children on the way and go to Ugbrooke. His Lordship will keep you safe." As he said that, their lovely house caught fire and the whole place burnt down to the stones in about two minutes. They both watched it happen. It was horrible. Thomas saw the creatures from the previous night running over the flaming timbers. They were screaming and wailing, seemingly lost. They tried to run away from the flames but were unable. They caught fire one by one and screamed like tortured babies as they turned to black ash.

"What are they?" asked Thomas in horror.

"I think the fire has solved the vermin problem," answered Charity.

Later that night when the family were spending the night under tents provided by the army and eating food provided by surrounding parishes, the villagers knew that it would be a long hard struggle to get Chudleigh back on its feet. Thomas looked over at the town with the smouldering and unfamiliar skyline. A few chimney stacks stood upright, looking black and dead and there were few buildings still standing.

"What a difference a day makes," Thomas said to no one in particular.

The next few days were spent in turmoil. Many came to help from surrounding villages and gifts of food, clothes and bedding. Charity was involved in many conversations with her women and those whose houses remained seemed strangely angry and disappointed. Charity was full of sympathy and suggested that perhaps theirs would be knocked down in the same way the fire-break house demolitions had been made. She convinced them that they would receive their insurance pay-outs too. Of course they never did. Charity and her fellow victims received theirs and the Prideauxs were able to buy the promised farm and still retain ownership of the Fore Street land.

Most were living under army tents for at least two nights before they were able to make a temporary home in the buildings behind where their houses stood. They needed to rebuild as a matter of urgency and were calling on craftsman such as Thomas to help.

A newly formed Relief Committee chaired by Lord Clifford, had responsibility for the rebuilding of the town and the fair distribution of £21,000 amongst those who had lost everything. Building contracts were awarded and Thomas was a beneficiary of these and was able to increase the income of their business which brought in good money and a secure future.

After the turmoil of the fire and the move, Charity forgot to intercept letters. This time he got the letter which announced the death of his parents. He immediately left for Modbury and slipcovered that they had wanted to see him as much as he had. He found it difficult to understand how each letter had failed to reach him. But, he took his inheritance and some of the good pieces of furniture and jewellery. On routing through the desk he discovered a book written by his father and the records left by his mother. He kept it safe from her. He didn't tell her about the inheritance either.

It was only years later that Charity reminded Thomas of the visit she had made to Lord Clifford prior to the announcement of contracts.

"It was highly unlikely that he would give you the work, when we were so new to the town. But you see I had proof against him that I told him I would make public if he did not help us."

"Is that why he let me purchase the farm so cheaply?"

"Of course, my naïve and silly husband. I wanted us to get on and you were quite happy to stay as we were."

"I would have been happy to continue on my father's business. We would have lived comfortably on that income."

"We would have lived in a narrow minded small community where your mother was considered a harlot and your father a child molester."

Thomas stood up quickly and the kitchen chair in which he sitting fell to the floor.

That was the first and only time Thomas ever raised a fist to his wife, but the appearance of their son John caused him to desist and Charity walked away laughing.

"What did mother mean?" John asked his father.

"Your mother is affected by our hardships John. Ignore her. Ignore us both."

Thomas went to the cellar and then over to the metal store which was protected inside and where he knew Charity still kept her records. These had been retrieved from the Fore Street cellar after the fire. Thomas had been surprised to discover when they opened it as soon as the scorched remains had been cleared from street level that every single valuable possession they owned including cash and gold was safely hidden in there. It was almost as if Charity had known they needed protecting.

Charity denied it but often referred to her files as a nest and her women as spiders.

He opened the file cabinet and looked at the files. There were so many that the older collections were completely covered in webs and dust. He reached for them and was horrified when several large – too large - spiders ran over his hand. He shook it furiously recognising the spider as a smaller version of the vermin creatures he had seen years before. The spider fell from his arm and screamed as it did so. Then it jumped back on to the files and cuddled up to them

So that was what was happening here. These terrible creatures were guarding the blackmail material. Thomas could not tolerate that. Suddenly he heard from his wife a shout telling him to come directly up and so he left the cabinet.

It seemed that John and Peter both felt restricted by the small friendly community in Chudleigh and wanted to travel around the country and see how other people lived.

Thomas spoke to his sons over and over again trying to get across to them that it was not necessarily a good thing leaving home and that having people surrounding you who wanted you to succeed was very important. He was thinking of his own youthful escape and how similar the two scenarios were. Perhaps God taught lessons where you don't expect. If it ended the same way he would never see his sons again.

Charity cried often. She had not raised her boys to leave her. She wanted them to live in the town or nearby where she could watch her grandchildren grow.

"I expect that is how my parents felt," he said to Charity bitterly.

The day the boys left, something died in both their parents. Charity was positive she would never see her sons again and waving goodbye to them as they waved from the back of the coach as it lurched up the hill towards Exeter was worse than seeing her house burn to the ground.

They had had two more children since the fire. When Mary was born on Christmas Eve, they were ecstatic and felt blessed with another Christmas baby. It was not so good when baby James was born in June and died in August 1811. Life was still complicated and unsatisfactory, even when you thought you had the upper hand, thought Charity as the cart took away her boys.

The files meant less and less as time went on. People died, relationships and friendships altered and blackmail information did not seem so relevant. They had the farm and the possessions and Charity and Thomas rarely had nice conversations. There were no grandparents and it had all been for nothing.

What had not stopped was the horrible tapping and scurrying sounds in the house, day and night. It was obsessing Thomas.

One day when he was alone at the farm he enlisted the help of some hardy men. The cabinet was taken from the cellar and dragged to the waste ground at the far end of the farm.

It was very heavy and as one of the men pointed out, appeared to be moving and shaking of its own accord. There was a general feeling of anxiety amongst the group as they cleared the area around the cabinet.

The door of the cabinet was opened and a flaming torch thrown in. The noise, reminiscent of the 1807 fire was loud and terrifying. Screams and the sight of fiery large spider vermin caused the other men to run away, but Thomas stayed. He stayed until every last venomous file and every last spider demon was gone.

He knew then that it was all over.

Charity was furious and became lethargic and depressed after the destruction. The files had been her lifeblood.

Charity died suddenly on Tuesday 10th January 1832 following a walk back from town with some shopping. She made it into the house and was found dead by Thomas when he came in for lunch. The doctor said that it was her heart and that nothing could have been done. Thomas was inconsolable. He felt that it was because she had never heard a word from her two sons. He sent up a silent prayer that they come home. No one had any idea where either of them was.

All for nothing.

Thomas carried on quiet with his carpentry business and his children and grandchildren made him as much part of their family lives as was possible. He had a housekeeper called Grace Swales who did for him. She looked after him well and grew very fond of him, but he had no special interest in her. Charity had been the love of his life and he wanted no other, in spite of her trouble causing.

His health became worse during the winter of 1841, following enforced bed rest after a spider bite became infected. On the morning of Tuesday 22nd February 1842 he coughed his last and passed away. Grace laid him out before his family came to see him.

His last words were, "Charity begins at home."

He was buried alongside his wife in the churchyard at Chudleigh.

THE STARLING TREE

*Featuring John Prideaux (1796-
1863)*

John was surprised that he was remembering so far
back, even though the pain and visual sights were so
current and so painful. He could see the broken
railing through which he had just fallen and the
heavy rain now splashing onto his cold and paralysed
body, but he was remembering the difficult path he
had travelled which had resulted in this sad event.

The 22nd May 1807 was an exciting day for John
Prideaux even though it probably wasn't for neither
his family nor indeed his hometown of Chudleigh.
It was a Friday.
He was sitting in school staring at the teacher, Mr
Bond. John usually enjoyed school but today was so
hot that his usually quick mind was stuck in stall
mode. He winked at his friend Elizabeth Lock, and
she grinned back.
Suddenly the door was thrown open and a
frightened looking child stood wide eyed in the
space it left.
"What is the meaning of this intrusion?" shouted Mr
Bond.
"A fire sir. There is a fire!" said the little boy.
"Where?" asked the teacher.

"Everywhere sir. The town is on fire. I think my house is on fire," and the boy began to cry.

John felt his heart beat quickly. Did that mean his house was on fire?

"Sir, sir, can I go home and see if my mother is alright?" he asked. There was a great clamour of voices asking similar questions.

"No, no, no. Sit down class; you must all remain here where it is safe."

Mr Bond was beginning to worry.

"In fact, stay here class and I shall go out and see what is happening."

Mr Bond left the room and as soon as he did, John climbed onto a table and looked out of the window. He saw black smoke and flames coming from the town and he could hear screaming. That was it, he wasn't staying a moment longer.

John ran out of the door and outside onto the street. The rest of the class watched and some followed him, while the timid stayed behind.

The sight which met his eyes was one he had never forgotten. Around him was a mixture of black and yellow and red and there was no sky. The air was choking and people were running in no particular direction. Everything seemed to be on fire.

He ran in the direction of his house past all the familiar sights which were now ablaze. No one spoke to him or tried to stop him. He thought he saw a dead horse across the street, but did not stop to find out.

When he reached the site of his house he was horrified to see his mother and father standing in front of their cottage with baby Peter and some of their belongings in the cart.

"Mother?" he said.

"Oh John," she pulled him towards her body and hugged him while she cried.

"Is everyone alright?" he asked, his voice shaking.

"I think so. Did you leave your brothers and sister at school?"

John said nothing, he had not checked before he left. He had been too concerned about his mother.

"Yes," he answered.

As soon as his mother let him go, John saw that they were never going to rescue his home. It was in the path of the fire which was now two houses away, it was all going to go. As the first flames hit, he saw the black, many legged creatures running along the beams and away from the heat. At first, he thought they were rats but they were more like giant spiders, so he ran away because they reminded him of the sleepless nights he had spent listening to clog scurrying.

Elizabeth caught up with him.

"I was worried about you John."

"My house has burnt to the ground and we have lost everything," he announced.

Elizabeth's face fell.

"How horrible. What about your family?"

"They are alright, I think. Have you seen the town?"

"They fetched me and told me to stay here. I saw the smoke and the flames, but they won't let me come out."

"You can't miss this Elizabeth, come out with me now. I will look after you, they will never know."

"I will come, they are all busy looking after themselves and trying to save the house, but I think we are too far away."

Mary jumped out of the window and went with her friend.

They ran across the grass and had to stop as a carriage began to turn in front of them. These coaches travelling with passengers from Plymouth to Exeter usually went through the centre of the town, but today were diverting around the back of the town through the dry fields.

"Are you alright?" shouted the driver.

"Yes, thank you," they answered.

The two giggled because drivers never spoke to them usually.

The town was even more ablaze. Men were pulling down houses in order to stop the fire. It was very exciting for the children with buildings crashing down and people crying. They watched until after four o' clock when the fire seemed to be mainly out. Lord Clifford came into the town and sent word around that anyone could come to Ugbrooke. By evening men and women came from other villages to help and the army sent tents.

The Prideaux family were to spend the night under one of these tents and Thomas was likely to be given more work to rebuild the town, he told his wife.

John remembered that his parents would argue a lot about how he came to get the work. They did move to the farm about which his mother always talked prior to the fire. Apparently, there was a large insurance pay out and they got to keep the Fore Street property too which they developed later. It was a very convenient fire for his family and few others too.

John followed in his father's footsteps and learned the carpentry trade as did his brothers. He was a very handsome young man and he enjoyed much female attention. Elizabeth had moved away with her family and so he entertained himself with the local beauties. That was until a chance meeting with Elizabeth at Exeter resulted in a more mature renewal of friendship and ultimately romance. She had sent John a note telling him that she was with child and they had decided to run away to London. After telling his parents that they were to marry, Charity had become hysterical and said that this was a trap women liked to set for men.

John and his brother Peter had heard stories of London and how a man could get rich quite easily there. Other town people had gone there in the past and as time went on the young men decided to seek their fortune. So, at the end of summer in he persuaded Peter to come with them.

"Please, please don't go!" begged their mother.

"Let them go if they want. They can always come home if it doesn't work out," said Thomas.

"If they go, I will never see them again," cried Charity, unconsciously repeating the cries of Thomas's own mother when Charity had encouraged him to leave Ringmore all those years ago. She was correct, they left Chudleigh for London and they never returned. They did not write and no word ever came back. Charity was devastated.

She did not know that they went first to Landkey near Bideford where John married the pregnant Elizabeth Locke in front of his brother and her family on Monday the 18th October 1824 one week before they went to London. Edwin Locke had a property there which he wanted managing by family. It fronted as a General Store but was used as a place to launder the spoils of burglary and murder. There was a great deal of money to be made.

But when they arrived in London, it was not all that they had expected. Used as they were to Devon and considering Exeter to be extremely busy, particularly on market days, London was horribly congested. It was filthy, smelly and full of violence and crime. John and Peter lost some of their possessions as soon as they arrived, although thankfully Elizabeth was spared.

Several people of questionable moral intent frequented the shop. They brought small items mainly, some valuable and some not so much. The shopkeeper, who went home after the shop shut and was called Jedidiah Winthrop, was a dirty and insolent man. However, he appeared to know the valuable of the property brought in by equally scary vagabonds.

"Edwin Locke will go through all of these accounts when he arrives but twice a year and God help us if it doesn't all add up," Jed told John.

Peter Prideaux got fed up pretty quickly of the place and soon found lodgings and a job with a builder. As Elizabeth grew in size, she became more frightened and complained that sometimes one or two of the men would make lewd comments to her. John was apoplectic when he heard this news and threatened to beat the man to a pulp. It took almost an hour for Jed to talk him out of it, warning him that John was likely to end up dead and thrown into the stinking river.

He and Elizabeth went for a walk one night by the river when the baby was only about a week away. They saw drunks, tarts and children stealing from the gents who were busy with the tarts.

"We must leave London," Elizabeth told her husband. "I am not bringing up a child here."

"We should give it a bit longer. At least until your father comes and then we can see how much we have earned. He promised us a good cut and the amount of money changing hands here is a fortune. We can set up on our own in no time."

"But I can't breathe here John. London chokes me."

Their daughter Charity was born in London and a letter was sent to Devon - to the Locke's. Edwin arrived a month later and soon after he discussed money and business with John.

"I thought I would be making more than this. There is a lot of risk involved."

"I managed before you got here, you have a roof over your head and that it is a bonus in this city. Be grateful for that."

Locke shooed   him away and huddled with Jed. Locke seemed menacing in this environment and so John went upstairs to his wife and child and told her that they would be in London a while yet.

They were awoken later when the front door was kicked in and several men ran upstairs and into their room. Elizabeth picked up Charity and held her to her bosom while John fought them in vain. By the time they left, John was badly beaten and Edwin was dead. Jed had vanished and the house was on fire. It was soon made clear that Lockes were out of business and John and his family must leave London or face the consequences.

So leave London they did and travelled to Staley Bridge where Elizabeth had heard that there might be some honest work. John told the villagers that he was a journeyman carpenter and work was soon found for him. No one enquired after his past. The family were happy and grew happier still when they had a son Edwin John a few years later. Life was quite normal until John had begun to notice the tree - not long after moving into his cottage.

To all intents and purposes, it was just an ordinary tree. A good old English oak tree with squirrels and owls and acorns hanging from its branches. It was a particularly splendid tree and on the first day they moved there. John saw a starling which they laughingly said seemed to be watching them.

The next day there were two sitting there. They laughed about that too and every day for a week as the starlings continued to arrive. The starlings would sit next to each other on the branches and do nothing. They sat quietly and never left the tree. John was pretty sure that they stayed overnight as he never seemed to see them leaving or arriving for that matter.

At first it was funny and they would take breadcrumbs and other small leftovers outside for their pet birds. They commented that they never saw the starlings leave the branches but whenever they looked for the crumbs, there was none to be found.

"Perhaps they sucked them up with their willpower, they look capable enough," laughed Elizabeth.

"I wonder where they are all coming from?" asked John.

"And why?" asked Elizabeth which was a better question.

By the time Edwin John was born, there were several hundred silent starlings sitting in the tree.

Neighbours had begun to notice the phenomenon and after initially laughing, soon began to talk in whispers about the Devil and hauntings.

"This has never happened before," said one.

"It goes against nature," added another.

The parson arrived one morning following Edwin's birth in order to arrange the baptism.

"There are a lot of birds in your tree Mistress Elizabeth," he said softly.

"I assume that is not a euphemism Parson."

The parson was shocked and he wasn't really sure whether it was because she knew what a euphemism was or that she had said it.

"No. I merely thought it strange that so many starlings should remain in one place."

"I am not a witch if that is what you are inferring."

"Indeed, I am not. I am making conversation while we arrange the baptism of your son. I presume little Charity was baptised in London?"

"She was not sir but we do want Edwin baptising."

"But you must baptise your daughter too!" more shocked than he thought he could be, the parson sat down.

"I shall if you let me know how that will be possible."

He told her and the deed was arranged for the following Sunday. He felt he must do this as quickly as possible before the Devil got hold of these Prideauxs and their children. As he left, he noticed that the silent starlings had now begun a synchronised chirrup and the tree seemed to vibrate with the sound. He pulled his cloak hood over his head and scurried away until the sound was no longer with him.

Elizabeth came out of the house and looked up at the tree. Charity clung to her hand and Edwin clutched her bosom. There were so many starlings in the tree, she could scarcely make out leaf or twig. As she looked the sound stopped and all was silent. She shivered and ushered the children inside.

When John came home later, she told him of the day's events and he said,

"I thought there were even more birds this morning. It's getting very weird."

"Ssssh," urged Elizabeth.

He ssshed and they heard the sound of children squealing and playing. John took up his heavy walking stick and went outside. It was dark and the lack of moon and proliferation of clouds made it seem darker. The noises were deafening and there was squealing and scurrying and snuffling.

"Foxes?" asked Elizabeth hopefully.

"No. Badgers I think."

The noises stopped and they went inside, more chilled than usual.

"I don't like Staley Bridge," said Elizabeth.

"You don't like anywhere," noted John and he slammed the door.

On Saturday night while Elizabeth prepared the children for their baptism by bathing them and making their best clothes presentable, an unearthly noise from outside stopped her.

John was with his pals at the inn but had promised to come home early. John was not a heavy drinker and would often only take a few drinks before returning. Perhaps it was because she was alone and peaceful that the noise shook her so much, but she was also freezing cold and shaking.

She looked out of the window and saw the tree aglow. She realised that the moon had come from behind a cloud and although only a fresh moon, it still had enough light to silhouette the hundreds and hundreds of birds sitting in the branches. Charity began to cry and so Elizabeth picked her up and went outside as if in a trance. Edwin was fast asleep and she felt safe doing so.

"Come on baby girl," she said. "Let's go and see what the moon is doing."

The moon was doing nothing, but the badger come fox come creepy noise making mammal was scuffing about in the hedgerows and squealing and clicking as it did so.

Elizabeth drew Charity tighter and Charity panted in fear.

"Mama, please get Papa. I don't like the noises."

The starlings began to chirrup and then louder and louder their noises. They soon drowned out the scuffing noises and the women put their hands to their ears.

"I hate you. I hate you!" shouted Elizabeth to the starlings.

John appeared in the lane and made her jump even more.

"Stop saying you hate things Lizzy. Thoughts make things happen and bad thoughts..."

"... make bad things happen."

Lord, her husband could be annoying when he wanted to be. But she calmed down a little and the noises reduced so she calmed down some more and the chirruping stopped.

"See," he said gently and pushed her back in the house.

They were up, dressed and shutting their front door on their way to church by 8 o'clock the following morning. The starlings had begun chirruping at first light and when the family began walking past the tree, they tweeted as they had never done to date. How so many starlings could stay on the tree and it not collapse was unanswerable. The anxiety levels of the Prideaux family were very high and their neighbours stared at them as they walked into the church.

Baptising was done and hymns sung and yet the starlings could be heard above them all. None of the congregation kept attention on any part of the service and were glad to leave at the end. Everyone filed out and one by one they looked at the oak tree. The starlings were hopping up and down and leaves were falling.

As John and his family walked out of the church, the flock rose as one and soared into the sky. It was an awesome sight as they swooped and swirled as one. Elizabeth and Charity became separated from John and Edwin as they became hypnotised.

This was a mistake. The flock came as a black cloud along the street and soon covered Charity and her mother. The other villagers screamed and ran to what they felt was a safe distance. John ran towards his wife and then saw that the baby was vulnerable and put him in the arms of a retreating woman he knew. He could no longer see his wife and daughter, just a fog of sparkling black wings and sharp little beaks which shredded his skin as he tried to grab his family. The birds swirled upwards and as they tornadoed towards the sky he saw that his family had gone with them.

"Demons!" shouted the parson as he fell to his knees in the lane.

"She must be a witch!" shouted the Edwin holding woman and she handed the child back to John as though he were on fire.

John cried and held the baby close. He looked into the sky and the birds and his wife and daughter had vanished. The villagers walked away muttering and John went home automatically. There were no starlings in the tree and no badger noises in the hedgerows.

He opened the front door and went in, unsure of his next step. Edwin was asleep in his arms and so he decided to lay him in his crib and find him some milk to warm. He would wake and scream the place down when he was hungry and John didn't think he could stand that. He went into the kitchen and took out the milk pail, putting some into a pan and placing it on the stove, as Elizabeth always did.

Elizabeth - what has just happened?

He stirred the milk and the back door opened. A young neighbour Mary came in.

"Are you aright John?" she asked him.

"No. Here stir this for me and feed Edwin when he wakes will you? I have to go out and look for my family. I don't know what else to do."

"Yes of course. People are out looking for them now John. They haven't found anything yet. They are talking witches and demons already."

John slammed the spoon onto the table.

"This village is living in the past with its ridiculous beliefs."

"Don't be mean John. They are worried about your family and are giving up their Sunday to help you."

John felt ashamed of his outburst.

"I am sorry Mary. I feel as though I am in a dream."

A noise of something falling stopped their conversation and they ran into the other room thinking that Edwin had fallen. He was safely sleeping and so John, closely followed by Mary went into his own bedroom.

There laying side by side on the bed were Elizabeth and Charity. They were both quite dead and completely covered in speckled black feathers.

John fell into a dead faint.

Within two months he was married to Mary. After the wedding, they decided to leave the village where tongues were wagging about the speed of the union. For John, it was practical. He could not look after himself or a boy on his own, so he must marry and Mary was willing. The locals were talking witches still and Mary not being a native of the place but an import from Wakefield was deemed to be the one responsible for the terrible deaths of Elizabeth and Charity.

They moved to Nottingham where John had the promise of some work and their son Matthew was born nine months after the wedding. The work did not last long and soon they moved to Leeds where John had heard there that he could work on the new railway.

They rented a back to back which was infested with rats and lice. They were thoroughly miserable and Mary and John bickered constantly. They had only been there a few weeks before John began noticing the starlings in one of the few trees he passed on the way to work.

"Christ," he muttered to himself.

John was depressed but would never speak of it. He really did not understand what it was he felt. He knew he was tired and that he missed his family back in Chudleigh. He thought of them often and had once started a letter but he screwed it up and threw it into the fire. So much time had passed now and he didn't know what to say to them. How could he write, I want to come home, find me a job and a house? But that was never going to happen. He couldn't go back as a failure. That was what he felt about himself. He was a failure. He couldn't go back, so what was the point in writing?

The starlings were collecting and increasing daily, seemingly in line with his thoughts. They   were silent, but he didn't want to wait for them to begin their chirrups.

When these feelings became too much for him, he decided the family should move town. He had always done that, ever since he got fed up with life in Chudleigh.

He couldn't escape the thought that Leeds was a horrible place. The house they rented in Saville Street was cramped, smelly and damp. But it was all they could get. Oh, to be back home near the fields and the flowers and the hills. These closed in streets of Leeds with so many people was hard to take. It was so like London and Mary working hard looking after the babies in the stuffy dark room was too hard to watch and he went to the inn at the end of the street.

There was less work on the railway than he had been given to believe and so John told his family that they would be moving to London. He was sure that his brother Peter would find them a place and some work. There would be more prospects for them down in London, he said.

That was an untruth. It was the starling tree warning him of trouble ahead and he didn't want to face it. There had been too many bad thoughts, John could see that now.

Thoughts are things.

John did not feel close to his boys. He couldn't understand them and Mary did not help with her nagging tongue. He was aware that he had turned her into this nagging woman as he became more closed down. He hardly communicated with her and she was left with little alternative but to nag. And every day more birds came to the tree.

The day they left Leeds in 1849 and moved to 52 Boston Place in Christchurch, St Marylebone in London the birds screamed and squealed in the tree in the small field at the end of the street. They left early one morning without telling the landlord or their friends and John told his family to get to the railway station   before the birds woke. Mary did not argue, having felt the same feelings of unease. As the train pulled out of the station and the dawn broke, they watched a dark cloud begin to follow the train. They noticed some of their fellow early travellers looking out of the windows and pointing. The cloud moved as fast as the train and some of the starlings began to land on the roof with a thud. Passengers just started a little with the first few bangs, but soon became more uneasy as the noises continued. Thud, thud, thud was quickly followed by scratching and chirruping and after only a minute or two the windows were covered in flapping birds and it was impossible to see out.

People were screaming and shouting for the guard and banging on the windows to scare away the birds. The guard arrived and tried in vain to take charge of a situation he had no experience of and no training for. The carriage was rocking and the well-travelled guard became red faced and panicky with this new experience.

John asked, "Will the train go faster? We might shake the birds off."

"As soon as we leave Leeds we will speed up. I have never seen this before. Have you?"

"I have seen starlings do odd things before but never on a train that is true."

The birds were making serious marks on the window glass and cracks were beginning to appear. Suddenly a bird came through the window and landed on the floor of the carriage, bloodied and screaming. Mary screamed and the boys cried. Passengers and guard alike held up hands in vain attempt to stem the flow of bloody starlings hurling themselves into the train. It was still difficult to see the scenery outside as the corpses piled up inside.

Thousands and thousands came and as the train sped up it seemed some of the later starlings could not reach the train and gradually the pile of birds stopped. The windows now were free of birds but the broken glass iced with blood and ripped feathers were a reminder to what had just occurred.

The passengers helped the guard shovel the bloodied birds out of the way. Their journey was shortened by the chore and what else could they do?

When they landed at London, John took his family and ran out of the station. Some of the other passengers stayed a little longer in order to report about the strange phenomena they had experienced.

Their new house was a tenement and they shared the block with a stableman, a Coldstream Guard, an artificial flower maker and men who worked on the river. It was another noisy busy place. There were so many more people living there than in Leeds and if John was honest, more people than the last time he lived there. Even he felt under pressure now.

One day in 1850 he saw a huge fire in Lambeth and he thought again of home, of Chudleigh. The smoke and fire was visible for hours even though it was the other side of the river. He was surprised how much it had scared him and also how much he wanted to go home to Devon.

There was such poverty and cruelty and in order to survive a man needed to conform.

John again found himself doing work for unethical landlords and there was no way he could get to show his considerable talents as a carpenter.

One day he was walking along a side street, avoiding the scurrying people pushing their way past each other. Even though the sun was high in the sky, these streets seemed dark and menacing. Thick smoke and buildings built too close together and the constant need to have his head down in order not to trip up over others made every journey too stressful. Suddenly he was aware of a hand grabbing his arm. He looked up and saw the owner of the arm was a dirty looking man, smoking a pipe and standing in the alleyway.

"Hello Johnnie. Long time no see," he said.

"Sparks!" answered John. He recognized the man from his earlier years in London. He had been avoiding some of his former associates since his return as he did not want to go down that road again.

"You haven't been to see us. We missed you! Come with me now, we have a job for you."

"I already have a job; I don't need any more work!" John knew that he was in trouble now. Sparks looked more menacing than he had ever done all those years before. He followed him because he knew there was nothing else he could do.

Sparks led him down by the river through ever smaller streets. Soon they turned into an alleyway, climbed some rickety stairs which clung to the side of a brick building and scrambled through a door at the top which led into a dark room. A couple of nasty looking men stood guard outside this door, but moved aside when Sparks nodded to them.

"I got him," Sparks announced to the men inside.

"Hello Johnnie!" A buxom young woman moved towards John.

"Remember me?" Of course, he did, this woman was well known to him. They had a dalliance when he first moved to London. Indeed, Sally was the one who had introduced him to this gang of thieves in the first place.

"Hello Sally." She stroked his hair and he looked uncomfortably over her shoulder to see the others staring at him with either indifference or contempt. The room was very dark and the lamps lit on the table or the wall only seemed to accentuate their look of evil. This was not a good place to be. There was a nasty smell of urine mixed with sweat. Then John noticed a squeaking noise.

There was a young boy at the back of the room and he appeared to have his hands tied up.

"Papa."

It was Matthew.

"What in the hell are you doing with him?" John turned on his former associate.

"We just want you to know that we can do anything we want at any time we want. You joined us and you tried to leave. I told you then that it was not possible. You do as I say or Matthew will suffer. You know I mean it Johnnie boy."

John looked helplessly around the room and knew he was finished.

"Let him go. I'm back in." he said, now defeated.

"Off you go boy. Don't tell your mother about this."
Sally had undone Matthew's bonds and was
smoothing his hair back from his face.
"Go home Matt and stay there until I get home."
Matthew ran out of the door determined that these
people would not see him crying.
"Now then Johnnie boy, this next job involves your
not inconsiderable skills. We both know what they
are."
Sally had moved right next to John and was smiling
at him.
John felt sick.
When John came home that night, Mary could not
get any sense out of him. Matthew had come home
several hours previously in a state of shock.
"What's happened to you both? John, the boy is only
thirteen!"
"You soften that lad too much. Leave me alone
woman!" He went upstairs, crashed about for a
while and then came down and out of the front
door.
It was several days before Mary got the truth out of
her husband. She was horrified and particularly
when she discovered that he had been doing illegal
work already.
"Oh John, we must leave this place!"
But John would not.
Mary took Matthew the next day and they left
London forever.
John moved to the Marquis of Granby cottages in St
Pauls with his friend George Oliver and his family.
Edwin married his Jane and moved away.
John never heard from Mary and as he had no idea
where they were, that was the end of that. He told
people that she was dead.

Whenever he saw a starling or indeed any type of bird sitting in a tree he would feel his heart race and he was generally overcome with anxiety if any of them twittered or flew away.

This phobia rose again spectacularly during the spring of 1863 as John leant against a balcony which George had arranged for him to fix. He noticed starlings settling on the hedgerows opposite. They landed one by one until hundreds of them were there. They twittered and sang in a dreadful chorus and gradually began to synchronise their sound. As they did so, the tune became one continuous hum which caused the people John saw on the streets to put their hands over their ears and scurry away. He felt his heart race and he couldn't concentrate. He pushed against the balcony in panic and the rail gave way with an almighty crack. John fell to the ground and lay still. He knew that he could not move and guessed that he had broken his back.

Some men came running towards him shouting,

"Mate, are you alright?"

John thought of Chudleigh and his parents and the day of the fire and as he did he was back there. He was running through the streets from school to find his home. There was his mother standing on the step of the cottage. He hugged his mother as if he would never let her go and she hugged him back. He went into the cottage and saw his siblings sitting around the table eating as his father came into the room.

"Come on in son," his father said.

"Why the starlings?" John asked his hallucination.

"Baby stars my little boy. I told you that good thoughts and deeds went to make stars and bad thoughts and deeds went to make baby stars that

turned into black birds unless they were looked after. Don't you remember? Only a joke John, only a joke..."
The men stood around the broken body of the carpenter.
"Stupid old fool, leaning on broken wood like that," said one and they heaved him onto a cart to take his body to the undertaker.

CHRISTMAS AT THE WORKHOUSE

Featuring Matthew Prideaux (1838 - 1888)

"Why do you want to talk to me?" asked Matthew of the young woman sitting by his head and holding pen and paper.

Miss Ellen Young, school mistress at the Hunslet Union Workhouse, put down her pen and considered her answer.

"Because Mr Prideaux, I am writing a journal of the happenings at this place. I write down my observations and thoughts and opinions but I so rarely have an opportunity to take notes from someone who is experiencing the troubles here."

"I would imagine that you speak to all of the inmates?" he answered breathlessly, for Matthew was suffering from Phthisis.

"I do sir but most are either too sick, angry or unable to process and reveal their true thoughts."

"Why do you think that I might be none of those things?"

"I overheard the way you spoke to Mrs Wilson." Miss Young lowered her eyes in case they betrayed the utter contempt she felt towards the incumbent Workhouse Matron. "You spoke as an educated man might."

"I am barely educated Miss, although I have always read as many books as I can lay m hands on."

"Your parents were well educated?" she asked tentatively. Some of the unfortunates who found themselves relying on the poor county handouts were not always the God- allocated underlings which some of the charitable people cared to imagine they were.

Ellen Young had become a non-believer during her time at the Workhouse, although her initial desire to work there had come from similar charitable beliefs. She wanted to help the poor unfortunates whom she had seen evicted from cottages they could no longer pay for due to loss of a job or the death of the family head. Now homeless and often sick and aged, they must take themselves and their few possessions into the workhouse. There, their possessions were taken from them in order to contribute to their care and families were split up at the door, often never to communicate in this life again. Ellen found it traumatic when aged couples were ripped apart while half hugging in a final goodbye. Children were taken screaming from their crying mothers, the older ones later sitting straight backed and starving in her classroom, eager to make a good impression on the soft and perfumed teacher.

If God existed everywhere Ellen thought - He did not exist in a workhouse. Therefore, He did not exist.

"My father was educated, not my mother, but she was a kind and resourceful woman as was my late wife. Both are long dead and my children are unable to look after me now."

"I see that from your records Mr Prideaux, although I believe your family have tried."

"They have, particularly my eldest daughter and the other children have been split up among my family. I will be dead soon and they will not have to worry about me."

This was said with little emotion and Ellen felt for him.

"Will you talk to me for a while?" she asked.

"Won't you get into trouble Miss? The bosses will not want you here and the nurses will come and make you leave."

"Not tonight Mr Prideaux, for it is Christmas night and they are all stuffing their faces with the food and drink that should be given to the residents here. I was invited but said I had a headache and have instead decided to walk about the place and talk to the people."

"Are you not afraid Miss?"

"Of the residents? No not at all. They will not harm me and to be honest most are locked up for the night."

"Except for us in the hospital?"

"Yes. You are all deemed too ill to go and observe their dreadful gluttony."

"In the style of Oliver Twist?"

"I knew I was right Mr Prideaux. I knew you were an educated man."

"Education matters not when you are about to die," he answered ruefully.

"Do you think so? I do not agree. I have a friend who has been to India and there they believe that the soul moves on to another life and takes all that has been learnt with it. And so, we continue until we reach enlightenment."

"I have read about it. It is about keeping your mind aware as you die. Or something like that," said Matthew.

"Something like that," said Ellen.

She adjusted her chair in order to move it nearer to Matthew's head and then passed him a drink of water.

"What is your earliest memory Mr Prideaux?"

"If we are to talk, call me Matthew."

"I will Matthew and you must call me Ellen, unless anyone else is listening."

They laughed. The silence in the ward was only broken by coughing or moaning and neither call was being attended by the absent staff.

"My earliest memory was being carried through the streets of Leeds clutching my mother and my elder brother walking alongside. I know that my mother was very cross. She held me under one arm and the feeling was of great discomfort. I think she was going to fetch my father from the inn and somehow shame him for allowing us to go without while he drank. My father John worked as a joiner. His family had been master carpenters for several generations and his grandfather was sought out by wealthy homeowners to do exquisite work on the timbers around their homes. But my father struggled to find any work at all. He did some work on the houses of his neighbours in the pay of the landlord. But the landlords did not want to pay much money and expected John to merely 'make do'. The neighbours however took it upon themselves to blame John for the amount of work he did. They blamed his shoddy workmanship and laziness instead of blaming their landlord for his meanness. John found it very difficult and often sought solace in drink, spending the little money the family had available."

An unfamiliar noise in the doorway of the ward caused them both to turn round, fearing Matron. However, there was nothing to be seen which could be illuminated by the lamps. Ellen turned back to her questioning,

"Have you got any really terrible memories?"

"I do remember a dreadful train journey from Leeds to London when the train was attacked by thousands of birds and left me and the rest of the family terrified of the awful flapping things for life. But then arriving in London I found out that was an even more terrifying place to be."

"When was this?" she asked.

"1850 Miss, very Dickensian and cruel. The streets were covered with horse manure and mud and there were people and horse drawn hackney cabs everywhere. Raw sewage ran into the same water which we also used for drinking. Prostitutes, beggars and thieves abounded on every street and commonplace crime and murder made it no place for a sentimental person. Cattle and sheep were driven through the streets and then sold and slaughtered in the markets. The slaughter men and butchers walked about the town, still covered in blood and successfully scaring the little children. There was a constant deafening noise and smog and smoke hung constantly over the city. Most people stank and the streets became just as smelly with each rain shower."

"How did your mother cope?"

"She hated it. I managed to find some work alongside Father and Edwin as a joiner's mate. We worked in many of the hovels where the poor lived and worked. All the repairs were paid for by landlords who were hard taskmasters. Father no longer seemed to care. Edwin was very like our father and the two of them often teased and upset the more sensitive me." Matthew smiled at the sad memory.

Ellen continued her jottings and smiled encouragement at the patient.

"I was only seventeen and Mother and I decided to leave London and seek our fortunes elsewhere. Mother took the money she had been saving for the last few years from its hiding place behind a brick near the fire place. She wrapped it safely in a small bag and hid it under her skirts. We stole away one Sunday morning and lost ourselves amongst the early market traders and late night revellers still on their way home. I vaguely remember my father standing in the doorway but saying nothing. The destination was Leeds where Mother had relatives and after two weeks of walking and hitching rides we arrived here. Mother knocked on the door of an old friend and through her contact we soon moved into the small house on Atkinson Street. I found work as a carpenter and Mother as a seamstress. This arrangement worked well for almost three years."

"Was that when your mother passed?" asked Ellen kindly.

"No Miss. It was then that I met my future wife Sarah Jackson when I was doing some joinery in the factory where she worked. Sarah decided that I was the one for her and she set out to catch me. Sarah's family had moved from Lincolnshire, where her father worked on the land. Work was hard to find there and he moved the family to Leeds where he knew there would be work. He worked with blue slate, his boys in the brickyard and his girls at the mill. When we married we all lived at Atkinson Street with mother. When Mary became ill with bronchitis, Sarah nursed her as she would her own mother."

"That was when she died?"

"She died on 4th May 1864 with Sarah at her side. Then a few months later Mary Emma was born fit and well. It was then that the hauntings began."

"Sorry. What?" Ellen held her pen mid-air, unsure of what she had just heard.

"Mother began to appear at the side of the new baby. We thought that she was just looking after her."

"You saw your mother's spirit?"

"You don't believe that to be possible Miss? And yet you are living in a workhouse all these years where the corridors are roamed daily by the tormented spirits of passed inmates?"

Ellen did not know how to answer without making herself look foolish.

"Well, I don't know. I'm not sure. I have heard stories naturally and some of the children pretend that they see ghosts walking about in the dark trying to scare them."

"It's not protected though, is it? I've seen them here regularly." Matthew slumped back against the pillows as though ready to sleep."

"Do you want me to leave, Mr Prideaux? Is this too much for you?"

"No, Miss. I might as well tell you my story as no one else is interested. Now that I have the time to tell my children our family story, they aren't able to come here and listen. Or they probably don't want to."

The noise by the doorway sounded again. It was a shuffling and knocking combination which was enough to cause Ellen to stand up and walk towards it.

"Hello?" she asked.

A small woman, dressed in workhouse garb came out from behind the curtain. She was bent over at right angles and leaning heavily on a thick wooden stick.

"Should you not be asleep now?" said Ellen.

The old woman stared at Ellen from underneath her greasy fringe. She spat and vanished into the dark.

Ellen walked back to Matthew's bed.

"You saw her, didn't you?" he asked.

"Of course."

"Well, she's a ghost," Matthew said and smiled broadly. Ellen noticed that his smile lit up his grey and thin face. He must have been very handsome before he got sick, she thought.

Ellen sat back down.

"How many children do you have?"

"We had a few," answered Matthew. "After Mary Emma, Sarah had two miscarriages and then carried a son successfully to term. We named him Edwin John after my brother who I miss even now. Another daughter was born and then George after two more miscarriages. Then, during the next ten years Sarah had several miscarriages and five further children, including twins."

Ellen acknowledged the way Matthew spoke. His speech neither matched his situation nor his last address, but Ellen declined to mention the fact. Matthew Prideaux must descend from different stock than she had first imagined.

"Did they all live Matthew?"

"No sadly. Charles was born sickly and was not expected to live. His twin Eliza died after reaching almost two years old and having constant nursing from her mother. Sarah had another miscarriage just before Eliza died. Sarah dealt with the doctors and the funerals. The children are buried in paupers' graves and flowers picked from the grass verges as none could be afforded. Sarah grieved for each and every one of our lost children. I would not talk about them, although I grieved in my own way."

"That is terrible Matthew. How I wish there was a more accessible route to doctors and nurses for the poor."

"It's a pity that the doctors we have don't know what they are doing most of the time. They are so arrogant and sure of themselves and blame God when their patients die so easily. They fail day in and day cut and expect to be treated with deference and respect."

Ellen nodded; she had as much respect for doctors as she did for the clergy. She pulled her shawl over her shoulders as there was a sudden cold draught.

"Are you warm enough Matthew?"

"I am fine. I expect you are feeling the spirit presence."

"Very funny. You can't frighten me."

"I am not trying to Miss. As I told you, there were plenty of ghosts in my house, but there are even more here at the workhouse. It seems to me that no one who died has left the place."

"They probably don't realise that they are dead."

"That's what I think. They haven't noticed that they have left the prison."

"Why did your passed family stay you with after they died?"

"Because they didn't want to leave or didn't know they were dead. We never did any of the silly tricks that others did to prevent the spirits of the deceased following them home from the graveyards."

Ellen nodded and made some notes. She was well aware of the customs but knew that these practices did not occur at the workhouse. The bodies were buried in the workhouse plot outside the grounds. First, they were placed in a cheap coffin where they were squashed in tightly. Then the coffins were kept in a side building until there were enough to fill the hole which was then filled in and left unmarked. It was no wonder that a spirit did not want to go there.

As if reading her thoughts Matthew said,

"The bodies are often kept so long here prior to burial that the spirits leave the body and begin to roam the corridors again. At home, there was one time when one of our babies had to stay in his little coffin for two weeks until there were enough to join him in his hole in the ground."

Ellen shivered again.

"Do you really think that is what happens Matthew? That there are ghosts walking the corridors?"

"Of course. Surely you know that Miss Young, you have been here long enough?"

Yes, she did know. She could feel them now, surrounding her and listening to their talk. They must feel particularly free to roam tonight with the rats away at their Christmas celebrations.

"That means the same thing is happening at all the workhouses around the country. They all do the same thing with those who have passed."

"And schools and universities and hospitals. There will be spirits all over them and I doubt they will ever leave because they won't understand."

"That is a frightening thought," said Ellen.

"I don't know so much. It depends where you imagine that leaving here at death takes you to. I think it takes you to where you expect to go."

"Where do you think you are going Matthew?"

"Because I am dying now?" he chuckled.

"I don't wish to offend you Matthew, but yes I suppose. A death sentence does rather focus the mind."

"I want to go back to Devon or Cornwall when I leave. And I do not believe for one minute that I need to go up to Heaven or down to Hell dependent on how good some ridiculous priest thinks I have been. I hope I find my Sarah and my mother there, but if I don't I shall begin again in my root country. Where will you go Miss?"

Ellen didn't need to think. "I am leaving here after Christmas although they don't know yet. I shall go to India with my friend and meet the great spiritual teachers there. Perhaps I shall stay there after I die this time round."

"Good for you Miss."

There came the sound of several heavy feet marching down the outside corridor towards the ward door. Ellen started,

"Oh. Why are they coming back tonight? I thought they would be feasting until well after midnight."

She began to rise from her chair.

"No wait here, you won't be seeing a warm body coming through those doors."

The ward doors swung open as if pushed by a firm hand. The footsteps continued but were made by no visible person. They marched along the centre of the ward and went out through the end doors which swung open in a similar way.

"They are active tonight. Why?" asked Ellen.

"It's Christmas so the veil is thinner and there are no bosses about."

"Oh, I see. I think I see. It's quite exciting, isn't it?"

"Do you want me to come and haunt you when I go Miss?"

"Not really. Or perhaps, I don't know. Just don't make me jump!"

Matthew laughed and beckoned to her to continue her questioning.

"Before I fall asleep and join the marching feet," he said.

"What happened to your children?"

"Agnes was sent away to live with my maternal aunt Mary and her husband George Kitchen at the Oatlands Inn. You know she went on the stage along with two of her Kitchen cousins?"

"Oh where?"

"Lots of plays at the Theatre Royal in Leeds and they had some dog act called 'Messrs Lamb and Kitchen and their Wonderful Dogs.'," he said with a flourish.

"I saw them!" said Ellen with genuine interest. "They were really very clever."

"They were indeed, Agnes always loved dogs. She still has them and she loves the stage. I expect she will be haunting the Theatre Royal when she goes."

"And what about the others?"

"When little Eliza died, I really noticed a difference in Sarah. She became pale and tired and had large black rings under her eyes. We were used to her singing and laughing and never being depressed. That had all changed now. We moved to 22 Ambler Yard in Holbeck as Sarah had decided that the last house was bad luck. I told her she was being stupid, but in truth I was more superstitious than my wife. It was me who put some lucky charms in the chimney breast and bedroom in order to ward off evil. I probably saw our ghost children more than Sarah did but I would never admit that. Then we only lived there for less than a month because Sarah's cough became worse. I have an idea that the dead children and my mother had been keeping us safe."

"What was the matter with Sarah?"

"She coughed up blood, the usual problem. She told me she knew that she was dying when we sat in our tiny kitchen one evening. She wouldn't go the doctor, because they never help. It was the end of summer 1884. The August evenings were still warm and the muggy air made Sarah's cough worse. By the beginning of September Sarah had taken to her bed. She was being nursed in turn by our girls but she was fading fast. 'Look after the babies Mary 'she told our eldest daughter. 'Of course I will Mama,' she answered. 'But you will get better.' 'I won't Mary, I am worn out. My spirit is already halfway gone. I saw my dead babies in the room last night.' Mary did not know what to say. Sarah told Mary that when she was dreaming that she saw many little children come into her bedroom after I went to sleep and they held out their fat little hands to her."

"Was she scared?" asked Ellen.

"Mary said not and I don't think Sarah was. She had a great faith unlike me. She said to Mary, 'Don't worry about me, my darling girl. All will be well.' And then she closed her eyes and died. There was a huge smile on her face and she looked like a girl again. It was 21st September 1884."

Matthew looked up from his bed to the pretty young woman jotting down his ramblings. Ellen noticed and asked him if he needed food or water.

"Water please but if you have any spare food then give it to the children."

"I will – I do. What happened to the children when you came in here?"

"Mary Emma wanted to marry her friend Arthur soon after Sarah died, but stayed looking after me instead, I got sick and could not work and so they all clubbed together to look after me. I signed myself in here so that they could have a life. She will marry him as soon as I die, I should imagine. George managed to find lodgings in Grape Street and Edwin lodged with his girlfriend and her mother. William and Thomas live with Mary and will live with her after she marries. They don't need me."

"I am sure they do need you."

"Perhaps, but if I hurry up and leave here, they will soon forget about me. I say, why don't we have a bit of an adventure before the nasty people get back?"

Ellen closed her journal and said,

"Adventure? What did you have in mind?"

"Let us get the spirits moving and marching to their Christmas meal."

"Wonderful idea, but how?"

"Fetch that wheelchair over here and while you do that, I shall pee in a bottle."

Ellen jumped up and left him to his business and brought the chair back once he said he was ready. She wrapped his legs in his blanket and put a pillow behind his back.

"Right, now take me to the morgue."

"No! Why? I am too frightened!"

"Well I am not frightened for I shall be there soon enough, so push me please."

"I don't think that is a good idea."

"I didn't argue with you when you wanted to write my story in your journal, did I?"

Ellen thought for only a moment and began to push hm. For if she was intending to leave the employ of the Workhouse and go to India with John in search of enlightenment, then she really should be prepared to take some risks at home.

She wheeled Matthew up and down corridors, conscious that they were being watched by live eyes and dead. The live ones peeked and sneaked as they went past but were much too fearful to follow. Past experience had taught them that to interfere in anything outside of their remit was – well, it wasn't worth it.

The dead ones seemed to scoot behind them and then every so often they would see a shadow or shape hiding in a stairwell or doorway,

"Ignore them," said Matthew.

"I am trying to," Ellen answered.

"I am so near the veil now Ellen that I can see and experience much more than you can. Most dying people are but they spend all of their time worrying about how ill they feel and whether Jesus or their mother will be there to meet them. They should embrace the process and take control of it."

"How?"

"By noticing their perceptual changes. This isn't the only life any of us have lived or will live. If we don't pay attention to our intentions and feelings when we are dying, we will go to where those scary feelings match."

"You are saying we can control where we go?"

"Of course we can. I never want to enter a prison or a workhouse or anywhere restrictive again and now I know that I am able to do it."

They arrived at the morgue and Ellen turned the wheelchair round and pushed the doors open with her bustle.

They were inside.

To her horror, she saw that there were four bodies lying on top of each other on a large table in the corner of the room.

"No respect you see," muttered Matthew.

"I do see. I think it is disgraceful. What now? Do we perform some kind of spell?"

"Not at all, spells only strengthen our thoughts. Once you decide what you want to do just expect it to happen. It will."

"I see. So, what shall we do now?"

"This."

Matthew poked one of the bodies and Ellen saw dust rise from the shroud which surrounded it. But of course, it wasn't dust - it was a spirit. The dust clouded above the body and then morphed into four separate shapes.

"Ladies and gentlemen, I want you all to collect some of our other spirit friends and move on to the room where the Master and his family and staff are stuffing their big fat faces with food that would have done you some good in your last days of your life."

The spirits flew and spun around Ellen and Matthew and soon the marching sounds began again.

"They are coming!" said Matthew in a theatrical voice.

The mortuary door swung open and nothing but marching boots entered the room. The new ghosts swirled above them turning the room green and glowing. The marching feet must have about-turned because the noise was retreating back up the corridor. Matthew beckoned Ellen to follow them and she did.

As they neared the Master's quarters some minutes later, the marching was in complete unison and the floor and walls vibrated with the sound. Matthew grabbed Ellen's arm and told her to push him into the stairwell from where they could perceive the scene better.

Master Atkins opened the door and looked up and down the corridor.

"There is nothing here!" he shouted back into the room.

Then he was pushed aside and thrown to the ground as the crowd of marching boots thrust past him and the green glowing cloud followed just before the door was slammed shut by a better-late-than-never servant.

The screaming and wailing which came from the room caused Ellen to put her hand to her ears and Matthew to laugh.

"We should go," she said.

"Not yet."

The doors slammed open again and people began streaming out, grasping their coats and their bags. They were screaming and terrified as they ran towards the main doors. Master Atkins followed them out exclaiming to his servants that the food and drink must have been poisoned and that it must be removed immediately.

"Give it to the dammed inmates," he shouted. "Let them hallucinate!"

"Christmas dinner for the workers!" laughed Matthew.

Ellen quickly pushed him back to his ward and got him safety into bed.

She tucked him in and said, "It has been a pleasure to meet you Matthew. We shall not meet again for I leave in the morning."

"Live your life well Ellen. I shall visit you in India - in your dreams."

She turned down his lamp and walked to the door clutching her journal. There under the sign informing the visitor that this was the infirmary, she turned back for a final look. Matthew was surrounded by a warm orange glow reminiscent of a Christmas fire. There were men, women and children looking down on him, some tucking him in and some stroking his brow. A woman whom Ellen assumed was his beloved mother held his hand and smiled at him like the angel she was. Ellen knew he was safe forever now and she cried softly for this enlightening scene that she would never be able to describe adequately to another soul.

CHERRY RIPE

Featuring George Prideaux (1871 – 1926)

Cherry-Ripe by Robert Herrick

Cherry ripe, cherry ripe,
Ripe I cry,
Full and fair ones
Come and buy.

George Herbert was born 23rd August 1871 at 5 Gorse Street, Hunslet. He was the fourth child of Matthew and Sarah Prideaux and their second son. He was also my great grandfather and I have his papers in my possession. I have transcribed some of the entries here - the ones I feel bring this particular event to life.

Some of the writings I have put together without dates as George wrote later in reference to his childhood and I felt it would complicate the tale to date the journal entries rather than remain chronological.

His son Clifford took possession of an oak chest which was always in George's house and although locked and no key found, Clifford broke it open. Inside he found papers and diaries and letters which he briefly read through before returning them to the chest. He also found a cigarette case and snuff box, within which were some pits which he guessed were cherry. Clifford remembered his father's interest in cherry tree cultivation.

I will relate through this story how this interesting little hobby began.

Soon after George was born, the family moved to 5 Essex Street.   Next door was home to Elizabeth Ogden who lived there with her sister and her niece. Elizabeth was deaf and dumb and received unfortunate attention from the children in the street about her affliction.

"I don't want to ever hear that you have been cruel to Miss Ogden," said George's mother Sarah. Her own sister was deaf and she knew from experience how horrid people could be.

Ten-year-old George said, "Mam! We don't do things like that!"

But of course they did. They followed Elizabeth as she walked to her charring job shouting things which they knew she could not hear. Once, George had barged into the toilet which the two families shared.   He had knocked, but of course she could not hear and she silently screamed in shame at being caught skirts up and sitting on the well-scrubbed wooden seat. George had been initially embarrassed and then found it extremely funny when he recounted the event to his friends.

He felt ashamed when he was told that the story had been relayed around the neighbourhood and Elizabeth would no longer speak to him.

George was present when three of his siblings Arthur, Charles and Eliza died. He was so excited when the twins were born and then to see Charles succumb so quickly and be followed to the grave by Eliza who died before her second birthday affected him deeply. Eliza was deformed and constantly sick and in pain. After her birth, George never picked on the neighbour again.

George worried constantly about the health of his mother. She often seemed tired and careworn. Her hair was prematurely grey and her face lined and pale. She coughed constantly and the coughing seemed worse during the night and in the morning. Even the smoke from the fire upset her.

When the third baby died, George really noticed a difference in his mother.

They moved to 22 Ambler Yard in Holbeck as Sarah had decided that the last house was bad luck. Matthew told her she was being stupid, but George knew that his father was more superstitious than his mother because he had seen him put something near the chimney. George saw the ghosts too but when he had tried to tell his mother his father had stopped him, citing her frailness. They were there for less than a month because Sarah's cough became worse.

Sarah did not recover from all this illness and death and died herself of capillary bronchitis from which she had suffered from for two weeks before she succumbed on the 21st September 1884. She was 46.

Matthew stayed at this address for a while before he too died at the Hunslet Union Workhouse on the 21st January 1888 of Phthisis

George's family was destroyed and they were all forced to move to new addresses.

Mary Emma had been courting Arthur Kay and as soon as she nursed her mother and then her father to their deaths, they married. Mary Emma and Arthur moved into 24 Grape Street and took the two youngest boys, Thomas and William in. She looked after them until they married and moved to Leeds.

"I don't want any of you becoming drunks just because we are living next door to the Queens Inn," she told them.

George moved as a lodger down the road at 77 Grape Street with Elizabeth Catton and Hannah Holgate. A couple of years later he moved to No 89 where he could live alone and soon had new neighbours who moved into No 93. They had a lovely daughter called Mary Ann Hobson and the two married in St Silas Church in Hunslet on 21st January 1893, five years to the day of his father's passing.

His sister Mary Emma and her husband attended as witnesses along with his two youngest brothers.

Soon after marriage they left Grape Street and moved to 7 Burniston Court where I pick up his story in 'A Christmas Story'.

But now I have got a little ahead of the story I want to relate and we must go back to Grape Street. The small amount of background story above may help you understand how George could be led so easily into a mystery and was very kind at heart.

There was a public house on Grape Street called the Queens Inn. It was frequented by all type of regulars, some of whom worked at Armley Gaol.

On one occasion George was working for the landlord as a glass collector and when he had a slack time, he hovered around the guards and listened to their tales of the Gaol. He was often shouted away in order to attend to his work and he answered the call because he needed the pennies.

He had a chance to learn more when one called him over,

"Boy! You been listening to us stories, have you?"

"No sir! Well yes sir – a little. I want to be a policeman so I was just interested."

"Police is it? We aint police, we are prison guards. We deal with the wrong 'uns after they been banged up."

"I know," said George.

"Oh, he knows!" said one guard.

"'e should make a good copper then!" laughed the other.

George wiped down their table - one of his allocated tasks.

"Do you do the hangings?" he asked.

"Hangings? No boy we don't do the hangings, Crown men does the hangings and let me tell you they are not very good at it."

"That's right, so make sure you don't murder no one cos you will end up swinging for half an hour before you die. It's not always a quick job."

George wiped the table as though he were trying to remove the paint from it.

"I am always good sir and I would never harm anyone, let alone murder them."

The men laughed heartily, enjoying their fun.

"I am sure you are. Now fetch us more drink before we die of thirst and if you are quick about it, I will tell you a tale that will keep you awake at night."

"Thank you sir," said George and ran away to the bar.

"Here you are," he said three minutes later. He had fetched ale, collected glasses and scampered back to the guards, anxious to hear their terrible tale before he lost them forever.

He gazed at the men with his big dark eyes.

"Sit by me 'ere," the bigger guard said, patting the bench.

The landlord shouted over to George.

"Give him five minutes boss!" answered the guard. "I knew his father!"

The landlord mumbled something but did not want to upset a prison guard, he might need his help one day.

"Did you know my father?" asked George.

"No, but I'm sure he was a good 'un."

George blushed and said, "Can you tell me your hanging story?"

"Impatient lad, aren't you? It was ten years ago in '76 when they were hanging John Johnson and they went through all the usual procedures and tests and everything worked fine. This hangman Thomas Askern was bad at his job and getting known for it."

"This turned out to be his last job," said his mate.

"It did and right that was too. I'm all for hanging murderers but not for being so cruel."

"What happened?" asked George breathlessly.

"They took him up the steps and led him on to the trapdoor where they finished strapping him and put the hood over his head. He didn't say anything to the crowd and then Askern put the rope round his neck and pulled the lever. Jones fell right through the trapdoor and so did the broken rope behind him."

George had not moved since the story began, eager to remember every detail.

"Was he dead?"

"No, he wasn't. We had to go through the black curtains under the gallows to find him all moaning and struggling in his bonds with his hood on and the broken noose round his neck."

"So, did you let him go free?"

"No, the law wants its Judgement. The law thinks it's God. We got the fellow a chair that one of the dignitaries had been parked on and let Jones sit by the gallows while they all looked for a better rope."

"That's horrible!" said George.

"It is and that's a fact. I felt a bit sorry for Jones so I gave him some cherries that I had in my pocket. The missus had given them to me to take to her mother, but I felt this man's needs were greater. He was real grateful and chewed on them until they had finished fixing the new rope up. Then we walked him back up the scaffold and they put the noose on him again. He said to me, "These pits'll be worth a bit one day!" and they dropped him again. It took him nearly 5 minutes to die, the poor bugger."

"What happened then?" asked George.

"I went and fetched the pits. The poor man had been spitting them out all the time he was throttling the second time. I suppose I thought they would be valuable."

The guard took a snuff box from his pocket and opened it.

"Are they?" said George, peering into the box.

"No and they brought me nothing but bad luck I think. I'm going to throw them away," he said snapping the lid shut.

"Can I have them please?" asked George.

The guards looked at him and the landlord shouted, "George, get over here now or go home and don't come back again!"

"You had better go boy or you will lose your job," the big guard said.

George clutched his towel and stared at the snuff box. The guard threw it in the air and George caught it.

"Go on. Bugger off," said the guard.

And bugger off George did, with snuff box pocketed and a grin on his face.

Reading through George's notes I see that he researched cherry trees and how to grow them for quite some time before he finally put one pit in soil that he had specially prepared. He only dare do one at a time in case it didn't work. Once he had exposed the pit to cold then it seemed that it must germinate. He had ten cherry pits in total.

George waited six months before he was sure that the pit had not germinated and then had to wait until he could try again. He was luckier the second time around and a year later had a tiny little tree in a pot in his house. He planted another to be certain and soon had a second little tree. He used seven pits over the years and got five trees.

He had hopes of sweet cherries and he wished that he was able to show his parents what he had achieved.

By the time he married he was only able to keep one tree and so gave the others to people with gardens, but did not tell of their history.

He probably didn't want them to know what happened with the trees at night. His own tree was in a bigger pot and he pruned it to keep it small and kept it by the window or moved it out into the fresh air whenever he could. The tree was healthy and responsive.

Now here is where the story becomes stranger. George writes in his journal that he would talk to the tree to encourage its growth and the tree would answer him back. George would ask questions with mainly yes or no answers and the tree would shake its branches in response.

At night when it was dark and silent George would hear whispers coming from the tree and as he tried to understand what was being said he realised that it was the twice-hanged man talking to him. It seemed that being hung once sends a person to their next life and being hanged twice keeps them in this life.

This night set off a series of changes in George's life.

He researched and asked questions about the twice-hanged man at Armley and became fearful that the murderer could now somehow control his thoughts. In order to protect himself George placed a crucifix in the soil next to the tree. He began to imagine that the tree was watching him – it certainly seemed to perk up and shake whenever he walked back into the house.

It was also getting quite big and friends and neighbours said he was silly to keep it in the room with him for everyone knew that plants take all your oxygen and can kill you when you are asleep. George wasn't dead yet and he had a great attachment to the tree and in spite of constant complaining from his wife Mary, he continued to look after it carefully.

The tree began to produce fruit and George collected the cherries and told his wife that the pits must never be swallowed nor thrown away but washed and dried and placed in the snuff box. Mary didn't complain at harvest time for the tree did produce a huge amount of cherries, far more than would seem likely for such a small tree. Of course the spring blossom was wonderful and during the early Spring through to fruiting season, neighbours congratulated George on his beautiful tree which brought colour and scent to the grim street. In the Wintertime George dragged the pot into the back kitchen and covered it with a sack to protect it from frost.

From time to time he would visit his other trees and noted that gradually they had failed and died off despite a far superior environment in which to grow.

George's tree continued to thrive and did not mind its life in a tiny and crowded Leeds house. In fact, the tree loved it there. On more than one occasion someone had tried to steal or damage the tree either with or without witnesses. They soon regretted the attempt.

One woman had jealously decided that the fruit should be hers and under cover of darkness took a basket and crept up to the tree. She took hold of a pair of cherries and pulled them lightly ready to place them in her basket. Later she told a friend that that tree began to pull back and soon she was in a two-handed battle with a small cherry tree on a late Summer evening. She swore that she heard the tree growl and then say, 'Clear off you thieving bitch.' She let go and ran back home crying.

Two drunken friends of George's thought it would be a lark to pull the tree from its pot and throw it across the street.

"Summat up with a bloke who wants to play with flowers," one said and grabbed hard hold of the tree. He fell back to the ground screaming.

"What's up?" asked his mate.

"It just bit me!" he said.

"Sure it did!" and his mate grabbed the tree.

He felt the pain but unlike his mate was unable to let go. He shouted and swore and tried to escape. It took half a minute before the tree released its grip and he could stare at his cut and bleeding hands.

"It aint got thorns, has it?"

"No! It's just smooth!"

"Well look at me hands!" The blood was flooding from his palms and they rushed home quickly to get help there. The man suffered infection and fever for the following week and then he died. His friend found it difficult to use his hands properly for the rest of his life.

Talk began after this episode and most would avoid the tree even when it was in full flower and sweet smelling, waving in the warm Spring breeze outside the front door of the Prideaux home.

A young man, keen to impress a pretty young girl and knowing nothing of the stories, crept to the tree with a small pocket knife eager to snip a few blossoms for a posy. He approached the tree in the dark and it snapped a branch at him so quickly that it knocked the knife from his hand and flicked it into his chest. Luckily the knife did not impale him too deeply and he ran away dripping blood.

Mary insisted that the tree be destroyed and thrown away but George was loathe so to do. Instead he rented a small garden orchard from a woman in Bramley village to whom he had given a cherry tree previously and the promise to plant more trees which would result in a crop of sweet cherries every year sealed the deal. She gave him permission to continue with his cultivation and there the tree went.

It appears that through the following many years, George spent a good deal of his time at the orchard treasuring his cherry trees and soon had ten producing fruit. As he brought each tree to harvest he kept many of the pits with which he could cultivate new trees. The trees were planted in his small orchard and the owner of

Wellington House on Broad Lane enjoyed the results of his labour. Some of her friends wanted to buy young trees from him and he would allow that on odd occasions as the payment offered was more than he could afford to turn away. These sold trees neither fruited nor survived.

George often talked to his trees and he wrote that they talked back. He apparently told no-one about his chats.

He was convinced that the hanged man was reincarnated in the trees – all of the trees. George wrote about the life the man Jones had had and how his mistakes had led him to murder and his subsequent execution. Jones was grateful that George was planting and caring for the trees, because that meant he could still live. He wanted to protect George and his brother trees in order that he could stay alive. George wrote, 'Jones wants to live and I am the only person able to make that happen. He will never allow me to stop.'

It seemed he told Jones that he was thinking of spending less time at Bramley because it was becoming difficult to spare the hours. The trees would shake and the branches grab him and not let go as he walked past. George was becoming scared.

By 1900 George and Mary had five children, although little Ben died less than two years after his birth. He died of Diphtheria after suffering dreadfully for weeks. Convulsions finally took him to his maker on Christmas Eve 1899.

"Why does Jesus want all these little babies?" Mary cried. "He takes so many, why does he want my little Ben too?"

There could be no answer to this. The authorities insisted on a post mortem and he could not be buried until after 27th December when they decided he had in fact died of natural causes.

Mary Ann would never forget the boy's death. His little body stayed in the front room until it was walked down to Holbeck for burial. They had hardly any money, but Mary Ann insisted that some flowers were carried with his coffin. George brought Christmas roses from his garden orchard. Mary still felt Ben's presence around the house, but did not tell George as he would have laughed. George would not have laughed. He often saw his own dear mother when he felt particularly tense.

George told his trees about his upsets and he swore that he heard in a whispered tone,

"Stay here then George. You kill my beloveds and I will kill yours."

George promised to stay there when he visited Wellington House orchard on Christmas Eve 1902.

Their luck changed the following day when they welcomed baby Clifford into their family on Christmas Day.

"Jesus has sent you another son to take the place of Ben," said George to his wife. Another three children followed and Jane arrived nine months after Ben's death. Nine births and one death was a very good average for the time, but George wrote that it was because of the Jones cherry tree.

George continued to look after the trees for years and seemed to be getting more concerned about the control they had over his life. But he went to the orchard regularly and cared for the trees, always mindful of what he spoke about and told the Jones trees of interesting facts and news of the war and his children and their marriages and so forth.

By the summer of 1926 George was becoming ill and less able to go to the orchard. His friend at Wellington House was also ageing and she visited the orchard less and less. The hedges were becoming overgrown and the stone walls tumbling down a little more each month. It was beginning to resemble an unattended cemetery and Jones had no one left to remember him.

George knew that Jones was becoming angry, but told the trees that he was ill and tired and unable to function as he had to date.

"Die then," he heard the leaves whisper as he walked away.

One time on 13th October 1926 George Herbert went to visit his son and his new wife with Mary Ann. He had been very ill with bronchitis for several weeks. Mary Ann blamed his constant smoking and noted that George had coughed through the winters of most of their years together.

This particular morning had been different somehow. George looked very pale and coughed constantly.

"George, do you think you should go today?"

"I said I would go and I will."

George sounded more forceful than he felt. He felt as weak as a kitten, but staying in bed had never made him feel better - not that he had ever had much time to laze about.

They set off and caught the tram to the railway station. Soon they were on board the train to Woodlesford which was not too far away and the journey took no longer than a few minutes. George was distant and seemed paler now than this morning.

After they walked to their son's house and spent a couple of hours there, his son and his wife were also very worried.

"I think you should see the doctor Dad. You seem so tired."

He knew his father had been laid off work for the last couple of days and that money was tight, but this was important.

"I will pay for the doctor, Dad."

George looked up and his eyes flashed.

"I am not so bad yet that I have to have a son of mine paying for me!" The anger made him cough all the more and everyone looked at him.

"Come on Annie, we are going home," he snapped.

His wife got up from her chair and gave her son a knowing look.

"Come and see us off George?"

"I'll come and see you to your own door, Mum. You should not travel on your own like this."

Mary was grateful and hugged her son. Annie waved them off from the doorstep and the three set off slowly to the station.

The bridge had to be crossed in order to get to the correct side of the tracks and the exertion seemed to set off George coughing.

"Have a cherry Dad, it's one of yours! The vitamins will do you good."

George took the fruit and accidentally swallowed the pit – something he had never done before. At the top step, he staggered onto the bridge and leaned on the wall where he coughed for a minute or two before he went very pale and slumped to the floor, eyes closed.

"Dad!" shouted his son.

There was no answer and George watched helplessly as his father stopped breathing and died in front of them.

Mary Ann stood in shock, hands over her mouth and frozen to the spot.

George shouted over the edge of the bridge to the station porter to come and help. But it was no good. George Herbert Prideaux died that day.

The Prideaux family posted a notice in the Yorkshire Evening Post on October 15th.

PRIDEAUX Oct 15 at 100 Elland Road, Holbeck.
George Herbert beloved husband of Mary Ann
Prideaux, aged 55 years – internment at
Holbeck Cemetery, Saturday at 3 leaving house
2.30. Friends please accept this the only
intimation.

The funeral was arranged and over so quickly
that Mary Ann and her sons had no time to cry.
It was only as she stood over his grave,
surrounded by her family and George's friends
that it became real.

"We have had a talk, Mrs P and all his friends at
the Club have had a whip round and are going to
pay for a marble flower pot to go with the
headstone. It is the least we can do."

Mary Ann stared at him and said nothing.

"Thank you very much," answered Clifford on
her behalf. That is very good of you."

The funeral tea was held at the club and
everyone went home. It was at this tea that
Clifford took the journals and chest as
mentioned at the beginning of this story.

The white marble headstone paid for by his
family stands proudly in Holbeck Cemetery.
When Mary Ann died in 1948, her remains were
placed there also.

The white marble flower pot paid for by his
many friends at the club stands alongside it.

However, the engraving the friends arranged to put on there, states the name 'Priddo' – so much for his fame.

Clifford read through the journals a couple of times and put the stories down to his father's imaginative nature and his ability to tell a tall tale. Perhaps he had intended to send the writings to a publisher or just liked writing things down.

It was twenty-five years later when Clifford and his wife and two daughters moved to a new house in Wood Lane in Bramley village when it dawned on him that the Wellington House which sat on the other side of the stone wall across the road from his front hedge housed the orchard his father had written about.

He vaguely knew the new owners and gained permission to look around the gardens citing Clifford's great interest in horticulture.

Clifford walked across the lawn from the front drive of Wellington House and broke through the brambles which covered a gate leading to an overgrown patch of ground. This was bordered by the stone wall, the wall which faced his house and Clifford swore he heard a voice saying, "About time too."

He walked on through the waist high grass, nettles and docks and noticed several cherry trees – all dead apart from one. The dead trees were bent over and broken and finished, but the central tree was still fruiting and healthy. This tree must be very old and Clifford wondered if this was where Jones now lived.

The tree responded to the touch Clifford gave as he stroked the cracked bark and he heard,

"Please save me Clifford, take the fruit and keep the pits. Plant them and keep me alive. I cannot go to Hell."

Clifford laughed at himself believing the voice and walked away.

"Please!" the voice begged.

Clifford turned back and opened the rucksack he had with him and filled it with cherries. The tree seemed to bow to him and said,

"Don't forget to plant them my friend."

Clifford watched as the leaves began to fall from the tree and spooked, he scurried back to the bramble covered gate.

He met some workmen striding towards him.

"Thanks for clearing the gate mate!" shouted one.

"Oh, going in there, are you?"

"Sure are. The boss wants us to chop down the trees and bring him the wood. He needs it for his fireplace."

"There's still a live cherry tree in there," Clifford told them

"Won't be for long. He wants the whole orchard cleared so it can be opened up for grazing." The man held a rope in the air.

"It's to pull it down," he said. "Like a hanging!"

To the sound of screaming from the orchard, Clifford walked swiftly down the driveway and back up the road to his own house. Later that afternoon he watched from the wall as the workmen tied the rope around the top of the cherry tree and held it taut as they sawed at its trunk. Twice they pulled and the tree would not fall in spite of its injuries with the saw. The third time it came down with a terrible crack and Clifford watched as smoke shot out from the truck.

"Please!" he heard.

Clifford walked back to his house and went inside and asked Agnes to put the kettle on.

Clifford kept the dried cherry pits he had taken from the old tree and placed them into a wooden box which he kept separate to the other pits, still in their snuff box. He closed the chest and never planted the pits in his wonderful garden full of roses and London Pride.

I still have the pits...

A CHRISTMAS STORY

Featuring Clifford Prideaux (1902-1963)

Christmas Day of 1902 was a special day for the Prideaux family who lived in Burniston Place.

No 7 was exactly like its neighbours, a back to back, two up and one down terraced property.

Burniston Place was situated off Elland Road in Leeds and consisted of eight properties facing each other, four on either side. The odd numbers were on the left and the even numbers on the right. At the end of the court, was the shared toilet and midden which completed the C shape. Burniston Place was on the corner of Elland Road on the north side. Elland Road moved west from New Princess Street in the centre of Leeds.

Two steps led to each house door from the narrow-flagged pavement and the cobbled street sloped to the middle. Here, a channel took the waste water to the drain at the midden and toilet.

Burniston Place was occupied by some of the very poor of Leeds who worked hard at making their low wages feed and clothe their families. But they weren't paupers and were proud people.

On this Christmas morning, Georgie Prideaux was wakened by a noise from the bedroom he shared with his eight-year-old brother Arthur, seven-year-old sister Annie and 2-year-old sister Jane. His parents slept in the bed at the other side of the room. A curtain drawn across the middle of the room, gave a small amount of privacy.

Georgie could hear his parents whispering to each other. He hoped he wasn't going to have to listen to the heavy breathing and bouncing again. He turned his head and forced it into the pillow. He put his arm over the upper ear and pressed down hard. Georgie had learned that this was the best way to keep out noises, especially if he hummed at the same time.

"You are going to have to wake the kids up George," said Mary Ann to her husband in hushed, urgent tones.

"Whatever for?" George was very tired. He worked all the hours he was offered at the brickyard in order to make the pittance which kept his family in the poor, but honest state they lived in. Christmas Day was his only day off.

"I'm tired. Let the kiddies sleep a bit longer, they will be up soon enough anyway."

He was thinking of the noisy excitement they would enjoy during the day. The few presents he and Mary Ann had managed to get together were hanging in little red stockings above the fireplace downstairs. He did not want the day to start too early.

"The baby's coming George, the baby's coming." Mary Ann tried to keep the panic from her voice. She had already given birth to five children and she was not looking forward to this one.

Labour scared her. She had seen a lot of birth and death in her young life, either attending her family or her friends. There was not always a happy outcome. One of her own babies had died at a young age and she often thought about him.

Especially at Christmas.

George sat up and looked at his wife. She was white and scared and he put his arms around her in comfort. "Alright love, leave it with me. Don't you upset yourself."

He jumped out of bed and put on his trousers. He was already wearing his shirt and underwear and when he threw a jacket on, it meant he was dressed in less than a minute.

The room was freezing cold and he could see his steamy breath in front of his face. Although there would be another hungry mouth and extra responsibility joining their family today, he was looking forward to the birth and quietly prayed for another boy.

He reached across to the window and opened the shabby curtains an inch or two. The glass covered with ice, had formed spidery patterns over the surface. He looked across their little street and could see a lamp lit in the bedroom opposite. John and Lena Monsheimer lived there. They were German, but alright in spite of that. John worked at the timber yard as a labourer and Lena could always be relied upon to help with any birth.

"Georgie!" hissed his dad.

"Yes Dad. What's the matter?" Georgie knew it was Christmas Day and was very excited now he was really awake.

"Get dressed quickly and then get Arthur and your sisters dressed and downstairs."

There was a cry from his mother and Georgie suddenly felt frightened.

"What's the matter with Mum, Dad?" Georgie spoke carefully, his eyes wide with horror.

"We will be getting a new member of the family today Georgie. You are going to have to be a big helping boy." This unaccustomed silliness in the voice of his father unnerved him even more.

"Georgie, do as your Dad says and take your sisters downstairs. You will have to help me and your dad all day today. I am relying on you Georgie love."

Georgie was pleased to hear his mother giving him orders. He loved his mother dearly and was very close to her. He went over to the side of her bed and grabbed her hand.

"Mum, are you alright?"

"Yes, my love. Don't you worry. I am just a bit under the weather and will need everyone to help each other today and that will help me."

Georgie felt more comfortable now that he had spoken to his mother. He told his sleepy siblings to get up and he helped them get dressed. They complained and cried, but he soon had them downstairs. Dad had already gone out and by the time the children were downstairs in the kitchen, their Dad was coming back in through the front door.

"Lena will come over soon," he told them.

The children were all excited to hear this news. Lena was always very kind to them.

George began to attend to the range and rattled the poker in the depths of the fire in order to bring it to life. Within a short time, the fire had brightened the room and there was water boiling away in a kettle. Bread was sliced, smeared with dripping and given to the children. They happily waited for their tea. What an exciting Christmas Day this was!

Within half an hour Lena arrived, smiling and carrying a large bag under her arm.

"I've brought some things I think we will be needing," she announced. "I have told Mrs. Horton and she will be along soon."

Georgie listened intently. If Mrs. Horton was coming as well as Lena, then great things must be going on. Mrs. Horton was the very old lady who lived with her husband at the end of Burniston Place. They kept the tobacconist shop which faced onto Elland Road and lived in No 3, which backed onto the shop.

Lena went up the stairs and smiled when she saw her friend crying in pain as she lay on the bed.

"Oh, mein liebling madchen! Lena ist jetzt hier. Alles ist gut."

"I don't think it will be very long Lena, it feels as though it is nearly here."

"A Christmas baby! He will be a blessing to you this child!" said Lena in her cheery way.

"Thank you, Lena. I am so glad you are here. But I am very sorry that I am ruining your Christmas Day," said Mary Ann, her voice full of strain.

"Mein liebling, do not cry. We will enjoy the day all the more with all the happy news! Now, Mrs. Horton is on her way. As soon as she comes I shall go downstairs and take die kinder over to our place. Then I will return to help and hold your hand. Everything is ready for Christmas and there will be more than enough food for die kinder today."

"Oh Lena," Mary Ann was crying with gratitude. "I have a chicken in the larder and a pudding which needs steaming. The babies must have their Christmas dinner. What about their presents?"

"George will give the presents to me and they can open them at our house. John will look after everyone. I shall cook your food over here while I am up and down the stairs and if everything is done this afternoon, you can all have your Christmas dinner with the new baby!"

It seemed easy for Lena to arrange all these things for her neighbours, but Lena missed having her own family. She had given birth to six children and not one of them had made it past five years old. She had plenty of love to go around.

There was more commotion downstairs and soon Mrs. Horton had joined the two women in the bedroom. Mrs. Horton had delivered many children locally. She was neither a nurse nor a midwife, but she knew what to do.

She was comfortably off and as her neighbours were all poor, she considered it an act of charity to help where she could. Mrs. Horton was 72 years of age, but did not look it. Her husband was 15 years younger than her and their friends guessed that had something to do with it.

Lena went downstairs and set about her work. As soon as the children were safely across the road and the chicken in the range, she was back upstairs to help bring new Christmas life into the world.

Georgie, Arthur, Annie and Jane were having a great time with Uncle John. He talked in a funny way, but was very kind. Dad had been going back and forth between the two houses and young Georgie was getting very worried about his mother. As the oldest boy, he felt responsible for the other children and the welfare of the family while his parents were so distracted. Dad stayed with them while they opened their presents in front of the fire at Lena and John's. Georgie and Arthur had been happy with their new clothes and a toy each. The outfits had been created by their mother from some second-hand clothes she had bought through the church charity. The girls had some hand me down clothes from their cousins, redressed with ribbon bows. They all had sweets, which went down better than the bread and dripping.

Naturally.

Georgie looked out of the window and saw his father walking across the road again, this time with Lena. They came in through the front door and seemed very pleased with themselves.

"Come home children!" he said. "Something very exciting has happened!"

The four children were ready in seconds. They remembered to give a big hug and kiss to Lena and John and clutching their presents followed their father back home.

"Dad it's snowing!" said Annie. Perhaps this is what Dad had meant. They stopped in the middle of the road, heads up, mouths open and eyes wide. Annie thought that the snow looked like fairies jumping out of the sky.

Arthur twirled round, his hands outstretched, looking up into the darkness. He noticed that the snow was sitting on top of the only gas lamp in the street, above number 8 opposite their house. It was all so lovely.

The young Prideaux family arrived back through their own door into the warm room. There was a smell of delicious food and the lamps gave a wonderful glow. The house may be tiny and they were very poor, but none of them wanted to be anywhere else on this magical day.

"Now come on children, your mum wants to see you all upstairs. She has another present for you."

This was news indeed. The children ran up the few steps and as soon as they reached the top step, George picked up his youngest daughter who was almost asleep.

The room seemed darker than usual and there were some funny smells.

"Come on in children," said mum.

Then they saw the surprise. Wrapped in their mum's arms was a new little baby.

"You have a new brother, children. Are you pleased?"

"Is he to keep?" asked Annie.

"Yes."

"Is he Jesus?" asked Jane.

"No Jinny, he isn't. We have not given him a name yet. We can decide now that you are all here."

"Did Jesus send this little boy to take the place of Ben because we all miss him so much?"

Mary Ann looked at George with tears in her eyes. Ben had died on Christmas Eve and had ruined Christmas for the family ever since. He had lain dead in his tiny plank coffin on the table downstairs, while the family waited for there to be enough coffins in the neighbourhood to fill a mass grave at Holbeck. Because of Christmas, Ben was with them for almost a week. Luckily the weather had been very cold. There were some terrible stories of summer deaths and the coffins having to be... Mary Ann didn't want to think of that anymore.

God had sent the perfect remedy.

Georgie saw that his mother looked very tired and drawn, but she seemed happy about the baby. He wondered who had brought it to the house and thought it very bad timing when his mother had been feeling so ill all day.

"Well Dad, what shall we call him?"

Georgie had been named after his father, Arthur after Mary Emma's husband, their uncle. They had looked after George when Mary Emma and George had been orphaned along with their other siblings. Mary Emma and her new husband had taken in the other children in order to save them from the workhouse.

The girls were named in a similarly thoughtful way. Annie, after her mother and Jane after Mary Ann's best friend.

George said, "I have been thinking about this. As you know children, our family used to be very rich and influential. We knew Kings and owned castles and much land before our luck changed. We still have some very rich relatives in Cornwall and Devon. If we visited, they would welcome us with open arms. Never forget that you are all better than the station you currently have in life. Our luck could change back at any moment. Remember that my beautiful children."

Mary Ann did not always approve of this way of talking, but was too tired to stop her husband now. George told anyone who would listen that they were only a couple of generations away from gentry.

"My grandfather and great grandfather were very good friends with Lord Clifford of Chudleigh in Devon. So, in their honour, I would like to call our new son, Clifford."

"Clifford!" said Mary Ann.

"Clifford Prideaux has been born on Christmas Day and is another blessing from God. He has come in place of your beloved brother Ben, who God needed back in heaven to help him. Clifford will bring us luck and all of his family will be special, just like us."

This was a promising speech and the family all beamed at the prospect.

Within an hour, the children were enjoying their second Christmas dinner with mother, father and Clifford in the bedroom. Chicken and potatoes followed by a Christmas pudding. The children never forgot this Christmas Day for the rest of their lives. Not just for the birth of their brother, but because it was the one and only time they were allowed to eat around their parent's bed.

"We should have two Christmas dinners every year!" announced Arthur.

His mother smiled and leant back into the pillows.

"Bedtime, I think," said George.

George had little trouble with the children this bedtime. They quietly snuggled into their little beds and Mary Ann slept heavily while baby Clifford snored lightly in his blanket lined box. Lena and Mrs. Horton had dealt with the soiled sheets and towels by taking them home to their own houses to wash.

Soon after the children had gone to bed, George's brother William knocked quietly on the front door. George opened the door quickly.

"Can I come in please George?"

"Of course, you can mate! Come inside, out of the cold. What's the matter?"

William took off his coat and shook the snow from it. His coat was shabby and of doubtful protection against the wintery weather. But poor people are hardened to cold and rarely complain. He took off his thin gloves and placed them onto the now cooling range.

"William, what's the matter?" George put his arm around his brother's shoulders. There was no manly holding back between these brothers. They had been through too much together.

William was crying and sat hunched in the chair by the fire.

It was a full ten minutes before George could get any sense from him.

"Lily has had the baby today. We called him William, but he is too early and he is deformed and the doctor says he won't last very long."

"Oh, William that is terrible news. I am so sorry. How is Lily? She must be devastated."

This boy was the ninth child for William and Lily. Five had already died. Two of them this year alone and to lose yet another child would be heartbreaking for them. But it was just so terrifyingly common amongst the family and friends they both knew.

"William, I don't know what to say." George decided not to mention his new arrival and hoped that nothing would give him away while William was so upset.

If they had money and proper food and housing and doctors that were any good, things would be different. But it was as it was and that was that. The two brothers had already seen so much death and sadness in their lives. They were almost numb to it. George thought again of his son Ben, dead these three years at only one year old.

"Why is life so hard George? Ever since we were born, it's been hard," sobbed William.

"I know," said George. "We are supposed to be grateful for what we have."

"Well some days that's too hard," William answered.

George handed over a whisky and said nothing else to his brother.

*

"What happened to William's little boy, Grandad?" asked Ann.

Clifford was telling his granddaughter about his first Christmas. Although only 5 years old, she listened to everything her beloved grandad told her. It was Christmas Eve 1962 and the family was together for a few days. The two of them stayed with each other as much as possible on these visits and Clifford told her the history of the family and showed her books and documents which she would treasure her whole life.

On this particular afternoon, her mother and siblings were in the same room, but were busy with decorations and sweets. Grandma Agnes came in and out with mince pies and instructions. The others listened only intermittently to the storytelling.

"It wasn't just William. We all had a horrid time. We weren't spoiled rotten like you little girl." Ann wriggled and giggled as he tickled her tummy.

Her mother looked up from her busyness and smiled.

"Tell me Grandad," Ann ordered.

"Uncle William and Auntie Lily had a baby son on that same Christmas Day, but he died on New Year's Eve."

"Did lots of babies die in the olden days?"

"Yes, and people too."

"Why does Jesus want all the people back?"

"He doesn't. We can all go when we want to go. The whole world is just a dream. You have dreams don't you Ann?"

"Yes."

"Well being alive is a dream too. You think up where you want to go and what you want to be and imagine yourself already there. Then one day you will be."

"Like magic?"

"Like magic."

"What happened next?"

"The years passed and there were three further additions to our family. Three more brothers for me, called Herbert, Albert and Wilfred. A larger house was required and the family eventually moved. The nine Prideauxs arrived at 100 Elland Road with great anticipation.

This house was exciting to the children because there was so much more room than at Burniston. Stepping in from the street still brought visitors directly into the room, but it was a lot bigger. This front room had a range topped by a large high mantelpiece which had velvet trimming with long fringes hanging from it. There were ornaments and pots and pans stacked on it. The range had a fender in front which had a seat at each corner. There was a door at the back of the room which led to the cellar. At the top of the cellar stairs were some shelves, one of which was made of marble.

On this slab Mary Ann placed butter, milk and anything which was likely to go off. The upward stairs led to two rooms where the family slept. George and Mary Ann had the tiny room at the back. The boys and girls shared the larger front room which was separated by a curtain.

The toilets were accessed by going out of the front door, walking along the pavement before turning right at the Thrift shop at the end of the street and immediately right into Tilbury Avenue. The toilets were along there."

"What if you wanted to wee right now?" asked Ann.

"We used the potty!"

Agnes pulled a face at her husband. The subject of weeing and potties was bordering on forbidden territory. The other children put hands to mouths and giggled. They had managed to hear this part of the story.

Clifford continued, "At the front of the house on Elland Road were the tracks for the tram, which ran into town or up Elland Road. The tram seat backs could be pushed to either side of the seat depending on which way the tram was travelling. Passengers like to travel forwards, not backwards. Directly opposite the house was the entry to Cemetery Road. That was a creepy walk if we went walking there when it was dark. We used to think a monster lived there. We called him Shudder.

At this new house, the family managed to get through the years happily together. Georgie and Arthur fought for their country during the Great War and came home safely although the experience changed them a lot. I missed joining up because I was only 16 years old at the end of the war. Instead I worked at the same brickyard as my father on Claypit Lane. It was a horrible job, but was apparently honest work, my mother said. I thought it was the most boring job in the whole world. Well, I thought that until I got my last job. You make sure that you get a job you like doing, young Ann. Not a boring one."

Ann nodded, her thumb going into her mouth.

"When my sister Annie married Arthur Askin and moved next door to number 98, it suited us all perfectly. Annie wanted to get married, but loved us all so dearly that she could not bear to be parted from us. She offered to help our mother with the ironing and soon was doing all her family's ironing as well as her own. That meant that she washed 36 shirts every Tuesday, 14 of them belonging to me. I insisted on wearing a clean shirt every day for work and another one every evening and I even changed my shirt on Sundays.

She hung the shirts around her house on Tuesday when she took her lunch hour and Mary Ann and Annie ironed them all on Wednesday."

"You said I was spoilt. You were spoilt," said Ann.

Her grandad laughed.

"I used to take Annie's daughter Mary into Leeds and she loved it when the tram driver let her move the back of the seats to face forward. That gave her mum a break."

"Were you very dirty Grandad?"

"No, I wasn't dirty. It was just that the girls all used to chase me and I wanted to look nice. Not like a tramp! I lived at my mum's house until I met your grandma, didn't I Agnes?"

Agnes, who had walked into the room said nothing, but did nod her head in agreement at her husband.

"All the girls found me irresistible, but I was very choosy and only went out with the pretty ones. And when I saw your grandma, I had eyes for no one else and married her as soon as I could."

"When did you get married?"

"Christmas, well as near to Christmas as they would let us. We got married on the 22nd on a Saturday because we weren't allowed to marry on the Sunday or Christmas Eve or Christmas Day. That was bad luck because I like to make Christmas Day the best day for everything."

"What about this Christmas Day?" asked Ann.

"I don't know what special thing will happen this Christmas Day," he answered.

"Its only tomorrow, so we had better think of something quick!" said Ann.

"It's snowing!" shrieked the children.

Everyone went up to the window to look. It certainly was snowing. They opened the front door and looked at the snowflakes coming down. The street lamp was reflecting every flake. The snow looked black when it came down and yellow as it hit the lamps.

Clifford smiled. He puffed away at his pipe and thought about all the Christmases he had had. He felt the sudden familiar pain in his stomach which almost made him double over. He wouldn't let anyone see. This was not the first time it had happened and he made a promise to himself that he would see a doctor in the New Year. That weird feeling came over him again and he looked lovingly at his family. Agnes glanced up at him and suddenly her heart hurt.

"Are you alright, Cliff?" she asked quietly.

"Fine love."

He smiled at her.

*

Agnes brought her head out from under the stairs and said. "Cliff, life does not get any easier."

Agnes picked up the cream sandals she had owned for a quarter of a century and checked the piece of newspaper she had carefully inserted in the soles to cover the hole. "They will do for another year," she said, to no one in particular.

She moved slowly across the hallway and up the stairs. The hallway was freezing cold and dark. Agnes believed in saving money for a possible future need.

The hall contained only a small wooden table which housed a bowl contain two bananas and an apple. There was also a black and white photograph in a frame of her two daughters, Dorothy and Ann. On the wall was a small mirror next to which there was a clothes brush. This brush had been used on many occasions by Clifford and their two children when they had lived there together all those years ago.

The mat covered a very small area of the floor and offered little comfort. At the bottom of the stairs was an old vacuum cleaner. It was brown and had a bulbous base. It made a horrifying noise when operated, as though hundreds of ball bearings were being shaken up. It was also almost useless and for that reason was rarely used. There were coats hanging on the hooks at the bottom of the stairs. A blue mac, a light jacket and an overcoat.

Agnes walked up the stairs, carefully holding onto the banister. Everywhere was painted brown in order to not show the dirt. Clifford had decorated the house when they moved here in 1955 and now at Christmas Eve 1993, nothing had changed. The carpet and the paintwork and wallpaper were exactly the same. The lino which was laid everywhere upstairs was of a green and brown mix, but covered in rips and holes. Agnes had put pieces of newspaper under all the rips. Upstairs was as cold as downstairs, but Agnes did not really notice it. The toilet was directly opposite the stairway and was a black and white unit with a high wall mounted cistern and pull chain. The toilet paper was medicated Izal which annoyed her grandchildren intensely. They could not understand why she did not use soft paper. The bathroom was tiled black and white and in her grandchildren's memories had never had hot water running from the taps, only cold. Any hot water had been carried upstairs from the stove in the kitchen.

The front bedroom contained two beds and had belonged to her daughters until they left home. After that the grandchildren topped and tailed whenever they stayed during their childhood.

Her and Clifford's bedroom was at the back and contained walnut furniture topped with old photographs and ornaments. The wardrobe housed beautiful dresses and a fur stole that no one living had ever seen her wear. Agnes stopped dressing herself up during the summer of 1963.

She sat on the edge of the bed and looked at the small alarm clock on the chest of drawers. It was three in the afternoon and outside was getting dark already. She had nothing to do and no one cared whether she did it or not. Agnes did everything as slowly as possible during the day in order to fill in the hours. Soon she would go downstairs and think about making herself some toast.

It hadn't always been like this though.

Agnes Stones was born in 1911 in a small house in the pit town of South Kirby. Her parents, Mary Lizzie and George lived on the same street and their fathers both worked down the mines. Mary Lizzie became pregnant with their first son when she was fifteen and she and George married when she was sixteen. They lived with Mary's parents in Sheffield and they soon had another son called George. Shortly after this they moved to South Kirby to be near her uncle and his family and Agnes was born.

They moved again to Sheffield and Dorothy was born.

As soon as the Great War started George, his friends and relatives all joined up with the fervour that was around at that time. 'Over by Christmas' was the cry as they all marched off to do their bit. Pregnant Mary Lizzie, holding four children was not so impressed.

Two years later George was dead. Shot in the head.

Now the children had to grow up very quickly. Their mother left early for work and the children stayed with their grandmother and sister in-law, who had also lost her husband.

Agnes at four knew what work was. She also knew what doing without and living in extreme poverty was all about. The mice which ran across the bedroom and ate the family's food, gave her a rodent phobia for the rest of her life.

Her mother soon had another relationship which resulted in a daughter she named Nellie. The relationship foundered and she met a painter and decorator who was the father of five children. He was a widower, following his wife's death from Spanish Flu. Mary Lizzie thought John would be a good bet and they soon married and had two further children. Now there were thirteen children and two adults all living in the same house. They all worked very hard trying to feed the whole family and pay the rent. The oldest boys worked in the mines and Agnes worked hard in the home. She did the baking, washing and cleaning and looked after all the children that Mary Lizzie kept bringing into the world.

Before long, the stepfather died and left her with nothing but debts and children. His first litter of children were sent to live with various relations while the other eight remained with Mary Lizzie.

What a life.

14-year-old Agnes continued working at home and also went out to work as a tailoress in order to bring in extra money. The boys were still working down the mine.

In spite of this, the house was lively and generally happy. They had trips to Blackpool and Scarborough and bought clothes 'on tick '. The latest fashions and many boyfriends meant that the very attractive girls enjoyed their lives to the full.

Agnes looked at herself in the mirror of her dressing table. She kept the curtains closed because she did not like any neighbours to see what she was doing. With the lights off it was hard to see her face clearly in the glass, so she turned on the bedside light. Clifford had bought her this lamp with its lovely red shade. It was an old-fashioned type with brown cord and not recommended for safe use these days, but she did not care. She looked at her face which was still strong and attractive, if a little thin. Her hair was thick and had only become grey in recent years. Her glasses emphasised her dark eyes. She wore a blue checked dress and a blue cardigan. Her children and grandchildren would recognise this outfit as being one she had worn for many years. Her summer outfits of brightly coloured dresses and green cardigan were similarly recognisable. She had been a beautiful young woman and if she had been given a different life, would have been able to launch a thousand ships of her own.

Clifford had fallen in love with her as soon as he saw her.

Agnes smiled as she looked into the mirror. She could see the reflection of Clifford sitting on the bed. He was smiling at her and she smiled back. When he died in their bed 30 years ago, they had held hands. He had not been the same man after he had been blown up during the war. The irony was that a bomb had gone off in Leeds while he was on leave and blown a wall onto him. He wasn't discovered for over a day and the delay meant he was late rejoining his unit and was marked AWOL. On his return to active duty, with only a small reprimand, he went through D Day and the rest of the fighting unscathed. Although Clifford was not a particularly religious man, just before he died he had sat bolt upright in the bed staring in wonder at the same place Agnes now sat and said, "Jesus!" Then he smiled and fell back stone dead.

Having no telephone of their own, Agnes had to leave her husband and run a quarter of a mile to the end of the road and ring for help. It seemed like only yesterday.

Agnes got up from the chair and walked back to the bedroom door. It was now quite dark outside and anyone else would have turned on their own lights. Agnes however, did not. Electricity cost money and she knew her way well enough around her home and so there was no real need for lights. Agnes did very little for her own pleasure.

She made her way down the dark stairs, across the hall and into the sitting room. She closed the curtains at either end of the room and thought about lighting the fire, but decided against it. Not much point now.

The room was crowded with furniture. At one end was a table around which her family had sat in the days they lived at home. It had also been the place where many meals were eaten when the grandchildren were quite young. They enjoyed their big family Christmas dinner around it. Nowadays, the family never visited. On the oak side board were the same ornaments which there had always been. There was a large standard lamp, a piano, a gramophone, a sofa and two fire side chairs. The black and white television set had been a gift from her son in law, but was only watched when she had a visitor. The décor was mainly 1950's shabby chic.

Agnes sat down quietly in the chair next to the fire place. She saw her long dead husband sitting in the chair on the other side. He picked up the pipe, filled it with tobacco and spent the next few minutes trying to get it to light. Agnes had been annoyed by this habit when he was alive, but felt comforted by it now. She closed her eyes as she leaned back and remembered the exciting Christmases when her daughters and grandchildren stayed. It was almost as though they were happening right now. She recognised the sounds and the smells.

Agnes got up from the chair, squeezed her husband on the shoulder and left the room. She stood in the hallway for a short time and listened to the noise outside. The children next door must be coming home from school. No, not school, it's

Christmas Eve. The letterbox rattled and a card fell on the mat. Agnes picked it up,

"Not even for me. They have either put on the wrong name or put it through the wrong door."

Agnes knew that the neighbours thought she was strange but she did not care. She stopped caring years ago about what people thought of her.

She walked into the kitchen. This tiny room was marginally warmer than the rest of the house and if she lit the cast iron stove, it would be very warm and cosy. But she could not remember the last time the stove had been lit. There was little point these days with only Agnes at the house and it seemed such a lot of work and fuss for only one person. The coal house was full of the coal which had been ordered and delivered in 1988, but no visitors meant that there was no one to fuss over and so the coal was never used. She looked at the old gas cooker which stood behind the enamel table and remembered that she wanted a cup of tea. She filled the kettle with a small amount of water, struck a match and turned on the gas. The stove would have been condemned years previously had anyone ever been called in to check it out. After an alarming flash, the gas was lit and the kettle began to heat up. The sink, of the old enamel variety contained a metal bowl which served as a washing up bowl. Agnes took a cup and saucer from the wooden draining board, took the teapot from the table and placed a spoon of tea inside. Soon the kettle began to whistle and Agnes poured the boiling water into the teapot and waited for it to mash. She dripped a small amount of milk into the cup and poured a thin stream of weak tea into that. Agnes knew she should eat something and opened the pantry door. Inside at the back she could see twenty bags of flour, at least the same of sugar, five large packets of cornflakes, ten jars of mincemeat, four pounds of butter and some marmalade. In front of this there was a loaf of bread and some cheese. She took the loaf and one of the packets of butter and made herself a cheese sandwich.

Agnes sat down at the table and began her meal.

Meeting and marrying Clifford was one of the best things that happened to her. Agnes enjoyed having a handsome husband and a nice house around the corner from her mother and her married siblings. When their first daughter arrived, they were thrilled and when Agnes was pregnant for a second time they looked forward to the birth of a son. Then war broke out in September 1939 and Clifford joined up, much to the horror of Agnes. Her handsome husband left her, she gave birth to a disappointing second daughter and Clifford rarely returned to their home until 1947. He had decided to stay on in order to help remove mines. Agnes let part of the house to serving soldiers in order to make extra income. Clifford returned looking much older and slightly weakened by his experience and their marriage was never the same again.

They both tried very hard to make their marriage work and after a few months managed to make some sort of a relationship. Of course, almost as soon as they settled back into a normal existence where Clifford left the house at six every morning to work as a stonemason, the rumours started about the houses in which they lived were to be demolished. Agnes's mother married a single neighbour called Herbert, in order that they could get a council house as a married couple. As single people, they stood little chance. Herbert was very sweet and caused Mary Lizzie no trouble at all. At the same time, Agnes and Clifford moved to this lovely little cottage in Bramley.

After Clifford died, Agnes wondered if her life was ever going to be nice again. It seemed that she had had so little happiness in life. She had no faith in God, since he had taken away everyone she loved and no matter how hard she worked, she had saved very little money. Still, here she was, 82 years of age, lonely, cold and miserable.

Thank you, God.

Agnes could hear noises in the sitting room again. It sounded like people talking, but of course it couldn't be so. She ignored it. Soon she could hear noises upstairs, the sound of running water and voices. She ignored this too.

This had been happening for many years and Agnes assumed that she was just remembering the visitors she used to have. She was probably projecting the memory into her house.

Agnes got up from the chair and went to the cupboard which was crammed full of old newspapers and Beano comics. There was a special smell every time this cupboard was opened. It was a sort of mouldy smell. She took out one of the newspapers and paid little attention to the date on the front of the paper, the 14th of June 1969. News doesn't change that much, just the characters. She spread the newspaper on the table, read it for a while and carefully folded it up and put it back in the cupboard. That will do for tonight.

She looked at the kitchen clock. It said seven o'clock, time for bed.

She made her way upstairs, walking quite slowly. She used the bathroom as usual and made her way into the bedroom. She changed quickly into her voluminous nightie and climbed into bed. No lights and no heating, Agnes was used to living like this. Her life was very quiet.

As a young girl, there was noise everywhere. The house was constantly busy. So many people living in such a small space meant that even the children were aware of their parent's intimate moments together. There were children crying, pots boiling and the seemingly permanent loud voice of her mother. It was also possible to hear the neighbour's lives through the walls. Those houses were built back to back and there were no yards. The front door led straight onto the street, which everyone in the neighbourhood used as a communal area. Washing hung in the street on lines going from one house to another. There were no secrets to be kept there. Everyone knew if a husband came back drunk or indeed whether he came back at all. They knew whose children were causing trouble and would have no qualms about clouting them without the need to call in a policeman. Agnes had hated all of the neighbourly intrusion and with that memory had become quite secretive once she had a family of her own. By the time she was widowed, Agnes lived almost as a hermit. She could leave the house and go for two weeks holiday without any neighbour knowing she had left. She began to do work in the garden at dusk or very early in the morning in order that she was not seen by anyone else.

One of her earliest memories was her mother giving birth with grandmother and the woman from down the road in attendance. When the last three girls were born, Agnes helped in the delivery. This experience paid off later on in her life when she helped her own girls give birth in this very cottage. It was such a pity that Agnes did not see them so much now. A person becomes involved so deeply with their own family and when they grow and move away it just seems unfair. She didn't like to think of it too much, because it was really quite cruel that none of her family came to visit her. It was Christmas Day tomorrow and she knew there would no family or friends arriving. Agnes wondered why her granddaughter Ann never came now. So heartless.

Agnes lay down in the bed. She still slept on her side of the bed. She had only shared her sleeping quarters since Clifford's death with her grandchildren when they were very young. It did not even enter her head to sleep in the middle of the bed and spread out like a star fish.

Now, listen, there were the noises again and the voices. They seemed to be in the same room as her, but that could not be so. It must be the children next door making too much noise and the sound of their voices was travelling through the dividing wall. Agnes thought she could hear the television on. There was plenty of music and the dull boom, boom, boom of some kind of tune. Agnes thought about complaining, but the last time she had gone round and knocked on their door, she had been completely ignored. She thought she had been speaking quite calmly, but the family carried on talking amongst themselves until Agnes had decided to leave. Once she had walked all the way into Leeds and into the council offices to complain about the noise and the staff had taken no notice of her. It seemed that now she was getting older, she was becoming invisible. When a person is young and vital everyone pays attention. When she was young and beautiful there was nowhere she went where people did not turn to look at her. Was it just the simple fact that older people are overlooked or was it that people did not want to be associated with her? Agnes could not work this out, it just made her feel very sad and angry. She thought about her own mother and could not recall her ever having been ignored. Mary Lizzie was always so loud that people had to take notice of her. Agnes sometimes wished she could be more like that, but she knew she could not.

"Is there anybody there?"

Agnes sat upright. She was sure that she had heard those words correctly.

The voices seemed to be coming from her sitting room. Should she go downstairs? What if there really was someone there? What would she do about it?

No, this was getting ridiculous, she would go downstairs. She swung her legs over the side of the bed and into her warm slippers. She put her shawl around her shoulders for the sake of modesty and quietly opened the bedroom door. The rest of the house was in darkness and she made her way down the stairs feeling her heart beating almost out of her chest. She quietly opened the sitting room door and looked around the edge of it to see if anyone was there.

There were people seated around her table.

It was dark in the room, save for some candles on the table and on the sideboard. There was a funny smell in the air of a sort of smoky perfume. What on earth were they doing in her sitting room? The shock of seeing the intruders emboldened Agnes and she moved into the room and across the floor. The strangers around the table turned to stare at her and one of the women began to scream. The woman sitting next to the screamer held her arm and told her to be quiet. A man who appeared to be in charge of the group, looked at Agnes and asked her if she wanted any help.

Agnes did not answer. Why where these people in her house and asking her if she needed help? Agnes could not understand this, it was a bad dream. She turned, intent on leaving the room and the house and fetching some help.

"No don't leave," said the man. "We don't mean you any harm. Do you mean us harm?"

This was crazy. Agnes could not understand what he was talking about and why he was asking such stupid questions.

"Is that you Agnes?" asked one of the women. "I've come to talk to you."

"Why didn't you just come during the daytime?" said Agnes. She really must be dreaming.

"We have come to help you move," said Grace. "Come and sit down with us."

"I'm quite happy where I am," answered Agnes. "I don't want to move. My daughters have tried to get me into those places before, but I refused to go. And I am not going now."

"She said that she doesn't want to leave and that she's quite happy here," the man told the others.

"But she can't be happy all on her own here. Come on Agnes, we'll help you see your husband again. Look behind you, can you see him there?"

Agnes turned around and saw Clifford sitting in his chair by the fire, smoking his pipe. Clifford smiled and held out his arms to her.

Agnes noticed that he had lit the fire and she went over to him and sat on the arm of his chair. She felt 30 years old again. She laughed and noticed how the room filled with light. The Christmas tree was up and the children and grandchildren were sitting around the room. There was food on the table and drinks on the sideboard. It was all as it should be. She must have fallen asleep after Christmas dinner and had a horrid dream. She jumped up, brushed down her beautiful dress and went into the kitchen to fetch some more food.

"Hurry up Aggie! I'm missing you already!" shouted Clifford.

He smiled at his granddaughter and said, "I told you, it's all just a dream."

Ann nodded and replied, "I understand now Grandad."

*

"Well, that went better than I thought it would. Everything should be all right now," Grace said to the others around the table.

"She looked like a proper ghost floating in the room all dressed in white. People won't believe that really happened," said the man.

"We know it did though. She is with her husband now, so he will look after her."

"The owners of this place should be much happier without Agnes walking about the house in her nightie all the time. They have been really creeped out about it. They have been seeing her for years."

"I don't know why they should be scared, she seemed like a really nice lady." said another.

"Apparently, lights were being turned off and taps turned on when there was no one to be seen."

"And it was cold all the time, no matter whether the heating was on or not."

"They kept seeing a grey lady floating about the place. Agnes lived here for years by herself before she died in 1988. She was starting to get a little confused in the months before she died, so probably didn't notice that she had actually died. That happens quite a lot."

They blew out the candles, turned on the main light and walked out of the house into the snowy Christmas Eve.